Praise for Thomas Dyja's

Play for a Kingdom

"Wonderfully conceived and eloquently executed. Story, character, and research have received equal effort—and together they achieve truly captivating results."
      —Caleb Carr, author of *The Alienist* and *The Angel of Darkness*

"Thomas Dyja knows how to mix his ingredients. In this innovative and original first novel he blends two staples of the American psyche—the Civil War and baseball—into a recipe for a very readable book. The battle scenes ring true. . . . And the baseball scenes ring true as well. Dyja's book is admirably wrought."
      —John C. Waugh, *Washington Post Book World*

"Dyja has crafted a deep and mature first novel realistically encompassing two pillars of American history and culture. Stirring and original. . . . If the baseball passages are deftly written, the battle scenes are yet more skillfully drawn. As Thomas Dyja proves with this impressive novel, peering into human desperation can produce insight and prose of unusual eloquence."
      —Charles Fountain, *Christian Science Monitor*

"Engrossing. . . . The band of soldiers whose stories Dyja tells form a microcosm of our country, circa 1864. The novel builds up considerable suspense and drama. . . . The overall impact of Dyja's panorama is devastating and memorable."
      —Diane Cole, *Newsday*

"Powerful. . . . Dyja's descriptions of battle are vivid and convincing. . . . [He] skillfully develops an array of characters and weaves a complex tale, so that the two companies [of soldiers] become microcosms of two armies."

—Tom Pilkington, *Dallas Morning News*

"Imaginative and suspenseful. Riveting in the vivid descriptions of the struggle at Spotsylvania. And there's a particularly affecting episode involving a company of black Union soldiers.

—*Parade*

"First-time author Thomas Dyja packs a lot of heat with *Play for a Kingdom*. [He] captures the glory of American's favorite pastime in the backdrop of America's bloody Civil War [and] takes the reader on a wild ride from the battlefields to the makeshift baseball diamonds."

—Denice Santangelo, *St. Louis Post-Dispatch*

"Dyja has created a sweeping novel of humanity on the battlefield, peopled with provocative characters. The author brings it all vividly to life. *Play for a Kingdom* is that rare treat—a novel that interweaves war and play, an ironic tale told with compassion. Watch Tom Dyja."

—*Santa Barbara News-Press*

Play for a Kingdom

Play for a Kingdom

THOMAS DYJA

A HARVEST BOOK
HARCOURT BRACE & COMPANY
SAN DIEGO   NEW YORK   LONDON

Copyright © 1997 by Thomas Dyja

All rights reserved. No part of this publication may be
reproduced or transmitted in any form or by any means,
electronic or mechanical, including photocopy,
recording, or any information storage and retrieval system,
without permission in writing from the publisher.

Request for permission to make copies of any part of
the work should be mailed to: Permissions Department,
Harcourt Brace & Company, 6277 Sea Harbor Drive,
Orlando, Florida 32887-6777.

Library of Congress Cataloging-in-Publication Data
Dyja, Thomas.
Play for a kingdom/by Thomas Dyja.—1st ed.
p.   cm.
ISBN 0-15-100267-3
ISBN 0-15-600629-4 (pbk)
I. Title.
PS3554.Y48P58   1997
813'.54—dc21   96-53875

Text set in Adobe Caslon
Designed by Ivan Holmes
Printed in the United States of America
First Harvest edition 1998
A C E D B

To my father,
and my son

...for when lenity and cruelty play for a kingdom, the gentler gamester is the soonest winner.

—WILLIAM SHAKESPEARE, *Henry V*, ACT III

PROLOGUE

———

A BLUE RIVER FLOWED DOWN THROUGH THE HILLS AND ONE-HOUSE towns of Virginia that night in May of 1864, under a moon that caught the sharp silver ripples of bayonets whenever the clouds parted long enough. It was a river in flood; Union soldiers four wide and twelve thousand deep claiming a land they thought was theirs, nearing the hamlet of Stevensburg at the sluggish pace of two miles an hour.

As always when a river floods, the victims believed the killing force to be contrary to the laws of God and nature, but that night the few men watching from behind their windows, mumbling to their wives, had honestly been expecting it since the weather held warm in April and the mud dried back to dirt. War had disturbed the natural order of Virginia every year since '61. Spring now brought the dogwoods to bloom and the flies and this Yankee flood into a land usually at peace with its rivers. Three times the rush of men had rolled through, then pulled back in defeat, and three times the few farmers and tobacco dryers stubborn enough to remain had started over again. This night they saw the ripples and shapes in the dark and hoped Lee could send it back one more time. One more retreat and the Yankees would stay north where they belonged. If not, the South would be forever under.

The river of Union men flowing down the road kept hopes as firm as Virginia's. Old veterans, some only twenty-one with just days to go in their enlistments, stared at the necks of the men before them and prayed they'd make it home through the death that hung in the still Southern air. They prayed for victory, too, and thought they might get it now that Grant had stirred some vigor into this army famed for its losses and the deadly incompetence of its generals. If the army did not love him yet, they knew he meant to win and they knew there'd be a cost. The first drives south had been parades of "On to Richmond," brass bands and laughing side swirls of lazy soldiers distracted by blackberry bushes or some stray cows. This year the sober quiet of men tired of war, afraid of defeat, and still wondering about their new general, muffled the scattered whoops of fresh conscripts. The raw men felt no duty, carried no honor, had never seen war. Instead, they were mostly thieves and cheaters at Bluff, loud cowards who marched off-step and placed bets on who'd hang Jeff Davis while the veterans shook their heads and prayed harder. This army—part killer, part coward, part gentleman, part thief—was a match for its new leader. Both pushed along with questions men didn't ask.

The campaign began with Wilson's cavalry galloping out of Culpeper around ten P.M. while thousands of men broke bivouacs east of the courthouse. Winter shacks and extra belongings had been burned days earlier in the happy bonfires they'd lit in Brandy Station, here in Culpeper and other camps along the fifty miles of Union-held Virginia, to celebrate the end of their waiting. Those who had wintered in Culpeper were especially glad to leave this town that had offered through clenched teeth her prized brick hotels and trim houses with views of the Blue Ridge Mountains. The soldiers were tired of the sneers and snubs of a people who considered themselves prisoners in their homes.

Wilson's vedettes were now spreading ahead like the foam of a wave in search of new shores that would only be less hospitable. The rest of the army had stepped off with drumbeats at midnight, Warren's Fifth Corps in the lead, and now, at two A.M., the thousand wagons bearing the Fifth's Maltese cross came behind with freedmen at the reins of mules fighting their yokes and the great weight of matériel they drew. The blue river streamed farther east, deeper south. Every wheezing mule and wheel that creaked, every canteen clanking on a gun and brogan shuffling in the dust, added a note to the dull roar of invasion. Sedgwick and the Sixth raised flags, then merged into this force driving on with one national mind. No one man, not McClellan or Grant or Lincoln, could take credit for this Union. The war's own progress had fused a nation with rails, commerce, and mass graves, and the army could only mirror a new and more uniform country as it surged forward, well fed and well clothed by the mechanical age it had made necessary.

THE
FIRST
MATCH

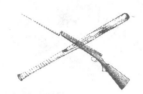

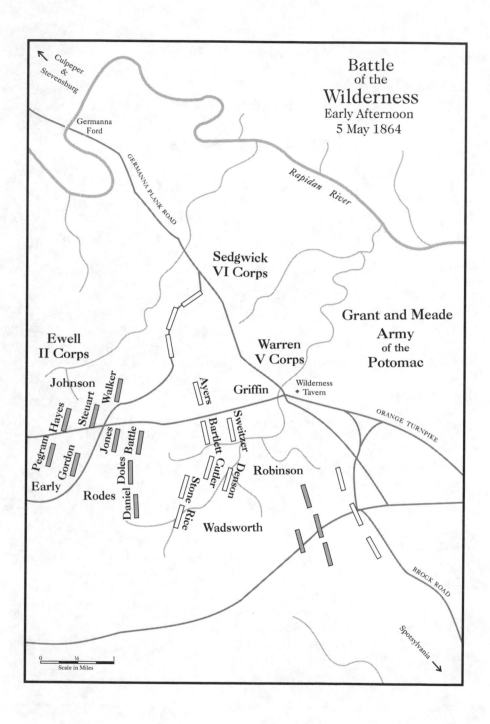

Battle
of the
Wilderness
Early Afternoon
5 May 1864

Culpeper
&
Stevensburg

Germanna
Ford

GERMANNA PLANK ROAD

Rapidan River

Sedgwick
VI Corps

Grant and Meade
Army
of the
Potomac

Ewell
II Corps

Warren
V Corps

Johnson

Walker

Steuart

Ayers

Griffin

Wilderness
Tavern

ORANGE TURNPIKE

Hayes

Pegram

Gordon

Jones

Battle

Bartlett

Sweitzer

Daniel Doles

Cutler

Denson

Robinson

Early

Rodes

Stone

Rice

Wadsworth

BROCK ROAD

Spotsylvania

0   ½   1
Scale in Miles

CHAPTER 1

___

UP TOWARD THE FRONT OF THE FIFTH CORPS, IN THE MOVE-ment's van, five rows of red dots bobbed atop the solid blue of caps and jackets. Amid Griffin's division, in Sweitzer's brigade, these remnants of a company detached for reasons as yet unexplained floated along with this Union tide. Their pants were scarlet, like the caps; loose trousers that white leggings forced into comfortable billows. The blue jackets trimmed with red fastened at top and bottom to show a vest the same deep scarlet as the pants. The moon caught fourteen gold buttons on each jacket; decorative flourishes that shone like small fires and bound the men of this company to their regiment, the 14th Brooklyn, now far in the back guarding wagons of bullets and food and counting down the days to May 21, the end of its three-year enlistment.

A thin man, clean shaven, cap tipped so the brim stretched down over his eyes, edged out just ahead of the group as though trying to get home that much quicker. Sergeant Dan Anson didn't so much march as spring along on his toes, turning his head side to side, slowly searching for clues in the dark. After the last mile of silence, one of the two men on his right ventured a question: "Where's this Grant taking us, Danny?"

The man who'd asked had a blond handlebar mustache with perfect twists. Unlike most around him, he'd also managed to keep his uniform clean since receiving a new jacket the year before. The ends of a base ball bat stuck out from the sides of his bedroll. Newton Fry was a handsome man and his bearing proved that he knew it.

Danny kept looking to the side.

"Going after Lee?"

Danny Anson took another scan around while Newt waited for his answer. "Nope. Grant's trying to miss him. That's why we're a-headin' toward the Wilderness again."

A few steps went by in silence. Newt Fry shrugged. "Maybe so." The thought of that eerie forest sank everyone's heart. This army couldn't take another Chancellorsville. While the 14th hadn't been there that day last year, they had seen the wagons loaded with men bleeding trails into the dirt, shrieking as they bounced along the road.

The third man cleared his nose to the side then wiped it on his sleeve. A stocky man, maybe five feet eight, he had a chin with a deep vertical dent and his thick legs rolled him along side to side like a ship in heavy seas. His name was Lyman Alder and he didn't want the silence to wash back over them. "What of our new generals, lads? Eh?"—a question asked of no one in particular, meant to take their minds off the many disconcerting possibilities they faced. The whole regiment had been shifted to a new corps when Grant came in, and now, with eighteen days to go, they were sent off on their own. Eighteen days seemed a very long time this dark night.

Danny wrinkled his nose like he'd just tasted something bitter, then spoke in a confidential tone, audible only to his friends beside him. "Damned engineer, is all."

"Lee's an engineer," said Newt.

"That's different."

Lyman Alder had his own opinion on the lieutenant-general, and he didn't mind who heard it. "Well, Grant's some hard medicine, I think."

On the left, a weathered, lined face smiled sourly. "I knew from the first ye'd have that Grant; yer butchers, the two a ye, and proud of it." Tiger Quigley snorted once, proud of his own joke. The man shambled along with his hair sticking all ways and his arms swinging at his sides. His mustache was thick and untrimmed; bristles curled into the sides of his mouth. Holding a stout laurel-root pipe between his few remaining teeth, he said, "So, Danny, have ye seen enough dead men yet?"

"I've dressed my last, that I can tell ya." Danny was an undertaker back in Brooklyn. Making the idle well-to-do of Williamsburg presentable for the Judgment had been a good living, but three years of brave men buried in shallow graves had made his job seem frivolous.

Newt quickly changed the subject. "The minute I step off the train, I'm walking straight into McCollins and ordering up twelve oysters about yea big." He showed with his finger how he liked them.

Tiger hawked and spit. "Ach. Ye got it all wrong, Newton. Ye're just a-wantin' the oysters 'cause yer lonely for that Mrs. Fry a yers." He looked ahead to see if Danny was smiling, which he was, so Tiger kept the floor. "No, Lyman Alder over there is the man with the goods for me. A steak, me boy. Three inches thick and cooked through till it's gray as Bobby Lee's coat." Lyman didn't look up. "Ye wouldn't give yer lifelong friend a gift for saving yer sad butchering life so many times? Yer a cheap sot, for true."

Lyman shook his head. "Oh, don't start with that. Newt saved me that day and it's a sorry show for you to claim the credit."

Newt opened his mouth, but then thought better of it, so he stuck a finger in and began chewing a nail.

Tiger smiled again, but not pleasantly. "The grocer has something to say, does he? The hee-ro. I been nice to ye, Newton Fry, keeping me mouth shut in the interests of us all getting on these last days, but don't be thinking I like ye." The three new boys in line behind them laughed.

Danny got in the middle. "Shut up both a ye. Horace Worm, ye got a poem?"

Someone in back cleared his throat, then chanted in a high tenor:

> *There is in Brooklyn town the very best of girls.*
> *Her name is Sally Edwards and she has a set of curls.*
> *They're not upon her head ye know.*
> *It's not so primer simple.*
> *She's got 'em oh so further down*
> *by another set of dimples!*

Everyone except Newt laughed.

Six or seven beat-up old houses appeared on the left, at a crossroads. No light came from inside. Danny Anson swore that he saw the curtains move, though enough windows were broken for it to be wind. One roof was bowed like the back of a dray horse. If people still lived there, they lived poorly. No livestock were visible, no smoke from the chimneys. Bullet holes dotted the walls. Stevensburg's only purpose now was to serve as a landmark. Behind it, a hill rose up with one tree, bare as the houses below, standing on top with branches pointing in each direction. Depending on one's mood, it either pointed south or north; invitation or warning. Just past that sorry village, the road climbed up a ridge and the Wilderness spread out beneath. Eyes accustomed to the dark could see treetops lacing the horizon and a forest cut by a narrow road that turned south into its heart. The line of men moved down onto the road and into the forest, whose trees formed walls on both sides, like levees barely holding back seas of pine.

In the wary silence of a night march, men imagined what waited for them behind that first, distinct line of trees. The obvious fear was of Rebels, but Rebels weren't the threat; the cavalry had cleared them aside. The greatest threat on a long and dark movement like this was the soldiers' own minds when men began fighting off thoughts born of fatigue, fear, and boredom. Memories of horrors they'd performed at Fredericksburg or Antietam floated up like hastily disposed bodies rising to a river's surface in the summer heat. Would Newt's wife see the mark of Cain on his brow? Could Danny's children love a father who has killed? The idea of a home turned against them made some angry, left others in despair, and reminded them all that they probably deserved whatever would be thrown their way when they returned home to a place nicknamed the City of Churches.

Under the best of circumstances, Lyman Alder thought too much, and now the pictures marched through his mind like their own invading army. He still saw the men who'd gone up during the glory days of the 14th: Fat John Porter; David Leigh with those tiny feet; Beaver Peter Ulster. Both of Beaver Peter's legs got blown off and that was a shame because he'd been a hell of a dancer. Three of the company's best. What was left and struggling toward Richmond were twenty out of the original one hundred; mostly the dregs of the company, save for a handful of brave men lucky enough to never have been hit or so unlucky that their injuries weren't bad enough to send them home.

Alder shook his head, briefly scattering the dead faces until a larger and more dangerous thought swept down. Since Gettysburg a new concern had gnawed on him during these endless empty passages that balance the fire of a soldier's life: Ernie, his one son, whom he'd last seen at the age of eight. The boy hadn't written for so long; months, by now. After Gettysburg and Lyman's injury, Ernie wrote constantly, first saying how much he missed him, then asking when his father would be an officer and if he'd ever carried the flag into fire. Lyman had sent back measured, appropriate replies that he'd thought were proper for a father trying to explain something about the realities of life to his son, but he realized now the boy might have seen through them in his heart to the testiness and distance that Lyman felt as he was writing. Finally the boy asked simply if he had been a hero and Lyman was forced to say no.

That wasn't the only reason why the boy wasn't writing anymore. His wife Victoria's last letter said that Ernie had been caught stealing from a dry goods store near his school. Her brother Albert, the police officer, had gotten the boy out and given him the lashing he deserved, and while the boy had settled down some, he still gave indications that without a firm hand over him, he might very well take to other forms of delinquency. Lyman's father—the "Alder" in "Alder and Son Meats"—had taken to waking Ernie up before five to help haul in the sides, the old man grumbling all the while about how Lyman had let the boy go spoil. The rest of Victoria's letter described a place he barely knew after three years away at war; familiar or not, that was the world Lyman would be coming home to. He couldn't say that the world he was now intimate with, the world of battle, was any worse. And that was the one thought he tried desperately not to have.

By 4:30 the sky lightened over the trees on their left. The whole army welcomed the day and relaxed, ignoring for a few hopeful minutes the possibility that the day they were embracing could also bring their death. Birds began calling back in the woods and wheeled about overhead catching breakfast on the wing. Men picked up conversations they had left off in some dark patch of trees. A German regiment marching behind the company sang about castles and victory, the first number in a concert that would go on all morning. A man in Company L held a hand up now to present his latest composition: a new set of words for "Dixie."

> *I wish I was in the town of steeples.*
> *Freedom there for all God's peoples!*
> *Eighteen days! Eighteen days! Eighteen days, Brooklyn land!*
> *A base ball match and hot clam chowder,*
> *Fetching lasses all a-powdered,*
> *Eighteen days! Eighteen days! Eighteen days, Brooklyn land!*
> *For Lincoln we have done our part, Hurray! Hurray!*

Now let us go back to our hearts
That live and die in Brooklyn.
Eighteen days! Eighteen days! Eighteen days till we're in Brooklyn!
Eighteen days! Eighteen days! Eighteen days till we're in Brooklyn!

Morning light had transformed the land they passed through. Dark ghosts at night turned into huckleberry bushes or dogwoods in young white bloom. Vines of wild pink roses crept through the blurry underbrush, dotting the gray and the light green. In their muddy camps of sinks and smoky fires, spring went unnoticed, but out here she was too obvious to miss. The Wilderness still hid behind this dressing of flowers. Though the forest didn't fully start until the other side of the Rapidan, here, on its outer edges, the closeness and bareness of the trees already disturbed some men. The first growth at this place had been cut down to stoke smelters, and now all the trees stood unnaturally the same twenty to thirty feet high and an arm thick, erect as if on review. The Wilderness was an opposing army of pine—silent, observant, and waiting for its chance to draw in and kill.

The road continued on through the forest until the woods broke onto a broad clearing miles wide. Heavy dew pulled the grass blades down and dampened the legs that brushed by. A bee zipped by Newt, who ducked, thinking it was a minié. Tiger chuckled as the bee flew on to a patch of daffodils. Two gentle hills bordered the road, which ahead bent left and out of view. On the right slope, Wilson's cavalry stood in clusters. Off on the left, where the road went, was the Rapidan. Griffin and his officers led the van of the Fifth Corps into lines on the slope to wait for the crossing here at Germanna Ford. It was nearing six. Lyman watched Black Jack Griffin giving orders. Farther beyond, the engineers were finishing one pontoon bridge on the left and making headway on another. It was clear they'd be here for a while. The new road with its pontoon edges stuck out like a spine, and the Rapidan, slow and brown, rolled on beneath it to meet the Rappahannock farther east. Most everyone sat down on the dewy ground, except for Danny, who stood with his legs spread, hands on hips, tilting his head back to see past his brim.

Lyman looked up to him. "See anything?"

Danny squinted through the sun. "Nah. Just the bridges."

Eighteen days. Lyman scratched the back of his neck, already getting burned, and thought about eighteen days. Too many chances left to die and too few left to be a hero.

Tiger Quigley had his knapsack off and lay sprawled against it, eyes closed as if sleeping off a night of dreggy lager. A reedy young man with the red braid of a second lieutenant on his shoulders and a wispy beard walked up to him. Seeing the sleeping soldier, the officer straightened. "Quigley, at attention. We'll be moving soon."

"Get buggered, ye whorehouse pimp."

"Soldier?"

Tiger opened his eyes. "I said, 'It's rugged. Me whole body's limp.'"

The lieutenant turned to Lyman, who said, "It *was* a goodly hike." Then a pause. "Sir."

Danny didn't even bother turning around as Lyman toyed with the lieutenant. He nibbled at the corner of some hardtack and daydreamed, staring off into the distance. The lieutenant put his hands on his hips. "Captain Henry and Lieutenant Stewart will be in attendance at the pontoons, so I expect decorous behavior of all men." No one indicated that they'd even heard him. The lieutenant cleared his throat and spoke louder. "I believe that's a reasonable request. Yes?" Still nothing. He dropped his hands. "Well." Pointing at Danny, he threw his last dart—"Sergeant, breakfast will commence on the other side." Danny brushed it aside with an uninterested nod.

Bugle calls sent all of Wilson's cavalrymen back onto their mounts, and the clusters of horses melted down into lines. Another trilling bugle roused the men up onto their feet and, led by the horsemen, they headed toward the crossing. The line took the road's left turn and down the bank to the pontoons. Calls of "Break Step!" and the indistinct rumble of thousands of feet scraping across bridges drowned out morning birds and a slight trickling made by water flowing past rocks. Captain Schuyler Henry and First Lieutenant Linden Stewart, commanding officers of Company L, 14th Brooklyn, stood to the side with their hands in crisp salute, their horses next to them.

At the front, Second Lieutenant John Burridge returned the salute, then quickly flicked his eyes back to see his company, their behavior the greatest evidence of his abilities.

His twenty or so men shuffled onto the bridge, dragging their rifles. Tattered and bad smelling, they stared at the ground, mumbling and swearing to each other in clusters of twos and threes. Not one of them offered a glance to the officers, let alone a salute.

The lieutenant felt his face flush. In this too-clear light of morning, Burridge had to admit that his company was a shabby group of men; that the fault fell on his wanting leadership was obvious and painful. He debated an angry command back, but that would only further signal his shortcomings. Instead, he clenched his jaw and stepped briskly onto the pontoon bridge.

CHAPTER

2

AFTER AN HOUR OF BREAKFAST AND REST ON THE FARTHER shore of the Rapidan, the army fell back in file and began moving again through the rising heat. Despite the young flowers and trees around them, this was no leisurely wander through the country-side; Grant clearly wanted the Fifth to steal a march on Lee. Warren's blue swallowtail flag streamed backward as it neared the crest of a long, slow grade. Knapsacks dug into shoulders, as did haversacks filled with three days of cooked rations and cartridge boxes neatly packed with fifty rounds of ammunition. A few men tried to fly a song now and then, but most had a job enough climbing the hill.

Unfortunately for the three young recruits—Teddy Finn, Slipper Feeney, and Wesley Pitt—nights spent watching the rat baiting at Kit Burns' Sportsman's Hall and stealing wallets hadn't prepared them for work like this. Sweat trickled down all men's brows, but it poured off Teddy's, and Wes rubbed his own burning thighs. Clouds of dust stirred up and settled into sweat to make a reddish paste on everyone's face.

Arch Feeney—Slipper Feeney—card dealer and pickpocket, rolled a lucky silver dollar through the fingers of his left hand and tried to appear lively. Short and sharp, but with the sloth of a bigger man, Slipper usually fidgeted away what energy he had, and he didn't have much left this after-noon. Working hard to keep up, he was worn down more than a boy just out of his teens should be from a vigorous hike. He stopped rolling the coin and turned to his neighbor, Teddy Finn, a thick boy his age whose face bore the soft flesh and odd mounds of an Irish prizefighter. "Can't see..." He took a breath. "Can't see how some of these old bastards here will make it.

Can you, Teddy?" He waited for a response from his friend. A few seconds passed before he realized that he'd been left to take full responsibility for his remark. Feeney coughed and spat a bit of froth to the side. "Yeah, all these old bastards."

Few punches had reached Teddy Finn's face, but they left marks of lessons learned, not defeats. He seemed toughened, not marred, though his wide, flat nose and round eyes were out of place with his stately *chasseur à pied* uniform. Teddy scratched his balls and tried to shift the weight of his backpack, but no matter how he moved, the haversack of rations still cut into his broad shoulders. Little rebukes of the sort he'd just given Feeney went a long way, just as a good cuffing for no reason kept a dog in line, and the opportunity for another one was presenting itself. Teddy pulled off his haversack and handed it to the boy on his other side. "Wes, take my sack here. Unless that Dutchman over there will."

Young Wesley Pitt, eighteen at the most, was only slightly smaller than Teddy, but a wide gulf of authority separated them. Wesley turned to the tall German on the end, an imposing man named Karl Udelhoffer, in his early twenties with a big beak of a nose and protruding cheekbones that swept back down into a pointed jaw. Wesley looked back to Teddy, who had the wicked grin he always had when he put Wesley up to a test. Wes Pitt had small eyes set deep in a broad ursine face and right now they cast about for signs that Teddy may have been joking. "Teddy, this fella..."

Teddy's eyes grew a bit colder. "Seems bully to me, Wes. What's the dilemma?" Slipper sniggered.

The German's cool blue eyes stole a glance at Pitt.

Wes held up Teddy's haversack. "Uh..."

Karl squeezed the boy's face with his right hand and pulled his ear up to within inches of his mouth, hissing, *"Sie können mir mal an den Sack fassen!"*

Teddy and Slipper burst out laughing, and Teddy growled an imitation of Karl, *"Zee kannen mirmala den auchgedauchenfutzen!"*

Karl's only retaliation was another run of curses and a final shove of Wesley's face as he let go.

Wes handed the haversack back to Teddy, but Teddy would not accept it. "I'm sorry, Wes, but I determinated that you'll be carryin' that sack a shit from now on." The two older boys howled another round of laughs, Feeney's especially loud and punctuated by coughs.

Wes flipped the strap over his cap and sunk down an inch lower on one side. He already felt he was tipping backward under the sixty or so pounds of cartridges, tent, food, clothes, blankets, rifle, and other necessities brought to remind him of a home back in Brooklyn that he didn't have.

Lyman looked back at Wesley Pitt with the extra load. "What're you doing that for? Finn runs a saw on you and you do what he says?"

Wes snapped back like a cornered rat. "Mind your own business, butcherman!"

Lyman grinned and held out his own haversack. "Well here, boy. You can take mine, too. Look, Tiger. We got our very own slave."

Teddy stepped in. "No, sorry. Wes here is most deniedly not no nigger. He's carrying the sack of the toughest man Brooklyn ever begit and its future mayor, that being myself." Slipper patted Teddy's wide back.

Tiger Quigley and Lyman Alder shook their heads and would have shared a good laugh if they couldn't imagine all three of the boys dead in a day.

The march continued. Wesley Pitt scratched at the leather band inside his collar. Half-empty packs and abandoned goods littered the road. Wesley's knapsack pressed on him like a piano, and the added weight of Teddy's haversack felt like someone had climbed on top of it. Wesley's head began to throb and white dots danced in his eyes. Clutching at his collar, he gulped at the air, which seemed too thin, as if he were getting the very last of it once everyone had had theirs. He never made the decision to sit down; three more steps and his body just broke rank, taking a seat Indian-style on the side. He wasn't quite sure where he was.

Karl stepped out after him. "This is not rest."

Wes was too dizzy to answer. A quick splash of tepid river water from his canteen helped him regain some sense, at which point he dumped the contents of his knapsack out onto the grass. Teddy and Slipper had followed his example and were now on their knees beside him making shoulder rolls out of their blankets when Danny kicked Slipper's aside. "If you ladies gotta simmer down, you simmer down, but you'll wear that goddamn knapsack! No man in my company is gonna look like a goddamn runaway nigger with his blanket tied over his shoulder! You'll carry your gear like soldiers!" He winked at Lyman, who was next to him, and whispered, "Make sure you get any food they leave."

Teddy and Slipper reluctantly rerolled their blankets, then divvied their things up as Wesley was doing, Finn having reclaimed his haversack. Lyman and Karl stood watch once Danny left, the German holding his hands behind his back and leaning over like a schoolteacher checking lessons. A small heap of underwear, a coffeepot, socks, spare shirts, canned food, and a Beadle novel piled up on the road.

Teddy glared up at Karl. "What are *you* osculatin', Dutchman?"

"Make sure you don't run, get firing squad for deserting, *ja?*"

"You think I'm some gutter bountyman about to hazardize my life for a weasely three hundred dollars?" Teddy tossed aside his writing set with all its pen nibs, paper, and ink and laughed. "Did you hear that, Slipper?"

Slipper hefted a tin of sardines and decided it was too heavy. "Yeah, Teddy."

Karl pointed a bony finger at the writing set. "You need that."

"My Dutch friend, lemme elucidate somethin' to ya. I don't *need* nothing. Someday you will memorize da fact dat you spent time wit Teddy Finn, who will den be the Dimmycratic mayor of Brooklyn. I'm being groomed, see?"

"So gimme that."

"And what if I don't?"

Karl's eyes narrowed over his beak, an eagle following a fat fish in a lake from high up. Teddy looked him in the eye as he reached toward his bayonet, hoping to distract him with his gaze, but Karl wasn't fooled. He tapped Teddy's hand with the tip of the bayonet pointing off his rifle.

Teddy weighed the odds. He'd stolen the pens anyway, so all he had to lose really was his hand. He chucked the desk a few feet to Karl's left so the German would have to leave to fetch it. Karl sneered, his drawn face especially ugly. "You watch it." Then he turned toward Slipper and pointed at the sardines. "Give me that, too."

Slipper lobbed it over. "Here, beggarman."

Guarded by Lyman, Wesley had only one more item to decide on. He opened his housewife and ran a finger over the thread and scissors and needles. He'd been told they'd need one of them, but so far he couldn't see why.

"You're gonna need that."

Wesley flipped it into the pile. "Whadda *you* know?" He shoved the surviving things back into his pack and joined the others as they trotted to catch up.

The pace slowed to a sensible level once the early warmth became a sodden, summery heat. Those who had been beaten down by the first hill caused the line to begin a tedious, undulating creep of a few quick steps and then a halt, over and over again. The march made five miles in four hours. By noon the woolen uniforms, smelling of every march, meal, and battle spent in them, hung damp off bodies as though the corps had forded a stream. The songs were desultory now and only "Weeping Sad and Lonely" rose with any real feeling. Last night's crisp blue flow had turned into a sluggish brown river like the one they had crossed this morning.

After a while the forest finally gave way to a broad, open field of four or five square miles. A white dot in the distance, like a single marker for a grave, grew as they neared it, becoming a two-story wood building on the road's left side, deserted and surrounded by weeds. The line stopped.

Tiger said, "Looks as empty as a nigger school, it does." Teddy and Slipper quickly agreed. Newt shifted around, as if uncomfortable under his pack. "And fancy as a nigger castle."

Newt put his hands on his hips. "Aw for Christ's sake, Tiger, leave off the Afri..." He caught himself. "Darkies."

Tiger took the pipe out of his mouth and extended a hand across Danny and Lyman for Newt to shake. "I'm much honored to meet ye, Mrs. Stowe. But ye look so much harder in the papers."

Newt sniffed and turned away, as Tiger popped a lazy, disdainful bit of spit into the dust at Newton's feet.

The delay, the open field, and nearly twelve hours of marching all pointed toward this abandoned building, Wilderness Tavern, as camp for the night. A few riders with corps flags rode out to a small, treeless farm exposed in the field four hundred or so yards to the southwest and established Warren's headquarters. The line started forward again, but instead of march-ing into the field, Griffin's own flags and the drums led a turn to the right onto an intersecting road headed west, the Orange Turnpike. Ayres took his men in, and the line finally brought the company quietly trudging up to the tavern on a slight rise looking over the westbound pike, a road that split the field and then the forest like a slick part on a man's head. The sun had done its climb for the day and hesitated before its slide down the west side of the sky and into their faces. Above the farthest point, where the road became a speck, trees formed a false horizon that only the turnpike's cut proved wrong.

Any morning breeze had long passed. Two huge crows flew a few feet over the ground, then settled to pick what they could from the soil. Someone moaned, a strange sound in the sunlight, but its biblical loneliness fit this empty land of bare pines spotted only by empty houses and farms in burnt fields. The moan became a voice—"The Lord said, 'I would pour out my fury upon them in the wilderness, to consume them!' "

A man with only one ear spoke up. "Isaiah, the one and very man who foretold ourn Lord's birth, said, 'The wilderness and the solitary place shall be glad for them,' and I'm standing by him, eh? Not that Ezekiel with his chariot on fire. Go on with that."

Lyman said, "Amen."

Two more hours of spiritless marching finally came to a halt in the middle of the forest. The line stood dead in the road until the orders came down to make camp here, a mile and a half west of the Wilderness Tavern. The lieutenant pointed to an area left of the turnpike, still between the 9th Massachusetts and the 62nd Pennsylvania, where the men drew a breath and dove into the depths of the woods. The sun inside suddenly dimmed to a mere source of light and the heat became a suffocating, tropical presence. The company was told to stack arms and make camp in a patch of thinner trees.

As Danny and Lyman parceled out duties, Louis Ferenczy, a firm Old World Hungarian, looked for a place to sit among the few thin fallen trunks. Though a quiet druggist now in Brooklyn, Louis had for many years led a soldier's life. Between Guyon and the Honveds in '49 and his other journeys with Kossuth, he'd had more days under arms than anyone else in the company and they knew it; he did mostly as he pleased. He eased himself to the ground among the loblolly pines, all fifteen to twenty feet tall, four or five inches thick, and small, but not small enough that you could walk over them.

Like these boys running around now in the army, they were young, easy to cut, but capable of stopping you dead. A man had to either chop them down or walk around them. Spills of violets held the ground in places atop the thin dirt left cold and drained by the countless trees. Dead leaves covered the entire floor; oak leaves, mostly, a deep blackish purple anywhere a standing puddle had kept the earth and leaves wet. The few standing oaks were mean and backward. This Wilderness was a desert of trees, as single-minded and frightening as any expanse of sand. Louis pulled off his jacket, pack, and haversack and cleared aside enough leaves for a small fire. Coffee, then work. The fire would also keep the gnats and mosquitoes away.

As he began to untie his coffee can from his knapsack, something seemed to brush against him. He looked down and there was a fine, soft green *Scudderia curvicauda* prowling with its bony legs through the dark hair of his arm, wondering what kind of field this was. After thirty years of collecting—he'd started at nine—Louis had more than enough katydids under glass; this was just a visitor. He offered a hand and the insect stepped on. Louis raised the katydid to the level of his small eyes, which slanted slightly at the corners. Veined wings, perfectly formed; antennae twitching for clues. A lovely specimen. Louis stretched out his leg, now sleeping and numb, and hoped he wouldn't have to stand up right away.

"What's that?"

Louis turned up and saw Second Lieutenant John Burridge pointing at the katydid. "Porridge" some called him. Like everyone else, he'd never warmed to this young man with his first beard and uncertainty, all of twenty-four. No one knew him in Brooklyn. His thin lips fit his thin body and his own thin conviction that he deserved to lead. The clumsy force of authority anticipating challenge only underscored his often inconsiderate words. "What is that?"

"It is *Scudderia curvicauda*."

"Yes. Of course it is." Louis could tell from Burridge's shifty eyes that the lieutenant had no idea what a *Scudderia curvicauda* was, but he would never have the courage to admit it. "Well, get rid of it. Your attention should be with making camp."

"Yes sir." Louis brought a beefy hand down hard onto the katydid, crushing it to his arm. Burridge winced. Jimmy Tice, Louis's tentmate, was walking by and made a girlish sound at the sight. Peeling off the insect by a wing, Louis dangled it before Burridge. "Would you like to arrange burial duty, sir?"

Burridge set his jaw and walked away. Tice asked, "Why did you do that?" He was a well-proportioned boy with black hair and an easy future in whatever career his wealthy father had waiting for him back in Williamsburg's Nineteenth Ward.

Louis said, "It was only an insect," and flicked it at Tice, missing. A poor goddamned insect, worth more than Lieutenant Porridge, Louis thought. He rubbed the earth, hoping to force up another, but he knew that he'd just killed the one gift he would get for the day.

Not far from Louis, Danny had a few men taking down trees while Lyman tried to convince Teddy and Slipper that they didn't need to put up their shelter tent on a sunny afternoon. One-eared Willie, the cook, dug a deep pit to fix some beans that Newt had carried with him, grocer that he was. On the edge of the new clearing, a beet-faced German named Caspar Von Schenk strode over to Louis and asked if he could boil some coffee with him. Before Louis could say no, Caspar had set his bulky Prussian frame onto the leaves and nudged Louis's can away from the hottest part of the fire with his own. Fires could attract pests as well as repel them.

Caspar used both hands to smooth and twirl the edges of his dark brown mustache. "So, beans for breakfast. I like beans." He drew a long white pipe out from inside his jacket. "You are a druggist; you will be interested in this oddity. Do you know that this is a genuine opium pipe used by Chinese mandarins of the fourteenth century?" Louis gave Caspar the responding grunt he was waiting for. "Yes, I received it from a delicious young girl from the Hoo-nan province." Caspar's slithery vowels made his stories of sexual conquest around the globe more repulsive than their usually unconsummated plots warranted. His round face was still damp from the march, so Louis held on to a hope that Caspar was blushing in shame or embarrassment at speaking of this. "Her feet, mangled most brilliantly, resembled large flowers available to her lover for pleasure *und* attested to a royal background. Of course, at that time I was fighting for . . ." Louis unbuckled his leggings, tugged his shoes off, and gave his feet a good rub. Flowers they were not, though a delicate peel of skin hung off the sole of one like a petal. "...*und* as a Christian I could not, but I did watch when..."

As Karl passed by with can in hand, Louis caught his eye with a quick roll of his own and a slight lean toward Caspar. Karl raised one corner of his mouth in a rare grin and sat as a favor. Caspar greeted his fellow German. "*Wie geht's, liebe Karl? Haben Sie Kaffee?*"

Karl patted his haversack. "*Ja, danke.* What lies are you telling now?"

"*Eine seltsame Geschichten auf einem Chinesische Mädchen.*" Caspar packed his last shreds of tobacco into his pipe of great import and lit it. "*Also,* Karl. What do you think?"

"All these trees and not enough good wood to make a table." They watched Lyman light his own fire. Flames licked up over the edge of Willie's cooking pit. The beans would go in soon. "If there is a fight here it will be a hell."

Patting his face dry with his last cotton handkerchief—a rarity in these days of Rebels burning their own bales on the docks and the starving Lancashire weavers—Lieutenant Burridge puffed out his chest and began a casual inspection of his men in hopes of calming his anxious stomach. Though the wires he'd pulled had put the red braid on his shoulders, they couldn't help strengthen his tenuous hold on this company.

Burridge recalled the morning's shame: the insolence of Quigley, Anson, and Alder; Ferenczy's patronizing; no one saluting as they marched past Henry and Stewart. Small things, but proof of his shortcomings; the latter episode surely taken note of by his superiors. As he was crossing, he had thought of Caesar's bridge across the Rhine. "...*sed navibus neque satis.*" He tried now to remember what was next. Was it "*tantum*"? "*Tantum esse arbitrabatur, neque suae populi Rōmānī dignatatum et statuebatis.*"—"He did not judge it safe, and ruled it below him and the dignity of Rome to cross in boats." Not a perfect translation, but a true rendering of the spirit, he decided, quickly forgetting a promise to himself to check his accuracy in the edition of the *Commentaries* he had stowed in his bag. The great men knew how to lead, Burridge thought. Caesar inspired his legions to do their duty, even when that duty meant death. McClellan could do that. So could the lowly sergeant, Danny Anson. But he—student of Latin and Greek, thinker, disciple of the law, consort to many well-placed persons, a man of limitless potential—couldn't get a soldier to sit up straight when asked.

His first stop was the fire of the three green b'hoys, who didn't know enough to make an effort at saluting. In Brooklyn, Burridge would have crossed the street in fear of the violence implied by their swagger, and that fear returned for a moment. His heart beat at Finn's harsh voice until he remembered the revolver pressing on his hip, a gun only officers were allowed to have. He tapped his fingertips lightly on the holster and moved on, passing the foreigners huddled together with their pipes. Gauls, he thought. The very descendants of those Caesar had conquered. Burridge imagined the punishments suitable for the Hungarian, finally settling on his being carried out of camp astride a rail, the rest of the regiment flinging slop at him and jeering. For all he knew, this trio of druggist, carpenter, and soldier of fortune could be plotting his death as he watched. Europeans, though, usually manifested blind obedience, unless in full retreat. Bred into them by centuries of kings and queens and coronets, they mouthed off sometimes, but they did the job. The officer's braid meant something to them.

Felix Cawthorne sat at the next fire. A prim toy soldier rubbed down some by a year in the field, he had been returned to ranks in '62 after a disastrous month as a corporal. A play actor, of all things. He babbled with Del Rio and Tice and tried to crack a square of hardtack with his bayonet. All three saluted Burridge and even asked his opinion about the army's next movements. Burridge enjoyed the warmth of their respect and compliance, but they were the three men deemed most worthless by the hard cases. Burridge answered that they were in for a quick march to Parker's Store tomorrow and then on to Richmond. Even these three looked skeptical. The lieutenant moved on before they asked anything else.

Willie Winston set the big pot of beans, molasses, sugar, and onion into the pit to cook overnight, then said, "Hey, John." Winston was a simple, energetic man. A shard of exploding metal had torn off most of his left ear.

"Smells good already."

"That's right." A harmless man, to Burridge's eyes. Huey Van Deuven, standing close enough to help if asked, but far enough not to botch up a much-anticipated meal, nodded at Burridge and the lieutenant nodded back. Another innocent. Huey had a long head, shaved on the sides and topped with a curly bush of hair. A janitor by trade, Huey left greater accidental destruction behind him on an average day than he cleaned up in a year.

The Worm twins stopped their usual debate to greet him as he went by. Pindar, a hunched, turtlelike accountant, was trying to convince his brother, rabbity Horace, that Francis Scott Key was indeed a man. Horace was a full two inches taller than his twin and better groomed despite the disreputable living he earned as a horse trainer, an occupational choice that had apparently placed him outside of the intimate circles of the Worm family. Odd men, but, as much as Burridge could tell, they supported him.

Others had it worse, he knew. There had been officers shot in the back by their troops or laughed all the way back to Washington, and certainly Burridge had never done anything so tragically wrong as Cotta and Sabinus. Caesar himself would have approved of his calm head during the proud and bloody days of Gettysburg, a performance that justified to him his less than patriotic reason for being here, namely to build a lucrative and prestigious legal practice back in Brooklyn based on his wartime rank. But Henry was his commanding officer, not Caesar, and he'd felt Henry's disapproval all winter, that look of vague annoyance whenever the captain's wandering gaze lit on him. It was unjust. If he had not triumphed, nor had he failed, and by now wasn't that enough? It had certainly sufficed for McClellan, Hooker, and every other commander of the Army of the Potomac. Of course, they'd all been knocked down a few pegs since.

Burridge knew from where the captain's distaste had really spun whenever he saw Henry and Stewart chatting together as if they shared a foreign tongue. Indeed they did—the language of wealth, privilege, and accomplishment, a classic language in which he could trade a smattering of words and a few phrases, but was far from fluent. This, he felt, was his greatest failing, and the blame for it rested on his father. It was not *his* fault; still, the resulting punishment was visited upon him. Sum up his many mistakes and his slipping grasp on the men's loyalty and the next step became quite clear: He would be returned to ranks. Burridge winced a little at the corners of his eyes and mouth.

He had that in mind as he approached the company's last fire. Oliver Stives, a long, Scripture-spouting loner with the wild hair and beard of Moses, sat next to Newt Fry and read the Bible out loud while Fry tried to ignore him. Next to them were Anson, Quigley, and Alder, and suddenly Burridge was twelve again, outside a circle of older boys on Wheat Hill, desperate to join and afraid of them beating him up. The four ate sandwiches of raw bacon between two slabs of hardtack. Burridge's stomach quivered. He walked on to make his own fire on the edges of the clearing, where he would cook his pork like a gentleman and wonder what it tasted like raw.

By five the boys had drunk their coffee and felt reasonably secure in this unnerving forest. Since one could only see twenty yards in, Captain Schuyler Henry and First Lieutenant Linden Stewart surprised them by their sudden appearance. An opening in the trees above let a shaft of sun beam through the gloom and Henry stepped into it. He was a short man, five feet tall, but well built. Bushy eyebrows and a thick, trimmed mustache showed him to be quite a hairy man. Now in his forties, Henry owned the North Brooklyn Savings Bank on Broadway and he had rallied this company together out of clients and depositors, so his authority extended beyond the military realm.

"Gentleman, I bear a message from General Meade, commanding."

Stewart bellowed, "Awlright, gentlemen, the captain is speaking. Up at attention." While the men tolerated Henry's posturing, knowing that there was some kernel of decency within his rule, Linden Stewart had earned universal disgust. Tall and broad, his stomach pushed open his tight jacket. His whole uniform, though new, looked as if he'd pulled it off a body on the field, a ghoulish act that he was not above performing for a shiny Reb buckle or some other souvenir. Many said he was a terrific shot, but no one could recall ever seeing him shoot a gun in anger. He had goggle eyes, damp, pasty skin, and was legendary for both his ability to consume more food than any other man in the company and his horrifying manners. Half of any plateful of beans or skillygallee would end up on his jacket. The men missed his brother Miles, who'd held the job before and had had brains and guts, now buried at Gettysburg.

Henry placed a pair of glasses on his nose and held a sheet of paper well out in front of them with his white-gloved hands:

SOLDIERS: Again you are called upon to advance on the enemies of your country. The time and the occasion are deemed opportune by your commanding general to address you a few words of confidence and caution. You

have been reorganized, strengthened, and fully equipped in every respect.
You form a part of the several armies of your country, the whole under the
direction of an able and distinguished general, who enjoys the confidence of
the Government, the people, and the army.

Danny pawed at the ground with his foot.

Your movement being in co-operation with the others, it is of the utmost
importance that no effort should be left unspared to make it successful.

Newt cracked his knuckles. He'd shoot this time, he decided. If he had
to, he would shoot.

Soldiers! the eyes of the whole country are looking with anxious hope to the
blow you are about to strike in the most sacred cause that ever called men
to arms.
    Remember your homes, your wives and children, . . .

Lyman saw Victoria's china face, Ernie rolling a ball on the floor of
their new house on Hooper Street.

. . . and bear in mind that the sooner your enemies are overcome the sooner
you will be returned to enjoy the benefits and blessings of peace. Bear with
patience the hardships and sacrifices you will be called upon to endure.

Tiger nodded, trembling some in his hands.

Have confidence in your officers and in each other.

Burridge looked at the leaves at his feet, cleared his throat, and wondered when Henry would take him aside for their fatal conference.

Keep your ranks on the march and on the battlefield, and let each man
earnestly implore God's blessing, and endeavor by his thoughts and ac-
tions to render himself worthy of the favor he seeks. With clear consciences
serve the Government and the institutions handed down to us by our

forefathers—if true to ourselves—victory, under God's blessing, must and will attend our efforts.

George G. Meade. Major-General Commanding.

Henry folded the sheet and put it back into his pocket. "All I can add is that I know you are indeed curious, and rightfully so, as to why we have been detached from our proud 14th Brooklyn regiment. Difficult as this may be for you to hear, I am not yet at liberty to reveal our purpose here near the lead of this offensive, as it is hoped by many that the need will not present itself. Know that your safe return to your families in Brooklyn is of primary importance to me, and I will make every possible effort to spare you any duty that I deem threatening. With that, gentlemen, I wish you luck and, like General Meade, God's blessing. Dismissed."

CHAPTER

3

EVERY PART OF NEWT'S BODY WANTED TO MOVE. HE TRIED to read the newspaper he had stuffed into his knapsack back in Culpeper, but he couldn't settle himself. A gnat buzzed up his nose and back out. He rolled over onto his stomach and reread the headline about the Fort Pillow Massacre. Forrest was a criminal for letting his Rebs slaughter soldiers who happened to be Africans. Even as he felt proud that he was fighting this war, he could feel his legs vibrating, his fingers drumming on the pages of the *New York Tribune.* He was lying when he said "fighting this war." What Newt said when he was honest with himself was "in this war." The memories of battle after battle returned to haunt him: Fredericksburg, Bull Run, and, most painfully, Gettysburg. He folded the newspaper and listened to Danny and Tiger talk.

"Ye can take all yer forests. I never seen a blessed tree till I set me foot in Brooklyn." Tiger stuck his bayonet quickly between the splays of his fingers. "Gimme the old peat and mud, I say. Trees are for rich men and animals."

Danny smirked and shook his head. "Never seen a tree, my ass."

"Fuck ye if ye don't believe me, lad." Tiger was not laughing. "Cut 'em all down, we did. The saint rid us of snakes; we rid ourselves of trees and the devil took the rest." He plunged the bayonet deep into the dirt. "And more."

Danny fell into Tiger's somber mood and nodded. "Well, we're through yer forest in another day."

"When do ye figure we hit 'em?"

Newt flinched. Tiger had voiced everyone's vague anxiety, and fear now formed into shapes in Newt's head. A line of yelling gray men growing larger, coming closer; white blooms of smoke. A man arching backward, arms stretched out to greet the morning of his death. Newt rolled onto his back, then his side, then his stomach again, hoping a new position would rouse some new thoughts.

A man with a long beard and battered blue jacket squatted down at their fire, the bottoms of his pants frayed up past the tops of his brogans. Danny recognized him first—he was a newswalker of the 67th New York, one of the men wandering from fire to bare glow of fire, following the sounds of men echoing in the forest to gather news and tell what they knew. They were also known for thieving, but this was a friend. If he *was* to hook the stray haversack, it wouldn't be from them.

"So whaddaya hear?"

"Well, Hancock's over at Chancellorsville. Same spot as last year." Heads shook. "Some of the boys from the 116th Pennsylvania are campin' right on the graves. Found 'em covered in flowers. Forget-me-nots." The newswalker poked a stick into the fire. "When they was diggin' in they kept bringin' up bones." Newt unfolded the newspaper and concentrated very hard on the fact that Edwin Booth was playing Hamlet at the Winter Garden. "Most everybody else is back at the Tavern."

"Anything from Grant?"

"Nothin' I've heard."

Newt considered writing a letter to his Mrs. Fry, blocking out images of hogs gnawing on human skulls with thoughts of what he would tell her. During the Peninsula he'd sent a letter to nearly everyone he knew. He thought briefly about pulling out his folding desk, a treasured parting gift, then rolled over again and looked at the fire ringed by Finn, Feeney, and Pitt. The youngest one, Wes, glanced at the man standing over him, then knit his fingers behind his head and leaned back into the haughty pose of some reclining swell. "Me and the boys come here ta be heroes, ya know? Somebody around here gotta be one."

Newt saw Lyman's head snap toward the recruits. He got up, pulling Lyman with him. "How about a catch? We still got some light here. I could go for a catch."

Lyman took a breath and nodded. Pitt was rubbing him raw, and the boy would be lucky if he didn't teach him a lesson for free before he saw his first Rebel face. They'd all intended to be heroes once; intended it the whole ride down to Washington, packed in trains like drunken oysters in a can. They'd meant to be heroes as they polished their shoes and pulled guard duty and drilled, wanted to make their wives and mothers proud as they marched south toward Bull Run.

Then they had their first smell of cannon smoke. They heard screaming they'd only heard from a baby. The cramps began. Throats dried up. Bleeding, weeping men ran past and a few of their own joined them. They told themselves they would run into the bullets, but the visceral certainty of courage was drawing out of their bones. Then the first man shit his pants, tears of embarrassment and fear creeping from the corners of his eyes. They heard whimpers and prayers, and nothing seemed so sure anymore; not victory, not heaven, not a glorious death. When the sword came down and those first bullets ripped by, the secret lesson was finally learned: Courage, so easily assumed a virtue of all soldiers, was by no means universal, even among those who believed most in the cause. As they watched a few men fire calmly into the fray, men who scrambled out under fire to pull in wounded friends, it became clear that some were born heroes and most could only hope to be near them.

Yet even those days were passing. Men unafraid of bullets had taken theirs early, leaving now just the ordinary thousands like the men of Company L, whose only extraordinary claim was that they knew some things few knew back in Brooklyn—that moments of sterling courage were rare on a battlefield and that most men just wanted to go home.

Lyman dug around for the base ball in his knapsack and found it tucked inside the folds of his rubber blanket, still as clean and white and hard as it was when he'd gotten it from Ernie last Christmas. He'd brought one out when he left Brooklyn, but some man-mountain in the Harris Light Cavalry had knocked the cover right off it the first time he'd swung. Lyman gripped this one with the pickle-thick fingers of his right hand and sniffed the leather.

The only thing he'd ever talked about with Ernie—when they talked —was base ball. He'd taken Ernie to his first match in 1860: The Excelsiors against Charter Oaks at the Excelsiors' new ground at the foot of Court Street. Creighton's first year with the club and Ernie had just turned seven.

Lyman had never taken him out alone and was a bit nervous at first, but once he had the boy on his shoulders drinking lemonade and asking excited, tentative questions about the match, he calmed down and began to show him off to the other men he knew there, even Hiram Cully. Ernie didn't know one player from another and, truth be told, he couldn't tell the Excelsiors from the Charters even after Lyman pointed out the *E*'s on their fronts, but none of that really mattered. What mattered was that when Lyman cheered, Ernie cheered, and when Lyman booed, Ernie booed. The boy drank in the people and the color and the green pitch, and he spent the next week chucking stones around the street saying, "I'm Creighton! I'm Creighton!" until Lyman finally bought him a real ball and taught him to throw. Creighton, who'd died from trying too hard, stretching three bases into four. Tore his bladder. That was a hero, Lyman thought. A damned fool hero who was gone like all the rest of them.

Back in '55, Hiram Cully had invited him to an Excelsiors match, one of the first ever. The club had just been formed the December before and though Cully said not many in the group got their hands dirty, they were looking for good men with prospects who enjoyed throwing the base ball. Cully had in mind a business venture, too, and a membership in the Excelsiors could help make them prosperous men. Lyman set his jaw, remembering the days when he was considered a man with prospects.

Alder Senior had forbid him to go.

The match was late enough—two P.M., past the end of a butcher's day—and the new sawdust had already been spread, but the answer remained no. Lyman still didn't understand why he'd listened. Simple fear was the best he could say now; fear he'd justified then as respect for his father's wishes.

Nine years later Hiram Cully and Lewis Porcher, the man who'd taken Lyman's place, were two of the richest butchers in Brooklyn and he was eating raw pork off the tip of a bayonet. Being a hero here, he decided, was as foolish as his other dreams, the boyish dreams of hitting a home run to win a match for the Excelsiors or owning his own business. Not meant to be. Lyman had called on Cully not long after the missed chance and nearly begged for another invitation, but it was not forthcoming. Cully had been much too friendly, an obvious attempt at softening the blow that conveyed no regret. Lyman was embarrassed, until laziness finally overtook embarrassment. Ernie never saw another match.

Lyman fastened the buckles on his knapsack. If he could only have that time back, he could do it all better. Like some of the battles. Pitt was right; they did need more heroes. But here in Company L all they had now was Danny.

Newt yelled, "Give it a toss!" He stood in a small field of stumps left by the clearing they'd done earlier, where Caspar Von Schenk was now attempting to lift both Worm brothers. With most of Grant's army camping around them, open space was hard to find.

Danny held up Newt's newspaper. "Do ya still need this, Newton?"

"All yours. Come on, Lyman." The ball came arching to Newt over a few campfires. "Paper says they're all starting up this week. Atlantics, Eckfords." Newt whipped it back.

"About that time. But I'll tell you . . ." Lyman caught it and windmilled his arm a few times before flipping it back underhand. "The sport has gone all to hell. Nothing at all like it used to be. I can't say that I'm a follower this day."

Newt sent it over with more spark. "You've been saying that for two years since Creighton died. Mind you don't hit Von Schenk here."

"It's not just Creighton." Lyman assumed more of a pitcher's stance, then shot it back, just missing the German, who'd finally gotten the two men off the ground. Caspar gave him a look. "It's the legal tenders they're handing out now. They play it for the money and that's all there is to it. Damned thugs out there now and it used to be a fine thing on a summer day. It's not a man's game anymore, Newt."

"That's the bull and you know it. Your man Creighton himself was the first to be paid, and if I remember correctly, you were the one arguing that he deserved it." He shook his hand to get the sting out. "Bully throw."

"No. You see, Jimmy Creighton, God bless his soul, was being honored. That's the difference. He didn't expect it." Newt laughed. "You know that's the God's honest truth. He bowled against the English at their own game and didn't ask for a penny. He was a sportsman."

Newt rolled his eyes. "All right now. Get into your work. Let's see one of those Creighton speed balls." Lyman got into his stance. "Remember the box is smaller this season. Four feet by three. You can't leave the box." Lyman took a small step with his right foot, holding his right arm back at a forty-five-degree angle to the ground; then, as he lunged forward, low onto his left foot, he brought the arm forward, letting go with a snap of his wrist just as his hand nearly scraped the dirt. The ball arched toward Newt, then curved across his body and down. "A snap pitch! Didn't know you were working on one of those."

"Jimmy Creighton took the game with him to the grave. Heart attack at twenty-one. The Excelsiors have never recovered and I'm glad of it." Lyman pitched a speed ball over.

"You and your Excelsiors, sent by God the Almighty to teach us base ball as it should be. The truth is, your Jimmy Creighton died of a torn bladder."

Lyman held on to the ball. "It was his heart, and as for the Excelsiors, they were never champions, but they were always gentlemen and sportsmen, which is more than I can say of your Eckfords. No, you let the Atlantics and the Mutuals have all the championships. The Excelsiors *chose*"—he pointed at him—"*chose* not to play for the championship in 1860 because the Atlantics *tainted* that season. The Excelsiors had honor and played like men, and they may be fading now, but I'll not forget them." He whipped the ball at Newt, who dropped it, surprised by the speech as much as the pitch.

Tiger clucked. "Oh-h-h, our star has the dropsy, does he?"

Newt was about to point out the six runs he recently scored in a match against the 9th New York when four or five pops, distant and far ahead to the west, froze everyone. Newt dropped his hands. "Shit." He wasn't ready. Not yet. They held their breath. No rush of fire, one or two more shots, spread apart.

"Just pickets," Lyman said. "Well, we knew they were out there some-where."

The slow, sad roll of "Tattoo" echoed through the woods, and a day and a half without sleep, of moving on impulse, and the energy of a new campaign, finally caught up with all who heard it. The newswalkers made their journeys back home to friends and regiments. Newt tossed the ball back to Lyman, then took a sniff at the beans cooking deep in the ground. Breakfast meant they were one day closer to home. The men who hadn't yet unrolled their blankets did so now with heavy arms, and new logs were added to the fires, re-creating the orange sunset blocked by the haze of trees. Random picket shots continued off in the thickening dark. What talk there was stayed low.

For a few minutes silence held the woods. Then a murmur rose behind them, coming from the miles of field surrounding Wilderness Tavern. A prayer meeting had ended with a hymn, a stately, simple hymn of thanks to a God who had not yet abandoned them, sung in deep bass and tenor tones.

Praise God from whom all blessings flow.

A few clusters of men joined.

Praise him all creatures here below.

The song jumped from outfit to outfit, a flame sending sparks to far, separate places then merging into one blaze.

Praise him above, ye heavenly hosts.

An indistinct moan at first to those at the edges, but as the number of singers grew, the song became clear.

Praise Father, Son and Holy Ghost.

Consoled, some offering true praise, others fond of hearing their own voices, fifty thousand men facing death at any moment united under the swell of Luther's hymn. The song engulfed them all; in the field, in the woods by Company L, at Warren's headquarters at the Lacy House. A thousand fires flecked the night. Stars met them from above and the song lifted as the smoke of battle does, riding the breezes between earth and sky.

Eternal are thy Mercies, Lord.
Eternal truth attends thy word.

Thy praise shall sound from shore to shore,
Till suns shall rise and set no more.

Burridge couldn't concentrate. The flickering firelight broke up Caesar's words. All evening he had continued to slip into one of his dour moods; the sight of Stewart sped the descent. Captain Henry wanted to see him tomorrow morning, and it wasn't hard to glean what the topic for discussion would be from Stewart's look. There were only three weeks left anyway. The return to ranks wouldn't last long, though the shame of it would.

Burridge flipped ahead some in the book. *"... omnia enim plērumque quae absunt vehementius hominum mentes perturbant."*—"What men cannot see frightens them more than that which they can see." There was much to fear in these woods—bullets, Rebels, snakes, treachery, failure—and none of it was visible until one had no choice but to accept the inevitable pain. He would become like Cawthorne, suspect in even the least matter of judgment, sniggered at. He'd always secretly believed in the singularity of his future, that the furthest reaches of his destiny fringed the Olympus of a Senate desk or White House chair, but men his age were becoming generals in this war and he had not.

Burridge stared into the fire and beyond, as the dark shadows of men trying to find their home regiments straggled past in a slow line. He could see a little office, dusty, in a corner of some faded wooden building near the river. Ashes down the front of his vest. Bits of food in his beard. Handling the paltry estates of the poor and keeping petty criminals like Feeney out of prison. Asking men like Stewart to lunch and claiming appointments before the bill arrives.

Burridge closed his eyes, resigning himself to the unpleasant days ahead. As unfair as Henry's decision was, he knew he deserved the blame. He was no Caesar.

Tiger wasn't sure what the sound was when "Old One Hundred" first spread through the Wilderness. He'd been hearing things ever since they made camp in these blasted trees. A soft voice saying his name and asking where he was. The baby wanted to see his da, she'd whisper, and a stringy bit of hair would scratch across his neck and he'd think it was her finger tracing his collar. Every small sound made him twitch. He pulled her likeness out of his breast pocket. Beautiful Mary Quigley. Black hair sleek and flat, tied behind her head, almost like an Indian. He was from Sligo, she was from Cork, but like every product of Irish soil those years, they were blighted both and joined thereby. They'd seen the bodies in the ditches, the naked children screaming from hunger and the rats sitting upon mothers too fever weak to move. At least the niggers got fed, he thought. And still they complained.

He wanted a drink just then, and he hated still having the taste for it. Every step his family had made in America seemed to splash into a puddle of whiskey. Only Mary and Lyman had put him on dry land.

Now there was just Lyman, if that. Tiger couldn't come up with a reason not to desert the whole nigger-loving Army of the Potomac.

Thoughts of battle kept Wesley Pitt awake; that and having to get up to shit every five minutes. He worried he'd freeze up in fear and his stomach balled up tight as a fist. Whether it was the food or the water or the thought of getting his head blown off by some butternut, he'd be in real trouble if he had to take a shit in the middle of a battle. He swatted a mosquito pestering his ear. Teddy said they called Rebs "butternuts" because their homemade shirts were all the color of butternut squash. Two more shots snapped off like dry sticks. He told himself that he'd been in scrapes before with Teddy and Slipper. They'd take the lead and he'd be behind them all the way, watching their backs. Knowing he wasn't alone, Wes gradually fell off.

————

The lieutenant slept little that night, and poorly when he did. By four, when the first dull outlines formed around him, he rose and picked his way through the trees, following what embers still burned from the evening's fires. The distance to Henry's tent wasn't far, yet Burridge couldn't remember a walk that ever took so long. In some ways, he thought, it was just the end of a walk he'd been making for twenty-four years.

He'd done well every step of the way. By far the brightest boy in the Williamsburg Grammar School for Boys, he was a natural genius, his father said, and he should have known, being a master. At six, John memorized bits of Ovid and Homer and would wait eagerly outside the parlor, rubbing the velvet of his short pants until Father called him to entertain the guests.

Though enormously proud to have a son of such talents, Master Burridge had never actually required proficiency in any particular discipline, so his son grew up content to devise new intellectual stunts far beyond his years, certain to amaze his father or anyone else whom he could impress into service as an audience. Whether or not he could truly converse in Latin or read ancient Greek was unimportant. He told himself that, of course, he could if he tried, but he never tried.

Young John Burridge skittered along looking for new things to learn a little about, creating an imposing facade of knowledge over a potential slowly eroding from neglect. During his first years at Columbia, Burridge began to sense a hollowness at his core. Though he could speak wisely about books he'd never read, music he'd never heard, paintings he'd never seen, which made him popular at late-night discussions with his fellow scholars, he had not become the kind of outstanding student he had expected to be. There was always someone else who had studied longer, who grasped the significance of some point in Thucydides that he had missed or could translate entire poems without a lexicon.

Burridge's hunger for respect, and self-respect, sent him to further horizons of knowledge rather than deeper into the heart of things. He convinced himself that his mind worked in that wider, more encompassing way; that his gifts were too great to waste on the life of a pedant, the life that his father had led. Burridge saw his greatness in something else, something larger than memorized verbs, something vital and active. He decided to be a lawyer.

In the world of law, his perception and acute memory served him well, as did his strength to charm people into seeing the image of himself that he wanted them to see. Others listened to him and gave credence to his ideas. He acted as though he knew his way, so it was assumed he did; his natural gifts helped him stumble along. Burridge had emerged as a serious comer in Brooklyn legal circles, and every night he wondered when someone would finally expose him for the poseur that he was.

Burridge stepped out of the woods. Griffin's headquarters were in a small clearing torn out of the forest and transformed into a settlement. Henry's and Stewart's tents clung to the outskirts, the former exuding a warm sepia glow. The captain's elderly African servant, Pompey, was fetching water when Burridge hailed him. "Hello, Pompey. Has the captain risen yet?"

"Course. You see that light; he be awaitin' for ye. Lemme tell de captain yo heah." Burridge straightened up. A man had to act like a man, he thought to himself. Before he could boost his spirits with any heartening thoughts, Pompey was back outside. "Captain say come right in."

Inside, the tent glowed with the russet luxury of a paneled room. Burridge wondered, as he did every time he came into this tent, what Henry's home looked like if this was how he went to war: the cot made with fine, light woolen blankets; the leather trunk now standing free as an armoire; the camp desk with its gold accoutrements, the cut-crystal decanter; the gold frames with likenesses of his wife and three children; the gold-and-marble washstand complete with mirror. The captain stood before the mirror, jacket off and sleeves rolled to expose arms carpeted with dense black fur. With one hand, Henry had pulled his nose up and with the other he was trying to trim his nose hair. His head was tilted back, his eyes were wide, and for a second he looked like nothing more than a startled pig. He took a snip, sneezed, then doused his face with water.

As he dried off, Henry finally spoke. "Good morning, Lieutenant."

"Good morning, sir."

"Solid progress we've made, yes? Since Culpeper."

Burridge nodded vigorously. "I hope the advance continues as well. This forest is no place for a fight, sir."

"It is certainly less than ideal. Like a prizefighter, pulling his blouse over his head. The army is ready to fight, yet blind for a moment, hmm?" Henry neatly refolded the towel and draped it on the stand, then he checked himself in the mirror. "Though I believe General Grant holds firmly to the tenet that any place is a place for a fight if the enemy can be found there." Knitting his forehead, he found a few stray eyebrow hairs and began applying himself to them as he spoke, "Lieutenant, I've asked to speak with you privately because we have a very serious matter to discuss."

Burridge winced at Henry's unwillingness to even exchange the customary pleasantries. "Sir?"

"I'm certain that you're aware how vital this campaign is to the existence of the Union, are you not?"

"Of course, sir."

"General Sherman drives from the west, Butler from the Peninsula. Our target is Lee. Warren's Fifth advances directly south toward Spotsylvania with Sedgwick and the Sixth behind. Hancock swings left, recrossing Chancellorsville. Burnside brings up the rear." Henry stopped snipping and turned to Burridge. "To cripple Lee's army, we must be prepared to perform whatever duties are incumbent upon us. Do you understand?" Burridge tensed, expecting the worst. Henry put down the scissors. "I have always had the utmost respect for you, Mister Burridge." He held up one finger. "Allow me a question. Why do you suppose we are on this detatched duty?"

Burridge swallowed. He realized that he hadn't given that question much thought, strange as it was this close to the end. "Sir, I can honestly say I've been preoccupied with the advance."

"Yes, you're right. And I must say you've done well with them. They're a fine-looking group." Henry motioned toward the decanter but Burridge declined, dizzy enough from the tension and suspense. "We cannot always wait for history to occur, can we, Lieutenant?"

"Sir?"

Henry put his jacket on, tugged at the hem, and lifted his chin. "At times man must, shall we say, create history. No matter the means." He stared at the lieutenant. "Would you agree?"

Bewildered, Burridge could not imagine what he was aiming toward. "Well, yes."

The captain smiled. "I was certain you would. Intrigues are sometimes a necessity toward effecting a greater good."

Growing curious, Burridge warmed to the topic. "Yes, Radamistus and Mithradates. Tiberius, Livia." He'd just about scraped his mind clean of examples. "The history of the ancients is quite a chronicle of intrigue."

"You've made a study of this, haven't you? And your profession must allow you to, shall we say, practice as well. Hmm?"

Henry leaned in with interest to Burridge, who avoided his eyes with the self-deprecating downward glance he made when some offered detail was happily mistaken for evidence of great knowledge. "I've read my share and . . ." Burridge smiled enigmatically. "Yes, I've done what an attorney sometimes must."

"Well said, sir. Very good." Henry put his hand on the decanter. "What I am about to tell you is strictly confidential. It is not to be shared with Lieutenant Stewart, nor with any of your men."

"You can be quite sure of that, sir."

Henry poured an inch of brandy into a small glass for himself and sipped. "Somewhere out there is a Union scout. A Rebel who has raised himself to a position of some influence within the Confederate army. Because of the extreme importance of our guaranteed success this spring, we need to establish close contact with him. We have a loose channel now, but it's too dangerous and it's not nearly reliable enough for our high command. What we must do is find him and create a means of constant communication with him so we can finally have an edge on General Lee." He returned to the mirror and combed his mustache, a large black brush that curled under his sizable nose and up along the side of his cheeks in one strip. "You will be the conduit of information, passing what he knows on to me so I can pass it on to General Grant."

Burridge folded his arms and leaned back. "Germanicus made use of such a man along the banks of the Weser."

"Is that so?" The captain nodded politely.

"Yes. It was crucial for the conquest of the Cherusci."

"Really?" Henry had continued to nod until it was clear that Burridge had no more to offer. "To return, we have passed information along to the scout and expect him to make contact within the next few days. I know Grant is hoping to get through this damn Wilderness without hitting Lee, but picket does offer some opportunity. All the scout knows is that you are in the 14th Brooklyn. As to my role, I've done a good deal so far, and that should now be clear. It explains why the company is on detached duty and why it is in the lead with Griffin. And it is why you will be given every opportunity to stand on picket duty. This is all I can do. All else rests upon your craft and courage."

The lieutenant caught the challenge in the last phrase. "How will we know who he is?"

"You're the only man who knows about this. That's part of the danger and the skill. Your men must not know." Burridge nodded. "There is a password. He will say, 'I've been to Brooklyn.' You will respond by saying, 'Did you eat at Howard's Halfway House?' He will say, 'Yes, it was very good.' Do you understand?"

"Yes, sir."

Henry strapped on his holster. It looked like it had never been touched. He smiled. "I have many roles in the war effort. This situation was shared with me, and when I heard the small amount known about this scout, I knew immediately that you were the man for this job." He tugged on his white gloves. "If we lose here, the chances of President Lincoln winning a second term are slim indeed and we will have a copperhead in the White House who will be very happy to negotiate a settlement with the Confederates. This is a crucial moment in this nation's history, and you are to serve a most important role in its resolution." He let that sink in. "Do you have any questions?"

"No, sir."

"Report back to me as soon as you've accomplished your first rendezvous. Good luck, Lieutenant."

"Thank you, sir."

The two men saluted each other. Burridge stepped out of the tent and was waiting for Henry to follow, but when he heard the captain brushing his teeth, he went ahead on his own. Pompey came by with a cup of tea for Henry.

Surging with confidence, Burridge had a wicked thought. "Tell me, is Lieutenant Stewart in?"

"No, sir. He out on his horse somewheres."

Burridge waited until Pompey went into Henry's tent, and then he stole a look into Stewart's lair, a place he'd never been invited into and honestly had never been curious about until now. Burridge was not surprised to find it as slovenly as its inhabitant. The cot was unmade. Clothes littered the ground. A burlap sack next to his trunk bulged with empty tin cans. Wax from a burning candle stub dripped onto his desk. It was a sty. What amazed Burridge most was that this man was an esteemed lawyer in Brooklyn. When he first joined the regiment, Burridge considered it one of the honors of the job to be near the legendary Linden Stewart. Stewart's reputation was built on a very visible case in which he proved that an extremely wealthy and extremely stupid man could not possibly have murdered his wife because he did not understand how the murder weapon—a flintlock pistol—worked. The defense was brilliant and Burridge had reviewed it in depth in preparation for a stirring discussion of the particulars with Stewart himself, a discussion that Burridge was now quite relieved to say had never taken place. Over the last three years, Burridge had lost any of the respect for Stewart he once had and now maintained a very wary distance. Stewart may have been a slob, but he was as dangerous as he was brilliant. He knew people, and despite Henry's affable nature, Stewart had his ear.

Pompey stuck his head in the tent. "He's coming!" Burridge quickly hopped out and just as he was about to ask Pompey how he knew he was in there, the African winked and said, "Something, i'n it?"

———

"Louie!" Tice took a tentative poke at Louis. "Louie, the beans are going fast. Better get moving."

Louis grunted. He'd been up for a while, lying in the dark, listening to the sounds of camp at four in the morning. Men shuffling awake and grumbling, coffee cans clanking, a few horses muffled by the cover of leaves and the dew and then the drums of reveille. He'd slept lightly, as soldiers usually do, and his dreams were of a drifting, idle sort: shaking hands with a bearded man at his druggist's shop; reaching into his pockets for his keys and finding them empty; an eagle tethered to the ground.

As he sat up, his back made an audible pop and the muscles along his neck contracted, pulling his shoulders nearly up to his ears. Other men were trying to stretch the damp ground out of their bones as they waited for their coffee to boil, shaking their limbs awake over fires, but these stiff mornings were happening to Louis too often now for them to be just a matter of sleeping on the ground, and the loud cracks from his knees as he stood did not cheer him either. He felt as though he was turning into a bundle of twigs; he allowed himself to stay hunched over and brittle until he remembered that he was only thirty-nine years old. Drawing in a deep breath of smoky air, he pushed his chest out and slapped his stomach.

A small run snuck between the trees nearby like one of the moccasins that slithered through these woods. Louis splashed some cold water onto his face and filled up a can for coffee. The level of camp noise rose. Pindar Worm accused Horace of taking too many beans and helped himself to a forkful off his brother's tin plate. Feeney made some loud mocking comments about Karl Udelhoffer's morning calisthenics, and in the center of it all, Willie doled out the beans. Before last summer he had cooked just for Danny, Lyman, and the rest of their mess, but with only four of them left and stray ones and twos left from the other messes of the company, Willie fed the company as one mess, whether they liked it or not. Mostly they didn't. Louis didn't like spending more time with the likes of Cawthorne than he had to, but then again eating with a live idiot next to you was preferable to sitting alone with dead friends, and there were certainly some men who didn't relish taking their meals with a man like him. Grant himself was one of those men; he'd made that quite clear when he'd had all Jews expelled from his territory in '62.

Willie scooped out some beans and heaped them onto his plate, then pointed Louis toward Lyman, who was gesturing for him to come over. Tiger and Danny greeted him with nods; Newt waved his fork. "Danny says we're going down Parker's Store Road and then straight down the Brock Road to Spotsylvania. What do *you* think?"

Louis put his coffee into the fire. "That's a good march for one day."

Danny spoke between mouthfuls of beans. "I'll say."

Louis stabbed a few onions with a bit of bacon and considered his words well. "We will hit Lee before then."

Danny paused for a beat, then put his spoon down as the tone of his voice deepened into a gentle warning. "Louie's right. We're fighting today, boys. Get yourselfs a-ready."

Newt tapped his fork on his plate a few times, then said, "Maybe not. We got the jump on 'em yesterday and this is a damn ugly place for a battle."

"Bobby knows these woods the way ye know the hair on yer prick." Tiger sipped his coffee. "I say if we're going ta do some shooting, for the love of Mike let's do it now and get it the hell over with."

Heads nodded around the fire and they finished breakfast in silence.

Wesley's head peeked over a bush. He'd only been up an hour and this was already his third trip to the sink. Teddy and Slipper had had their laugh when he'd taken off again, but Slipper had gone twice, too, so Wes didn't see what he had to laugh about. From his hidden vantage, he could see more and more officers striding around, including Burridge, who was now talking with Danny Anson. Men throughout the camp started to toss water on their fires and stamp out the coals in preparation for moving out. Picturing himself left behind by the whole army and squatting in the woods as thousands of Rebs watched, Wesley tried to hurry, grabbing nervously at one of the few leaves left on the bush. Riders came by, picking their paths over the stumps and through the standing trees, and most men now had muskets slung over their shoulders.

Burridge called the company to fall in. Wes finished as best he could and buttoned up, though the stirrings of a new disturbance in his gut told him that he was finished only for the time being. As he mulled the possibility that he would be doing this for months or even years, Slipper's panicked face scrambled past him in search of a new bush. Cheered up considerably, Wesley straightened himself and went into the clearing with a smile.

The men were in lines as straight as they could manage around the stumps and trees. Rifle shots picked up again as dawn neared and the fog began to clear.

A deep bovine bellow called out of the trees for Burridge as he finished. All heads turned toward the source—Henry and Stewart stood off to the northwest, Stewart following his call with a loose wave. The lieutenant jogged over to report to his two superiors.

Newt put his pack down. "So, Danny, what exactly are we doing?"

"Sittin' here until the Fifth gets pulled out an' the Sixth comes down to cover its own ass. I'd load up, if'n I was you; everybody oughta. Them pickets ain't gonna stop Lee if he puts his mind to making a move, and ye don't wanna be caught with your trousers down around your ankles." He turned and put a hand on Slipper's shoulder. "Do ye, Feeney?" Slipper had just returned from his visit to the sinks. "If ye need to go ta hospital for that quickstep, ye'd better go now."

Feeney pushed Danny's hand away. "Nobody's leaving me behind."

Lyman tore open a cartridge and poured the powder down the muzzle as he watched Burridge talk to the officers. Henry indicated west with both hands, then pointed to the edge of the 62nd Pennsylvania, a barely visible tinge of blue on the right, and over his head to the 9th Massachusetts on their left, again only dots of blue between the trees. Every minute a cluster of shots would sound from the turnpike.

As he ran his hand along the wood shaft of his Springfield, Lyman realized that the Sixth would never get there quick enough. The humid air, the shots, the current of anticipation; it was inescapable. They'd be fighting today. Their surroundings changed from a random point on a map into a battlefield. Lyman stuck the minié in the muzzle and plunged it down with the ramrod, feeling the raw vulnerability of human flesh armed with only a single-shot rifle. If either of the two other regiments drifted away even just a few feet, Company L would be alone and out of contact. They did still have the log defenses, but Lyman preferred hunting to being hunted.

He looked back at the three officers. Stewart stood next to Henry, mouth open, his arms folded and appearing to rest on his belly, and Burridge across from them nodded his pathetic agreement to whatever ill-conceived plans they were ordering. Lyman replaced the rod and fixed a percussion cap on the hammer. He was ready to go and a bit more confident now with a loaded weapon in his hands, though a Spencer repeating rifle would have made him feel positively invincible. He drummed his fingers up and down the length of the muzzle.

In the distance, Henry and Stewart retreated on some bureaucratic pretext to their usual command post safely behind lines, while Burridge returned with the news. "General Griffin will have us move north toward the pike to advance"—the veterans grinned and nodded to each other at this example of Griff's manly confidence—"in support of his skirmishers, so load weapons and . . ."

Danny interrupted. "We did."

Burridge saw the cartridge papers scattered on the leaves. "Well-l-l, good."

It was just past five. The sun had not risen high enough yet to push through the canopy of pine, and a dankness made by rotting leaves and moss floated up from the earth. The fact that there was no breeze omened a hot day. Ahead, the 62nd Pennsylvania disappeared into the trees. Burridge signaled to his company and began leading the two short lines of red-capped soldiers through the forest, trailing behind their fellow *chasseur* regiment. Straight movement and the usual close order were impossible; instead, the lines flowed along, separating, then re-forming whenever they could.

After a few minutes of disorganized progress, the lines halted square up against the 62nd. Burridge turned the company to the left so they were facing due west. Danny double-checked their bearings on his compass. Sounds from the turnpike filtered into the woods now and a surge of quick-time marching scraped across the dusty road. Caissons of horses galloped by, pulling something that sounded like artillery.

Burridge dressed the line. The ranks were nine across, files two deep, each man in the front eighteen inches from the ones next to him and the same depth behind, except where trees forced men apart. Anson rechecked the lines with him and shrugged to say that it was the best they could do in there.

More shots.

An officer from Griffin's command strode through the bushes, checked the line, then saluted and moved on. In a few seconds the officer trotted back past them to report to Griff, which meant they had to be far on the left flank.

Then the drums started. Officers called out the advance and the drums set a hard, throbbing pulse that another burst of shots broke after a couple beats.

Burridge cried out, "Forward March!" and Company L stepped off.

Lyman looked into the sea of trees. No miniés had whizzed by, no puffs of smoke, so they were well behind the skirmishers. He turned to look behind, but beyond the panicked look on Pitt's face lay the same waste of trees they were walking into; no landmarks, nothing distinguishing he could look for again if he had to move backward. His one reference was that forward was west, but as trees and bushes jostled men into each other and apart, the thin tissue of visual communication between soldiers strained and the directions of the compass meant nothing. The 62nd had already vanished. He could hear another regiment—maybe the 22nd Massachusetts or the 9th—shuffling behind them in support. Firm directions were imperative here. Setting marks, Lyman aimed himself toward bushes and bent saplings ahead, side-stepping trees and staying the course as best he could.

Eyes flitting across the distance, Burridge searched for his glory and wondered whether it was about to creep whispering out from behind the pines. Most scouts he'd known of—Union and Confederate—had been greasy characters who'd stoop to donning a frock or slitting a throat from behind to accomplish their mission. The prospect of traffic with such a type added a fillip of personal fear to the danger already underlying his duty.

A shot snapped off to the right. Burridge's head snapped toward it.

Was he there? Burridge shifted directions, imagining some barefoot campaigner in a slouch hat. He added a beard, then took it off; exchanged the gray jacket for a brown homespun shirt.

A harsh whisper called his name.

Was it him?

"Lieutenant!"

A rough hand shook him from behind. Anson's. The sergeant pointed left. "This way."

Burridge nodded.

The company crunched on through the leaves, fifty, then a hundred yards, in a measured pace made slower by the trees and farther wanderings left and right along Burridge's erratic path of advance. The scout could be anywhere. A black crow's feather sticking up in the litter drew him north; muffled words from hidden regiments nearby sent him southward again.

Then movement. Every man turned. A few hundred yards up. Things falling onto the leaf cover.

They listened for voices. For screams.

Nothing at first. They tried not to breathe. Then more movement and a dry splash of leaves. The lieutenant began to sweat. This could be, had to be, him.

Then the dull *thock* of a minié hitting a tree. Burridge stopped and listened for his name. There was silence. He waved them forward in whatever direction he was facing. The company took a few more steps. A shot. Another dry splash.

They were close enough now to see that just branches and treetops were being shot off. Burridge signaled for them to keep going.

Fifty more yards, slowly, then a shot. Danny waved a halt. Silence now took them, and they stood still in expectation of many things.

Danny moved first, motioning to Burridge that they were headed too far left. The lieutenant immediately waved him off, but the men waited for Danny to move. Danny looked back to the right, then the left. He rechecked his compass while Burridge stood impatiently, arms folded across his chest. The sergeant shook his head with a deliberate firmness, then mouthed the word "No."

The woods remained silent. Burridge did not move. Sergeant and lieutenant stared at each other until the power represented by Burridge's red officer's braid finally stood out against the gray trees. The sergeant threw his hands up and pointed toward Burridge.

The company followed.

Wesley Pitt gripped his Springfield so hard his arms had begun to cramp. One second he felt like the toughest man in the army and the next he was scouting a place to hide, but mostly he was dazed; hunched over and gnawed by a fear his rifle couldn't fight. He'd thought about this moment since the day he'd signed up and it was nothing like he'd pictured. These first steps toward battle had none of the pomp that he had hoped for—Porridge didn't give a speech; there were no Rebs in sight or horses or flags. Disorientation at not knowing where they were or where they were going merged with his disappointment.

Ten more yards. The rasp of Caspar's tense breathing set a rhythm. He told himself that he could handle this, that he wouldn't run. A look at Teddy smiling the kind of smile he had before he knocked somebody's face in told him that Teddy wouldn't run, either. It was like old times in Brooklyn. Some of those nights in alleys and back rooms Wes had wanted to run, but he always stayed to get his licks in because Teddy and Slipper were there to back him up, and the truth was he liked getting his licks in, too. Just the thought of shooting settled him down. He gazed into these baffling woods and wondered where the Rebs were.

Something snapped nearby.

Wesley aimed his gun into the trees, but no one else was stopping. He couldn't understand it; Rebs coming and no one stopping. All the fear eating him pushed outward. He was on fire. Every sound exploded in his ears, every sight burned into his mind as if his last and then passed as the next last vision burned in. Feet tripping along, hands sweating on the musket, pumping heart—Wes felt he'd fly apart if something didn't happen. He was sure they were going too slow, so he upped his pace until every step nipped Alder's heels.

Shots! It was much too fast now for Wes. There was no time to breathe, no time to grab back his legs. The impulse to run welled up, but he couldn't say if running back in shame would be worse than running forward to death.

He silently begged Burridge to charge, to let him burn off this energy and find whatever was waiting for him. But they kept slowly walking. And walking.

Wes couldn't hold back. Pointing the gun over Lyman's shoulder, he let go and pulled the trigger.

The explosion roared into Lyman's ear. He went down screaming in shock and the others did too, even Danny, hitting trees and grabbing at themselves to see if they had been hit. Danny crawled over to Lyman. "Are you hit?" Lyman was pressed face first into the leaves, trying to dig himself into the earth. "Lyman, are you hit?" Danny flipped him over. Lyman's eyes were squeezed shut and his teeth chattered. Danny put his hand on Lyman's cheek.

Lyman opened his eyes. "I don't feel shot."

Danny looked around. Men were either sprawled on the ground or holding on to trees except for Wesley, who just stood there, shaking as he tore open another cartridge. A dense cloud of smoke hung over them, trapped by the trees and the heavy air. Danny pointed his rifle at Wesley's head and pulled the hammer back. "If you ever shoot without an order again, every goddamned man here has permission to kill you on the spot! No court-martial. No guardhouse. We just kill you. Do you hear me?"

Wesley whispered a yes. Everyone got up with wide eyes and shaky hands.

More picket shots cracked off ahead.

Burridge counted his men. He caught Danny's eye and the two exchanged a glance longer than any they ever had before. For once they had the same thought—that this company was played out, a spent bullet that could at best bounce off the enemy and then fall. Even the few fighters in the group were questionable now. Burridge nodded once. Danny took out the compass, but it was broken, smashed when he went down.

He flung the bits away. In every direction there were gray trees. When they'd known where the pike was, where west was, it had been easy to connect the shots to their source, but now the shots could be a sign of continued skirmishing on the road, or they could mean the company was being flanked. Danny shrugged his shoulders.

Burridge had no better idea of where they were. Even if the scout was out here somewhere, they'd never meet because he'd gotten the entire company lost. Swallowing his embarrassment, the lieutenant picked a direction based on the shape of the smoke cloud only now starting to dissipate and pointed toward it. They continued the advance slowly, in what they hoped was the right direction.

The company crept on for another hundred yards. Danny kept sneaking looks at the treetops, hoping for some sign of the sun. A crow nagged at them from somewhere above. The sounds from the unit that had been behind them were now off to their right. Only the new men didn't understand that they were lost.

Another round of shots, closer now. Slipper stumbled ahead, mumbling, "We're all here. Everybody's together. We're all here."

Another round came, and another. Now it was a continuous series of crackles until single crackles gave way to a solid roll of shot and the constant rumble of fire. It wasn't just pickets anymore.

Lyman turned to his left. The 9th was gone. They were alone. A cannon report shook the woods and then another. Burridge waved them on to keep walking.

Branches began to fly off the trees ten yards ahead. Danny yelled, "Stay calm!" as the spent bullets kicked up leaves.

Wes was sure that this was the elephant. He also noticed that his diarrhea was gone.

Volleys replaced the chaotic firing. Flecks of blue materialized suddenly in the trees and added depth to the two dimensions of the forest. More branches dropped. Danny signaled a halt and Burridge followed with the verbal order. A few more yards and they'd be close enough to take a minié, though from here they couldn't hit any Rebs. Burridge looked to Danny, who ordered them into volley position. Griff himself would have to order them into those woods any farther. Not with seventeen days left. Not when they were played out. The front file knelt down; those behind stood. A voice, hard to tell whose in the roar, shouted, "Aim high!" Hammers were pulled back. Burridge and Danny both brought their arms up, ready to give the signal to fire.

Something rustled toward them, getting closer from the right side. They froze. Suddenly Burridge couldn't remember the password. Which restaurant was it? He pictured it; had eaten there once with his intemperate uncle. It had an *H*...

Danny had taken aim and was about to pull the trigger when a blue runner dashed out of the woods. "Who's in charge here?"

Danny swiveled his gun back forward and kept an eye on the runner. After an uncertain moment, Burridge saluted. "I am. Where are you from?"

The runner panted as he spoke. "Ninth Massachusetts. Wouldn't've found ye lads but for yer caps. Listen. Reb column on the pike. Griff wants us ta stay put." Given a breather, he seemed to regain his bearings. "You boys is pretty far back here. We're probably another fifty yards up and getting it good."

Burridge looked puzzled. "How did you get on our right?"

"How did ye get on our left?"

Danny stared at Burridge.

The runner's mouth was already black from cartridge powder. "I'd stay right here, I was you. Not much else on yer left. Don't wanna get flanked." As soon as the order to halt had been given, some men had knelt down and begun plunging into the dirt with their bayonets, and as soon as the runner said the word "flanked" the whole company was digging in.

Wes made a few halfhearted stabs into the ground and tried to shove the loose dirt away. Though he felt stupid for the shooting, he also felt different, as if he'd taken a step that Teddy and Slipper hadn't and gained some piece of manhood that they were only thinking about. He knew what the gun sounded like in his ear and how it bucked back hard on his shoulder. He'd almost shot one of his own men, but he could've run just as easily and hadn't, and that was worth something to him.

After checking to see how the veterans did it, Teddy and Slipper took out their coffee cans and started bailing while Wes used his tin plate, and in a few minutes they were already a good foot deep along a six-foot line. The low piles of dirt on both sides began to look like shelter as the miniés kept flying. At two feet down Teddy stopped to wipe off his forehead and then out of nowhere started laughing, as if he'd remembered a joke. Slipper asked him what was so funny.

"No, don't bother me, Feeney. I'm conjurating a pitcher." Teddy spread his hands before him, as though introducing some heroic vista. "It's young General Pitt, terrorizer of both armies, leading his troops inta battle."

Slipper hacked away at a thick root with his bayonet. "The boy's scared. He's gotta learn."

"Well, he knows how ta handle his rifle, which is a statement I'm not so certified I can make about you."

"What's that mean?"

"Well, you got that scrofulous yellow face you had the night we interduced Francis Dolan to St. Peter and his missus."

"Teddy, I don't know if ya wanna be talking so loud about it, if ya know what I mean."

"McLaughlin hisself paid us the gold for that work."

"Sssh! Jesus Christ!"

"Stop fretting like a hot corn girl. These green leeks don't know nothing about politicos. If I was you, I'd keep an eye on Wesley here."

Wes couldn't tell if Teddy was setting him up again. He'd been waiting for a good word out of Teddy since the day he met him, but Teddy had just called his best friend a coward, so who knew? "He did go down, didn't he."

Teddy laughed. "Hear that, Slipper? 'He did go down.' Wes, you sent that old man flying!" Wesley's embarrassment gave way to the skewed kind of pride one has when he's done something so heroically stupid that it verges on courage. He joined Teddy in laughter and for the first time they were laughing at one of *his* exploits.

Eager to press on with Teddy, Wes whipped a rock into Lyman's pile of dirt.

Lyman fired a rock back. "What the hell are you sons a bitches laughing at?"

"Lighten up, old man."

"You think shooting my fucking head off is funny?"

"We'll take care a you. Don't worry them gray hairs." Wes looked to Teddy for approval after that one. Teddy winked and nodded.

Lyman was out of his trench and in a second had pulled Wesley up to his face by the front of the boy's jacket. He spoke in a harsh whisper. "Listen, boy. You think I'm a straight old bastard, but lemme tell you somethin'. I've shot men in the belly and had their lunch on my shoes and I ain't gotten a shilling out of it. So don't think I'd blink before putting any a you under." Lyman let that sink in. "Now get back to work."

Out in front a yard or so from the line of trenches, Burridge cut halfway through some saplings about three feet up their trunks and began to bend them over, twining them together where possible. Anson stood watching for a minute with a few others at his side and decided that he'd never understand Burridge. "What're ye up to here, John?"

Burridge started as if he'd been caught playing when he should have been practicing his piano. "Oh, this is, uh, this is something that the Nervii did." He got blank stares in return. "Against Caesar. In Gaul. They bent the trees over like so and wove them together with bushes attached to create a barrier against the Roman cavalry."

Danny made a quick appraisal. "Well, I don't think we have much to worry about from any Roman cavalry." Burridge began to blush. "With this forest the Rebs ain't gonna be running horses, either, and our boys'll have a hell of a time shooting through it." Danny hacked down the trees and handed them over to the other men with him. "But the bushes are right. Let's get some green bushes and lay them around the front so's if there's a fire, the whole thing won't catch." Burridge nodded agreement and carried out the order.

CHAPTER

4

T HE NEXT FEW HOURS WERE SPENT CROSSING AND RECROSS-
ing the unguarded border between boredom and fear. The veterans were generally sedate. They'd seen enough to know that
every battle had its surprises, and they wanted nothing so much
as to just get this one over with. A cursory inspection of their
trenches by Stewart and Henry provided some distraction, as did
another inspection of their line of battle from Warren and Griffin
themselves.

By ten o'clock the thick heat tugged everyone down into a heavy torpor
that only the thought of battle could dispel. They were always moody when
fighting loomed, but the humid weather exaggerated the swings. In a proud
voice, Von Schenk read dispatches about Prussia's incursion into Denmark
out of Fry's newspaper while Karl glared, fingering his rosary. Pindar Worm
counted the cartridges in his brother's box while Horace sketched a filly on
a piece of letter paper. Burridge spent his hours wondering whether Stewart
was discussing with Henry the company's morning wander in the woods. It
looked terrible to have gotten so twisted, and Stewart was sure to take any
opportunity offered to undercut him with Henry. Burridge's face flushed.
He could only hope he hadn't lost his chance.

Newt read over what he had written so far.

Dearest Wife,
I take pen in hand to write you this letter. I trust it finds you and the
Children healthy and in want of Nothing. We must be grateful to Mr. Isaac's
Generosity that your needs have been met in such fullness. The Lord has

*kept me well, so please do not begin to Cry in the manner you so often
Describe in other letters. I eagerly await my Homecoming and the sight of
your Face. But there is nothing I can do to make the time pass with greater
Swiftness. Nor can crying move the time. If you recall our Sojourn to Ni-
agara, you will remember that a month can be a very short time indeed!*

He doubted that the memory would help her, but he had to try. She
had cried when he had left and, from the sound of her letters, hadn't stopped
since. As the time passed and nothing happened to break the tension, Newt's
words consoled him more than they would ever comfort her.

*The Generals promise certain Engagement today in the Wilderness,
which is a Forest that you have never seen the likes of and, God willing,
never will. The boys are Resolute that we shall leave the war with the
Honor of Co. L, 14th Brooklyn held high above us and I could not agree
more. The Union and all that a free Republic holds dear demand our efforts
to the very end and I shall endeavor to do my part. How else are we to
realize the goals that Bishop Joycelin speaks of and that we all keep nearest
our Hearts?*

Newt saw the tanned face of the screaming Reb coming at him at
Gettysburg. The image of blood spraying out of the man's chest made his
heart beat and fear clutch his throat. Newt did not want to kill any Southerners; behind every one of the few shots he took there was a prayer. At the
same time, he didn't want to offend anyone on the Union side. He never
spoke about slavery in camp, afraid of getting into a fight with someone of
Tiger's mind. Or Tiger himself. Newt had learned his lesson after Lincoln's
proclamation. He'd come close enough to some fights to know that he didn't
want one.

*Please be Strong as well and pray for the Lord to give this army strength
in equal measure. The Bravery of those at home is surely felt by us.*
*I could describe this place, but it is of such sameness that it would be a
waste of your Time. I eat well, crave oysters, and am glad to report that
my Shoes are faring Admirably. It has been Hot the last few days, which is*

to be expected in this part of the country at this time. I hope your weather in Brooklyn is more pleasant. Some of the "Men"—I will be generous and call them that—are having trouble without their whiskey ration, but we will do fine anyway. Gambling is also present. It is typical of a certain sort.

How are the children? I am eager to see them and would ask another photograph but for the fact that I am home soon and will see them myself!

A minié pitched into the earthworks in front of him, and he decided to finish the letter later. There was no mail going out today anyway. He rolled up the tablet, with pens, ink, and stamps inside, fastened the buckles, and exchanged the leather tube for his bayonet, but briefly running his finger first along the wood of his base ball bat for luck.

With the bayonet, he began to even the walls of his trench, four months in winter camp now gone like a good dream. He'd had the silly wish that somehow they'd skate through until the twenty-first without facing fire, that they'd pull them off the line and Newt would be able to tell himself that he just hadn't had the chance. But here they were again and Newt was still holding his chips, wondering if he should ante up and play a hand. To distract himself, Newt began to lightly whistle "John Brown's Body."

"Shut ye face, ye nigger-loving bastard!"

No secret who that was. Newt wondered when exactly he and Tiger began to hate each other. They'd never met in Brooklyn. Tiger was a friend of Danny and Lyman; they'd run together as young men, though how Lyman and Danny had fallen in with an Irishman was a mystery to him. Tiger came over during the Hunger and grew up, they said, in Tapscott's Poorhouse. A hellhole, that was, a human bog full of half-naked women, drunken children, and not a one of them putting a hand on a tool. When he was a boy, he'd been told to lay a course wide of that pit.

Newt had met Lyman at a base ball match. They'd chatted pleasantly about the match, then learned they were both in the food business. He and Lyman had nice houses with gardens, took the *Eagle,* and subscribed to Appleton's *New Cyclopedia.* It made sense for *them* to be friends. Tiger was another animal entirely—a drunk who let a room under a cigar store. They'd gotten on well enough, though, for a while and much to Newt's surprise;

after all, Tiger was an Irishman. The change came after Gettysburg, Newt decided. It made him angry that after Gettysburg Tiger didn't think the same of him. He began to whistle again.

More bullets slammed into the works, sending Newt into a ball at the bottom of his trench, and suddenly the morning's light shower of miniés became a full storm. The Rebs tested the flanks for ten minutes, and then the line returned to silence, save for scattered pops before them and thicker fire off to the right.

As he crept down behind the berm, Felix Cawthorne lifted up his cap and immediately smoothed down his hair.

"Today is very hot day, *ja?*" Down at the other end of the trench, Von Schenk sat wheezing in the heat. "I would prefer to expire from cold; it is more gentle. I have seen such deaths." Cawthorne did not want to hear any more. He slid his cap back onto the familiar grooves it had worn into his hair and brow and turned away. "We should be grateful to God we are alive at all *mit* Porridge. He will kill us all."

Such talk made Cawthorne nervous. He scratched his cheek. "I advise you to keep such sentiments to yourself."

A harsh snort burst forth from the German's nose. "I advise you to *blasen mich.*"

Cawthorne didn't know what this meant, but the sneer on his neighbor's face and the area of the body Von Schenk had cupped with his right hand made words unnecessary. "Burridge *ist ein Affenschwanz.* An ape's prick, *ja?*"

Should he report this insubordination? Or arrest the Prussian this moment? Cawthorne fidgeted with the buttons on his cuffs, then his vest, as Von Schenk waited for his reaction. All he had to do was open the buttons, reach into his vest, and there would be the gun. He'd found it after the ambush in '62, and no one had taken it from him. There'd been too much confusion. This was his secret and, anyhow, he deserved to keep it. He'd done what he'd been told to do. He'd certainly need it if he wanted to haul this human cannonball before Burridge. Who would then do nothing.

"*Ein Affenschwanz.* You know as we all did that he had lost his way. Any man here could have done better."

Cawthorne swiveled his head back and forth, even more uncomfortable as he silently agreed with Von Schenk. The German was right, but other men may have heard him and might tell Burridge that he'd agreed, or worse, that he'd said it. There was only one course of action. Securing his revolver with what he hoped looked like a scratch, Cawthorne crawled out of the trench without a word to Von Schenk and went searching for Burridge.

———

As slow as the wait had been, so the shift into action was sudden. The hours of digging and cutting were over, and the men advanced at noon in two columns toward a new line of battle, a half-mile through the rough pines and scrub oak. Reb miniés hit any Union man they could find and there were no trenches to hide in, but the proximity of other troops reassured the men of Company L that at least they weren't orphans anymore.

In fact, the troops were so near that it began to cause problems. In the dense woods, the brigade on their left inclined to the right instead of bearing straight on, driving all of Sweitzer's men, including Company L, far to the right as well. When they halted a few hundred yards short of a clearing, the company found themselves next to the 22nd Massachusetts in the second line of Sweitzer's brigade. Burridge and Danny saw no reason to push into the front.

The shots were loud and rapid now. The battle would be here, just up ahead a few hundred yards. Officers darted through the lines, and even Stewart and Henry had deigned to join their men. Soldiers buzzed among themselves, and their nervousness blended with the great energy needed for an undertaking as huge and risky as this clash. The whole army's spirit had shifted from a walk to a trot, and it was itching for the whip. Columns were re-formed into lines, and they closed up ranks forward through an old cemetery.

Burridge could see the trees thinning and a pale, milky sun ahead as through prison bars. Though no one wanted to fight in these woods, the report from Henry was that they'd run into the Rebs on the turnpike and Grant wasn't about to back away from a chance to give battle. The real work of the campaign was about to start. Was the spy really out there, he wondered. How would he find him now that the fighting had begun? One of his men scribbled a note onto a shred of paper and pinned it to himself. Fry and Del Rio were doing the same. The puffs of rifle smoke from the front line were now visible. Maybe he'd meet the scout after the battle, behind a thicket of trees during the empty hours of a burial detail. If both of them survived the next few hours. Ahead, a company of the 9th circled a priest, a bloated red-faced man wearing a snowy white robe and balanced on top of a tombstone as he swore out a list of causes for sure entry into hell. A boy, maybe sixteen, broke down and wept.

Burridge turned away. In five minutes that chaplain would be safely hidden and nipping at a flask. In the front of their line, alone, Lyman Alder sat staring intently at a photograph, looking like an American Hector taking off his helmet for a quick return to humanity before he wages war at the walls of Ilium. Was he wondering if he'd ever see his wife again? Remembering the day they met? Burridge envied the gaping absence a husband must feel without his wife, but the shame of his quick visits to Bowery whores pushed that thought aside.

Alder looked up and caught the lieutenant watching him. Burridge tried to look away, but he was found out. The butcher brought up a good-size oyster, then spat forcefully in his direction, all the while holding Burridge's gaze.

After Burridge skittered away, Lyman tucked away his photograph of Victoria, slipping it safely next to his base ball. He rubbed the shoulder where he'd been shot and yawned. He yawned when he was nervous. He couldn't figure out why, just as he couldn't figure his steadiness under fire. Though he hadn't expected to fail in battle, he was still surprised that he'd never hesitated, especially when he considered that he was not a fighting man back in Brooklyn and conspicuously so in a profession with more than its share of men inclined to violence. Every time he saw Danny running out ahead shooting, Lyman just went out there and did what he had to do. He took no credit for his steadiness in the same way that he no longer blamed other soldiers for coming up short if they'd tried their best. Now even that effort was becoming too much for many. He found it hard to believe that there was once a time when they'd all laughed at men for ducking bullets.

Lyman rubbed his shoulder again. The bullet had hurt like nothing he'd ever felt before and it had only been through muscle. He wondered what it would feel like to get hit in the gut. A sharp memory of pain coursed through him and he pictured the Washington hospital he'd lain in for months, waiting to see if the wound would go septic. Screaming, moaning, crying—all the human sounds of the battlefield had echoed through the ward from boys who'd thought death couldn't reach them in a U.S. hospital just a thrown stone from their elected representatives. All day and every night there'd be new voices; some yielding to the inevitable, others fighting a final, desperate battle without weapons.

For a week Lyman had felt the mark of death on his head. The reporter from the *Eagle*, Whitman, had given him a jelly and proffered an unwanted kiss of sympathy on his lips, but it did not improve his condition. The terror of Gettysburg and its pain still held the ground.

Then the letters came. Simple letters from Victoria and Ernie about what they did all day—a description of a visit from her sister, a report on what he was learning in school; things he'd barely listened to when they'd said them at home. Every letter offered a reason to wake up in pain amid the smells of gangrene and kerosene. He finally stopped waiting to die. Whatever sign it was that marked a fading man rose off and he heard the call of his family urging him to rejoin the land of the living.

Those days burned in Lyman's mind as much as the demands of Ernie's letters. The hem of Death's robe had brushed his arm. Knowing his son, making him a man; providing a better life for his wife—he wanted to do these things and more but he wondered often, as he did again in this trench, if they would know him when he came back. If he really wanted to go home. If they would want him home. Had he changed too much or not enough? Could there ever be another chance?

Drums and bugles turned all heads to the front. Men wrestled down their hearts and dropped their packs—only guns and last letters home went into battle. Newt gave a final squeeze to the handle of his bat as he lay his pack down next to Lyman's. The troops had rolled up a hill of fear and now they were about to be sent flying down the other side at full force into the Rebs. At the highest point, there was a pause, swords raised, young eyes opened wide, old legs set to run.

It was one o'clock. From the reserve position in the fourth line, the company watched the first two lines under Bartlett as they plunged scream-ing forward up a low rise that blocked any view of what was beyond, then disappeared. Sweitzer's first line followed. As soon as Bartlett's front went over the crest, a storm of smoke and shot erupted that quickly became one continuous roar, and dying screams and cries tore through the blasting and the thunder. Burridge led them through the trees and headstones to the lip of the clearing, about forty acres of low corn stubble surrounded completely by a dark gray wall of trees, as if a park had been specially created for this day. The pike cut through the field east and west, dividing it in two. Across the clearing, Rebel muskets bristled and bloomed smoke. The miniés whizzed past their heads, and a huge white cloud of smoke rose over the hill and settled there into a fog only slightly stirred by a weak breeze. Teddy hollered at Wes with a mad grin, "We're in the thick of it, buddy! We're gonna be right in the heat!" but Wes could only wince at the bullets shredding the air around him.

Henry, still lurking back in the trees, got the order to follow the 22nd and 32nd as they shifted to the north side of the pike and he passed it on to Burridge. The lieutenant screamed out the order to his men, most of whom were on one knee and bent over to make as small a target of themselves as possible. Louis and the older veterans were on their bellies. He screamed at them all again, but no one moved except Cawthorne, who, though trembling, forced himself forward.

A few endless seconds passed as the men held their ground against Burridge's order. The lieutenant stood immobile too, shocked by a disobedience so instinctive that it seemed without malicious intent. Back in the woods was one thing, but under fire such behavior could earn them all courts-martial. Only Danny got them moving. At his signal, the men got to their feet and attached themselves to Cawthorne and their commanding officer.

The short line scuttled behind the lieutenant along the edge of the forest while miniés ripped by in front of their eyes, past their knees, into the stock of rifles. The fire was heaviest at the pike and a couple of the men stopped to return fire. Danny couldn't reach them in time to stop them from shooting, but he shoved them ahead before they could reload. Men from the two Massachusetts regiments dropped on the road, their bones shattered and their guts torn apart by thumb-thick miniés.

The company halted in the trees on the north side of the pike, behind another brigade, led by Ayres, preparing to go in. Burridge ordered them onto their stomachs and to fix bayonets, and he was relieved to see them do so.

Lyman took stock. Henry and Stewart were nowhere to be found, as was expected. On the south side, blurred by smoke but still visible, Bartlett's men and Sweitzer's had poured over the hill into a gully and up the other side. The Rebs laid into them with a hot free fire, but the Feds were keeping right on and pushing them back deeper into the western edges of the forest as the sound of thousands of rifles cracking off at once shook the trees. Licks of fire appeared within the chalky smoke, started by bullets igniting the dry shucks of corn littered across the field.

Another "Forward" rang out with bugles and drums, and the first line of Ayres's brigade stepped off in sharp marching order toward the northwest. They went twenty yards down a slope in best textbook style, a fine wave of well-tested regular army men in perfect lines splashed with a white-turbaned Zouave regiment—New Yorkers, some in red fezzes, their blue jacket fronts swirled with an odd red shape on each side, pantaloons flapping, bayonets shining. All filed ahead under limp flags, a comforting, beautiful sight in this place of fatal confusion.

Then the Rebs opened fire. Lyman's stomach tightened as the volleys slammed into Ayres's men just when they stepped onto the flat stretch that led to the gully and beyond to the woods opposite. Men flew, collapsed, wailing, but the lines pressed on toward the woods. The regulars made a slight left shift and now faced due west. Flanking fire burst from the trees on their right. More men fell into the grass and tan stalks. One fez rolled a few yards on its edge, then fell flat. The brigade pressed on.

Walking wounded began to crawl back toward the line. Two bareheaded Zouaves dragged their captain by his legs since he had no arms. The men had wrapped their turbans around his chest as bandages, but they were peeling off. The captain's red kepi lay over his face. Lyman guessed he was dead. A private staggered back, wiping bits of brain off his jacket, a large piece of someone else's bone embedded in his neck. A goateed man in a tall, leather shako clutched the gushing hole in his midsection, a shocked expression on his face. Scores of others lay in the field, out of their minds with pain and screaming.

Over the treetops to the southwest, smoke swelled into round cottony bolls where the pines left enough space for it to escape. The light breeze tugged at them and drew them up with an invisible hand. It was impossible to say who had the edge there. More Union boys, Wadsworth's, stormed in from the south wall of trees behind the first wave.

Here on the north side of the pike, Ayres's first line had smashed into the woods, and the chaos in that corner of the clearing was just visible from the company's turf on the eastern edge. A loud cheer went up and Ayres's second line charged in, led by more Zouaves—Garrard's 146th New York in their extravagant light blue jackets and billowing pants, all trimmed with gold cord and decorated with gold *tombeaux* on the front. Gold tassels on long strings hung off their red fezzes, bouncing on their shoulders and backs as they ran in. Lyman remembered watching them play base ball once; they had a good nine.

The brigade streamed down the slope followed by two Pennsylvania regiments, and once they hit the gully, Reb volleys slammed back from both sides again. Artillery could operate in the clearing, so a Union gun on the south side of the pike added its deep, shattering pulse to the hell, trying to dampen the two sides of fire Ayres's men were facing. Its northerly angle sent the shot straight into the backs of its own men and pinned down those it did not kill.

Single screams and miniés kept on tearing at the exploding roil of smoke and fire. Just when Wes thought it couldn't get any louder, the sounds would reach another level. He couldn't swallow. Jimmy Tice blinked incessantly. The gun smoke now obscured the farthest ends of the field, and there was no telling how far Ayres's boys had gotten, though the cannon was pretty far up. Louis pressed his face into a patch of violets full of his grandmother's smell. The smell of Pest in the spring.

The flanking fire kept right on at Ayres and the shooting grew more and more heated. After a few more minutes the brigade began to fall back, chased by the devilish screeching of a resurgent tide of Rebels. A few stray bands of twos and threes led the retreat, then fives and then full bands of men running and offering their backs to the Rebs and arching in graceful curves when hit.

The flames ignited by bullets on the south side of the field had crossed the pike. The gun crew down there tried to fight off the advancing Rebs, but a bout of close fighting and clubbing muskets left it in enemy hands. Lyman hadn't seen any Zouaves falling back and the shooting a hundred yards ahead proved they were still down in there, now somewhere between the counterattacking Rebs and the Confederate line. The smoke thinned enough for Lyman to see patches of light blue uniforms and red dots of fez swirling through gray and brown homespun, like cardinals and jays swooping in and out of a flock of rock doves and common sparrows.

Lyman marveled for a moment at what good men those were. Then he took a glance at his own company. The toughest had always known they'd have to watch out for the slackers and he'd been afraid of seeing how they'd all play under fire, but now even the hard cases were looking gun-shy and the weak were little but fodder. Cawthorne tore at his cheeks. Newt was shaking uncontrollably. Karl stared ahead without blinking. These men, his friends, were breaking apart. They didn't care if their fear showed, save for Tiger, who was smiling. Lyman had the same sickening realization that Danny and Burridge had shared after Pitt had shot his rifle: This company was finished. He forgot about doing damage and started to worry about getting out alive, briefly ashamed during the few seconds he could spare, the terrific din and horror of battle blasting his thoughts into smaller and smaller pieces.

A high Rebel yell sliced through the torrents of rifle shot on the south side. Union men were falling back there, too. There were light snaps in the fire before them, as though someone had decided to pop some corn as a midbattle treat. The cartridge boxes of the injured men who couldn't walk were being caught by the flames and exploding into them, one bullet at a time; others were consumed by the flames before their bullets turned against them. Two Confederate regiments now surrounded the captured gun.

The order came to go in. The 146th and 140th New York were trapped in the gully and the company was to help them get out by flinging themselves into the onrushing Rebs.

Tiger held Huey's head between his two hands and bellowed hysterically into his face. "Go in screaming!" all the while spraying flecks of white foam. He grabbed Teddy and did the same thing, his face contorted and red, and though he had petrified Huey with his mad advice, something lit in Teddy's face when he heard it. The meaty kid started chewing his lips and nodded like a woodpecker knocking his head into a tree trunk.

Louis swallowed hard. Stilling his body, he listened for the tolling of Pest's Inner City Church bell, the sound of death to him since he was a child; the bell he'd somehow heard in Brooklyn the same night his mother died in Hungary. He listened, but there was no bell and he knew it wasn't his time. He gritted his teeth and stepped forward.

Wes tried to breathe, but he couldn't get deep enough into his lungs for much more than a pant. Every moment of Wesley Pitt's past life was falling away and he was left stripped naked at this moment of judgment. He hadn't seen his brother since he was four and his sister for a year, but all he could picture was their faces and the white house they lived in then, and more memories flowed into his head that he wanted to see for maybe the last time. He hadn't thought of his dead parents in years, but now he saw them both clearly. His bearded father sat on the edge of his bed reading a poem out loud—"Sweet and low, sweet and low, wind of the western sea, low, low, breathe and blow, wind of the western sea!"—and his mother stroked his head because he had a fever and he was a good boy. And as he felt like a son for the first time in many years, he began to feel like a man.

The soldiers gripped their rifles and had their last cogent thought for no one knew how long. Danny stood between Lyman and Tiger. He turned to Lyman with a smile and said, "Be a hero, my friend."

Some general up in front of the Massachusetts regiments raised his sword. And lowered it.

The bugles sounded and with a single cry made of different words and tongues like the roar of Babel, they ran into the fray.

Lyman set his eyes ahead and immediately stumbled over a hummock of grass and corn stalks. A massive pulse of fear jolted through him upon the impact, pulling him up and ramming him forward. The miniés came in as a hail and he tried to resist the futile impulse to bend forward as though striding into a storm. A wall of fire was ahead at the gully. He could see Burridge streaking forward too far beyond them; he'd be useless. It was up to Danny to get them out alive. Lyman leaped over two embraced bodies and reminded himself to breathe. Slipper tumbled to the ground. Miniés ripped by. Another body stretched across his path, and the image of its face ground to meat by footfalls and bullets stuck in his head as he leaped over it toward the fire in the gully, screaming himself into the murderous state necessary to survive.

Wes ran in wailing, "Sweet and low! Sweet and low! He clasps the crags with crooked hands! Close to the sun in lonely lands!" at the very top of his voice. He was being born for a second time in another place of blood and pain, in the shattering way that men deliver men to life, running out of himself, flayed of all thought. A Rebel yell raked across him, Wes turned Tennyson's lines into threats of slaughter and a primal claim—an abandoned boy crying, howling, that he was still alive.

The colors, the fire ahead, and butternuts spun into a blur of possible dangers that Lyman tried to run into headfirst, but he found himself nearly sent sprawling by the shock of this battle. No matter how many times he'd seen combat, he could never get used to it. A numbing shroud fell over Lyman, and he was tired enough to stop right where he was and yield to the sleep and safety he wanted among the mangled Union dead.

Lyman caught Caspar's voice bawling and wheezing, *"Das Feld muss er behalten!"* Bullets hit everywhere. Lyman looked for the Zouaves and saw only Newt crying, "Oh God! Oh God!" and shooting into the sky. Tiger was screaming, "Mary! Mary! Mary!" over and over, and someone else shot as wildly and wastefully as Newt. Another pair were huddled together on the ground. All these men were past fighting. Burridge was out in front, far from the men, his head cocked to one side as if he was listening for a single sound. Lyman had to find Danny.

Wes could see them. Rebs. Beards. Faces. Snarling. He had left his mind and become action. Color flashed in blue and red and white and gray and brown and green, and the taste of cartridge sulfur dried his mouth. He could not name the colors or taste or friends. Known faces gave him a good feeling and those he didn't know across the dividing fire made him angry. That was all. Pictures and poems fled as he shot and killed and learned that he was meant to kill and lived to kill.

Louis heard Von Schenk crying out Martin Luther, and he let the beautiful martial song run through his head as he stole a guilty moment of appreciation for the hell around him. Though a man of healing, he loved these moments when life exploded through the veins. It was a sick and terrible thing, to revel in the feeling of killing, and at thirty-nine, with creaking knees and two sons the age of most of those dying here, he was becoming embarrassed by it, hating battle and yearning for it as an old man lusts after young girls.

Jogging ahead, Louis saw fire and death and the Union flag, and he gave himself over to the joy of battle and a hymn from a faith that considered him damned. The stately pounding of "A Mighty Fortress Is Our God" became his own song as he neared the shore of the flaming pool separating North and South.

Cawthorne stood as still as a tree and right in Lyman's way, so he pushed him to the side and continued to the front. He found Danny edging more and more into the flames, with no one behind except for Tiger, who'd raced up to catch him. Frenchie and the Dutchman were up close and so were Pitt and Finn. Lyman had no idea where the rest were; probably hiding behind dead bodies or crawling back toward Union lines. It was a pathetic showing. A few Zouaves fell back out of the gully, but only a few, and some Company L boys were running with them. It was a terrible charge and a failure. Burridge had somehow managed to survive so far, but he was not shooting as much as looking at the Rebs.

Lyman shot, reloaded, then ran toward Danny, calling his name. When he was a few feet away and almost into the fire, Danny and Tiger finally heard his voice and looked back. Both of their faces were black with cartridge powder, and Danny's big teeth stood out as he grinned to see his friend.

Then a minié crashed into Danny's head and another followed, and blood and brain and chunks of skull flew everywhere, over Tiger, over Lyman, and Danny was dead. His body flopped into the fire.

Lyman froze, but only long enough to know how deadly it was to freeze. He focused on the clean line that a shard of bone had cut into the left arm of Tiger's jacket. Everything moved three times faster than it ever had before. Boxes of cartridges exploded in the fire like crackers on the Fourth, and swollen beyond their limits, burnt bodies began to burst, too.

The animal in Lyman had died. Reduced to just a man, a fleshy thing hunted by lead bullets, he looked ahead and saw dancing, grinning faces, black and bearded, between the gaps in the curtain of flames. It was a perfect hell and he was ready to surrender to it until he thought of Danny's body roasting there.

"Be a hero, my friend" burned into Lyman's mind. He aimed his rifle through the fire at a man with thick black hair cut with a bowl, who was aiming right at him. They locked eyes. The Reb's eyes were big and soft, like the rest of him, and Lyman could tell he was staring at him in turn because he wasn't squinting to aim. A fallen Reb between them shrieked as he beat his flaming arm, more a torch now, into the ground in hopes of putting it out. Both Lyman and the Reb looked toward the burning man, then caught each other's eyes coming back up. In two seconds they exchanged all they'd ever need to know about each other. Lyman took the chance. He aimed his gun toward the ground and pointed into the fire.

The big Reb had a thick chest and a square jaw that seemed to be working some tobacco. Lyman could swear he heard the word "Brooklyn" coming from the Rebel side. The Reb slowly lowered his gun and nodded at Lyman.

Immediately both men started screaming, "Stop! Stop!" and pushed down the muzzles of rifles belonging to their own troops.

Tiger shoved Lyman away when their muzzles crossed and roared from his twisted battle face, "What the fuck are ye doing, ye goddamned asshole?" For a second Lyman couldn't tell who it was, nor could he recognize any friend from foe along the banks of this river of fire. Tiger's shouting restored the common identities to Lyman's world.

"Cease fire. Getting the wounded out of the fire," he yelled at Tiger, who grumbled. "Danny. For chrissakes, help me get Danny!" Tiger finally understood what was happening and, bending over, began tugging at a pair of brogaued feet jutting out of the fire. "Is that him?"

Tiger nodded. They dragged Danny out, but he was already charred beyond the point where anyone could recognize him. Lyman stroked what there was of Danny's swollen, blistered face. Jimmy Creighton died at twenty-one, he thought. Men on both sides put down weapons to pull bloated, flaming bodies from the heat. The few remaining fighters of Company L happily took the excuse to help wounded boys to the back, even when they were beyond any hope of survival. Even when survival was a torture.

Jimmy Creighton died at twenty-one. Lyman took Danny's arms and Tiger had his legs. Lyman knew he wasn't returning to this battlefield today, nor was Company L. He looked back briefly to see if the Reb was near, but with the flames dying now, deprived of human fuel, Lyman's partner in peaceful rebellion had disappeared.

———

Company L, like much of the army, went through the hours after the attack as though in a fog. Most of Sweitzer's troops had been relieved, so Lyman and Tiger added Danny's body to a long ribbon of dead in a clearing, and after a good-bye made quick by the fear of grief, they rejoined the rest of the company and thousands of other Feds crossing the turnpike, which was now choked with ambulances headed toward Fredericksburg. Once across the pike, they continued to shift south. They'd only lost Danny; a major loss to be sure, but such a low casualty count from such a hot battle spoke of something less than a full effort. The rest of Sweitzer's reserves had fallen back from the fighting soon after they had, so the shame was not theirs alone, but like all of Warren's army that afternoon, the fact that they hadn't been humiliated was a feeble salve for the wound left by not winning. Union and Rebel troops were now in a standoff in the Wilderness.

Off to the right, not far from where they'd been, another attack was under way; down to the south, on their left a distance, artillery throbbed low and irregular, like an erratic heartbeat. Skirmishers kept the Rebs busy in front. Few words were spoken as they dug entrenchments not far from where they'd started that morning. The work was slow and having done it once already that day with little cause, they did only the barest minimum, making the trenches just deep enough to hide in, as they did once they were finished.

Wes was on the brink of slipping off on a stolen nap. Teddy's rambling version of his battlefield valor droned on in the background, and Feeney mumbled to himself as he slumped in a corner. Wes had let his eyes slip closed and was about to go down when a new fact snapped him back awake. He was a killer now. He'd broken a few legs and brawled some, acted tough and always tried to seem the killer, but he'd never actually killed a man. Unsure of what to make of this aspect of his new self and no longer so sleepy, Wes dug in a little deeper and tried to unstick the damp, itchy wool of his pants from his legs.

Lyman never felt good after a scrap. The initial grateful rush that swept through every man once he realized that he'd survived usually wore off quickly with Lyman, and especially today. He became very quiet as random faces appeared to him; faces that his eyes had seen and his memory caught but that he had never registered in the fight. The young Rebel boy with the sad eyes of a hound dog. A fellow in a straw hat, freckled and missing a tooth. He focused on the faces and the lives that had finished that day, some of which he'd finished himself. The big man with the black hair. Lyman imagined what that man's life was like—a farmer, maybe, with a son and cows and a homely wife back in Georgia. For all the regrets he had at these times, Lyman had never wished the dead back or prayed to retrieve a minié from a Southern heart, but today he hoped that big Rebel was having a cup of coffee in front of a fire.

Lyman felt guilty for his gentle thoughts about a butternut on the day that Danny died and he felt scared, too. Without Danny they were lost in this Wilderness. They'd never spoken about it, but Lyman had always had the feeling that Danny meant for him to take over if he went up. Lyman had felt queasy about toying with the idea of leading these men, shambles that they were, while Danny was alive, but maybe, he thought, it was finally the time for the wreath to be placed on his head. Maybe this was his second chance to make good. Being a sergeant wasn't the same as joining the Excelsiors, but then Alder Senior would hardly ask a sergeant to sweep up blood-soaked sawdust.

The lieutenant could not escape a sense that his inability to find the scout was, even amid the confusion of war, nothing less than a failure. A shuffle behind reminded him of the company. They were waiting for a new sergeant. Burridge knew it was a terrible thing for Anson to die. He had been a great soldier; a constant reproach and his salvation from many difficult situations. No salvation today, though. The men had never balked that way before. Only Danny Anson had gotten the company to move—no amount of screaming or punishment from him would have stirred them.

Of course he was well within his rights to mete out some punishment now, if not send them all up for regimental courts-martial. He pictured Tiger Quigley digging his own grave while a firing squad stood by, a few impatient toes tapping through the last foot of dirt. If he hadn't been struck dumb in the field, he could have begun shooting at them himself; that would have wakened them up. He imagined a glum Alder balanced on one leg atop a box of hardtack, weighed down by signs declaring him a thief. Still, for all these pleasant thoughts, the lieutenant had never ordered such a punishment, uncertain as he was that anyone would carry out his orders. Besides, he thought, time spent safely in the guardhouse would probably be welcomed by most of the layabouts in his command, even if a court-martial meant death or prison.

Who would be the next sergeant? The man would have to be someone that would help turn this unit into a fighting force again. The only person qualified, the only real choice for the job, was Lyman Alder. The men looked up to him, though some of his glory was reflected off his closeness to Anson. He was strong and quiet, with equal veins of kindness and brutality.

He was the last man Burridge could select. What he wanted was someone who would look up to *him*, someone who would be his man, who knew less than he did. The choice was obvious: The only one fool enough to follow him unforced back in the clearing was Cawthorne. Even this afternoon he had told him—wholly unbidden—some meaningless insult Von Schenk had slobbered his way. By now Cawthorne had had the shine rubbed down and would be immensely grateful for the favor. He was unsure of himself despite his theatrical regular army manners so he would never challenge Burridge, no matter what unusual activities the assignations would entail. He'd be satisfied to merely appear in the role of sergeant. Henry and Stewart would approve as well.

He called the troops to order. "Men, after the sad death of Sergeant Anson, whom we will all miss very, very much, I have the honor to name Mr. Cawthorne to take his place." Cawthorne had the surprised and arrogant look of a child who'd just won a spelling bee as he shook hands with Burridge. "I'm sure you will give him the same respect that you proffered Sergeant Anson."

Von Schenk laughed. A few other men caught the giggles, too, which balanced the muttered swearing of Tiger. The lieutenant pictured the fat German spread-eagled across a wagon wheel, tied by his thumbs and ankles, squealing as the wheel was turned.

Cawthorne held his chin high and let descend a solemn certitude befitting battlefield honors, his dramatic silence muffling the squeal of pride that was bounding through his still body. An old actor once told him the three secrets of the trade: Do what you're told; Step forward; and, Have the best costume. Cawthorne reflected now that he'd done all of those things and though he'd often despaired, he was finally being rewarded.

He let his gaze drift down to his trousers, covered in dust. Fry was the only other man Cawthorne had ever noticed caring for his own uniform. How, he wondered, could a man be a soldier without a uniform? When a man has a role, he wears the costume. And a revolver was now part of his costume again. Cawthorne let himself smile. Pulling out the gun right here would be ill-advised; he would savor the delicious moments of a pleasure deferred until everyone was asleep.

———

There was no moon that night; only stars and hazy air pungent with the smells of gun smoke and sweet decomposing flesh held low and captive by the forest. Burning trees lit the sky like torches. As fresh assaults to the north and south rolled on, the men of the company drank some coffee, ate a piece of bacon or two, if they had any left, and did their best to grab an hour's sleep. Angry at themselves, angry at each other, they barely spoke except to trade what little they knew with the passing newswalkers. When the volleys abruptly stopped across the whole field at nine, their uncomfortable silence around the campfires became more pronounced. Horace Worm, uninvited, began a tune from the 14th's winter theatrical at the Culpeper Academy of Music, but he quit one line into the second verse. The whole day, every yard marched and bullet shot, had led to this inconclusive evening. A poor showing on the field, their leader dead and replaced by a fool, their brotherhood strained if not torn already, no one knew where exactly they were and everyone was too tired to care all that much. They just wanted to get home. Seventeen days had become a very long time.

Rebel artillery picked up over their part of the line as wagons brought up more ammunition to restock empty cartridge boxes. Throughout the woods and the wide clearing, wounded men bled away their last hours alone within earshot of thousands. Fires finally reached injured men unable to move, who'd been watching the slow advancing flames for hours and imagining their inescapable burning death. Their insane shrieks were the sharpest sounds of all. Orphaned companies called out for their home regiments. Stray groups of those wounded still able to walk, lost for hours in the smoky maze of forest to the south that had seen even hotter action that day, wandered by groaning or, even worse, silent, as though already walking in that other, better land.

Stives read aloud from his Bible—" 'Because there were no graves in

Egypt, hast thou taken us away to die in the wilderness?'" A shabby man, limping by on a leg bandaged with torn strips of uniform and a crutch made from a thick branch, stopped with folded hands. Newt sighed at the sight; yet another of Wadsworth's men with horrible tales of the battle at the Plank Road intersection, regiments lost in the trees and smoke and underbrush; fires. A whole procession of men like him had been stumbling by all afternoon, telling the same stories, and Newt had had about enough of them and their hard luck. The wounded man shared a prayer with Stives, then came to Newt and with a tired whisper asked for directions to the Fifth Corps hospital. Newt gave him a vague wave toward the back, then tucked down into his trench and asked the Lord to take away these wretched signs of what battle could turn him into.

———

There was thunder at sunrise. Confederate artillery blasted open on the right side, followed by the lightning of another Rebel yell. Union boys met them with a high battle scream of their own, and the fight was on again amid a frantic song taken up by the birds; a thick and constant whistling that seemed inspired by the Rebel howling and the unnatural noises that had rocked through the forest these last days and nights. After a few hours of listening to this din, the company made another dash toward the flames across the same field they'd crossed the day before.

For Lyman, it was the loneliest advance ever; with Danny dead, his back felt cold and unguarded save possibly for the eyes of Providence. After a slow walk halfway down the decline and a crawl to the gully, Lyman clawed a few yards up and held back, as ordered, from charging the earthworks before him, but the sense of solitude was so strong that he turned his head back and saw the bulk of the company flat on their stomachs behind him, breathing shallow, frightened breaths and doing nothing to save their own lives. Tiger was nowhere to be seen. He had flung himself forward the moment they'd stepped off; removing himself from this company, it seemed, in all ways. Newt was far back, pinned down with the rest by heavy Rebel fire. Lyman had the disappointing feeling that his friend was happy for the excuse to lag. The Hungarian had gone forward, but he'd already staggered limping to the rear, apparently shot in the leg. The ranks were thinning.

Lyman could now hear the Southern voices hollering to each other and screaming when hit. This close, the Rebs became men. Closer or farther away, they could be dots of color, animals, madmen, ghosts. Trapped here between the duty to stay up and orders to stay back, Lyman tried to listen to the miniés and not the men who shot them.

Burridge was now the only Yankee as far up as he was, which was little comfort; Porridge had taken to staring at the enemy instead of shooting. Even now, the increasingly worthless boy was lying on his stomach, squinting through the gun smoke, rifle idle. Lyman asked him why they didn't either pull back or go in and the lieutenant just shook his head.

That was the moment it became clear to Lyman that they were no longer soldiers. That they were no longer men. They were being left there to kill and be killed, and whoever was running the Rebs was doing the same thing. A war for principle and honor had become blood sport and they were being forced to play the game. Lyman fired a round and loaded another, just a butcher plying his trade.

———

Eventually they were removed from the field in a welcome, orderly retreat. On the way, they stopped to pick up their knapsacks piled among the debris; the big white *14*'s painted on everything kept theft by other regiments to a minimum. Lyman went through his knapsack to make sure everything was there, and when he came across the ball, he tossed it up a few times. A perfect white ball. He held it in his hand as they walked back and squeezed it hard as he thought of what he'd just done in the field.

As he squeezed, Lyman said it to himself—He should have been made sergeant. It definitely should have been him and not the bandbox soldier who almost got them all wiped out at the second Bull Run. The only explanation anyone had ever come up with for why Cawthorne was here was that he was a bad actor and had been sent here to die by an angry playwright. Newt had seen him once as Old Tiff in *Dred, a Tale of the Dismal Swamp* and said that it was very likely.

Maybe it was better this way, he told himself. It had never been his place to lead, neither here nor in Brooklyn. All his life he'd taken orders and carried them out without a complaint because chained to his constant desire for more was the suspicion that he'd bungle things if they were ever handed over to him.

He tucked the ball away.

———

Company L, 14th Brooklyn, Army of the Potomac, had now spent two days in battle, charging under heavy fire, stepping over bodies, digging trenches, and trying to steal sleep and food whenever possible, lost somewhere in the dissolving order of Grant's forces. Louis's return from the hospital, limping slightly on his leg, the surface wound dressed in gray bandages, brought some cheer. The second night anchored in, though, and a thundering of cannons on the right sent whispers of the army flanked along on the same breeze that brought the odor of rotting flesh into their faces. Anyone with a pipe lit up both to screen the putrid smell and to deflect the swarms of mosquitoes and biting flies. Burial duties went into the woods now that the sharpshooters were gone, and a deepening pall of darkness and decay settled over them. By nine the guns to the north had silenced, and since the company hadn't moved, it was clear the Sixth Army had held their ground somewhere short of them. Grant had turned out to be like every other Union general, and the Army of the Potomac was about to turn back north once again. At least they'd march to Culpeper in good order, not in a Chancellorsville rout.

CHAPTER

5

————

THE GUNS REMAINED SILENT THAT NIGHT. NOT LONG AFTER twelve, Burridge got the men to their feet and ordered them into columns for the pullout that all assumed was a prelude to retreat by the whole army. Led by torches and restocked with bullets, they marched back deep into the forest toward the line they had held on the first day.

The morning passed with skirmishing all along the line, including one right at Company L, but both sides seemed to know that nothing would be settled that way. Like two dogs after the worst of a scrap, they watched each warily, nipped, and growled, but wanted most of all to lick their wounds. A heavy Rebel cannonade tore into the woods around noon, setting everyone on edge for another charge, but this one never came.

The men took the lack of any solid activity on the front to mean that this fight was over. The generals were giving them a day to catch their breath and they took advantage of it. Feeney dealt a less than friendly game of Bluff that let him ease another $2.50 out of Newton's pocket while others wrote letters, cleaned their fouled rifles, and allowed themselves to dream undistracted dreams of home. Midmorning Lieutenant Burridge was called to see Captain Henry, leaving Sergeant Cawthorne in charge.

Leaning over the barricade, chin resting in hand, Lyman watched Huey sort through the litter of leaves for souvenirs. Whenever time permitted after a battle, Huey searched the field for some strange, unusual object that he could present Phineas T. Barnum for display in his museum to earn not only fame for himself, but free admission for the entire 14th Brooklyn regiment upon their return. So far, the closest Huey had come to a true oddity was a year ago, when he found a leg bone sticking up from the ground with a clean, perfectly round bullet hole through it. Huey had decided after some debate that he would never be able to prove that he did not drill the hole himself and, more to the point, he had confided to Lyman, it was not something that he felt little babies should see. Barnum's Museum had shown Huey the wonders of the world and the bone of a shot man was hardly wonderful.

Tiger's shaky voice chased after Huey. "Whaddya looking for, laddie? Looking for that General Tom Thumb? Eh? He's a-sitting with his buddies Grant and Meade, so don't go bothering yerself."

Lyman was surprised when most of the men joined in laughing. Huey appeared surprised, too, and stopped for a second before he continued his search. Unless someone's peccadilloes endangered your life, you let him hunt for oddities or quote Scripture or sing off-key—that had always been the rule.

Of course, hard words from Tiger no longer surprised anyone, especially not Lyman, who'd been listening to them on and off for fifteen years. They simply meant Tiger needed a drink. When they were fifteen or sixteen, Tiger would slip into a foul mood over the course of a few days, sniggering at private jokes and spitting until he'd finally light into a passing dog, at which point Danny and Lyman would perform the indicated treatment. Lyman would slip out the window, Danny would hook a bottle of whiskey, and they'd all three meet at the riverside. Tiger would have three drafts for each one of theirs, and they'd let him scream into the wind and battle trees. Those were adventures for him, too; Lyman had to admit it. Tiger's wildness was infectious. Too much so for Alder Senior—he hated Tiger.

But that was years ago. It was time for Tiger to take care of himself. Newt had managed to do that, almost to a fault. They'd met at a base ball match; Lyman saw Newt as going somewhere up, and after Hiram Cully, it was nice to know someone going somewhere.

Huey kept on turning over leaves and picking up strange-looking rocks. Lyman pictured him presenting Barnum with some freak of man or nature as a band played and a crowd cheered. Huey took a very long and pensive look at a chip of wood. Lyman had to give him credit: No matter how much blood was spilled, Huey was out there looking for wonders among the world's most ordinary stuff. Still Lyman wasn't so sure he could be satisfied with that, a life of beef prices, gossip over the counter, and spirited discussions with Victoria about new doilies for the parlor chairs. Lagers at Piggy's as he watched Tiger throw his life down the hole. A suffocating feeling swept over him, the kind he had when he thought of what it would be like to end up in some Rebel prison. The great men, he thought, didn't live like that. They didn't sift through the litter looking for glass to call diamonds.

Huey stayed out in front until Burridge came back. The lieutenant called them all together for his announcement—"Gentlemen, the army will be pulling out of the Wilderness." There was some scattered limp applause. Burridge stared at the men until they were quiet. "We will join Colonel Herring of the 118th Pennsylvania, who is assembling the rear pickets, and guard the movement."

Groans rose from everyone at that news. Lyman slung his knapsack over his shoulders and formed into line with everyone else. So that was it: Once they wrapped up this bit of picket duty tonight, they'd be on their way back to camp and then home. Huey wouldn't find his oddity after all. It seemed so sudden after these endless years. Lyman had been thinking about going home for so long now, had come up with so many pictures of how he'd feel when he finally knew that his soldiering days were over, that the news they were pulling out took a long time to sink in and when it did, he thought of blood. He'd see no more of the human kind. He'd see no more heads bursting, except in his dreams; no more torn flesh or pleading eyes. Leaving now meant that even if he'd been made sergeant, he'd not have had the chance to use the title. It meant Danny had died two days away from freedom.

The company marched ahead to their next position, through a forest showing its scars. Where cannonballs had blasted holes in the trees, the sun hit fallen leaves and needles full force for the first time in years. In other places, the nearly solid volume of fire had cut down everything above four feet. The land seemed naked and embarrassed, as though forced to expose itself. Smoldering piles of logs and leaves, stretches of charred ground, and black, pointed trees bare of all branches and green spoke of the fires that had burned in the woods.

The sight of all this ruined nature further withered Lyman's mood.

They had done little other than contribute bodies to the earth. Lyman wanted to feel as though he had made a difference, that his shots and wounds and sore feet and deprivations had meant something in this historic struggle, but after yesterday's pointless scrap, he felt as if he'd just been keeping a place that could have been as well filled by some other butcher from some other city in some other state. The government he'd helped elect had put him into the war machine and now it was taking him out like a worn part. He could have reenlisted—they were fairly begging men to—but the regiment had voted long ago and Lyman was no longer sure of why he was there anyway. As the army had accomplished nothing, he'd accomplished nothing, leaving behind only burnt wastelands, fatherless children, widows, men with no arms. He'd been a hired gun; yesterday had confirmed that shameful thought.

And so he was just an ordinary man, facing the pieces of his life. His son was a thief. His marriage was empty because he had emptied it of anything other than responsibilities. And in his fear he had waited too long, because now they were leaving and there were no more chances.

No chance for victory. No chance to be an officer, to storm a position, to save a life. Lyman heard the clock tick in the parlor, the heavy thud of a cleaver on wood. The *tink* of empty glasses. The sounds of his life.

————

Colonel Herring had sad eyes set back far into his face and a trim mouth hidden by a well-groomed, sweeping mustache on top and a goatee below brushed into the shape of a whisk broom. Great ornamental twists of golden ribbon rose from his cuffs all the way to the elbows of his uniform jacket's dark blue. The colonel stationed the men on the right side of the pike, a little farther beyond the field they'd charged through two days before, closer to Sedgwick's positions, with orders to drive ahead a mile or so and clear out anything they hit. Behind them, the exhausted army slowly wheeled itself away from the line, and the first troops and wagons drew back east along the pike. Burridge asked Herring if he had any idea of where they were headed next, but Herring simply shook his head. Henry hadn't seemed to know much more in their meeting that afternoon. The army was pulling out; where exactly they were heading no one knew, the captain included. All he knew was that rear picket duty was the opportunity they'd been waiting for and that Burridge should make every possible effort to find the scout. As they spoke, Burridge looked for some sign that Herring knew about his mission, but saw none. With a warning to stay awake and a mournful gaze that Burridge felt lasted just a second too long, Herring turned toward the main body of his skirmishers.

They were alone now, in the woods, with the sun only starting to fall in front of them. Spread out across a hundred yards, they pushed ahead through more stretches of humbled forest. Low piles of dirt and small markers made from pieces of scrap wood showed where some bodies rested. Stives inadvertently kicked a marker aside as he passed, so Lyman angled over, stopped, and stooped to replant the short board, just a cracked-off length of hardtack crate, maybe one inch by three inches and a foot long, with a few words scratched on it in pencil.

JAMES HARRIS—23—A GOOD MAN & FATHER—MAY 6, 1864 A.D.

Lyman stuck it back into the dirt and drove it in deep with the butt of his rifle.

Though most of the forest had been thinned by the battle, a broad swath as long as their picket line lay ahead, still tall, washed with green, and apparently untouched. Before they entered, Burridge passed the word to remain silent and be extremely careful. The day had been mostly sunny much of the way and the tattered forest allowed light, but once they stepped into this border of trees, the gloom they had felt that first day returned.

After a minute of walking, they hit a particularly thick stretch of trees with a heavy canopy blotting out the light. No birds sang in the stillness and a weighted silence wrapped the men. They were spread out and staring straight ahead as they walked, afraid to turn and see their own growing concerns about this place confirmed on the faces of the men next to them.

Lyman knew this spot was perfect for a bushwhacking, so he tensed and padded forward on the balls of his feet to keep down the noise. The trees packed closer and closer together, men having to almost squeeze through them, until Lyman could see what was nearly a solid wall of trunks, a natural vertical barricade, with light streaming through the chinks in firm rays. Ten feet to his left, the light poured into the forest as though a door were open there. He recognized the quality of the light, a spreading triangle of thick orange gold broken at parts into separate beams by branches overhead. It was something he could touch. Gnats flitted through the motes of dust swimming in the liquid gold. Though it was late afternoon, Lyman could think only of morning; that's where he knew this light from, early morning; a summer morning when he was just nine or ten. As his father had called him back into the shop to help finish the day's sausage, the same light had streamed through the open back door and into the kitchen, beckoning young Lyman out toward the dense patches of roses and tiger lilies in the fields behind their house. Lyman had stood by the door, squinting out toward a day meant for chasing rabbits or throwing rocks into the river or collecting flowers for his mother, but before he could do any of those wonderful things, he had felt a thick hand grab his arm and drag him away, slamming the door shut behind.

Lyman had seen that light other mornings since then; thousands of mornings he had wasted by heading straight to work without a good-bye to his wife and son, thinking only of another day of cutting meat and doing his bloody job. He'd missed more chances than just that Excelsiors match with Cully. Resting the butt of his rifle on the ground, he leaned on the gun and considered the light. Burridge whispered frantically to him, but Lyman chose not to hear and the lieutenant stopped. In the silence, that trembling, honeyed light became a presence. Lyman extended his arm and began to touch it, but that wasn't enough. This light was a gift. His only job was to step forward into it.

He inched closer, unmindful of all the deadly possibilities that could be in that opening despite the harsh renewed whispers of Burridge, and now Cawthorne as well, ordering him to stop where he was.

But he wouldn't stop. Not today. It was too beautiful. Green pine branches laced together and arched over the entrance like the very gates of heaven. He edged up to the opening, took a breath, then stood full before the light and whatever it would show him.

The color hit him first. The rich green of a grassy field rolled a hundred and fifty yards to another wall of trees. The sun tipped the blades with light and the breeze set them all a-shimmer. Beige clouds, white at their soft tops, floated by against a deepening blue sky. Violets flowed out of the trees and into a large stain of purple circling much of the glade. Lyman reminded himself to breathe. He knew that he should have been scanning the trees for Rebs, but this place seemed too good for shooting and there was evidence that he was right. Despite the horrors this forest had seen, no bloated bodies drew flies in the corners, no blood seeped into the dirt. It was a private place that had somehow defied the worst of man and nature.

Newt and Louis came in next, their rifles sweeping wary arcs across the field. The lieutenant tried to stop any other men from entering as he stared into the woods, but drawn by the light, the entire company filed into the field and offered themselves up to possible destruction in this corral. Louis saw it for the killing floor it was and crouched close to the opening, the exception among these men as hungry as Lyman for beauty and another chance. Their fatigue catching up with them, Tice and Feeney curled right up to sleep. The Worm twins sat and let the light warm their pale skin while others prowled along the perimeter investigating with curiosity, not caution. Huey spotted a rabbit.

As Lyman looked across the field, he could only picture one thing—the Excelsiors' grounds on Court Street with its same expanse of clean grass and exact limits. A ball field was a world within the world, too, he thought, with its own rules related in some ways to the rules of life, but a world that offered immediate rewards and penalties. No one had to tell a ballplayer he was doing well or not; if he performed well and played as a gentleman, the fruits were evident. As Lyman saw it, there was only one thing to do on a spring afternoon on a grassy field and it was a very ordinary thing; what any man would do on a field like this with his friends. He dug into his knapsack and took out his base ball. There was consolation in a game of catch.

Without asking to be covered, he strode farther into the clearing, then called over to the group of men clustered near the entrance, "Newt! Come on and have a throw!"

Cawthorne blocked Newt by pressing his rifle against Fry's chest. "You'll get us all shot!"

Newt looked over Cawthorne's shoulder to his friend, who tossed the ball from hand to hand, smiling the easy, sure way Lyman smiled when he held a base ball. That was the man he'd met in '59, on top of his game, ready with an answer. Courageous. Fry wanted some of that. He smirked as he pushed the play actor aside. "Gimme one a those speed balls, Lyman."

Tiger hissed over, "What the fuck are ye doing!"

Lyman lobbed the ball to Newt. "Season starts this week. I'm gettin' ready to go home."

C H A P T E R

6

NEWT AND LYMAN HAD A WARM-UP CATCH BEFORE LYMAN started to throw hard. Every man held his breath, waiting for a sharpshooter's bullet to drop one of them, but nothing happened after a few tosses, so the company relaxed to watch the battery work. Newt rubbed his palms. "Time for the speed ball, Lyman. Gimme the best ya got." Lyman wound his arm back and as he came down on his left foot, he shot the ball hard into Newt's hands.

A Southern voice drawled through the clearing. "Do you call that a speed ball?"

They all fell to their stomachs, yet every man knew it was a wasted precaution. Whoever saw them could take them out one by one, like a firing squad.

"I said, do you call that a speed ball? You must have better weapons than that, sir."

Lyman searched through the trees, but he could see nothing. Though the voice sounded friendly, he was sure the Rebs were toying with them and a leaden guilt settled into his stomach. He had led them all in here to get wiped out. The wisdom of Burridge's decision to pass over him for Cawthorne seemed confirmed. A couple of Union men got off shots in the direction of the voice, which hollered back, "Damn! Don't shoot! Don't shoot!" Burridge scrambled over to stop another round. Though the lieutenant's reaction surprised Lyman, he was glad of it since, to his immense relief, these Rebs were obviously deserters and there was no need for more blood here. While he was grateful that there'd be no scrap, the sight of surrendering men gave him the feeling one had when watching a trained bear. They were on his side, tamed, but who wanted them? Lyman dropped his shoulders. "We'll come out!"

Burridge had the same thought, but it took him further. If the scout was in here with a group of deserters, the whole plan was dead. Trees shook across the way and there was a rustling. Gray and brown figures emerged from the openings in the wall. Lyman counted them as they came out— twelve. But they didn't have their hands up as he'd expected.

Slowly, with guns level, the Rebels started across the field in a line. If they were deserting, it was on their own terms, and the chance remained now that they weren't. The mood swung back to caution; Union men cocked their guns. At any moment, if any one man on either side took a shot, there'd be a short and pointless bloodbath and everyone knew it.

Fear balanced Lyman's gladness to be with equals in the field and the natural thrill of two groups of men possibly doing something that was illegal in the eyes of both armies. If they did anything less than kill each other, they'd be court-martial material, liable to face firing squads or, at best, prison for life. With just days to go in their service.

The Rebs got closer, close enough so that Lyman could make out faces. And there he was. The big black-haired Reb, a couple steps out in front of the rest. Lyman stopped short, amazed to see him here.

The Reb stopped and so did the Rebel line. He reached into his pocket. Even Lyman raised his rifle. Though this was the last man he wanted to take aim at, Lyman wasn't ready to die for any mistaken dreams of friendship.

The Reb carefully drew back his hand.

Lyman pulled back the hammer.

A white handkerchief spilled out of the pocket.

Lyman's heart dropped at the thought that this man was a deserter, but at least he didn't have to shoot. He exhaled. "Are you surrendering?"

The Reb looked down. "Hell no. Truce." Lyman smiled, lowered his gun, and restrained an urge to rush up and shake his sizable hand.

The moment Cawthorne had first heard the Southern drawl, his hand had been drawn slowly down to his hip. The revolver perched heavily upon it. Distracted as they'd been making traitorous overtures, no one had noticed him pulling the Adams out of its holster, and now he had it raised shoulder high, squinting into the line cut between the sight and the heart of the big Reb talking to Alder. His own heart beat faster. He began to squeeze the trigger, his eye squinting a little more. The sight quivered with his effort.

Then a hand shot into view, grabbed the barrel of the gun, and pointed it downward. "I gave no such order!" Burridge planted himself in front of the sergeant. The shock of the action and the lieutenant's mad face, angrier than he'd ever seen him, frightened Cawthorne into silence. He breathed heavily through his nose, collecting his thoughts. What had happened? His lieutenant was preventing him from shooting a Reb. It made no sense. He tried to wrest the revolver away. Burridge held firm and the two tugged at the gun, moving only inches between them until the lieutenant ripped it away.

"Sir!"

"Let me handle this."

"My sidearm!" But the lieutenant had already turned away, Felix Cawthorne's prized possession in his hand.

A thin, good-looking Reb with some gold on the shoulders of his worn gray jacket and shiny black hair parted down the center said, "I propose we drop our weapons at our sides. A few men on each side will keep guard." It was his burnished plantation voice that had first spoken a couple minutes before; minutes that seemed like hours now to the anxious Feds. The Confederate officer strode forward toward Burridge with a slight upturn in one corner of his lips. He stopped and extended his hand. Despite the missing buttons on his jacket and the long tear up the leg of his trousers, he had managed to maintain the dash and manners of a well-bred Southron. "Lieutenant Sidney Mink. Twelfth Alabama."

Burridge hadn't imagined the rendezvous would be so friendly, and public. He hesitated for a second before shaking. "Lieutenant John Burridge. Fourteenth Brooklyn."

"I know." Mink nodded. "I once made a most pleasing visit to Brooklyn. We recognized those red legs."

Burridge had been listening so hard for those words that when he heard them he nearly jumped. His reply was immediate and sounded as though he was reading it off a chalkboard back in the Williamsburg Grammar School for Boys. "Did you eat at Howard's Halfway House?"

"Well, I was fortunate to visit so many of your wonders. That fine Academy of Music and the Athenaeum. Fine structures. In a fit of bad humor my host also brought me to hear your Reverend Beecher sermonize at that . . . What's the name?"

"Plymouth Church. But did you eat at . . ."

"Of course! Plymouth Church. A most beautiful edifice." A few beats passed, during which Mink scratched his temple quizzically. "Now that you mention it, perhaps I did take a meal there. In fact, I can say with some certainty that I did. Yes, yes I have. It was very good."

"Good," Burridge replied, with some nervous nods of his head. His eyes flitted from man to man, from the treetops to the ground as he tapped his fingers on his legs and wondered what would happen now. Whenever he lit on Mink, he saw the Reb looking hard at him, and he realized that Mink had been staring at him the whole time; the deep-set eyes were fixed on him and he began to feel their pressure. Burridge couldn't move and could barely breathe as the spy appraised, he guessed, his worthiness, his courage. The lieutenant forced down a swallow. Then the edges of Mink's lips turned up again, slyly. Though the eyes did not relent, their force suddenly became pleasant, the sort of boyish jostling that he had often envied among his inferiors. Their acknowledgment settled, he wanted the connection to continue. Burridge had never seen such a wonderfully dangerous man in his life.

Mink smiled slowly, showing a perfect set of teeth. "I believe we may be well met, sir. Very well met."

As Mink and Burridge spoke, Lyman went to the man he'd had his own peace with now for a day. With a respectful formality, he introduced himself without offering his hand. "Lyman Alder."

The big man nodded, moving slow as if it were a hot August day and staring at the ground in some combination of what seemed humility and embarrassment. He was built like a barrel and his head, topped with that mop of black hair, was wide and strong like the rest of him. "Micah Breese." Like many of the Rebs here, he had a white *14* painted on his canteen. Others had one on their knapsacks.

"We run into you fellows before."

Micah waited a few beats, his eyes on the incriminating *14* before he said, "Yep."

Lyman hunted for something to say but, instead, he held up the ball. "You boys play?"

"Have. Not much of late."

Mink, who was listening to them, stepped in. "I played some innings some time ago in New Orleans. I'm more of a cricket man myself, though."

"Any more of you play?"

Micah nodded again. "Some. Not many."

Mink had a wicked smile. "Well, why don't we have ourselves a match?"

The image of a firing squad popped into Lyman's head; the inevitable result if they were caught by their own troops. Rebel capture meant even worse; starvation or typhus in some prison camp. But when he looked at that green field, all he could see was the Court Street Grounds. Fear would not keep him away this time. Lyman turned to the company and asked them what they thought.

Newt was shaky at the idea. "Do you trust them? They got Brooklyn gear."

A flickering image of a Southern face framed in blazes appeared to Lyman. "I think they need to catch a breath as bad as we do."

Cawthorne piped up. "So they can kill more Northern men and rob *their* bodies."

"What makes you think they want to kill you any more than your cowardly ass wants to kill them?" Lyman looked at Newt. "You're our best man."

All these muffins around Newt were below him as players—it would be an ugly game—but he could tell how badly Lyman wanted it and there was the added benefit of keeping these Rebs away from their guns. He said yes. Lyman clapped his back.

Stives and Tice were against it; they couldn't conceive of fighting men exchanging anything but bullets and hatred. The three recruits were for it, though, suspecting that this was some odd test of courage that they couldn't back down from. That made five. Huey and Del Rio decided they were too tired to play and grumbled nervously about their suspicions. Willie said he'd do some trading.

Cawthorne still had objections. "This is a most serious contravention of the codes of conduct. It is traitorous behavior in the theater of war and it will mean courts-martial for every one of you."

Burridge rubbed the back of his neck. He had misjudged Cawthorne completely, read three moves when the great opponent had read four. Cawthorne wasn't on Burridge's side; he was on his own and no one else's. The sergeant went on with his histrionic bluster. Burridge had done nothing more than establish contact and the scheme was already in jeopardy thanks to his poor judgment. Germanicus on the Weser, indeed. All he had remembered with Henry were the names; the plottings of Tiberius and Livia had returned to the mists of the unfamiliar the moment he'd last closed his Tacitus. "Shut up, sergeant." He turned to Lyman. "I'm in."

Tears of anger formed in the corners of Cawthorne's eyes. "Sir, I respectfully request the return of my sidearm." He seemed equally capable of bursting into flames as he was into tears. "Sir. Again I respectfully . . ."

"After the match."

The group stood in shocked silence, surprised by the quick and forceful decisions. Reassured by the lieutenant's participation, the Worms said they liked the idea, but neither man knew how to play so they offered Pindar's accounting skills to keep score. Lyman and Newt had seen Karl hit some long balls in matches last summer, so it didn't take much to convince him, but Von Schenk showed no interest.

Lyman could see Rebs shaking heads and shrugging shoulders, too, especially the two tall ones. Micah did the talking and cajoling inside their group, but it was Mink who finally turned to announce that they had a nine.

Tiger wasn't sold so easily. "How do we know ye aren't out to ambush us?" He pointed at one of the stolen knapsacks. "Again."

Mink smiled, as if pitying Tiger for his question. He raised a hand and said, "Brock."

There was a rifle shot, then a minié zipped out from near the opening and into the dust before Tiger's feet. Everyone turned toward a thirteenth Reb kneeling there, reloading. Like some of the other Rebs, he wore a checked homespun shirt and a gray fatigue cap, but high cavalry boots riding over his knees most distinguished him. "That, sir, is how. Brockington there. If it was in our minds to kill you, we'd surely have done it by now. Same's true of you, and you well know that."

Lyman pointed to the sun. "Think we have enough time?"

Mink squinted toward the sun. "I'd say we have until eight. Do any of you have a bat?"

Newt unrolled his blanket and presented Mink with the stick. "Still, let's keep it fast. Call high or low, but no waiting for your pitch. Take a good toss and it's a strike; three bad tosses on purpose and the batter takes first base. That's how they're playing it this year in Brooklyn."

"All right."

Newt had a thought, too. "Make it a fly game."

"And that is . . . ?"

"You have to catch a hit ball on the fly for the hand to be out."

Lyman didn't like the fly game, even though the Excelsiors and all the best teams were playing it. To him it stressed physical prowess more than necessary. One bounce was fine with him, but everyone seemed to like the idea of a fly game and Mink agreed to it, so he gave in. They paced out the forty-five feet between the box and the plate and ninety feet between bases, but then remembered that they needed bases.

Micah pulled his haversack over his head. "Here. Use these. Ourn's empty anyways."

Lyman took it and the other three offered him. "You boys have any 'backy?"

"That'd be about all we have."

"Well, I think we got some boys who'd trade up some belly for that."

"That'd be fine." Lyman didn't expect a show of gratitude and none was made. "Listen. We ain't so good."

Lyman laughed. "Neither are we."

Mink had one more rule he wanted in. "This is the South, so *we* are the home nine."

Lyman and Newt shrugged at each other. "Fair enough," Lyman said.

Louis still had to decide if he wanted to play. Lyman and Newt stood over him, arms crossed. This base ball was a boy's game, he thought, much like one he'd played when he was a schoolboy in Pest, called *meta*. The game they called cricket was closer to it, but still it was bats and balls. Louis remembered playing on soft spring days in fine clothes, when he wanted for nothing but a good swing. That was before the flood in '38, though; no one in his family had want for anything before then. He could hit the ball well in those days, and he probably still could. The thought of floating along on some memories and displaying a new kind of prowess settled the issue. He handed his gun to Del Rio.

Newt gestured toward his leg. "What about that? Can you run?"

Louis blushed. He had forgotten the injury, such as it was, in the excitement. What had sent him limping to the back yesterday was an old leg that had simply fallen asleep, and the kind of pain that lingered in the Hungarian's bones went far deeper than any bullet wound. "Yes. I will not be fastest, but I will try to hit far."

Lyman smiled at that.

There had been games once, and dances. Jigs and a piper when the crop came in. Dim memories, those. Sitting on the grass, off to the side, Tiger Quigley chewed on some hardtack as Lyman pleaded with him. But no one plays games at a time when people fight over a dead rat's carcass for food, and you don't much want to play them after you've seen such a thing. Prizefighting was the only sport that made sense to Tiger. Besides, there was no reason to play a game with men who'd stripped the corpses of your dead friends and left them naked for the hogs. "Sorry. I'm playing no game with the likes of them. No, sir. Danny wouldn't have it and I won't, either."

"I ain't happy about the gear, Pete. I know how you feel and I ain't saying we should chum up with them. We just need a rest here."

Newt smirked. "Leave him be. He can't play anyway." Lyman shrugged, then the two turned away without another word.

Tiger boiled inside. If there was one thing he would not stand, it was Newton Fry thinking himself better than Tiger Quigley at anything, be it shooting, shitting, walking in a straight line, or playing base ball. He'd taken a few turns at bat in his day and was lucky to be standing after each, but he'd never admit it. He popped up. "I'm in."

As Tiger trotted past them toward the field, Newt nudged Lyman in the ribs. "Told you it would work." Lyman knew Tiger was right. Danny would never have done this. But Danny was dead.

Under the light of a setting sun red and round as a new cricket ball, nine men in gray and brown stood in their positions. The home base had been set near the northern edge of the clearing, halfway between each side. Circled by the wall of trees and the violets, the grass looked more inviting to Lyman than any field he had ever seen. The beauty of the place and the remarkable thing that was happening burned away any strange mist clouding the scene in his mind. He couldn't imagine a better way to celebrate the end of his fighting days.

Lyman scanned the defense. Far back in left was a tall, slick fellow, the battle-worn remants of a riverboat gambler under a handsome, though ripped, hat of black felt. Center was a lanky type whose long face belied some Indian blood, and a freckled kid in a wide straw hat was in right. A squirrelly, short man with waves of curly hair, clucking like a chicken, had third. At shortstop was a hairless man, bald to his eyebrows. Mink stood on first and a bearded man wearing a Confederate fatigue cap was a few paces off second. Micah was catching and the Rebel pitcher was a mean-looking one with a stringy gamecock on his shoulder, a small man squeezed into the very essence of nastiness most Union men expected in a Reb. Pindar squatted on the side with a piece of letter paper in his hand to keep records and an empty pipe in his mouth. There was no way to know if these Rebs could be trusted; all Lyman had to go on was a feeling about Micah Breese and it would have to do. He stared hard, so he could remember it all, then set the order.

Newt stepped up first, a position he considered rightfully his given that he'd once played in a match against the Stars, a match that, he was never shy to point out, saw him make two runs. It felt wonderful to be for once fully confident, to know more, to be more able than anyone else around, and he knew, for one, that these tattered, barefoot Rebels hardly formed a nine worth fearing. Though their hems were frayed and their seats no longer scarlet, his Union boys had the satisfied glow of a recent meal on their faces and uniforms that matched. This was a sure thing, and no one had seen one of those since the first Bull Run.

Newt went up swinging, the bat swooping in from high above his head like a cresting wave being somehow sucked back into the ocean. His shallow pop put him on first. After a few pitches spent appraising Karl's stiff Teutonic stance, Newt took off for second and came all the way home on the German's liner into left. It was that simple. Thick Teddy Finn powered a double, scoring Karl, and he was caught out at third only because he was trotting there backward. Newt had a smile at that; typical of Lyman to cluck like a mother hen and shake his head. The capper was Tiger embarrassing himself with a weak trickle to first.

Wesley Pitt finished it with a pop to short, but two runs an inning would be quite enough, thank you very much, thought Newt. All in all, one of the most enjoyable halves of a frame Newt had ever spent, even if he'd end up in prison for it.

	1	2	3	4	5	6	7	8	9	R	H	E
UNION	2									2	3	0
CONFEDERATES										0	0	0

Lyman pulled off his jacket and went to the pitcher's box, feeling the ball in his hand with its perfect weight; any lighter and it would never get over, any heavier and it would be a rock. It had been a sweet-looking thing when still white and new, but the fresh green scuffs had begun to give it character. Lyman liked that. Every mark on a base ball was the story of a safe hit, an out, a play at home base—a round and indecipherable record of time spent playing. After a quick sniff of the leather, he was ready.

The first Rebel batter, the squirrelly fellow, came up to Lyman's chin at best. He was small, compact, and blessed with long wavy hair, a beard, and mustache all the same light brown and all parted down the middle. Lyman admired the way he moved; quick, yet fully considered and limited to only the minimum needed to effect whatever it was he wanted to have happen. Pindar Worm, sitting Indian-style on the side, stopped the Reb before he could take a swing. "Please tell me your name." The Reb whistled suspiciously back to the others for approval. "It's just to keep score, you understand." Pindar waved the sheet of letter paper.

Mink said, "Go ahead. This is mere diversion."

But the Reb still wouldn't give his name. He stood, eyes flicking from one corner to the other. Micah caught Lyman's eye and glared as if trying to divine evil intent. Lyman nodded back and Micah, still watching Lyman, said, "G'wan."

The Reb had a reedy thin voice that seemed to be on its way toward becoming a birdcall itself. He leaned toward Pindar's ear. "Lemuel Haddon."

Pindar nodded. "And how do you spell that?"

Haddon hung his head down, as though he'd forgotten a lesson, then looked Pindar right in the eye. "Don't know."

Pindar waved him toward the plate. "I'll figure it out."

Lyman checked his fielders. Newt bounced around from foot to foot at short, and Wes, in his lumbering way, did a similar dance at first. Feeney at second and Karl at third were each straight up and down, but the similarity ended there. Karl was firmly rooted to his spot and appeared ready to burst into some form of calisthenic activity at any second, while Feeney's inert stance came from pure apathy. In the outfield, Louis and Teddy paced back and forth not too deep in right and left, respectively, and Tiger stood far back in center with his arms folded. Burridge rubbed his hands together behind the home base. Lyman hoped the lieutenant was ready, because he would be throwing hard as much to cause him pain as to strike the Rebels out.

His first pitch was outside of where Haddon liked it, but the Rebel took a big swing anyway and missed. Lyman came inside with the next and Haddon swung wildly again and again he missed. Seeing no reason to fool around here, Lyman put some real heat on the third pitch. Haddon was just starting his swing by the time Burridge caught the ball, shaking his hand as if burned.

One out. Lyman turned to Newt and winked, trying hard not to smile. In all his days of playing base ball, he hadn't struck a man out, and while this Haddon certainly wasn't Joe Oliver, it gave him the same feeling of glorious triumph that he'd had when he first put on his uniform. Next up, the tall Reb in the black hat announced himself to Pindar as Mansfield Covay, taking pains to spell it to him in a very pointed manner. A lefty, Covay wore a once-white, round-collared shirt that buttoned with a large square sweep near his left shoulder, and though Lyman believed that calm, indifferent looks like his were usually a sign of great abilities, two clumsy swings at low speed balls told him otherwise. Clearly, the Rebs were not players. Lyman decided to put on some spin and come in with one of the snap pitches he'd been practicing for the third. As he let go, he pictured it lofting high, then curving down irresistibly into Covay's zone, where the Reb would swing and miss again.

But Covay did not miss. He timed the pitch and slammed it way over Louis, good for all four bases and a sure boundary in cricket.

Lyman shook his head. A fluke. A lucky shot. Any strong man who'd handled an ax could clout a pitch as bad as that one. Newt jogged to his side. "Don't do that again, huh? Lay off that snap pitch. Nice enough of us to play with them; we don't have to let them win."

Lyman looked in at the next man, the pitcher, Albert Arlette. The hairless Reb called out, "In the name of Jesus Christ, go forward, brother Arlette!"

Covay and the Indian laughed. Arlette just scrunched up his face, spat, and said, "Amen!" loudly in their direction, which brought more laughter. Only five feet five or so on his best day, he was down to his undershirt and suspenders, and a heavy growth of whiskers, along with a paste of dirt and sulfur, blackened his face. Arlette took two practice swings, then set in the box, squeezing his lips into a determined line. Lyman went fast and right down the base with the pitch, which Arlette sent over Teddy. Only a strong throw kept him at third. Harlan Deal, the tall Indian, stuck his small pipe into the breast pocket of his rough butternut shirt, dug in on the right side of the base with his left foot, then put Lyman's first offering far beyond Quigley's reach in center with a swing as lean and powerful as his body appeared. Rebs 3, Union 2.

When a bullet hit a tree next to him, a man liked to think it was luck; the second bullet meant someone had him in his sights and he'd better find cover or shoot back. The Union boys were too surprised for either. If they'd been expecting a fight, they'd all be clapping right now and steadying Lyman. Instead, all Lyman heard was a stunned silence until Tiger hollered in, "What the hell are ye doing out there, Lyman?" A sour taste rose up from Lyman's stomach as he went back to the box, the fear of losing now elbowing at the fear of getting caught.

The hairless Reb, one E. Simon Weed, put his fatigue cap on his bald head and folded his hands in murmured supplication before popping out on a speed ball. The Rebel lieutenant Mink chatted some with Burridge, then ground a single to left. The inning closed with three quick strikes that a bearded, shaggy Reb named Kingsley could only lunge at. Newt put a good face on it all, reminding everyone that they were only down one run. Lyman kept his head down, examining his fingers as if they were the cause.

Even among friends, stepping in the first time can be a daunting moment and Lieutenant Burridge didn't have any friends. Like most of the men playing, he hadn't swung a bat in a while. In fact, he'd never swung a bat in an actual game. When he was young he'd watch other boys playing two o'cat by Wheat Hill and sometimes even summon up the courage to stand around hoping for an invitation to play, but hoping as well that he wouldn't be asked so he could save himself the embarrassment of playing badly. Invariably passed over, he would go home, find a bat-size stick, and reenact his own games on the street, by himself. As he went to the base, Burridge knew he had a nice swing; he just didn't know if it would work in a real game. Burridge tugged at each of his shoulders, rocked back and forth to find a good purchase in the dirt, then grit his teeth.

As soon as it left his hand, it was clear that Arlette's first pitch of the second inning would come in low and outside, missing the lieutenant's high mark. Burridge took a deep breath, relieved that he did not have to make a choice, then scrunched back into his constricted stance, legs close together and arms tight to the body. With someone who had quick wrists and the knowledge of what to do with it, the stance could provide great torque and sharp hits to all fields. Unfortunately, Burridge had only practiced the swing against the family cat.

Arlette's next offering looked good to Burridge at first, then it seemed to be way outside. In the space of a second, the lieutenant decided to swing, changed his mind, then changed it again and took a hurried frightening slap at a strike. Burridge closed his eyes and took a breath, his hands shaking. He'd never known one second to contain so much action, excitement, and fear. Right on top of his first contact with Mink, this was giving him palpitations he hadn't even experienced under fire. He took another breath. Certain he'd gotten the jitters out, he watched Arlette's next pitch come in across the plate, at which point he swung, just edging the ball with his bat.

Burridge knew he had to get on base so he could talk with Mink. Concentrating, he swung late again on the fourth pitch, but got enough to send it rolling toward Mink's right. The slow roller seemed to freeze the Reb at first, and though he did get his hands on the ball, it was too late to catch Burridge.

Mink tossed the ball back to Arlette as he turned to Burridge at first.

"I can hit like the devil himself, but the kindest thing you can say about my fielding is that it is, well, the word would be 'suspect.'" He stayed close to the bag, near the runner, as if planning to pick Burridge off, and continued in a barely audible voice. Burridge, still catching his breath from the sprint and the tension of the at bat, had now learned enough to read between the lines. "Hit the ball to me all day—I'd make half the plays, at best." Mink watched him until he returned a significant nod.

Their contact and mode of meeting finally established, Mink asked Burridge his first question as Louis took a few practice swings. "Is this one any good?"

Burridge shrugged his shoulders. "I don't know."

"Why then did you place him after yourself?"

"I didn't make the order."

Louis took a ball high.

"Do you mean to tell me that one of your *soldiers* told *you* what position was yours?" It hadn't struck Burridge before that he wasn't the captain of his own team; he'd been content to let Alder suffer the details while he tried to figure out how to save the Union. As Louis took another ball, Mink suddenly dropped his air of Southern good cheer and said with an earnest seriousness, "That's your job, son," like a well-meaning older brother handing out advice, though he was no older than Burridge and had the same smooth skin. The eyes had become a pair of cold darts in Mink's mask of youth; the eyes of an officer, of a man who could execute. Mink knew how to play this situation. Louis hit a towering pop to Covay for the first out. Just before the first pitch to Feeney, Mink said, "Make yourself first baseman. A man can just stand there and watch what happens. *Talk* to people." Feeney grounded a sure double-play ball to the hairless Reb Weed, who, instead of tossing to Kingsley, took the short trot to second and barely forced Burridge without even a look toward first.

Burridge sensed that his education was only beginning.

Lyman told himself that he was batting last because the shank of the line needed his bolster, but the jitters began as he stepped to the base and he had to admit that he wasn't a Leggett when it came to the bat. He held his hands high on the handle to get more control, but more often than not he dribbled grounders to second or, if he was lucky, looped a hit to shallow right. The sorry truth was that he'd most likely fare better on a cricket pitch, where even the slow single was rewarded with a run.

Lyman looked out to the field. Every Reb was now staring at him, wondering what he played like, if he was good; remembering him now for something other than the color of his uniform. They were massed against him, but their faces were becoming distinct to him now, too. The two teams were slowly dissolving into eighteen men of two sides. It happened whenever unfamiliar nines faced the first time; boys from other parts of Brooklyn came into focus the same way on fields back home. There were faces, ways of walking and talking, that made a man take an instant dislike to another man without a word being spoken—Arlette, for example. Everything the man did made Lyman want to deck him. Those were the ones you tried to beat. And then there were the men you wish you had on your own nine, like Breese. While Micah Breese hadn't said a word since they started playing, even if his canteen might have once belonged to a tentmate or friend, Lyman had considered him more than just another Reb since that first meeting amid the flames. They'd been pushed together twice; fate, and Lyman's curiosity, had to be attended. "So where you boys from?"

" 'Bama."

Lyman swung and missed at the first pitch, even with his belt and just where he'd asked for it. "Whereabouts?"

"Opelika." That meant nothing to Lyman, who just got a piece of Arlette's change of pace and ticked it foul.

Lyman turned back to Micah. "Some fight we just had."

Micah stared straight ahead at Arlette and waited a second to reply. "Yep."

The third pitch was a speed ball. Lyman's swing wasn't even close. Twisted around by his effort, he could see the boys on his side scowling as the Rebs celebrated. Breese dropped the ball at his feet and walked away.

Embarrassed by his sorry at bat, Lyman pushed harder, but the Rebels added two more in the bottom of the second and Lyman couldn't even take credit for holding them to that; only a lucky catch by Tiger kept them in view.

	1	2	3	4	5	6	7	8	9	R	H	E
UNION	2	0								2	3	0
CONFEDERATES	3	2								5	6	1

No one spoke to Lyman as the Union boys came in from the field. He took a place not far from home and watched the others group in twos and threes, grumbling, prodding the grass with their shoes, and staring at him. Teddy said he was afraid of getting any closer to the trees for fear of getting hit by a Rebel minié; Tiger told him he'd be more likely to get hit by a Rebel fly ball off of one of Lyman's floaters. Newt stood over him. Lyman was hoping for a pat on the back, but Newt just told him again to stick with the speed balls, then walked away. He rubbed his shoulder and said to anyone listening that he just needed to get the blood going. Teddy folded his arms and said, "What I can't figure is why he got us inculculated into all of this so's we could lose is what I wanna know."

Lyman didn't have an answer. He wondered if he was just rusty or whether he really was this bad a player. For the first time, he thanked God that Alder Senior had kept him home that day years ago, because the embarrassment of muffin play like this would have killed him. Then again, no one else on the Union side was tearing the cover off the ball, either. None of them were playing badly, it was just that the Rebels were playing well. Lyman considered yet another surprise of war—why hadn't anyone told them that Rebs could play base ball? Why hadn't anyone told them what it was like when a friend's head exploded before your eyes? Why hadn't anyone told them that they were here to kill and die, not to win? There was so much that they'd all imagined, but so little that they really knew. By now they should have known not to underestimate the Rebs. Lyman sat alone and watched as Karl, Teddy, and Tiger all failed to move Newt along after a lead-off double; watched as Breese played on without making the smallest signal of friendship to him. A bit of sport and a balm for the soul was slipping into yet another defeat. Lyman pulled up a clump of grass and let the blades slip through his fingers.

	1	2	3	4	5	6	7	8	9	R	H	E
UNION	2	0	0							2	4	0
CONFEDERATES	3	2								5	6	1

The bottom of the third began with Alder quickly getting Weed on a pop out to Newt. Mink followed with a single to center. Burridge, now at first, welcomed him with a nod. The Rebel put his hands on his hips and seemed to again appraise Burridge. *"Tibi similitudo viri magnae eruditionis est..."*

Burridge wasn't sure he heard him right. "What?"

"Salve, amice." Kingsley took a ball low and Burridge scratched his head, not sure of what to say. *"Deponeram te eruditum lingua Latina esse quippe qui tibi talis similitudo sit..."*

Burridge tried to quickly translate, but he wasn't very deft with spoken Latin. Mink had said something about him looking like a professor. His stomach lurched; how could the man know about his father? *"Immo possum legere illam,"* he managed, *"quamvis non possum dicere volubilis."* Kingsley fouled off the next pitch.

"Where did you study?"

Burridge looked down his nose and said, "Columbia College" with a smug nonchalance.

"A fine institution. Fine. At Harvard, we'd have said, *'Ita possum legere, cum non volubater dicam,'* I believe."

Burridge's small triumph became an embarrassment, as though a lovely dinner partner whose giggling attentions he'd held all evening revealed to him afterward the presence of a large green ort of spinach on his teeth. Burridge scrambled to recover. "Columbia *me docuit bene, gratias."*

Mink smiled, and to Burridge's relieved surprise it seemed genuine. "I'm certain Columbia gave you a fine education." He delivered his next sentence slowly, so Burridge would catch every word. *"Si volubiliter non potes dicere, nostrum opus etiam difficilius erit. Hic litterulas non mutamus."*

Before Burridge could answer Mink's claim that his problems with spoken Latin would make their job difficult, Kingsley two-hopped one toward Feeney, who raced to second, just edging out Mink.

Angry to have been put out, Mink stood at second for a moment with his hands on his hips, his belt hanging loosely around his waist. Burridge took his measure again in light of the mounting evidence that Mink was not only more than another squirrel-hunting Reb, but more of a man than most he knew in Brooklyn, including himself. Mink was a good leader, he spoke perfect Latin, hit well, was good-looking, attended Harvard and so was probably full of that righteous Massachusetts abolition, was unmistakably well-bred, and was performing a dangerous duty for his nation. As the Rebel spy trotted back across the field, Burridge sighed as Caesar had before Alexander's statue, envious and intimidated.

The Rebs made it 6–2 in the third. The freckled boy, Caleb Marmaduke, a cheerful teenager too old to be a mascot but too simple to be considered a man, doubled in Porter Kingsley. Lyman roused and did his part for the Yanks in the fourth. He singled home Wesley and—if not for a perfect throw from center—Louis's huge home-base collision with Breese would have meant another run. As it was, the Hungarian was out and hammers were cocked and triggers gripped until Micah congratulated him for a hard effort.

By the fourth, Lyman had been through the order twice and was getting a sense of what each Reb liked to swing at. Haddon popped to Newt off a low outside toss. Covay liked the ball inside, so Lyman got him to swing at two speed balls on his hands. To mix it up, he came slow and outside for the third. Covay went with him, lunging at the pitch and dumping a single into left. Arlette swung at whatever Lyman offered, in his zone or not, so this at bat Lyman missed low on purpose and Arlette could only hit a high hopper to Newt. Feeney was standing on the base, waiting for Newt's throw, but the shortstop took one look at Feeney and ran it over himself. Now there were two out, a man on first.

Lyman felt a rhythm now. No one had taken a good scup since the second inning and the ball was going where he wanted it to go. Though the rest of his nine were clearly still disheartened by the unexpected resistance of the Rebs, Lyman was certain now that they'd weathered the worst. It always happened; David might beat Goliath once, but if Goliath had had a few more at bats against him, the Bible would probably record a much different score. The surprise was over and now the tide was ready to turn. A run or two on the Yankee line and there'd be a contest again.

The thought of a good close match got his blood going. He wound up high for the first pitch to Deal and let loose a hot speed ball that cuffed Wesley, the ball skipping off the boy's fingers. Arlette took second on the passed ball. Wes brought the ball back to Lyman, shaking his aching hand. "That was some pitch. Let's try it again."

Lyman grinned. Maybe the other boys were feeling the same thing. Ever since Burridge asked to switch places with Wes, he'd been oddly reassured by seeing that bear's face behind the plate, even if the boy had nearly blown his head off the day before. Why did he seem so familiar? There was no mistaking him for anything but a big boy. Time had not yet sculpted the baby fat away from the muscles beneath his arms and legs, and at times he moved awkwardly, as though trying to shed the child's smooth shell off the man's body inside. When everyone was ready, Lyman wound up for another one. Deal just got around on the pitch and lined it over the infield to Tiger's left for a hit. Arlette was nearing third when Tiger picked it up; Newt saw they had a play and screamed at Tiger to throw him the ball, but Tiger ignored the cutoff man and instead whipped the ball toward home, where a good throw might have caught Arlette.

Tiger's throw bounced high and up the line, and the Rebs took back a run. The Yanks got to within three with another run in the fifth. They were keeping pace; if the Rebs stumbled, if the Yanks could get within two, there were still enough innings to play. The Rebel runs were coming harder and if they could stop them here, Lyman was certain that the turning tide would become a wave. The important thing was to keep the pressure on. If the Rebs kept hearing footsteps, they'd surely begin to worry about getting caught.

Mink opened the Rebel half of the fifth with a long fly out to Tiger; Porter Kingsley followed. In two at bats, Porter's tentative pokes at Lyman's offerings had achieved nothing, so Weed urged him to put his faith in Jesus and close his eyes when he swung. The result was a double down the left-field line and a brief Psalm of thanksgiving from Weed.

Lyman winced. The sound of paper rattling made him look to the side, where Stives was furiously flipping through the pages of his Bible, apparently investigating the frightening possibility that God was on the Rebel side. A brief scan seemed to reveal nothing to Stives, but evidence appeared on the field to Lyman. The next batter, Caleb, slapped a hopper at Karl, who held the slightly confused Kingsley at second with a wave of the ball, then threw it away high over Burridge's head. In obedience to Mink's screamed orders, Kingsley ran to third and Caleb reached second. Micah then ambled to the plate and drove them both in with a three-base hit between Teddy and Pete. Rebs 9, Union 4. Lemuel's grounder to Newt made it 10–4, and by the time Covay finally popped out to Louis in right, Lyman had just about thrown it in with all the rest of the Yanks. Somehow the Rebs had beaten back the tide and pushed it even farther out to sea, and in just five or six of the dozens of pitches he'd thrown. Maybe David would always win against Goliath.

	1	2	3	4	5	6	7	8	9	R	H	E
UNION	2	0	0	1	1					4	8	1
CONFEDERATES	3	2	1	1	3					10	12	2

Down six runs, Lyman's competitive urges yielded to the simple motions of the game. The sun had dropped below the tree line and the orange sky over right field melted into an azure blue in deep left. Those soldiers not playing lounged in the grass paying some attention to the game but enjoying most the freedom gained from sharing a peaceful place with their greatest fear. The occasional shot from pickets at other points in the line sounded too much like the crack of ball on bat to startle them. Though Cawthorne and Von Schenk ostentatiously ate some bacon and refused all contact with the Rebels, other Feds had succumbed to the lure of tobacco and their curiosity about these exotic Southerners and started trading. Lyman had noticed Huey creeping a little closer each inning to Denton and the gamecock perched on his rifle, and Willie had been exchanging cooking tips with a long-bearded fellow sporting a broad-brimmed hat while they measured out coffee and tobacco on a blanket. Most fraternizations Lyman had been a part of had featured good-natured banter and tales of shared battles, but the game seemed to keep these men from excessive chatter. Nothing needed to be said. As an aimed gunshot spoke volumes about a man's intentions, so did his willingness to play.

Burridge's intention at this moment was to go to the right side and let Mink muff another ground ball. Their work had not yet been done. So far, he had been unable to take his eyes off Mink, how he casually placed one hand in a pocket and crossed the other behind his back, or how densely black his hair was. Burridge fouled off two pitches from Arlette, then got under one, popping it high over Sidney Mink's head. Burridge took off toward first, expecting the error, but Mink caught it and grinned at the Yankee now standing baffled on base. "If memory serves, I said I'd miss half of them, Billy Yank. Not all of them."

Burridge wandered back to his side. Louis limped by—faking, was the lieutenant's guess. A serious injury would have kept the Hungarian out, yet here he was, now hitting a single. Feeney then came sprinting back from the opening in the wall of trees to slap a crisp two-hopper that the Reb shortstop couldn't handle. Burridge looked at the setting sun and Mink below it, glowing in the red. He had never been so intrigued by a man before and strange as it was, he leaned back into its pleasure, registering only occasional moments—Alder popping out, Fry loading the bases on a dropped fly, Karl the German singling to center. Struck not only by the looks, Burridge saw something dark about Mink. Secrets lived inside there, one of which Burridge was privy to already, and there was the reward of more to someone who could get close enough. They were dark secrets, Burridge guessed—darker and more intimate than his own. At the inning's end, he realized that he still had no information for Henry.

Two Rebs made quick outs to start the sixth, a fact which did not faze Burridge because Mink was due up fourth. The hairless one, Weed, was up next. Union boys left and right were telling Alder to put him down, but Burridge couldn't wait another inning. Weed played the first pitch of his at bat right at him. With a growing sense that this perfect situation would not last for much longer, the lieutenant fluffed Weed's ball.

The serious look on Mink's face as he went into his stance confirmed Burridge's thought: It was time for business. The hair on both sides of Mink's part had slipped down and formed two halves of a crescent framing his face. He couldn't go to Burridge again after this last error, so he motioned for a high pitch and, as though warning that the next ball would be coming right at him, Mink stared at Slipper. Slipper, ready for this kind of fight, stared back.

The Reb was true to his look and a hot grounder came right at Slipper Feeney, who was bracing himself on second. Before Slipper could meet the challenge, Newt streaked out of his position and square in front of him to field the ball and force Weed himself. Feeney and Mink both howled, "Goddamnit!" and Burridge stopped before he said it, too.

The Yanks went down easily in the seventh, so the lieutenants quickly had another chance. Burridge stepped in and immediately bounced a single up the box past Arlette.

Much relieved, the lieutenant ran to first and said, *"Salve"* to Mink.

This was the moment. Burridge wondered what Mink would tell him: Troop locations? Battle plans?

Mink didn't look at him while he spoke. "Listen very closely. *Septem milia interfecti vulneratique.* Longstreet *teritus;* Anderson *suscepit. Denuo* Hill *aegret;* Early *suscepit.* Wadsworth *mortuus."* Louis fouled off the first pitch. *"Cras mane* Rodes *Earlyque progressuri primo in meridiem, deinde ad orientem via fani ad nemus umbrosum. Spotsylvaniae in acie stabimus."*

Louis fouled off another one. Burridge struggled to remember it all, translating into English to feed his curiosity, then clumsily turning it back into Mink's perfect Latin. Wadsworth was dead. Rodes and Early would be first off tomorrow. *"Septem milites interfecti vulgatique.* Longstreet *feretis,* Anderson *suspexit. Deinde* Hill *egit..."*

"No, it's *'Septem milia interfecti vulneratique.* Longstreet..." Louis lifted a high fly to center. "Shit."

Deal pulled it in and as Louis trotted out to right, he could have sworn he heard Burridge and Mink murmuring Latin.

		1	2	3	4	5	6	7	8	9	R	H	E
UNION		2	0	0	1	1	2	0			6	13	2
CONFEDERATES		3	2	1	1	3	0				10	12	3

Four runs was the worst kind of difference, Lyman thought. Five runs this late in the match meant it was all over; three had you in the thick of it; but four made you hope, and it was a cruel, impossible hope. Down four felt like something you wanted badly was being dangled in front of you, just outside your reach. If they could just keep the Rebs from scoring again. If they just got one run in the eighth they'd see what happened then. He bore down and got Porter Kingsley to go without much of a bother, but Caleb put up a fight, fouling off a handful before finally lining out to Newt—two outs right away. Lyman posted two strikes on Breese, but the pressure to keep them in the game began to heat his brain past concentration. Lyman shook his head a few times as if trying to clear it. Wes called time and trotted to the box. "You know, this would be a good time for that big snap ball you got. You haven't thrown it since the first inning. No way is this homely old boy lookin' for it." Lyman nodded, cheered that someone had faith in his pitch.

As Micah swung and missed his third strike, a cheer rose and crested over the field, a cheer that Lyman initially took for another daydream. It had the resonance and spontaneous charge of the excited crowds he'd heard and been a part of many times at Excelsiors games, and had often privately listened to in his head while imagining some personal feat of base ball valor. Three batters in a row and a strikeout on his snap was certainly worth a cheer, and Lyman basked in what he thought was dreamed-of glory until he wondered why it hadn't stopped.

The cheers kept coming.

They weren't from Horace or the other spectators, or the men playing, either. The cheers came from a mass of men, behind them to the southeast where the Union soldiers were on the move, and unlike the quick release of sporting appreciation, this cheer rolled on and grew in strength. Men of both sides passed each other on the pitch, cocking their heads. These weren't the wild cheers of a battle won; though they rung through the forest with the same joy and congratulations, they were controlled and free of the exultant trill of death avoided.

These cheers meant something was happening, and whatever it was caught fire with Lyman; he could see it had the same effect on the other Union boys, too. Slipper rubbed dirt on his hands and screwed himself up for the first pitch of the eighth inning, which he promptly arched over Weed into center. Newt hollered out, "Get into your work!" as Lyman took the bat and the cheers kept rising around them. A pulse of energy surged through the Yankees. Men smiled at each other as the whole Union army seemed to urge them on.

Arlette peered suspiciously out of the corners of his eyes and the Rebs all tensed. The outfielders set deep to guard against the long ball, but Lyman's choppy swing placed a single in front of Caleb, and the Union had two men on with no one out.

The cheers, from both within the field and outside, echoed in the trees. The sun had long waned over the horizon and over them now was a blue sky dotted with a few bright stars. All the Union men were on their feet now, clapping.

Newt swaggered up to the plate to face Arlette. Lyman hollered out to him to keep the ball on the ground—as sound a strategy in this sport as it was in cricket—but he knew Newt wasn't about to listen to any advice right now. Newt let two pitches miss high, then the third came in big and fat and straight into Newt's favorite place. Lyman got ready to run.

Newt curled back and swung.

The ball took off deep to left, and for two seconds it looked gone, but wind and reason kept Lyman from cheering. With no sting on it, Covay camped under the ball and there was one out.

Lyman sagged, and he could feel the other Yanks sag with him.

Karl was next. More patient than Newt, he waited through some close tosses until some grumbling started among the Rebs, then he shot the ball deep to center. To Lyman's eyes there was a lot of heat on it. He shouted ahead for Feeney to head home, but Deal ran it down and they had to scramble back to their bases. There were two hands out.

Until now the unexplained cheers had only come from the deeper joined voices of the North, but now they were answered with Rebel yells and howls from the facing lines. The entire Wilderness was cheering, and the men in the field had no idea why, but they made the cheers their own. Mink and Arlette assured the fielders that they were out of the inning. Southern players nodded to each other.

It was up to Teddy. Lyman didn't like him, but that didn't mean he wouldn't root for him. Teddy spat into the dirt and ripped the first pitch into right center. Lyman screamed, "Go! Go!" to Feeney. He was right on his heels round third and he nearly passed him on the way across the plate. It was Rebs 10, Union 8, with the tying run coming up.

Cheering continued from both sides. Catching his breath on the side and out of the action for a while, Lyman wondered what the cheering was for. Was it that all those offering huzzahs and tigers were still alive? A tribute to valiant enemies? Whatever the cheers meant, Lyman stopped asking questions; the sound hung over the field as a happy change from smoke and screams of pain.

With the match in his hands, Tiger took his stroll to the plate, saying one sentence—"We're going south, lads"—over and over and nodding as if he'd known it was happening all along. The phrase hopped from man to man as Tiger grinned and said, "That's why they're a-cheering. We're a-coming for ye." Then he swung late and hard on an outside pitch and sliced the ball down on the line in right. Rebs 10, Union 9.

Lyman pounded Newt on the back; with Wesley up next, the tide had surely—finally—turned. If they kept the heat on, chased them back the way Meade should have at Gettysburg, they'd take this in a rout by the end. Before he could yell some instructions over to Wes, just as Arlette wound his arm back, Tiger took off for home.

The screams on the field didn't get through the roars of two armies urging Tiger forward and his lungs reaching for what wind he had left.

It wasn't close.

Tiger was out by five steps. Newt pulled at his hair, wailing, "You idiot! You idiot!" and when he demanded an explanation, Tiger, wheezing, barely able to speak, said, "At least I try, laddie."

Lyman felt that jab as sharply as Newt seemed to.

	1	2	3	4	5	6	7	8	9	R	H	E
UNION	2	0	0	1	1	2	0	3		9	17	2
CONFEDERATES	3	2	1	1	3	0	0			10	12	3

Burridge had spent the last few innings repeating the message over and over until he was finally certain that he had it memorized: Seven thousand Rebels killed or wounded. Anderson had taken over for Longstreet, who'd been hit, and Early had assumed Hill's command because he was ill. Rodes and Early would be off southward tomorrow morning, then east on Shady Grove Church Road so the Rebs could make a stand at Spotsylvania.

He counted down the Rebel order; Mink would bat sixth. Burridge silently cheered when the long-haired third baseman singled and after a strikeout, the German made an error on a grounder by the pitcher. A pop out made it close, but when Alder hit the hairless Reb to load the bases, Burridge relaxed, guaranteed another visit with Mink.

Mink did not wait to take advantage. He stroked the first toss into left for a single. Two men scored.

As Mink jogged toward him with a smooth, composed gait, the handsome figure he cut refreshed the importance of the message. Though it was hardly the kind of world-changing news he'd been imagining would be his duty to carry, it had to have no small value if Mink was risking his life to send it. The Rebel left the tip of his foot on the base and said, "Christ, I love to win."

Kingsley missed the first pitch and Mink continued the conversation in Latin. *"Ad nuntios mittendos hoc non multum valet. Alia ratio mihi cogitanda est."* Burridge deciphered Mink's sentence. The scout wanted to try another way of passing information because his Latin was not good enough. Burridge's shoulders sank. *"Tibi tua lingua latina sufficit—tu alius Tacitus es, sed Ciceronem requireo, ille qui possit dicere."* Burridge nodded, placated by Mink's flattery that he was a Tacitus, but not a Cicero; a man of the written word, not the spoken. *"Valembimus."*

The next pitch was fouled off to the left and while someone retrieved the ball, Mink kept the conversation going. "So, if I may ask, what is your father's profession?"

Burridge blanched.

Ever since Mink had said he looked like a Latin scholar, he'd been fearing this question, a question he had feared other times while sitting in good leather chairs in other men's offices, as he sat at tables glittering with silver and crystal. The only response he had ever devised was to mumble the word "headmaster" into his hand. He looked at Mink, expecting the arched eyebrows and the bemused, pitying expression he'd seen in those offices and around those tables, but the Rebel stroked the stubble along his jaw and said, "A man of learning. A fine vocation, sir. And yourself?"

Wonder glowed off Burridge's face; a grateful wonder that this superior person found value in a man he had come to scorn, but whose existence would always be bound to his own identity, his own name. Would the honor extend to himself, he wondered. "I'm an attorney."

Mink smiled and inclined his head with what Burridge, as objective as he could manage, had to call deference, or at least admiration. "Another fine vocation. I'm certain the ladies are taken with a man who cuts such a strong figure."

The effect of all this attention on Burridge was intoxication of the finest, smartest, sharpest sort. Few men aside from Henry and Stewart had ever asked him about his father, himself, anything about his life for that matter. Yet here was a man of aristocratic breeding and wealth, a man who spoke that envied language with the sweetest, purest, oldest dialect imaginable on these shores, eagerly asking for even more information. Suddenly Burridge found himself telling his life story in exactly the kinds of opulent, heroic terms he employed in telling the story to himself.

And Mink appeared interested throughout. Flattered, Burridge continued to offer more information until the ball was finally tapped to him for the last out.

Standing off on his own between innings, Burridge had a slight pang of regret for talking so much, but it was also an exhilarating feeling that he was grateful to Mink for, even if the questions were simply the product of good breeding. It dawned on Burridge that Mink was exactly the kind of man he wanted to be.

	1	2	3	4	5	6	7	8	9	R	H	E
UNION	2	0	0	1	1	2	0	3		9	17	3
CONFEDERATES	3	2	1	1	3	0	0	2		12	15	3

Playing this game was much more fun than Wes had ever thought it would be, even if the Rebs were loose with the rules. Everyone was on the same nine, but they were equal. You did your part so that everyone could win, and there wasn't one fellow who did all the deciding. Though down by three, the cheers that had shaken the birds out of the treetops and some life into Yankee hearts buoyed them up in the top of the ninth. They'd nearly done it once, so why couldn't they do it again? Alder told him to wait for a good pitch. Wes started to think maybe he wasn't such a bastard after all.

Arlette's first three throws were low, but Wes liked the next one up near his shoulder where he'd asked for it. He liked it so much that he slammed it way deep to left for a home run that kept the match tight. Rebs 12, Union 10.

Lyman rushed up to Wes and put his arm around his shoulders after he touched home. "That was some all-fired wallop, boy! You're a regular Leggett, you are!"

"Leggett, like hell."

The shy, but happy, expression on Pitt's face rang that familiar chord in Lyman's memory, and Lyman couldn't shake the thought as Burridge struck out, Louis doubled, and Feeney moved the man to third. All of a sudden it was Lyman's turn.

A voice whispered in his mind. A fine game, it told him, as he let a ball go low. It's enough that you played and tried your best. If you flunk here, it's of no account.

He swung and missed. One and one.

Lyman wanted to win. It would be nice to win, but it probably won't happen, so don't get up to the hub in it. Control yourself, it said, as he missed again.

One more strike and it was over. Or a hit. That would be fine, too.

He saw himself jogging home with the tying run and was still watching himself haloed in triumph as the ball skittered to Weed and then on to Mink to end the game.

	1	2	3	4	5	6	7	8	9	R	H	E
UNION	2	0	0	1	1	2	0	3	1	10	19	3
CONFEDERATES	3	2	1	1	3	0	0	2	X	12	15	3

Evening in this hidden field had turned to night, and the darkness brought back creeping fears of what could happen now that the game had finished. No handshakes were exchanged to celebrate a match well played; the brown, gray, and blue of opposing nines became again the uniforms of armies engaged in civil war. Not everything had been forgiven between the sides, but it had been proved that they could trust each other for the length of nine innings. By now the cheering on the road had lost its glow of joy as the fact of future battle hollowed it to a simple roar. If they stayed together now, the only reason would be to introduce that war into this place of secret truce. Both groups of men quietly edged toward their guns, though Huey did summon up the courage to ask Arlette a question. He pointed at the Rebel's shoulder, again decorated with the rooster epaulet. "Does that bird there have a name?"

"Goes by Lou."

Huey rubbed his ear on his shoulder. "D'ye think I could pet him?"

Arlette stole a look at Lou, as though reading the bird's reaction to Huey's question. Finally he nodded. "Reckon so. Lou don't be having no diff'rence with no Yankees. It's other birds he down on."

Huey took a half-step toward Arlette so that he'd be within reach, then smoothed Lou's mussed feathers down into a handsome black coat. Lou trembled at first, but Huey soothed him with restful sounds and the rooster settled down onto his Rebel perch to enjoy the petting. Huey settled down, too, and smiled like the boy he was. "That's one nice chicken."

"Tain't no chicken, son. He be a fighting gamecock. Don't let him fool ya."

Arlette's warning gave Huey pause for a second, but he couldn't believe such a thing of a good bird like Lou.

Burridge stood close to Mink, expecting some sign of further plans from the scout outlining where they'd next meet. Mink hoisted his rifle over his shoulder and saluted him. "A fine match, sir."

His patience with Mink's subtlety was wearing. Burridge came to the point. "Do you think we'll ever have the chance for another?"

Mink's hard stare stopped him from going further. "Mars is a strange god, lieutenant, of whom we should not ask too many questions." He patted himself over to see if he had everything he needed to reenter the war, then answered Burridge's quizzical expression. "I wouldn't be at all surprised to see you again some time soon. On picket duty." Relieved with even so vague a reply, Burridge nodded. "A shame your good men had to lose. *Postea, rationem victoriae reportandae tibi monstrabo.*"

Burridge returned the salute and as Mink drifted into the gray, he worked through his last sentence. "Next time, I'll show you how to win."

Lyman tugged at Wesley Pitt's shoulder. "You're Wesley Pitt, aren't you? Andrew Pitt's boy?" He'd finally placed him—the orphan son of a dead neighbor. Ten years before, little Wesley had stood behind the counter and watched him grind sausages and cut meat as Mrs. Pitt gossiped with his mother.

Suspicious, Wesley pulled away and said, "Yeah."

"Don't you recognize me?"

"You're Alder. Lyman Alder. So?" Lyman was waiting for more. Wes gazed longer, trying to put a meaning to this name and this face.

"Lyman Alder the butcher. Remember?"

Another wave of memories, like the ones that had struck before battle, washed over him. A man with a huge silver cleaver cutting a slab of meat into chops, smiling at him. Wooden tables stained with blood; sausages hanging from racks in great loops; flies. "That's right. Lyman Alder. The butcherman."

The two shook hands for the first time.

Burridge recognized that he could not entirely alienate Cawthorne. Not that he was willing to offer him another chance to regain a place in the lieutenant's good graces, but for his own good he had to smooth whatever overpreened feathers he'd ruffled this evening. Cawthorne was liable to talk. Rather than extend his hand, he extended the Massachusetts Adams toward the sergeant. "I appreciate your rectitude, sergeant. And I appreciate your deference to your commanding officer and your support. You may not agree with all of my decisions during our time together, but I don't have to remind you that it remains your duty to carry them out. In this case I felt the men needed a rest, as uncommon a rest as it was." He smiled in apology. "Here's your sidearm."

Cawthorne sniffed once and held still for a second, as though he were considering whether or not to take the gun, but then his hand snapped out and took it from Burridge before the decision seemed to have been made. "Thank you, sir."

"It's a handsome weapon. A pleasure to hold."

The sergeant nodded and tried to appear humble. "Yes, isn't it?" Happy to be reunited, he hefted the gun in his hand, then slipped his palm comfortably around the handle like a man slipping his hand around his wife's waist. He seemed to be placated, so Burridge took his leave.

Willie called over to Newt and Lyman, packing up their bat and ball, to ask if he could trade the *New York Tribune* for a *Richmond Examiner*. Newt agreed, then strapped his bat and blanket back onto his knapsack. Wes handed Lyman his share of the tobacco.

There was no stopping night. It hung in the trees and drifted into the field, consuming the land with black as a blizzard does with white. The Rebels surrendered to the force of darkness and melted back into the forest, invisible once again, to join their own cheering forces. The Yankees stood as they had two hours before; alone, and in the middle of a wood. To the south, burning forest showed the way they would follow with a pale light that fought against the black and gave Teddy something to look toward.

On his knees, Lyman gave the ball a final look before he shoved it deep into the pack. It was full of green stains and had a dent or two from the good scups men had taken. As he replayed some critical moments, wishing he could take back a pitch here and there during this defeat now souring in his belly, Lyman felt someone standing behind him. He turned and looked up at the hulking figure towering over him. It was Micah Breese. Breese gave him a short, slow, and respectful nod. "Nice time. We grateful to ye."

Breese was already a few steps away by the time Lyman responded. "Don't shoot us, now."

The Confederate looked over his shoulder as he walked. "Don't make us."

THE
SECOND
MATCH

———

CHAPTER

7

———

OFTEN, AT THE STRANGEST MOMENTS OF OUR LIVES, THE
deep and well-used ruts we travel do not allow us to consider the
extraordinary circumstances we have recently experienced. Only
once we are clear of them, and safe, do we begin to understand
the profound impact they may have. On this hot, moonless night,
the men of Company L, 14th Brooklyn, approached the remainder
of their picket duty with an enthusiasm that they were unable and
unwilling to question. So many horrifying things had happened to them in
their army years, so many gruesome scenes and moments inexplicable to any
human mind, that they ascribed their mood to Grant's decision to head
south. They put aside at first their encounter in the woods as a single blossom
in the otherwise thorny tangle of this war. As they held their individual
positions many yards away from the nearest man, each soldier kept alert with
the usual thoughts of home, now sprinkled with stray images of a grassy
field and base ball players, and the renewed pride of being part of an army
that was pressing on.

Close to one A.M. Colonel Herring pulled all the pickets out to follow
the tail of the Fifth Corps headed south down the Germanna Plank, then
Brock, Roads. As the company fell into the line of regiments just removed
from the woods, the men realized they were all smiling on a sweltering night
of slow marching that promised more battles ahead. Each had believed that
he was the only man who had revisited the meeting with the Rebs during
the five hours of lonely duty, but the much-improved mood they all obviously
shared, and which was not reflected on the faces of the other regiments,

made plain that every man had held on to his memories of the field and, in fact, that something quite wonderful had happened there.

Now that the van of the march had passed on far ahead, only the orange embers of full pipes and a spray of stars lit their way over a dusty road barely wide enough for two columns. As it had been for the entire corps that night, their progress was sporadic at best, torturous at worst. After the dry weather, clouds of dust spread a feeling that the fires of battle had frightened spring into yielding this land to her impatient and unforgiving sister. Horses and wagons pounded by, forcing the men onto the narrow margins of grass along a forest edge covered with sleeping stragglers.

After the earlier cheers, silence was not necessary on this march. Those of Company L not swamped yet by fatigue finally began talking to each other again, lifted by a shared subject beyond death, cowardice, and the ineptitude of their officers. Lyman and Wes spoke more than most as they marched along next to each other.

"Teddy and the Slipper are fine fellas once you get to know them. They'd do anything for me. We've had some times, I can tell you."

Lyman's reply had a paternal tone, which he was happy to take out of storage. "They're a rough set for you. Knowing your father, God rest his soul, as well as I did, I can say that he wouldn't have approved of their poltroonery."

Wesley's memories of his parents, though fresher now than they had been in years, were still clouded by the vivid Eastern District hells foremost in his thoughts. "Yeah. Well . . . Listen, have you seen those Union Grounds? You would go for them in the biggest way."

The voice of Stives moaned up from behind them. "Whose son art thou, thou young man?"

Wes gestured back with his head. "What's he on about?"

"I never know." Lyman shrugged. "I don't know about those Union Grounds, either. Sounds like another way for one rich man to get a whole lot richer."

"It's not such a bad deal. We went skating in there once, because in the winter they ice it over, and they have bands and restaurants and a Chinese pagoda and everything you want."

"And you pay for the privilege."

"Sure, but what's the difference?"

"Is it a nice field?"

"Sure. I mean I never been to a game, and they got it all walled off so's nobody can sneak a free look, but I know a fella went to an Eckfords match there and he seemed to like it fine."

"But what does any of this have to do with base ball?"

"Nothing. Why does everything have to do with base ball?" Wes coughed from the dusty cloud stirred by the marchers. "The fella who laid out the coin makes a dollar and you have a good time. What more do ye want?"

"It used to mean something to be a base ball player."

Wes mumbled, "*You're* gonna be the green one there now."

Teddy Finn grumbled loudly about all the meandering around they were doing. More of a city boy than any other man in the company, Teddy didn't like the dark, and the reason he gave himself for this uncharacteristic fear made perfect sense—a person can sneak up on you before you can do a thing about it. It was a sensible concern for anyone who lived in a big city like Brooklyn and a wise one considering the kinds of places he went, but the truth was, Teddy was just plain scared of the dark.

The wounded and dying men screaming for death didn't dent Teddy much; he'd been listening to screaming all his life. If it wasn't his mother screaming under the belt, it was one of his brothers or sisters getting a taste of a fist or a knot of pine or whatever else their father could lay his hands on, and Teddy had done his share of screaming, too. As soon as he had gotten out of the house in Irish Town, Teddy had promised himself that he'd never scream in pain again, so he pursued a career of making other men beg for mercy in the ring, the alley, or wherever else the bosses said there was work to be done, and he had no plans to stop until the day every person in Brooklyn looked up to him for favors. At twenty, he could claim that few men in town would knowingly cross Teddy Finn, which still left the dark to contend with.

Teddy wanted to be distracted and tonight he was stuck next to Karl, who had never hesitated to show his disgust for him. In the last few years, Teddy had become accustomed to the deference accorded in the Eastern District to a rising star, so he was fascinated by this Dutchman who visibly disliked him. Teddy could tell they were about the same age, and while he figured the odds at 10–1 against Karl in a fair fight and 25–1 in a dirty one, the man showed no fear, a quality that drew Teddy to him more than any sign of friendship ever could. Teddy wanted to get something on the Dutchman that would give him the edge, but he also had a thought he would never have admitted: He'd seen worse enemies become best pals when the circumstances were right.

Cunning and boyish fear put Teddy on the offensive. "I been conjertating on this one thing for a while, Dutchman, so mebbe you can clear it up. What I wanna know is why ya got it out for me?"

A minute or two went by and Teddy was beginning to think Karl was giving him the silent treatment when the German finally spoke. "You don't belong here."

"I'm fighting Rebs just like you." That Karl didn't argue the point explained to Teddy what he meant. "Oh, now I'm onta ya, Dutchie. You don't fancy the Irishman, eh? All them whiskey bottles and taters? I say you're the one that oughta float back to Dutchland or wherever the hell you're from."

"There is no *Deutschland*. There is states fighting each other *und* there is one big state that wants everything. Like here."

Caspar had been listening and now that Karl had struck on to a topic near to his heart, he couldn't hold himself back. "How the circle of life comes around. Yes, Karl? How ironic. Here you fight for the big federal government, but in *Deutschland* you are part of plucky little Bayern, land of Louis the First and Lola Montes—a romance fit for a Southern gentleman. I think you are rebel at heart, Karl. Or you are becoming Prussian."

Karl shook his head. "This *America* is good idea." He tapped his temple. "But it will fall apart *und* not because of Johnny Rebels. *Everybody* is rebel here. Nobody wants think about everyone. Only themselves."

Caspar smiled and nodded. "So you *are* a Prussian."

Felix Cawthorne walked these miles alone, contemplating what he had witnessed in the clearing. Excuses and explanations fluttered through his mind—it was harmless; a much-needed rest; good for the company's spirit—then each was slammed by the certainty that this match was dangerous. What if they were caught and he was implicated? He'd wanted no part of this adventure and Burridge could not force him to, even if he commandeered his revolver permanently. In his years backstage, Cawthorne had discovered another rule of life: Make friends with the man who pays Hamlet, not the one who plays him. He decided that someone would have to be told. It was the right thing to do.

———

Holding on to the tail of the march, the picket detail had by first light only just passed the intersection of the Brock Road and the Orange Plank Road, scene of some of the heaviest fighting in the Wilderness. Spring had surrendered nothing here to summer; the gains had been forceably taken. Life and any promise of it had been shorn from the trees and burned from the bushes. Branches and limbs lay about, coated with soot and dust save for the green buds that would never open. This bare cross of roads, once an intersection and a reason for battle, had become an unwitting memorial to the death it had caused.

Though the last light of yesterday had shown the men green grass, a white ball, a brown bat, and gray uniforms, the morning sun now lit only gray and the men had changed as much as their surroundings. Lyman, Wes, and a few others had tied handkerchiefs over their faces to keep out the dust and now looked like dusky wives in purdah. Teddy got a look at Tiger, who hadn't assumed the veil, and let out a howl; he was nearly pitch-black, creased with thin white lines of wrinkles, and while every man had been dyed that night by the stirred soot, Tiger's transformation brought the most laughs. Newt feared an impromptu minstrel show, but Tiger immediately set to wiping himself back to whiteness.

Along the sides, men sprawled in heaps and cuddled together in spoons, sleeping survivors of an inferno, waiting to complete their passage to the next circle of hell. Willie shoved aside a snoring Pennsylvania boy just starting his first beard so he could light a fire and boil a can of coffee. The smell soon woke the boy up, and Willie ended up sharing the can and a slab of hardtack with him. "What day of the week is it?" the boy asked.

Willie smiled. "Sunday."

———

By eight they were three miles farther along. That much closer to the heavy artillery and crackling fire of rifles that had just opened down the Brock Road. For Burridge, though, the war was to be found back in that secluded field; it was his first real chance to affect the war's course and he hadn't lost sight of that for a moment. He couldn't say if the Union command already knew that Wadsworth was dead, that Early and Anderson were injured, but if they didn't, he was convinced the knowledge only he possessed would change the world. Only he knew of the surprise that would be waiting for this army at Spotsylvania if the race south wasn't won, and for a moment he toyed perversely with not telling anyone the facts he had learned. Burridge grinned like a guilty child until the thought of Sidney Mink reminded him that such boyishness would not do if he were to follow in those steps.

All through the night and morning, Burridge had examined every face in his command for signs that they knew what he had done with Mink, and none appeared. As heroic as this duty was, it had risks that were less than glorious. He'd made it clear to the men that they were never to speak of the match to anyone, and as much as he held them in his hands during this dangerous duty, they also held him in theirs. Though a risky position for an officer as disliked as he was, Burridge decided that they'd enjoyed twitting the rules and they were at least speaking to each other again; they'd bear him up.

Next to Lincoln pinning medals on his chest, Burridge thought about Mink. Along the road were thousands of men all blurred into one general idea of a soldier, but Mink's penetrating stare hovered before him in all its fascinating particulars. Why had Mink been so interested in him, Burridge wondered. There were many unflattering explanations, but Burridge could only see the sincerity in Mink's face. The warm sense of Mink's acceptance spread over him again and it felt so good that he became uncomfortable. He'd revealed himself totally and a morning-after search for regrets crept over him. Would there be rumors of the horrid sort that dogged Caesar and King Nicodemus?

Mink's face comforted him; such untoward thoughts were absurd. Surely Mink was a man of quality, one who could be trusted. It was meet, he thought, that noble minds keep ever with their likes, so he had his own list of questions for Mink: Where did his family's money come from? What did he do for a living? Who were his favorite Romans? How did he manage that crowd of bumpkins?

The line marched along crisply now and for this Burridge was very grateful. He had much to tell Captain Henry. Within his mind lay the fates of thousands. John Burridge had finally found the perfect calling, and he had Sidney Mink to thank.

————

Lyman guessed from the sun that it was after eleven. The next battle continued not far to the south and no one could say yet when they'd be shoved into it. They were all sitting just across from a house and a scatter of out-buildings called Alsop's Farm, nestled between the tines of a fork in the Brock Road. The house was once trim and white, maybe three rooms inside, smaller than Lyman's house on Hooper Street, with a snug porch at the door, big enough for one man to sit on and whittle for a summer's evening. Of course that wasn't possible anymore; the two armies had skirmished through here just hours ago, and the buildings that hadn't burned down were pocked with bullets. Dying flames ate at what was left of the house. Black clouds of flies swarmed over the carcasses of mules and horses, swollen and putrid in the summery heat. Great scoops of earth had been torn out, and most plants higher than a healthy blade of grass were trampled flat. Cannons, set free from the constraints of the Wilderness, rocked earth and sky.

Bodies lay scattered about the yard, the flies only beginning to light on eyes and other damp, cooling flesh. Karl noticed men of the 14th among them, proof that the regiment had been through here and hit hard. Willie had a chat with some of the wounded boys as Tice and Huey tried to get news out of one man they knew about how the regiment was bearing up. Lyman pumped another, a fellow butcher, for facts about this skirmish. The 14th had been pinned down behind a fence near the house—the story was that a shell had exploded in it while the family was eating breakfast—but the boys had finally worked themselves free into a thatch of woods not far away. The man asked Lyman when the company was coming back and Lyman could only shrug. While the rest of the regiment was getting hit, they'd been happily reliving their base ball match; the thought sunk into Lyman and made his shoulders sweat some in shame and in fear of getting caught.

It was no secret where the battle was. The pop of rifles and bolls of white smoke rose over the trees to the south and west. The road left of Alsop's headed into the forest again. The road on the right was little more than a dirt path bordered on the far side by forest, but clear on the left. After their spread, both roads jogged left, leaving a gap through which the men could see a broad field contained by a ridge at its farthest just over a mile from where they were. A burning building plumed black smoke about halfway up. Long lines of men swirled by, marching past down both roads, preceded by flags that identified the left line as Crawford's and the right, plodding along the dirt path, as Griffin's. Some groups had blackened faces, clearly parts of units re-formed; others were fresh. There appeared to be no organized advance from either side, North or South, on the field that Griffin's line was doomed to explore. Men were simply poured in until they buckled or fell. Blue and gray dots—many more blue than gray—spotted the ground a mile off, and just now a thin line of blue fled back into the safety of the woods on the right.

Yesterday had seemed an end to many things for the men—the Wilderness, the battle, their active duty; but this hated forest and the fight waiting for them ahead proved they were starting again the cycle of fear, desperation, and relief. Knowing the 14th had been through action without them made them sullen and curious about when they'd rejoin it. Tiger trembled as he lit another pipeful of tobacco. Slipper lay on his back, white as the sickly clouds scrabbling over them, hands folded across his chest. Del Rio pointed at Feeney. "He gonna peg out. Look at heem, like he at the undertaker."

Teddy stuck a finger under Feeney's nose. "Naw, he's breathin'. He got the constitutional of a horse."

"Quickstep will kill heem before any bullet does."

Slipper's waxen face didn't move. Tice wandered back after a fruitless forage through the farm, shaking his head. "Nothing." Lyman lay down on the grass. "Say, are we ever goin' back to the regiment?"

Lyman pulled his cap over his eyes. "Ask Porridge."

"Gone. Said he had to see the captain."

A sharp stomach cramp made Lyman wince. It could have been hunger, but it could also have been the thought of going into this new fight under Cawthorne's lead. "Choice time for a visit."

"So do you think we'll go back to the 14th now?"

"How the hell should I know?" Willie turned the pages of the *Richmond Examiner*. "Anything worth reading in there?"

"Says Lee got a hundred thousand men."

Tiger spat and smiled. "Not anymore he don't."

The laughter was tired. Newt asked when they were getting mail, but no one knew. Willie said they were low on coffee. Men and wagons streamed along both forks of the road toward the shooting as all of Herring's picket detail waited here for orders. No one asked if they were going in. The Wilderness had made it clear that everyone was going in every time there were two Rebs to rub together.

As the afternoon began to drag on, Del Rio stood up and held a stick in his hands like a bat as he demonstrated to Horace what was wrong with Mink's batting stance. "You see, he hold the bat like thees."

Horace nodded. "Yes, I see."

Del Rio shifted his hands to a different position. "But everybody else hold it like thees. See?" Worm suddenly looked startled. It was a strong reaction, Del Rio thought, but then Horace Worm was easily excited. "Yes, beeg difference." A voice behind him asked whom he was talking about. Del Rio answered without turning or paying any attention to Worm's widening eyes. "Meenk. You know. Who we just played."

Linden Stewart came around to face Joaquin directly. "Played what?"

Flustered, Del Rio could only think of the truth. "Base ball."

All eyes focused on Del Rio and Stewart. Just as Cawthorne opened his mouth, Pindar said, "Yes, the 9th New York State Militia. If you'll recall, the regiment had a match against them in April."

"*Sim*. Meenk, he is, uh, one of them." Joaquin gestured randomly toward the south, then realized where he was indicating and pointed west, then back north for good measure. "Ninth. You know. Them."

Completely puzzled, Stewart went to Cawthorne for an explanation. Cawthorne was only too happy to put down the button he was sewing onto his jacket and help, but Pindar stepped on his words. "Sir, when are we headed back to the 14th?"

Stewart could never resist the opportunity to display his exclusive knowledge of the war's secrets. "I have it on the highest authority that Lieutenant Colonel Herring's pickets will move in support of General Crawford's advance." Heavy firing came from the woods in the direction Crawford's troops had gone. Stewart gestured toward Stives, now kneeling and beseeching the heavens. "That's Stives, correct?" Pindar said yes. Stewart looked him over, keeping a careful distance, as though examining a decidedly unappealing and guilty defendant whose case he had been forced to take.

Since observation of his devotion was Stives's primary religious goal, he was sensitive to others' eyes. When he saw that it was Stewart bearing witness, he leaped up and clasped the lieutenant's hands. "You must be warned! Something is happening!" The men of the company traded nervous glances.

"And what might that be?"

" 'If any man have an ear, let him hear!' The seals are being opened!"

Stewart extricated his damp hands from Stives's. "Do consider me alerted." He now pointed at Willie's *Examiner*. "What's that?"

Willie smiled and swerved toward the gray area he often inhabited between simplicity and simplemindedness. "What?"

"That paper."

"This?"

Willie's strategy, if that's what it was, worked well. Stewart rolled his bugging eyes. "Yes, that."

"Found it."

Stewart held out his hand and beckoned. "Let me have it." Willie reluctantly surrendered his paper, then asked when he would get it back. Stewart rolled his eyes again as he rearranged his manhood. "You're not getting it back, Winston. It's contraband. I'll take possession." Lyman figured he was on his way to the sink and wanted something to read. Stewart turned to Cawthorne. "Now, you want to speak with me?"

"Yes, sir. If we may do so in private."

Stewart cased around in a broad way, but in the middle of a clearing, privacy would be very hard to find. "Why don't we simply step away."

In a low, urgent tone, Lyman hissed at them all again to keep their mouths shut about the game. "Do you want to die in prison? Huh? Or get shot? Do you? Well, so keep yer mouths shut! You may not think this is serious, but Stewart'll slice off all our jewels if he finds out. If Cawthorne don't tell him."

Officers continued to push more troops down the right path, and now Lyman could see the head of this new line start to crumble as the Rebs' sharpshooters on the eastern side picked them off. Confederate artillery opened up from behind the burning building. Union guns responded and a thundering duel of cannons took command of the skies. The whistling and the throbbing bursts set everyone's nerves on edge.

Newt leaned over to Lyman and whispered into his ear. "Where's Burridge?"

"I don't know. I don't trust him."

"Me, neither. He's been an odder stick than usual lately."

The whole company watched Cawthorne and Stewart as they talked, distracting themselves from the cannons, not noticing Burridge's arrival. All Burridge saw were the backs of heads. "What does Lieutenant Stewart want?" he asked no one in particular.

Tice answered. "Don't know. Cawthorne took him aside, though. Del Rio almost told him."

Lieutenant Burridge knew he had to take action. But what could he do? Apparently the return of his revolver had not placated Cawthorne.

Tiger Quigley growled up at him from where he sat. "Watch." He tugged the bayonet out of his rifle, then turned toward Cawthorne and Stewart. "Oh, Felix! Felix!" The sergeant looked. "Ye forgot this!" He flung the bayonet like a knife so that it plunged into Cawthorne's jacket right where the sergeant's heart would be found if he were wearing it. "Aww! Bad luck, laddie! Me own fault!"

Burridge realized that he was nodding and quickly stopped himself. Still, he couldn't find it in himself to reprimand Tiger. The Irishman was so willing to kill on his behalf. When he'd seen Stewart, the lieutenant's instinct had been to race back to Henry in order to suss out what Stewart was up to, but now he saw he had no need of that. The men of Company L, Tiger Quigley especially it seemed, would indeed be his cover and protection. "A fine toss, Quigley. But let's not be too strong. I believe a close eye will do."

Lying on the ground, pretending to be dead, Slipper explored the nagging thought that Del Rio could be right, that he *was* dying from the quickstep. Totally exhausted, sucked so dry from trip after trip of giving back what small chunk of hardtack or sip of water he'd take that he wasn't even sweating, Slipper had forgotten what it felt like to be well. He'd been this sick once before, a whole feverish summer spent lying in bed; his mother, when she'd bothered to come up, wrapped damp rags around his belly and his head. Slipper never held that against her—she was busy with his nine brothers and sisters, and he could only command such attentions as a sickly child who didn't contribute to the family coffers deserved. His father worked at the sulfur plant on Ross Street, so every corner of the shack smelled like the stuff, and now Slipper had to force down an impulse to gag every time he ripped open a cartridge. Alone in an attic and sick, Archie the Runt had listened that summer to the workings of the Feeney family churning on just the same as they had with him down there pushing for his plate of soup or slopping the pig, and he realized that he was always to be on the tatty fringes of whatever place he went—if he'd ever be able to go anywhere. On Sundays the whole Feeney clan would troop off to Mass without a good-bye, and while they received the blessings of the Holy Eucharist, Slipper lay condemned to the sheets of his solitary hell, reciting all the parts and prayers of the sacred drama he was no longer able to attend, his precise soprano Latin echoing off the papered walls.

Newt called over to him. "Feeney! Wanna play a little Bluff?"

He could hear the smile in Newt's voice. He could also hear that Newt wanted to do something other than worry about the guns. Slipper decided to let him stew. He opened his eyes. "Ya hog every chance in the match, so now ya think ya can beat me, huh?"

Tiger enlisted as a surprise ally. "Aye, that's right, Grocer. The Finn boy and you set out to make me and Feeney there look like muffins. Yer no sport, for certain."

Newt was glad to have Tiger walk onto his turf. "And you're no base ball player. Stealing home." He shook his head. "That lost us the match."

Wes agreed. "Then I hit the long ball right after. We would've won."

Tiger gave him the kind of dirty look he usually reserved for Newt. "Ah, the hero speaks! Boy, ye've not shown me anything when it counts."

Lyman had had enough. He was already getting edgy about the coming battle and his patience for Tiger had nearly worn through. What had happened to the Tiger Quigley who every year brought flowers to Mrs. Alder on her birthday, who'd taught Ernie to swim, stood at his side when he married Victoria; Lyman knew and, sadly, he was caring less and less. "Shut up, all of you! For chrissakes, we're all on the same side."

"Shut up yerself, Captain. There's no sides anymore. It's every man for himself." Wes stood up, ready for a fight, and while Stives warned them to keep holy the Sabbath day, Tiger sneered indulgently at Lyman's defender. He bowed. "In honor of the most Reverend Stives and our Lord's holy day, I offers ye a hymn." To the stirring melody of the "Battle Hymn of the Republic" and the ominous rhythm of cannon and gun, Tiger sang:

Lyman Alder has a chicken and his name is Wesley Pitt.
Wesley'd rather be in Williamsburg but ain't got guts to git.
So he talks about how tough he is.
He thinks he is a man.
But we know he will run.
Wesley, Wesley, he's no man yet.
The fellow's merely Teddy Finn's pet.
Young Pitt will never be a soldier

Till he can shut his mouth.

CHAPTER

8

———

To everyone's great annoyance, Stewart had been right—the pickets had been assigned to support General Crawford's troops down the left road past Alsop's. The afternoon brought a lull to the field and the ridge, called Laurel Hill, but around four o'clock Company L and the other picket regiments staggered a half-mile into the woods to take their place behind Crawford. These woods were thinner and broken up by small clearings dense with underbrush that were no easier to forge through, but gentler on the soul. Crawford's two lines of Pennsylvania Reserves, who'd already weathered a storm of Rebs earlier in the day, were stationed near the rim of a gradual three-hundred-yard decline. Two hundred yards behind them, Company L was between the two Massachusetts regiments on the right flank. The other regiments were positioned on Crawford's left.

Though it had been clear back at Alsop's that battle was inescapable today, the usual apprehension had simmered on a low flame because no one had the energy to stoke it, but with dusk now approaching and a few hours of comparative rest, the men could face—had to face—what was coming. Wes had noticed earlier in the day that he didn't have the quickstep anymore, a happy improvement that didn't keep his stomach from tying itself into a tight little knot. Caspar, burned a crimson to match his trousers, sucked on his pipe and stared off into the pines.

Leaning back against a tree, Newt was composing a letter.

Alsop's Farm
Virginia
USA
May Eight, 1864

Dear Bishop Joycelin,
It is with Humble Heart that I address this letter to You. I have written to You in past times and though You have never responded, I take great Comfort in knowing that You have read them and have prayed for me surely, as beseeched. To have lived so long in this War can only be a sign of <u>Holy Providence</u>. I hope You are well also and in the Lord's hands.

I take pen in hand today for the Reason that we are soon to be engaged in <u>Conflict</u> once again with the Confederate army—the representatives of an <u>evil</u> and <u>degraded</u> society which I am sworn to defeat. I beg that You will find <u>pity</u> for a member of Your flock who is in fear for his Mortal Soul as he performs his hallowed duty as a soldier in this Army of the Righteous—the army of the United States of America. So many first sons have died these years, and still the <u>pharoahs</u> will not let the Africans go. As my wife, Mrs. Helen Fry, and myself have often heard You say, the Africans are Men as well in God's eyes and so must they be in ours. They must be free whilst the Lord has also Commanded us that we shall not kill our fellow men, and I have been torn <u>mightily</u>. Will I be damned for judging the Lives of other Men, even if it is for a Cause Devoutly held? Or, on the other hand, if I choose to follow the Fourth Commandment, will I be damned for not Fighting for justice?

I have seen so much, Your Eminence. The evils of Slavery are <u>everywhere</u> around us here and I have witnessed for myself its wrongs, however I have also seen young boys spilling their Bowels upon the grass and grown men whose Minds and Spirits could better serve the African become as wild beasts, and settle this most Moral question with their physical bodies. There is no guidance here among <u>degraded</u> Men. The chaplains are more concerned with saving <u>their own hides</u> than our Souls. You are the only person I can ask. Is there a way for Me to save my Soul? I have prayed <u>fervently</u> on this, but have received no response.

Your Prayers for strength are most appreciated and a return letter which would include some Divinely inspired direction would have a value to me,

here in Virginia, which You, in Brooklyn, cannot understand. As I am to
be mustered out in a few weeks, a rapid response is <u>*Vital.*</u>

    I remain most humbly,
    Your obedient servant,
    Mr. Newton Fry
    14th Brooklyn Rgmt
    Army of the Potomac

After an afternoon of rest Slipper's guts felt better, but now he had to think about Rebs again—Rebs with guns. He sat on the ground next to Wes, who was nervously picking at the crop of pimples that had grown on his chin between the stray hairs. Slipper opened his cartridge box and examined the bullets. "What am I doing here, Pitt? Huh?"

Slipper had never uttered a comment this personal to Wes in all the years he'd known him, so Wes kept his mouth closed. "I mean it." Slipper took out a cartridge, gave it an appraiser's look, and began tearing off the paper. "I ain't no soldier. Alls I ever wanted was a free and easy. Man comes in, feels at home, has a lager." He poured the powder on the ground. "Now I'm getting shot at." He held up the revealed minié. "With these."

Slipper Feeney was a man to watch out for back in Williamsburg, but here his survival depended entirely on whether or not the others wanted to wait for him, and Slipper's only revenge was to take them at cards. Wes wouldn't be afraid of him again, and was surprised that he ever had been. "Aw, you been in scrapes before. I seen it myself."

Slipper propped his gun up in front of himself. Grasping the muzzle with both hands, he hung his head between his arms. "I can't do this, Pitt."

The pathetic admission set Wesley wavering. He was getting spooked now himself. He looked about for Teddy, who was clenching his fists and grinning at the Rebs he couldn't see but still very much wanted to kill. It heartened him, but not enough so to kill the feeling Wes had; the same feeling he'd had under fire; the same feeling he'd had as a boy watching the grave diggers lower the two pine boxes holding his parents into the ground of the Cemetery of the Evergreens. He wasn't sure he could care for his needs even if he *was* a killer now. He remembered being angry that it was sunny that day, instead of rainy and sad; sunny like this day.

Lyman sat down next to them. "How you?"

Wes didn't want this new friend to think he was anything less than completely ready to go in, rifle blazing, so he balled up his fists like Teddy and said, "Aw, we're itching to get in there."

"Bullshit. You two are so scared I could smell it twenty yards away." Wes tried to deny it, but Lyman wouldn't hear him. "Let me tell you one of the secrets of being a soldier. You're always scared. Every son of a bitch here is scared."

"Tiger ain't."

"Tiger's scared of something else. But look at Von Schenk. He's been smoking that pipe for six hours now, by my count. Karl's done three rosaries. We're all scared. You think you're something special, but you're not."

Wes slugged Slipper in the arm. "You heard him. Buck up."

For the first time in days, Felix Cawthorne felt something close to calm. An odd time to feel so, he thought, when they were waiting to fight, but he'd never been one to fret about going onstage. As long as he knew what he had to do, he would do it. The ones who got scared were the few strange ones who believed that they actually *were* the characters they were playing, as if slipping on some ragged shawl could make a man Othello. It was distasteful.

Gruff words with the taint of Irish burred just behind him. Cawthorne flinched. He imagined Tiger Quigley's message to him earlier that day. But would silence have kept him alive and out of prison? Who could tell? Lieutenant Stewart did not believe him, he wanted proof, that was secondary to the infinite relief of being on the record. *That* could be banked at the North Brooklyn. Regardless of what transpired, he had told the truth to a superior officer. There'd never be another match; the subject would never come up again; and he had cleared himself of blame. Cawthorne realized that this purity of conscience was the cause of his unusual serenity.

A runner stopped before him, saluted in a twitch, then delivered his message—the company was to stack packs and dress the line. The sergeant began to tremble slightly. He thanked the runner and saluted him away before the boy noticed. He recalled a dream two years ago. It was a gala night, the gold boxes and buntings and shimmering silk dresses caught in the lights and made it clear that fame and fortune met here regularly. They were playing *Henry V* and he spoke the lead. He was about to stride forward to deliver a speech—"Let he which hath no stomach for this fight," it was—only he had forgotten his lines. A man in the stalls coughed. And only more silence. He woke up with that silence in his mind. Later that day he was returned to ranks.

As he was about to begin tearing at his mutton chops, Cawthorne remembered that he had his line for the moment. He ripped his revolver out of its holster and went in search of Lieutenant Burridge.

"Bellum, bellum, belli, bello, bello, bella, bella, bellorum, bellis, bellis." Burridge scoured his mind for as much vocabulary as he could. Though the *Commentaries* were useful, he had to have more for the next meeting. Standing in the middle of the forest, soon to go in, the lieutenant wondered where they'd next meet Mink. Two lines were forming here between Laurel Hill to the southwest and a rise about a mile and a half as the crow flies to the northeast. The Union line was bowed forward and the Reb was cupped back to take the blow, making for a standoff; the Union had interior lines but the Rebs held the possibility of turning their flanks.

Henry had asked many questions about Mink, but base ball was not among the topics discussed. As it was, he had sketched the rendezvous as a solitary meeting between himself and Mink. It was a *splendide mendax*—an honorable lie. Risky though it was, Mink's idea of a match was genius incarnate but hardly something the captain or any other officer would approve. After all, Mink was in truth a Union man; speaking with him was not fraternization. Forty men playing in a field *was*, and more of that could bring the war to a halt.

Someone tapped Burridge on the shoulder. "Lieutenant!" Burridge snapped back to the battle at hand. It was Cawthorne. "Lieutenant, we are ordered to stack packs and dress the line." Imagining him dragged to a gallows, Burridge thanked the sergeant and politely requested him to perform the duty.

The line moved up closer to the front. Now Lyman could see the backs of Crawford's Pennsylvania Reserves through the trees and the rapid dusk. All was ready for battle. A silence descended over this section of the forest. In other woods around this area north of the Spotsylvania Court House there was scattered skirmishing and cracks of rifle fire, but not here. As in the moments before a storm, before the first gusts of wind test the trees, a stillness held. Minds begged to know where they were going, if they would live. Hearts pounded. Eyes strained into the dark to see butternuts out in the distance. The birds, the crickets, and the tops of tall loblolly pines held a moment of prayer in tremulous silence.

Lyman had done well all day to keep his thoughts in check, distracted by Pitt's sudden change. He'd held to the standard iron gauge of military duty, allowing only for memories of the match, but as the battle neared and death ripened in the air, Lyman felt his mind push forward into the darker regions of fear. His first thought was to have Danny returned to them, to glimpse that old familiar face. Lyman tried to guess what Danny would do in this coming scrap, but the only answer he got was that whatever it was, it would have been the right thing.

The barrel of Cawthorne's revolver clicked in the stillness. Lyman sensed the hundred thousand men of Grant, the hundred thousand men of Lee, and his one face among them, just one face among the thousands. The reservists ahead, motionless in blue, seemed a flock of roosting birds waiting for a fox to set them flying. He had his flock, too, and there were countless others, all together on this violent migration. One bird didn't matter anymore.

Lyman could still remember the days when it was a good thing to be a common man, when it was believed that the natural attributes of an American were enough to carry him forward, when the United States was a place where every face had value and every hand had to tend this garden and do its planting. A place full of men like Micah Breese.

He remembered Brooklyn the way it used to be—a nice town where you knew everyone. Everyone gave a whistle about who you were, how you were, what you did with your life and your hands; but now it was filled with people like the reservists; spokes on the gears of a huge machine that was grinding away to make money. If a spoke snapped off, they just replaced it. "Union" meant something else now, a faceless country, a consuming whole that united everyone together like the numbered employees at the sulfur plant who worked *for* the company, not *with* each other. Failed lives were taken care of by the government so that no one had to help them or show them their best selves. Grant could send a wave of boys in to be slaughtered, and he'd get another ten thousand in the morning. And Lyman's was just another life handed over to the nation, to be guided by its manifest destiny.

He wanted to run up and down the line, screaming his name and his wife's name and what it felt like when Ernie was born and how he liked his eggs and every other thought and fact that belonged to him and no one else—the things he added to the lives around him, to this nation. He wanted a light shining on him in this darkness to catch the cleft in his chin and the swirls in his beard and the color of his eyes. In this place where he meant nothing, he felt a duty to identify himself, to say his name where names no longer mattered, but Tiger's words came back. "There's no sides anymore. Every man for himself."

An order floated back, muffled by the trees, but clearly "Forward March" from the motion of the birds. Lyman hated this, as much as he hated going in at the Wilderness. He didn't want to be a paid murderer anymore. Better things remained to be done in this war, and in this life. He knew it for a fact; he'd learned that in the hospital and he'd just seen it playing ball.

Once the Reserves had moved up, Company L and its two fellow detached units made their first steps into the darkness. The woods here were not as tight as in the Wilderness, so slats of dark blue sky knotted with stars alternated with the black trunks and tops of trees. It was dusk, the time of shadow and things seen from the corners of the eye. Movements sensed, shapes unknown, and all the secrets night wisely veils scuttled through this graying forest, preying on the fears of men.

Rather than comfort, Stives offered a low pulse of doom as he pushed through the underbrush. "We do not know when the hour will come. We do not know when the hour will come," he moaned as a chant. They were coming up to the edge of the trees, where the ravine slid down to a snaggled field of thorny bushes, stunted trees, and briars and a small plot of cleared land someone had tried to farm. The Reserves ahead were wrestling through it and Stives kept on his cadenced call—"We do not know when the hour will come."

Lyman turned back toward Willie and whispered in a hoarse voice, "Shut him the fuck up!"

They left the forest and entered the clearing. A weak moon tried to light their way, but only added shadows to the vague black shapes of bushes and banks of thorny vines. A few hundred yards ahead, the shadowy figures of the Reserves splashed through a small stream cutting the ravine.

Willie pleaded with Stives to pray silently. "Ollie, the Lord'll hear ye any ways ye pray."

Stives could only stare ahead. "We do not know the hour."

"Then pray that we win, goddamn it, and stop praying that we all die!"

"We do not know the hour."

Willie snatched a quick look at the sky and said, "Forgive me." Then he threw a solid left into the baker's belly that doubled him over and left him crumpled on the ground; out of breath, out of voice, and out of the battle, which he had wanted all along.

Across the ravine, the first lines were now hitting the rising slope and the new wall of trees. The Rebs were in there, somewhere. Tiger stopped in front of a thin shape, shrouded in darkness; it looked like Mary, wrapped up in her shawl. What would he say to her now? He remembered his words of that spring morning, that last morning, last sight of her—"Now what are ye doing here? Git back home with ye, ye know ye can't come. Just one, and that's all." He nearly kissed the heavy air. "Now git back, lass. I got work to do." A furious cheer erupted from the woods. And then his final words, so bitter now—"Soldiers' wives'll be watched for, I promise ye so. They'll take care of ye." Guns suddenly burst and the flash of muskets showed Tiger a young tree wrapped in suffocating vines. He was ready for war again.

The storm had broken. Huge flocks of birds shaken awake by sound and bullets swarmed into the sky. Herring stopped his detail just before the small freshet and dressed the line as the men stared into the blackness that had finally fallen over them. Licks of fire sliced the night. Streaks of light created by the two firing sides revealed the changing silhouettes of distant heads and shoulders, rifles, waving swords amid the constant bars of trees.

The second line of Reserves flung into the fray and the roar of shooting rose.

Lyman yawned, then looked next to him at Wesley. "You still standing?"

Wes nodded and shook his head at the same time so that it seemed his skull had unhinged itself from the rest of his body. "Yeah. Yes. Oh yeah."

"Stay close and you'll be fine. Just do what I do."

The shooting had peaked and now began to trickle off. Then the sound of a mob rolled out of the trees, black shapes running toward them.

Lyman snapped his gun to his shoulder. So did Wesley.

The whole line tensed and hammers cocked as the shapes drew nearer, swinging arms and rifles like a wave of charging madmen. All the officers screamed out to hold fire, and soldiers ready to shoot realized that if these were Rebs, they'd be yelling like banshees instead of just looking like them. The shadowy hulks were on them in a second, showing their faces, still twisted by fear and desperation, to be those of the Reserves, who had been repulsed by the strong Rebel force lurking in the trees. A few heads turned and more than one man wished he had the courage to be a coward, but in a moment all eyes swept back to the front and the silence and the gloom. A passing flag slapped Lyman in the face; he was saying, "Stand firm. Stand firm. Let 'em run." Before anyone could even strain to peer into the woods and imagine what waited, a howl rose to the moon from the Rebel lines and a new wave of shapes came storming down the ravine and into the clearing.

Screams of "In volley order!" echoed down the Northern side. Burridge and Cawthorne were screaming, too, trying to get the men in two lines as quickly as possible. Lyman's voice was lower and cut through the nearly uncontrolled wailings of the surprised Union officers and the screeching Rebels. "Work together! Work together! Standing shoot first, then kneel. Kneeling stand, then kneel again!" He shoved bodies back and forth, pushed men onto their knees in the front line and turned around just in time to hear Burridge's order to fire.

The first volley illuminated the field with a great bank of white light, as though a bolt of lightning had struck. Wes could see for the shortest of seconds the stunned expressions of wounded Rebels caught in the deadly burst. The Rebs hadn't got off a shot yet before the second volley slammed into them and their screams of pain now drowned out the bellowed orders in the lines.

Lyman didn't have time to ask what Danny would do; his own battle instincts took over. He called for another volley as a line of red fire and silver white exploded from the other side of the ravine. Since the Rebs were aiming at the first light they saw, they shot high over the men crouching on the incline and their bullets ripped into the ground above the company. The Brooklyn men delivered another volley into the Rebs, who were now falling back, and Burridge gave the order to fire at will.

Slipper tried to slide away in the confusion, but Karl caught his arm. The boy was crying, "I can't! I can't!" and his body was going limp when Karl finally slapped him. "Shoot your fucking gun!" he howled, a screaming order that in Slipper's frenzied mind was just another voice of hell, another jailer in the cell of madness he was building as the armies clashed. Feeney slid onto the ground and the German pressed a foot down on his back, the battle cries directed now toward his prisoner, who could not hear. Slipper had passed out.

From the Rebel side, a volley sliced the field, and the Union men returned it with a heavy random fire that pushed the enemy farther back. The shooting ebbed again. Only single shots now cracked the night like angry stars come crashing down to earth. The scrap had been too sudden, too intense for Lyman to even think about how sore his arms were or how fast his heart was beating, but as the silence held for a minute, and another minute more, he rubbed his wounded shoulder and tried at once to take a calming breath and still remain alert.

Though Newt found shooting at vague shapes in the darkness easier than aiming at men, he still shot high through the skirmish. When he heard from the bishop, he'd abide by his response. Until then, frightening as this fury of black night and exploding white had been, it provided a perfect cover for the quandary his conscience left him in. He took a sip of water and prayed for safety.

Cawthorne stood trembling with Del Rio and the Worms, fixing his hat, scratching the broad swatches of hair on his cheeks, patting his stomach and each limb in turn to make sure they were all still there, and all the while delivering a few lines in a stunned monotone:

That he which hath no stomach for this fight,
Let him depart; his passport shall be made,
And crowns for convoy put into his purse:
We would not die in that man's company
That fears his fellowship to die with us.

Horace, pleased to recognize the lines, said, "*Richard the Third!*"

Pindar shook his head, "*Macbeth*. We saw it years ago with Father at the Brooklyn Museum. Davenport played the Scot and *Toodles* was on the bill as well."

"No, I've never seen a play with Father. Maybe you had the good fortune."

Before the discussion proceeded any further, Herring pulled the lines back a hundred yards. The men, unwilling to turn their backs on an enemy who they could hear breathing, talking, moving up ahead, walked backward up the gentle rise until ordered to stop. Lyman's mouth had gone dry, and as he worked his cheeks and tongue, trying to raise a little spit, Wes leaned over to him. "Are you still standin'?"

Lyman couldn't help but smile. "Yeah. That was something, wasn't it?"

Wes nodded. "You just keep throwing that snap, OK?"

Lyman smiled again, seeing the boy in the softness of Pitt's face, a round chubby face that Ernie's could very well resemble when he turned that old. Lyman knew the look, too; a look of admiration and openness that had often scared him when he saw it on Ernie because of its high expectations. He pictured Ernie giving the same look to his uncle Albert and resented both of them for it. From Wesley, though, the look made him feel valuable: Pitt had seen him in action. He knew how hard soldiering was, and *he* thought Lyman a good man.

The realization surged through him. Back there, in that sweet green field, he had finally stepped forward and made a moment count; he had stepped into the Rebels and begun a base ball match in the face of both armies. He hadn't planned the moment. He'd just done it and made himself a hero, of sorts. He smiled as the injured wept below in the ravine. He had walked under that green arch and taken charge, had elevated himself to the place he'd wanted to be. In the same place, in the same body and same mind, the man who'd been an abject loss stood straight and gave his name the value that he'd been waiting for someone else to vest it with. Lyman laughed in wonder that he had ever been ruled by a small, twisted knot of fear. He should have been sergeant.

Wes looked at his friend, who'd suddenly bolted up straight and was breathing through his nose like a bull set to charge. "Are you feeling right?"

"Of course I am. Take a look at Cawthorne there." He pointed to the sergeant, whose lips were moving rapidly as he continued to click the barrel of his revolver, fumbling with bullets, dropping some and leaving those that fell.

"Nobody listens to him anyways."

"Someone has to be in charge." And it would be me, Lyman thought. No waiting. He'd just started that match in the forest; just picked up the ball and let 'er rip. No more waiting. "Don't worry, son. You're gonna be fine."

A slight pause had tricked no one into thinking that the fight was over, but the Rebs swarmed back in a wild firing sprint that caught the Union men unawares. Though they got off one volley, it didn't even slow the yelling onslaught, and the Rebs smashed into them with the speed and fury of a stampede, throwing the whole clearing into one vast melee of screaming killing men reduced to their most primitive selves. There wasn't time to shoot or think. The moon and stars caught tips of bayonets before they plunged deep into hungry stomachs, and swords as they cut through arms and throats. Few shots were fired when loading a gun took half a minute; a man could die ten times by then. Rebel knives ran slick with blood. Butts of muskets swung like clubs and shattered skulls, spraying brains and teeth. Men bit and clawed, they pulled at eyes, ripped into flesh, tore beards off, and all the while they screamed. They screamed in fear; they screamed in horror at what they saw and what they did and what they had become.

At first Wesley was glad for this kind of fight; he could punch and kick and stab. The bullets, cannons, and other mechanical ways to die that he'd seen so far gave no warning; they had no faces; they stole life from you instead of fighting you for it. Wes dove into this grapple like he was back in Dangertown beating up Polacks who dared to enter Greenpoint. He stabbed the first few with his loose bayonet, but the iron stuck in a Reb's stomach and he lost his grip on the blood and was left with only his hands and his musket, and the Rebs kept coming, their eyes bulging in the frenzy, mouths wide. One grabbed at the straps of his cartridge box and began pulling him down as another stabbed at him. Wes knocked the first away with his musket, then scratched at the hands of the one on his straps. He scratched, and then he tore, digging in like a cat, breaking skin, mangling tendons, and another came as this one was falling. The white eyes shone in the night and the Reb howled sounds that only Satan could understand.

Wes realized that this was no bar fight. He saw that he would have to take every single one of these bastards if he planned on seeing another day. Teddy wasn't coming with a chair to bust someone's head, the coppers weren't on their way—there was no one to stop this and the fact was nobody wanted it stopped. The Reb lifted his musket high over his head and smashed the butt down into Wesley's jaw. Wes turned away just in time for the blow to glance off his mouth, but it still dropped him to his knees so fast he didn't have the chance to taste the blood.

He whipped both arms up straight into the Rebel's crotch and brought him down to his level, finishing him off with a knee that made something crack in the Reb's head. But the fight wasn't over and they kept coming. Wes pushed himself up, blood pouring from his mouth, to keep fighting for his life, the only good reason he saw now for becoming a killer.

A Reb had both hands around Lyman's throat, close enough for Lyman to smell the fetid breath and years of sweat. Choking, Lyman leaned forward and bit a chunk out of the Reb's face, then spit it back at him, screaming his name as though introducing himself to the man who'd just tried to kill him. The Reb sank down, clutching at his cheek. Lyman's knuckles were already bleeding from landing on bone and metal and anything else they could reach, but he screamed the only words that entered his mind: "Lyman Alder."

A bayonet glanced off his forehead and blood began dripping into his eyes. Lyman roared his name once again and swung his rifle into the belly of another man, stabbing the Reb as he fell. The light was on him. He was sure he was at the center of this fight, a storm of savage men. He wiped his face on his jacket and tried to stave off the soreness throbbing in every part of a body completely flexed. As he slashed down at a kneeling Reb, Lyman saw, thought he saw, for a flash Micah Breese, and as quick as the thought came it was out with a scream—"Lyman Alder!"—and a kick to the head of this man who refused to stay down.

Stray pistol shots and the sharp ring of meeting swords skipped over the dense fog of sounds. Louis heard none of it. He heard his heart beat and his breathing, and a rhythm only the earliest men had heard; the rhythm of waves crashing, of seasons passing, of migrations and molt and the dancing of the bees. Preserving the Union had no part for him; he was guided by a more ancient god. The rhythm pushed him on to acts of violence he had never dreamed of and soon, if not tonight, that rhythm would stop. Fatigue would hit, the pain would rise, and Louis Ferenczy, the Lion of Comorn, would be a warrior no more. But now he stabbed at the gray jackets, threw young men onto the ground, and relished this final celebration of a part of life that he knew was coming to an end.

Pindar Worm fell, unconscious from an elbow thrown by a frantically swinging Reb who was knocked aside before he could finish the job. Jimmy Tice simply collapsed from fatigue, from nerves that could not handle fighting against endless brutal hatred. Men stepped over his body when they could; otherwise they stepped on top. Death wakened Slipper Feeney as no smelling salts could do. He dragged himself back through stomping feet and falling bodies to a place near Stives, where the two sat like they had paid admission for the spot, each man weeping in his shame.

Newt had thought this was the perfect battle to hide his secret fears, but God was angry. Like Saul struck blind, he had been found and made accountable. He cried for help, but no man could expect help here; not this night. He cried for mercy. As he pulled himself to the lighter edges of the fray, broken by the strain of staying whole, he asked why he was being punished for being good.

Tiger jammed a bayonet up the soft area underneath the jaw of some Rebel. The eyes crossed, the tongue was pierced, and the true horror was that this man would live. Quigley pulled the blade out and pushed the man aside for dead. Tiger saw every man in the Rebel army surrounding him, coming at him—Bobby Lee, Jackson, Longstreet. Every Reb he'd ever seen went filing past, even the ones from the base ball match. Their friends the Brits had killed his father and brothers, had let them starve while food sat on the docks at Cork. He put his meaty hand over the face of another and squeezed as the man slashed at him. The government had lied. Lincoln, too; especially Lincoln for freeing the niggers while freemen suffered. It was all their fault this was now a nigger's fight. Tiger shoved the bayonet in this one's belly. They were all enemies. Tiger tried to take twice as many Rebel souls to make up for the Yanks he wasn't supposed to kill.

A man backed toward Burridge, a canteen with *14* painted on its side slung over his shoulder and two hands held up to ward off a musket blow. Too blurred by unrelenting combat to realize the man was wearing gray, the lieutenant stood next to him and deflected the rifle butt with a swing of his own gun.

Burridge looked over to see whose life he had just saved. It was Albert Arlette. Burridge's scream may have been taken as a war cry, but it was as true a scream of horror as had been heard that evening. Neither man struck a blow. Instead, they each grabbed someone else, someone they didn't know, and ended their life.

————————

When Lyman thought it had to end, it got worse. Bodies piled up into barricades, falling from sheer exhaustion. He began to feel dizzy, seeing things he couldn't possibly be seeing, men who couldn't be there, the Rebels like Breese and Haddon and Mink. As the blood slowed on his forehead, he slowed down as well, and the other grapples, too, became grotesque dances through the field. Men clutched at each other, trying to kill or maim, but death came slowly now, in drawn-out couplings. The shroud was falling and Danny couldn't save him. It was every man for himself.

This was when he usually quit, when the call for strength greater than what he believed himself capable of came and he pointed it on toward an-other man of proven steel like Danny Anson or Alder Senior, but tonight weakness meant death, not just dishonor, and Lyman was not ready to die. He saw Ernie's face and Wesley's face; Victoria's long hands. Wesley's voice repeated, "Keep throwing them fuckin' snaps!" and he screamed out his name again, to tell everyone that he was still standing.

Someone in blue or gray saw a large movement on the left side and began screaming, "We're flanked!" The dreaded word spread like a fire and the reaction it caused had no grounding in the battle itself. There were no lines to flank, no ranks or files. The ravine was one seething pot of blood mixed with bodies and soldiers trying to stay up, and now every man thought he was about to be set upon from two sides. Tiger detected the movement himself. There were definitely men headed toward their flank, but he could tell by the sameness of the moonlit uniforms that they were Union troops. Tiger relaxed for a moment. Then he looked more closely and saw what appeared to be dark skin and black curly hair beneath the fatigue caps. Nigger bastards! His mind burst to flame. Cowardly nigger bastards not fit to see white men's blood! *They* were the ones who deserved the bullets. *They* were the true enemy, and Tiger decided to take a few down to hell with him. He picked up a Union flag draped on a body and called men to rally behind him.

Lyman saw Tiger waving the flag a few feet away and charging off to the right, but those new men were showing the Stars and Stripes too. Wes and Louis stood next to Tiger, clearly swept up in his fury and ready to go. A few other men joined, good men about to storm their own troops and kill, and be killed by, their own men. Lyman forced his knee into the groin of the Reb he was wrestling, a kick that on other days or even ten minutes before would have been stopped, but now it landed and hard enough to crumple the vomiting Rebel down to the ground. Momentarily free from attack, he made his way over wrestling bodies to this ill-conceived unit. Lyman grabbed on to Tiger's arms. "Stop! Those are our boys!"

Tiger shoved him away. "Git off of me, ye bastard! I'm taking these boys in!" Tiger pointed the flag again through the mass of mauled and mauling men.

Lyman tore the flag out of his hands. "No, you're not. I'm ordering you to stand here!"

"*Yer* ordering *me*? Go fuck yerself! Come on, boys!"

"They're Yanks, goddamnit!" Lyman hauled Quigley to the ground. The two rolled over wounded men, into puddles of blood. Another soldier hoisted up the flag, but before he could lead the detatchment much farther, the Rebs hastily loaded what rifles they could and bore down upon the regiment of Union flankers, firing and tearing a final supreme yell of exhaustion and fury from their bellies.

The Union regiment laid two volleys into them. What Rebels were still left standing afterward ran to the safety of the ravine's far side, and the Battle of Laurel Hill was over. Lyman and Tiger kept on fighting.

———

When the sporadic shots of men who somehow hadn't had enough died down, the stillness that had preceded the engagement settled back over the clearing. Throughout the field, men sank to the ground. Some knelt in thanksgiving, others lay among the dead and wounded of both sides, wondering if, in fact, they were all—even those still breathing—dead. Frantic searches began for friends buried in heaps of bodies. Men would briefly look at each other, shake their heads, share the common thought that neither had ever seen action like this, then look away in shame at what they'd done and their joy at having lived.

Pulled apart from Tiger, Lyman now sat between a Rebel whose jaw had been knocked off, leaving his dead body in a state of constant scream, and a Union boy grasping a ramrod sticking out from his stomach. That boy was dead, too. Lyman couldn't move a muscle. His shoulder, always just a little sore, now felt as it did the moment it had been injured. He didn't try to clean the blood off from his face. Leaden though his body was, he lifted his head up a bit and saw the field writhe with bodies reaching out for help or fighting death. The movement was just a ripple through the layer of black that now coated the whole clearing, a solid layer of fallen men. He had been saved, he thought, but then he corrected that—he had saved himself, and Wes and Louie. And Tiger.

Horace tapped his shoulder with a frantic insistence. "Have you seen my brother? I can't find Pinney and I must find him."

Lyman couldn't imagine finding one man among all these bodies now, as even the moon slid away in embarrassment at what it had just witnessed. A whole family of brothers had joined up with the 14th at the start and they'd all been killed. And the three Egolf brothers with their dog, Leo. Two dead and the other a cripple.

When Lyman looked up, Horace was still standing there, waiting for some advice, encouragement, reassurance, in a slumping pose that showed none of the usual bounce. Lyman gestured off to his left. "Last time I saw him was over that way."

Horace reacted as though Lyman had found Pindar and brought him back to life. "Thank you! Thank you, Lyman! I know I'll find him!" Horace picked his way through the bodies, checking faces and searching for a pair of red trousers.

The moans and cries of the injured, so similar despite the thousands of individual pains they expressed, merged into one chord that faded before numb ears, like the cicadas' chirruping wall of sound, forgotten as the summer night goes on. No longer an inferno, the field now was purgatory, where deliverance was possible, even if it meant death. Officers tried to rally soldiers into a defensive line of sorts in case the Rebels returned, but there were no men to follow orders; only ghosts who roamed and slept amid the battlefield and hoped that morning, hours away, would turn them back to men.

The urge to crow drained out of Louis as quickly as every spark of energy had faded in his bones. His knee throbbed and he found a handsome laceration in his side that he hadn't even felt before. He closed his eyes. The screams of some poor boy stood out from all the others and Louis thought of days before, when he'd listened to other boys scream at the hospital while he had faked his wound. The void he'd felt since then was filled now, a debt was paid, and he had claimed a dozen lives at least for that one leg. Deep in his memory he heard other more familiar screams: the cry of shawled women and girls, standing in the snow as flames consumed their home; a man kneeling, muffling wails with his hands; the tears of a boy old enough to feel shame for his weeping and anger at those who stood around them and laughed. As rarely as he heard these cries, he knew them as he knew his blood and the sound of his own breath in his ears; they were cries that always echoed in his mind and he turned his attention to the pain in his side to silence them.

Louis tried to savor the battle that had been his best. He hoped for more action to soothe that strong fighting pulse still beating, but the sharpness of his pains and the softer edges of his heart called out for rest. For good.

Burridge wandered through the human wreckage searching for Sidney Mink. If Arlette had been here, so must Mink, and the lieutenant could only pray that he would not find him lying among the dead. The thought of losing Mink now left him breathless. Stepping over some blue-clad bodies still twitching in their final throes, he kept on searching, reviewing the facts he'd passed on to Henry and wondering if they had led to this in some way, if destinations and lists of casualties were enough to cause this kind of slaughter. Death was necessary here, but Mink's death would be too cruel a blow to this nation. Too cruel a blow to him.

He paused, nudging aside an arm to clear his path. The arm flopped over and there it was: a familiar crescent of hair framing a staved-in face. Burridge bent over the corpse, dressed in gray with the same epaulets as Mink had worn, and looked into its pockets for some identification.

"Anything good?"

Burridge looked up at a bedraggled Union man, also picking the pockets of the dead. The lieutenant started to slide away like a rat caught in a coach lamp but he was struck with a better idea. "My brother. I think it's my brother. He went secesh."

"Jesus." The grave robber crouched over to help. "Oh Jesus. That's a tragedy if it's true."

Flustered, the lieutenant was immediately suspicious. "What do you mean, 'If it's true'?"

"I mean, if this is your kin."

Burridge turned away and dug into the pockets for the wallet. The man's name was Russell Purchase. "Not him."

"Thank God. Hope ye find him."

"I hope I don't." The man wasn't listening anymore. He was busy going through Russell Purchase's pockets.

Tiger and Lyman sat a good ten feet apart. No words had passed between them, though they had drifted toward each other during these moments of numb calm. Quigley picked his teeth, as if he'd just finished a pleasant meal, fairly cogent from the shock that battle left. Lyman pulled his knees up and put his elbows on them, resting his face on his upturned hands, while Wes sat next to him slopping blood and probing his mouth for missing teeth. Though Wes was delivering a slightly deranged monologue about what had just happened right in his ear, Lyman was paying attention to Tiger. Every so often one of them would sneak a look at the other, waiting for some sign, some signal. Each man was convinced that his friend had finally turned a corner, and it seemed that they were destined now, after all these years, to make their journeys apart.

Lyman flipped a rock off a Rebel buckle. The ping turned Tiger's head and their eyes met. Both men saw Danny Anson between them, Danny's head being blown apart. At the same time Tiger was remembering the Danny that whored with him after Lyman got married and once climbed the front of a five-story building for the hell of it, Lyman saw the man who'd convinced them to sign up to save the Union, who'd never forgotten they were in his hands.

Wes tried hitting the buckle, but he couldn't get close in a dozen throws. Lyman and Tiger stared at each other, watching Danny's spirit smile and die a few times, hearing Wes thudding rocks off of bodies, until they each turned away.

Holding Pindar in his lap, Horace smoothed his brother's hair and wiped the sheen of blood and dirt and sweat from his face. He sang a quiet song to Pindar; not the operatic tunes he'd sang in the theatrical but a simple melody in the lullaby voice their mother had had years ago.

> *Sweet child of mine, you are rocking*
> *In arms that will hold you all night.*
> *The birds in the trees are now flocking,*
> *And sleep in the silver moonlight.*
> *So close your eyes, little dear one.*
> *In morning I'll be your first sight.*

Pindar's eyes slowly opened, like those of a child wakened as he's being carried to bed. He put his arms around Horace, who wept happily as Pindar held on to him. "It's my brother. I have my brother back."

CHAPTER 9

THE MIRROR WITHIN NEWT, WHERE HE LOOKED FOR HIM-self, had been warping for some time, but tonight it had shattered into thousands of sharp pieces, and as he collected them, each gave a painful and true reflection of what he really had become.

He had always liked mirrors before, always looked in them to check the part of his hair or the cut of his trousers, receiving in turn a crisp, definite outline of a handsome man aproned with conviction and success; a man the world approved of. Now left with only slivers of a self, he couldn't name that stricken and defeated man staring from the shards. It wasn't Newton Fry, who'd courted many Brooklyn ladies until he found the perfect one, a Mrs. Fry whose beauty he saw as a suitable complement to his. It wasn't Newton Fry whose grand plans for Isaac's Grocery were already in motion toward future wealth. It wasn't the father of four children, a member of Bishop Church, owner of a home.

This Newton Fry had fearful eyes that belonged to the coward Jonah, cast into violent seas at God's command. His bleak, worried face shirked the call to make His divine intentions known. The Lord had found him hiding on a false ship of moral courage and brought this storm of battle to blow it all away and show the truth. At the very kernel of his soul, he was a coward.

Herring's pickets still jutted out into the ravine, exhausted and vulnerable to any charge the Rebs could muster. Across the blackened field and the crust of dead, the Rebels could be heard whispering, scuttling back and forth in a constant threat of sudden dead-of-night destruction. Fry squeezed himself into the smallest possible size while other men stared off into the dark. He reviewed his life and wondered whose it was. The Newton Fry he saw had no right to all those things and people he so treasured and lived more to enjoy than to defend. He had only posed as a man who fought for God and wife and country. The company wouldn't have him now; Mrs. Fry would turn her head if she could see this dirty thing that had no pride. What else had he lied about in his twenty-seven years? His looks? His love of God? His business acumen? Every aspect of his life was put to trial and Newton Fry signed the writ for them to hang.

Once the shock of battle passed and the Union men finally admitted the startling fact that a force of Rebs still faced them after such a hellacious encounter, they listened to the pleading orders of their officers to leave the wounded and the spoils of the dead in order to re-form. Lyman got the detachment from Company L moving. He had leaped at the chance to make his presence known to Burridge and Cawthorne; just another soldier for too long, he was ready to give orders and lead a charge. He'd been preparing for this longer than Cawthorne had, and now, waiting silent on his belly, he congratulated himself for his successful attempt at leading these men. He'd put them into position with energy and authority. He'd checked to see if anyone was played out or simply gone. He'd been solid and the men had reacted well outside of Tiger, who never listened to anyone's orders anyway. He'd acted quickly, before Burridge and Cawthorne could take control, and all the lieutenant could do was approve the formation. Cawthorne had cav-iled, but Burridge saw Lyman's work for what it was and let it stand. Lyman played it as he had back in the clearing and young Burridge fell in line; after all, the boy *was* only twenty-four. Lying on his stomach, Lyman knew that this was now his company, as it had been Danny's before him.

Lyman wondered at the cords of muscle through his arms and over his back, flexed thighs and biceps and calves as if he'd just discovered how these familiar pieces of his own body worked. He breathed, conscious of the shallow sips of air and the deeper, sating drafts; he tasted the acid residue of bile that had sunk back earlier that night. His other senses were just as fresh and sharp. The world had become at last knowable and a place to conquer. His delinquent boy seemed merely spirited; his unhappy wife would warm to renewed attentions; Alder Senior and Tiger would be handled just as easily. Each solution had occurred to him many times, but now Lyman took a long, cleansing breath, tensed his arms, and found the strength to believe.

With the right side of the line angled to protect their flanks, the company bulged ahead with the rest of Herring's detail into the ravine, moonlight sparkling on the broken swords and buttons that graced the drifts of dying men. Herring had ordered quiet, but the silence didn't fool the Rebs. Instead, it let the Union boys hear the shuffles of Southern troops, the hoarsely whispered orders and sounds of preparation for another battle.

Lyman listened to the Rebs, and a quick scurry across the way cleared his head momentarily of the kind notices he'd been giving himself. Wes flinched at the sound and Lyman raised a hand to calm him down. He heard Willie coughing, someone shifting their legs back and forth—probably Louie or Tiger. The Worms whispered to each other. There were twelve days left and to Lyman every flinch of every man was a personal obligation.

At three they heaved themselves onto stiff legs and moved in parallel lines to the left, out of the front. As they came through Sedgwick's pickets at the tail end of the detail, the company looked more like straggling wounded than active soldiers. The battle in the ravine had marked them all with welts, cuts, and torn jackets, but as they came through, they saw the expressions on Sedgwick's men, looks they had forgotten because they hadn't seen them in a while—awe and pride, approval for a battle well fought, concern. A collective impulse stood them up straighter, made them step lighter as they saw reflected in their fellow soldiers' eyes that they were soldiers too, and brave.

For men without sleep in so many hours, the order to bivouac seemed too good to be true. Safe behind Union lines, the company reclaimed their packs, laid out their rubber mats, and dug in for as much sleep as they'd be allowed. Four hours later they were up and drinking coffee under another strong Southern sun, but the four hours was worth ten. Their incursion the night before was the talk of the Union lines, and as the regiments of Herring's picket detail were sent back to their brigades, the boys of Company L were eager to return to the 14th, wherever it was, so they could tell some stories. The two lines had stretched wider through the pines and fields north of Spotsylvania Court House and solidified. A salient, like a horseshoe, now anchored the Rebel right, and though it fused the end, it also gave the Union a way to turn them. A tension began to smolder. Every man knew the two lines would clash—and clash—until one side finally broke through.

Sitting on a stray box of hardtack, Wesley tried to pour coffee into his mouth around the sweaty rag Lyman had handed him last night to stuff into his bleeding cheek. A strip of the cloth four inches long dangled from his lips. Next to Pitt, Lyman sported his own new bandage—a broad length of white undershirt he had torn off a dead Vermonter and wrapped around his forehead, now slashed with red where it covered the wound. The two sat quietly, squinting at the sun, with Lyman occasionally handing Wesley pieces of weevily hardtack he had managed to snap apart with his heel and Wesley taking them without acknowledgment.

Four men came by, grunting as they carried a wooden box with a stout bronze gun atop it. Setting it down, they flexed their hands and fingers and stretched their arms. The gun seemed to be a miniature of a big siege cannon, short and wide with no barrel to speak of. Lyman had never seen anything like it. "What's that?"

One of the men, the youngest it appeared, a redhead with wild hair and freckles, patted the gun's pug snout. "This here's what they call a cochorn mortar."

"Yeah?"

"Yeah." He lit up as if he were showing off a new toy. "Shell goes clean up into the sky . . ." The boy described a sharp curve up and down with his hand. ". . . then it comes full wallop right down on some fool Rebel's head." Lyman didn't like the looks of it. Didn't seem fair, somehow, but neither were cannons. "We tried it out yesterday and them Rebs were running for cover like God himself was hunting them with lightning." The other three men were hefting the box again and called to the redhead. "You take care now." Lyman touched his bandage as a salute, and even that made his head throb a little. Was it better to never see the man you killed than it was to see him too closely?

Not far from Wes and Lyman, Horace placed a blanket over his brother's shoulders and checked if Pindar had eaten something, an inquiry that Pindar ignored because he was too fascinated by the explanation Feeney was giving him as to why there were fifty-two cards in a deck. Horace was about to scold Pindar when Burridge announced the unwelcome surprise of Linden Stewart. The second lieutenant called them to attention with a small smile that led everyone to believe they were going back. He was actually happy about something else. "Gentlemen. Lieutenant Stewart has given us our orders for this day. We will remain here, attached to Colonel Smith's brigade until further notice." A loud and angry groan went up from the assembled troops. "After serving on picket duty this morning..." The groan became cries of disbelief. "After serving on picket duty this morning, the company shall have the balance of the day in reserve in recognition for their valor this past evening."

Lyman jumped in as soon as Burridge took a breath. "Why the hell are we going back out on picket? Why aren't we going back to the regiment?"

The answer to that question was the reason Burridge was smiling—they were going back out to find Mink. Unfortunately, this wasn't something he could share with the twenty irate soldiers demanding a valid explanation for their extended duty. He made no response to the question but stared hard at Lyman. The butcher was clearly stepping forward. Burridge decided that as long as Alder didn't make a show of it, he would let him play at being Anson for these last two weeks. Cawthorne could use his sidearm, give orders that no one would listen to, and, in short, do whatever he liked as long as he didn't report the matches. The other men would stifle any talkative urges the sergeant might have, they would follow Alder like dogs in a pack, and Burridge could continue their true mission.

Unsatisfied by Burridge's silence, Lyman made a higher appeal. "Lieutenant Stewart, maybe you can tell us why we aren't goin' back."

Stewart shook his head and smacked his fat lips as if he was about to sit down to dinner. "I have no idea, sir. But Second Lieutenant Burridge has an idea. Don't you?"

Burridge ran through all the ways he could take this, none of them pleasant. Cawthorne could have told him about the match and now Stewart was hanging him out to dry for his lie to Captain Henry. Or Stewart could have figured something out himself, or overheard the soldiers talking. Or he could be fishing. There was one more possibility and it was the one Burridge chose to proceed with—Stewart was talking about pure tactics and was testing him. "Well, um, I certainly have no more information than Lieutenant Stewart has." Stewart's left eyebrow went up. "But I would surmise that Colonel Smith wants an experienced unit to work with his picket detail at this crucial juncture." Stewart still had his eyebrow raised and was now working his tongue around his mouth. "Would you agree, sir?"

"I think you underestimate your knowledge, Mr. Burridge."

"Possibly you overestimate mine, sir."

Stewart chewed Burridge's reply for a second, then said, "The lieutenant could very well be correct in his reading of the plan." He looked directly at Lyman. "And we have no choice but to follow the orders we've been given. Are we finished?"

Burridge stepped in before any of the dozen questions thrown at them from the lines could be heard distinctly. "Yes, sir." Stewart nodded, then stuck three fingers and a thumb into his mouth in order to dislodge a piece of fatty pork from a molar. "Dismissed."

––––––––

The Rebel lines were six or seven hundred yards away, through forest as dense and lifeless as the Wilderness had been. Burridge scanned the trees. He knew Mink had to be out there somewhere. His four-stride lead on the rest of the company was interpreted by the more optimistic among them as a small show of bravery.

Though nearly identical to the Wilderness, here small clearings occasionally opened, and the trees did not harbor the same palpable sense of evil as those first miles of woods. There were military reasons as well for a less eager advance: Now that firm lines had formed and blood would surely be shed when they met, to stand picket meant to serve as an ornamental defense. If they were fired upon, it was their duty to run and let the skirmishers and full army take over, just as the fingertips do not land blows, but yield to fists and arms. Still, two long bristles of guns lined these woods; anything was possible and the risks were not forgotten.

The birds had greeted the pale withering morning long before, and now only random chirps and the occasional weak cry of an eagle echoed through the sparse tops of the loblolly pines. As the men warily trudged on, one bird seemed to be following them, or really leading them along. Its call came from the trees overhead, and always just ahead of them. Louis looked for some flash of color in the gray and green canopy, but none appeared. It was a hearty call, friendly in a way, and Louis thought it might be a mockingbird. Even Lyman, no great lover of nature, noticed the persistent singing, and what was strangest to him was that it sounded familiar. He trotted over to Burridge. "Do you hear that bird?"

The lieutenant wasn't interested. "Yes. So?" He turned back to the trees ahead.

"Doesn't it sound just like that birdy little Reb? He was always whistling. Haddon. That fellow."

Burridge's broad smile surprised Lyman. "Keep your ear on him and let's follow."

"You think they'd bushwhack us?"

Burridge remembered Albert Arlette turning away and attacking someone else the night before. "No. I honestly don't think they would."

Lyman grinned. "I don't think so, either."

The lines were close enough that ten minutes of walking, now veering left at Burridge's command, brought them to the center of the no-man's-land between the entrenched forces and another clearing of short green grass streaked with longer blades that looked like wheat. It was possible their fraternization with the Rebs would be found out, but the chance was small—they were the ones responsible for finding such things. They let their guns droop as they squinted toward the Rebel positions. The birdsong stopped and across the way, on the fringes of the field all of a hundred yards away, was a line of Rebs moving toward them.

Burridge didn't have to look hard to see Mink leading the group. He had on a new pair of trousers, probably taken off a body, and a tired look on his face, but the same black hair cupped his forehead and he nodded slowly. He was even more striking than Burridge recalled, and the lieutenant restrained himself from rushing forward and clasping Mink's hand in his own when Mink smiled.

The first instinct of the Union boys was to welcome familiar faces, even if they belonged to Rebs. Among a combined body of nearly two hundred thousand men trying to kill each other, seeing people you knew after a battle still alive and relatively healthy was always an event worth celebrating. After looking about to be sure of their privacy, Lyman, Huey, Louis, Wes, and a few others stepped forward to shake hands; then they got a good look at the Rebels' condition. Harlan Deal had a bandaged hand. Lemuel, who had by now dropped out of the trees behind the Union men and rejoined his company, had a bandage of his own around his head, stained with a large red blot. Unwashed for weeks and having taken the worst in a recent encounter, they all were tired and hurting, every man bearing bandages and bruises. The Yankees stopped short and many turned their heads away.

Lyman found Breese, who as usual was looking at the ground, and suddenly remembered that he'd seen his face the night before. He'd thought it was just his imagination caught in the swirl of battle, as usual spewing forth faces and snatches of songs and lines from letters he'd received. But it became clear at this moment that they'd been fighting with these men twelve hours before. The shocked looks of the others revealed that they had seen them last night, too, and had dismissed the sight as Lyman had.

When Breese finally looked up, Lyman said, "Did we . . . ?"

Breese nodded.

"Aw, Christ."

The two lines of men stared at each other, shaking their heads. Del Rio crossed himself and pulled his cap off, and soon every soldier removed his hat and bowed his head in silent prayer.

Mink broke the silence with an offer. "Another match, gentlemen? In fact"—he put a finger to his chin as though a terrific new idea had struck him—"since we seem fated to meet each other, I believe a series is in order."

Burridge asked the next question as politely as he could. "Do you think you boys can, uh, play?"

Mink put his arms over the shoulders of Tidrow and Kingsley, who shied a bit to the side, away from him. "These boys are the fightinest, play-inest sons of bitches you ever gonna meet and they'll kick your asses back to Washington city."

Wes blurted out, "Like hell you will!"

"I think there's a taker right here. Anyone else?"

Lyman nodded. He had one demand, though. "It's our turn to be the home team." Yankees calling themselves the home team in Virginia was not a pleasant thought to men like Mansfield Covay. The Rebs had a brief conclave, until Mink finally turned and accepted the terms. The second game between the Yanks and the Rebels was on.

History bears out the theory that war is a natural activity of man, but history also shows that playing games with balls is as natural and universal to man as its distant, martial cousin. The difference is that men do not have to be ordered to play a game. On this May morning, no one had to tell these two groups of soldiers to stack their arms; a few held their weapons only to guard against intruders. At seven the sun was already hot and bright, flashing white like a shell stopped in midexplosion. Most of the Rebels lay down in the grass on their sides and tilted their caps over their eyes, Willie and Huey waiting for the Yankees to take the field before they edged over. Jackets and packs piled up on both sides. Lyman and Wes had a few practice pitches while the other men went back to their positions. From the pitcher's box, Lyman saw a wall of trees, but on the side and behind him some well-size evergreens broke up the rhythm of thin pines. Brockington stood guard off toward the Rebel lines. No clouds this day; only sun and blue sky.

Lieutenant Burridge came up next to Felix Cawthorne, playing the role of victorious chieftain offering a palm to his vanquished opponent. "You have no problem with this, I trust? Our last days have been no easier..."

"I act at your orders, sir." Cawthorne folded his arms and stared off at the horizon, enjoying the lieutenant's surprised silence.

"Well, good. Good. Thank you." He pointed toward the pitch. "I'm going to, over there..."

"Yes, sir." Cawthorne surveyed the field. He had his orders. He had to find some proof.

Sitting cross-legged with Horace beside him, Pindar whittled a fresh tip on his stubby pencil, ready once again to keep score. Since the battle, Horace had rarely left Pindar's side and Pindar, to everyone's surprise, seemed glad of it. As the accountant began to draw the grid, he stopped and turned to his brother. "Horace, how does this work?"

Lemuel, who was standing over them, whistled, pointing at himself, then pointed at the first line on the grid and whistled again.

Horace gently took the pencil away from Pindar. "See, Pinney, this way." He wrote in Haddon's name. "Each man goes on a line." Pindar nodded as though he understood the words, but not what they meant. Horace looked up at Lemuel. "He got hit in the head." Haddon let out a sad, loonlike call and pointed to the bandage on his own head, nodding in sympathy. Then he stepped into the batter's box.

Even with a bandaged head, the curly-haired Reb led off with a mean little swing on Alder's second pitch and popped a two-base hit next to Louis to open the match. Covay, whose white hat now sported two prominent bullet holes, struck out, bringing up Albert Arlette with one down.

Seeing the man whose life he'd spared now standing under the sun, Burridge tried to twitch away the strange conflicting feelings that set upon him. He was both gratified to see Arlette and angry at himself for not killing him. There was shame, too—had it been an act of kindness or of cowardice? What the lieutenant wanted most was for Arlette to strike out or fly out or make any kind of out that wouldn't take him near first base, but Arlette did not comply. He ripped the first offering into left for a single, making it first and third.

Burridge nodded to the Rebel as he took his base. Arlette made no sign that anything existed between them. Before Burridge had time to feel insulted or relieved, Arlette broke for second and took third when Pitt's throw went into center field. A run scored, followed by Arlette on a sacrifice fly. The men in the field were beginning to groan as they had in the first match, losing already by two. The hairless Reb was next and his grounder looked simple enough to Burridge. The German fielded it cleanly at third, then he flung the ball toward first. The lieutenant watched and readied himself as the ball came toward his head, but it continued to rise on its path and his fingers only nicked it as it went by. The mutterings of his teammates faded in his mind—Mink was up.

Mink's new trousers were an improvement over the split-leg pair he had two days ago, but they needed a patch in the rear end and a couple of washings. Like his namesake animal, Mink had a long, sinuous body and a flowing motion at once graceful and rodentlike. He spit on his hands, slicked back his hair, and stepped in against Alder, whom even Burridge could tell was rattled at this point. Sidney Mink had no mercy, though. He slapped a speed ball so hard that it rose a cloud of dust off the dry hard ground as it bounced between Newt and Karl.

He took his base and stared ahead at Kingsley while he spoke to Burridge. *"Sepissime tibi metam contingendame est. Tibi multa dicenda habeo."*

Mink may have had much to tell him, but getting on base often, as Mink was telling him to do, was not his first concern. "Are you well?"

"Of course." Kingsley swung and missed.

"I'm glad." He had questions to ask. *"Habeo quaestiones tibi."*

"Such as?"

He tried to construct the phrase "Captain Henry" in Latin but gave up. *"Praefectus vuit scire motus* Anderson." Kingsley missed again.

"Yes. And?"

Burridge asked his next question with the blithe pleasantry of a Savannah evening formal. "What business is your family in?"

Mink's warm expression chilled in an instant. "What?"

Burridge realized he had made a mistake; Mink apparently felt that personal questions were entirely his province. Burridge asked again, this time in an apologetic tone. "I just wondered what field of business *your* family was in, as you know mine."

Kingsley popped up on the infield. As they waited for Lyman to catch it and end the inning, Mink said, "Cotton. Whatever else?"

The etiquette of subterfuge was as remote a study to him as the language of wealth, and Burridge cursed his ignorance of both. While he sat regretting the question, the first few Yanks of the inning got hits, and soon he was up with the score tied. Burridge ground a slow roller to left that scored Pitt and gave the Yanks their first lead.

Mink was not entirely pleasant at first base. "Nicely done," he said with a dose of sarcasm that surprised Burridge—why should Mink care who won these matches? "Now, before you pepper me with your questions." He shifted into Latin. *"Audi. Cum tabulis geographicis informationes tibi dabo."*

Burridge furrowed his brow and stared at the spy. How could Mink use maps to give him information?

As Louis fouled off a pitch, Mink looked down at the ground, pulling Burridge's eyes with his. They were standing on a dusty patch that was free of grass and covered with a good inch of loose dirt. *"Ecce."* Mink looked up and drew with his toe a line in the dirt that roughly resembled the lines of Laurel Hill. *"Heri."* Louis missed the next pitch, so Mink rapidly scratched in the locations of the Rebel troops, then pointed at Burridge with a quizzical expression and looked back down to the rough map. Burridge narrowed his eyes and licked his lips at this taste of the sort of espionage he'd been expecting. These were enemy troop locations. *"Ubi foederati exercitus est?"* Where are the Union troops, Mink asked. Was that something he should tell this man in Rebel gray? Mink's jaw tightened at Burridge's pause. As a Union scout, he decided, Mink needed to know where his real allies were. Burridge added the Union positions he knew with the shredded toe of his brogan. Mink nodded, then, after giving Burridge a moment to memorize the positions of the whole Rebel army, he casually wiped it away with his foot, as though playing in the dirt.

Louis hit a liner straight at Covay before Mink could share, or learn, anything else.

	1	2	3	4	5	6	7	8	9	R	H	E
CONFEDERATES	2									2	3	0
UNION	3									3	4	1

The Rebs went down one-two-three in the second, and the teams quietly traded sides. As Teddy came back in, Caleb Marmaduke stopped him and pulled two battered cards out of his pocket. In a low conspiratorial whisper he said, "Y'all should take a gander at these." Teddy flipped them over and saw naked women. The first had long dark hair draped around her face as she reclined on a velvet couch like an odalisque, arms raised, hands linked behind her head. The second woman was larger and sat on a wooden chair with her legs crossed, a leashed monkey on her shoulder. Potted palms framed both models, and while their expressions showed more boredom than arousal, their effect on Caleb was great. He was near quivering as Teddy nodded his head in passing interest; he'd seen his share of whores and as whores went, these were no beauties. "Ain't they purdy?" Caleb held up the odalisque. "This here one is Sheba and the other one is Cleopatry. Got 'em off some dead Yank." Teddy looked at Caleb. With his smiling freckled face, checked homespun shirt, and straw hat, the boy looked more like a scarecrow to Teddy than a soldier. "No offense. Ain't they beauts?"

Teddy shrugged. If this were Brooklyn, he figured he'd send this hay-straw up to Slappin' Mary and have his wallet before the boy could find his pecker. "They're healthy."

"Ain't they?" Slipper was already standing at the plate. "Talk to ya later." Caleb trotted away. Teddy laughed to himself, then pictured the fat one with the monkey, Cleopatry. On his second thought, she was a brick after all, though he'd've called her Sally.

Lyman came to the plate with Slipper on second and no hands out. The Yankee bats were working today—when the Rebs scored one, the Union put across two. Some days you could just tell, and Lyman was certain today was a day his nine could not be beaten. The only way they could lose was to give it away. As long as they didn't stop to think, they'd take it.

Lyman felt generous. He greeted Micah with a nod and asked if they were all OK, to which Breese just said, "Yep." Micah Breese had said little to anyone other than Haddon this morning, yet every Reb kept his eyes on him, a sullen bull at the other end of the corral. Micah's dour mood affected all of them. The catcher let a slow pitch slip through his legs, putting Feeney on third. He tossed the ball back and shrugged at Lyman, peeking out from the corners of his eyes toward the woods around them. Lyman had been doing the same. They both knew what could happen if they were caught.

The deep furrows in the Reb's forehead and his late reactions on the field spoke to Lyman of great exhaustion and the kind of lonely, hardened sadness soldiers know. Men sometimes got that look after reading fresh letters from home with news a man could do nothing about. This morning the man might have read that the cow had been foraged by Yanks, some relation had died, or a cousin was seen selling herself back in town.

Between pitches, Micah stopped and looked at him, his mouth slightly open, breath held. Lyman inclined his head toward him and opened his eyes a bit wider. The moment held and just as Lyman expected Micah to speak, a series of gunshots cracked off in the distance toward the Union lines.

Every man froze. How would they explain this? Lyman could feel the chains on his wrists already. He watched each body slightly incline toward where their guns lay, then his eyes swung back to Micah, who was staring at him; their gaze held as they listened together.

Two more shots. Seconds passed with no sound or movement. When the silence seemed firm enough, Lyman shrugged his shoulders and said softly, "That's pretty far off, anyhow."

Micah nodded. "I think we OK."

Lyman turned to the pitcher and, as if released from some spell, all the others relaxed, too, and the match resumed. The Yanks put across two in the second and the Rebs one in the third.

As Burridge took his place with one out in the bottom of the third, he decided to try Mink's slapping swing, a technique that had worked very well for the spy so far. He took the first pitch, then hacked down at the next with a violent clubbing motion. Though he made contact, he also lost his footing and slipped down in a puff of dirt while the ball rolled weakly but safely into left.

Laughter burst through the field, Rebs and Yanks both pointing at Burridge and reenacting his sorry swing to any man of either side who'd missed it. Though he'd accomplished his goal, he'd done it so artlessly, so boyishly and desperately, that the familiar flush rose on his cheeks. His only consolation was the superiority he felt before this proof of the lower unity of thugs.

Covay pointed at him. "Did ye kill it, Yank?"

Deal said, "He look like he was a-butchering a fat sooka."

Wes asked what a *sooka* was and Tidrow, the Reb cook Willie'd been trading with, explained that it meant "pig." "Deal there be half Creek Injun. His maw. Lot a them in our parts. In fact 'Opelika' be Creek talk for 'large pond.'"

Deal rolled his eyes. "Like hell. That ain't even no word and if'n it was, it'd mean 'large swamp,' 'cause that's all they is our way—piney woods and swamps. Any land worth having is haved by that Mink family over there."

Burridge detected the sharpness of things gone too long unsaid in Deal's tone, and he was very curious as to how Mink would reply. Mink tried to diminish the tension with a mask of good nature in keeping with the moment, but the Indian kept on staring at him.

Burridge was fascinated by the new bit of information. "Do these boys work on your plantation?"

Mink cocked his head a little, squinting one eye as if trying to bring Burridge's motivation into focus. "You have more questions than a bride on her wedding night." Burridge began to blink rapidly and Mink broke into a smile. "Well, if it matters so much, friend, I'll tell you. These boys raise a little corn, hunt vermin, live out in the woods. Our niggers work the cotton.

No white man will work beside a goddamn nigger, doing the work of dirty niggers." Mink tried to redirect Burridge's eye to the crude map before them, but the lieutenant only stared at the scout.

Louis dribbled a roller to short, so Burridge took off toward second, wondering all the way if Mink meant what he'd just said or if he'd been playing Confederate gentleman for any eavesdropping Rebs. He could easily enough understand not being an abolitionist. Loving the African had, to Burridge, always been the province of the blessed, those few who actually had the strength to do what every man was supposed to do, and merely attending Harvard didn't raise one to those heights. No, what surprised him was the Rebel vehemence of Mink's dislike. Those were hardly the words of a civilized Christian elevating a savage race, the avowed mission of so many loudly protesting slaveholders. Where did Mink fit in? Burridge couldn't shake the incongruity of a traitor to the Rebel cause holding such views, risking his life to hasten their extinction. Was it all an act? Was Mink really interested in his life? Was he really a Union man, or was that all he cared about? Confused, he tried to separate the Union hero from the Southern aristocrat, but what confused him even more was the realization that he really didn't care to. Mink had called him friend. Burridge continued his interrogation into the fourth. Mink's skidding roller slipped the German's reach, allowing him to continue with his idle-looking scribbles in the dirt showing the heaviest Rebel batteries. Burridge stole glances down at the map as Kingsley went through the motions of a strikeout. "Which are your favorite authors?"

Mink was ready for him, with the right blend of flattery leavened with what seemed to Burridge genuine interest. "I'm more curious about *your* favorites."

Giving his opinion was one of Burridge's most beloved activities and he seized this chance here. "Well, I must say that Virgil ranks among the Pantheon. Homer, of course."

"Of course. What about the *Commentaries*?"

Burridge's heart pounded. "I brought them with me!"

"Don't you agree they're a bit dry?"

To anyone else, Burridge would have delivered his well-oiled discourse on the hard beauty of Caesar's prose, but Mink's words made him think again and he admitted to himself that the *Commentaries* were hard going sometimes. In fact, they were often boring, a truth that Burridge had always felt to be outweighed by the pleasure of being seen with the volume itself in his hands. "Yes, often they are. I enjoy Lucan."

"A minor figure. My dear mother recently sent me Long's translation of the *Thoughts* of M. Aurelius Antoninus. That, sir, is a fine book."

Burridge had once struggled through a few pages of the Greek; Mink's interest, though, made it worth another look. "May I borrow it?"

Mink paused for a moment, then lightly clapped Burridge on the shoulder and said, "My pleasure."

Back at the home base, Caleb Marmaduke scuffed his second pitch foul, right toward Denton Cowles and Lou the rooster. In an unusual display of maternal instinct, Lou fluttered off Cowles's sloping shoulder and nestled on top of the ball as if it were an oddly shaped egg. Everyone laughed, but they laughed much harder when Lou took a strong peck at Cowles, who was trying to pull the ball out from under him. Arlette tried, too, and got the same treatment. Huey had better luck. He smoothed Lou's feathers and said, "If that was an egg, Lou buddy, we woulda et it by now." Then he calmly reached under and pulled out the ball. Deal said Lou was getting as soft as his owner, and Covay nodded and made an obscene gesture in Arlette's direction.

As Caleb continued his at bat, Huey stayed with Arlette and Lou. "What's with those fellas?"

Arlette scratched the dense black whiskers on his cheeks and said, "People don't like when a man change. Rather he was dead than him be different."

"Why's that Weed got no hair?"

Arlette smirked, then scratched again. "Says Jesus took it from him. His Paw took him for ta be dunked when he was maybe sixteen or so—he was a full man, if'n ye know what I'm saying. Preacher dunks him in the river and up comes Weed, every bit a hair gone—eyebrows, legs, every way. Folks said it was a miracle. Married the preacher's daughter, he did, then."

"You believe it?"

"Dunno. Can't see what Jesus'd do with that boy's hair, but it *did* do the job on him. He believe like the Lord hissef."

Huey stroked Lou and shrugged his shoulders. "Guess anything can be true if you believe in it."

Lyman dug in for his turn at the plate to start their fourth with the score 5–3, Yanks. The match was passing quickly in a comfortable, well-paced rhythm. The play was high quality, considering, yet if asked Lyman would have had to admit that he found this match frankly more than a little boring, a scratchy affair of singles and errors that failed to satisfy his taste for big hits. There was good reason for the speed, for the urge to swing away and run; the stray sounds of two armies now constantly reminded them of the risk they shared. The trading on the side was just as clipped, largely because Tidrow and the Rebels had nothing left to trade. Willie was handing bundles of coffee out gratis now. Huey tried to interest Cowles in the collection of tattered clippings, mostly animal etchings from Van Amburgh's Menagerie he'd been culling from every paper he'd gotten his hands on since '61. Cowles seemed unimpressed, so Huey began hunting for relics.

As much as he wanted to speak with Micah, Lyman told himself that he'd seen the limit of their friendship. A man had to respect another man's quiet and, anyway, these moments of truce they had created were a reward in themselves. Breese would remain a mystery. Lyman touched his bandage, took a level practice swing to show Arlette where he wanted it, and decided to turn his attention to winning the match.

He'd let two balls go outside when Breese said, "You ever know a Mistah Yellis Wade?" It was said so softly and diffidently that Lyman wasn't sure who Breese was speaking to. He turned to him, pointing at himself. "I said, did you ever know a Mister Yellis Wade? He a neighbor. Lived up in New York for a time."

"No, sorry. Brooklyn's a big city."

"That he said. Said he thought maybe New York and that Brooklyn would come out with us."

The sun can come out after a rainy morning, Lyman thought. He recalled the talk of secession. There were certainly enough copperheads still there to go around. "Well, we didn't."

Breese shook his head once. "That's too bad. Yo' head hurt?"

"Not so bad."

Breese coughed. "You ever et at Howard's Halfway House?"

An odd question, but Lyman had once. "Yep."

"Mister Wade said it was fine."

"I figure so. It's a nice chop they offer." Lyman swung and missed an outside pitch.

"Who you boys with now?"

Lyman paused for a second. Was there anything dangerous in what he was about to say? It sounded harmless to him. "Warren, but we're detatched now. We're stuck out on picket with Smith's Brigade, Sixth Army."

"What about Warren?"

"He's good enough. Kind of man who cares how his handwriting looks, though."

The Rebel nodded. "We got those. Where you think you going now?"

Lyman ticked the ball foul on the right side, so Mink had to chase it down. "Don't know. Might be settling back with Warren farther down the line. Course, maybe we'll try to turn your left round where we were last night."

"Good luck to ya there. But I got it on good word that the fight's shaping up where you say. And Marse Lee, God bless 'em, ain't happy about it." He shook his head. "We're up a bit more on the right. Just all a yourn keep your heads down, huh?" Lyman nodded. "Hope you and me don't get catched out for this."

Lyman lined a single to center and scored a triple by Karl, the specifics of what he discussed with Micah already fading, but the talk with him still very fresh.

	1	2	3	4	5	6	7	8	9	R	H	E
CONFEDERATES	2	0	1	0						3	4	0
UNION	3	2	0	2						7	10	2

Tiger gritted his teeth and waited for fretting old-woman Lyman—the man who'd tried to slam his nut last night—to throw the next pitch. Tiger was glad to be this far out in center. His only regret was that he hadn't been able to leave the world with a few less niggers. As Haddon came up, he asked himself why he was even doing this. Out of loyalty? But to whom? He felt as alone as the day he stepped onto that ship in Cork harbor.

The crack of the bat snapped Tiger back just in time to see Haddon's hot liner fly over Newt uncontested for a hit. Tiger smiled at seeing Newt's downcast eyes. Maybe he'd stay so that Fry would always know that someone knew the truth about him and his sort.

Covay now came to the plate. Though his beard was overtaking his once perfectly groomed goatee and mustache, the left fielder retained his air of riverboat elegance and now seemed to Tiger a most forbidding character; he was sorry he hadn't taken care of him last night. Tiger rated him and the Indian as the Rebs' toughest numbers. The dirty little pitcher Arlette looked to be feisty as a rat, too. As he watched the Hungarian chase down a long fly out, he felt the stone certainty of an absolute fact weigh in his stomach; the same sense he'd had on many an afternoon in Brooklyn that a decision had been made somewhere beyond his control. On those days, he knew he'd end the night drunk. Today he knew he'd be grappling with one of these three before the end of this match.

Louis kept one eye on the batter Pitt and the other on the two *Bombus fervidi* he'd been watching flit from thistle to thistle in this thick grass. "Bumblebees" they called them here. Louis decided that he enjoyed this base ball. He saw why Lyman and Newt were so taken with it; the logic, the limits, the meeting of physical and intellectual skills. It was beautiful, as well. In the course of the war, he had caught himself more than once admiring the folds of fabric draping over legs that were running to their death, and this same classical fullness and grace was brought to life here. In the pleasant indolence of right field, he watched both the red and gray trousers curve and billow as the white ball zipped from man to man with the same playful zeal as the bees. Nothing had made him feel that way in a long while. Aside from battle.

Wes lined a single and bounded off toward first. Louis looked back down, but the bees were gone, so he set to observing the larger, more dangerous species surrounding him. The Rebs waited for Burridge to pick up the bat, standing in groups of twos and threes talking, for the most part, except for Breese and Haddon. They stood silently close up next to each other like some great plodding ruminant hosting a parasitical, yet very welcome, bird on its back. Haddon whistled once in a while, which Breese, arms folded and head down, seemed to enjoy. Lyman stood by third base, his arms folded like Breese, watching with the same commitment and natural intensity that he applied in battle. What concerned Louis about Lyman was that he took everything too seriously. He was driven, but without abandon. Always in control and about to burst. And now there was Burridge at the home base, quickly becoming Louis's nemesis. Occasionally the lieutenant stared at the Rebs for long stretches, barely seeing what was happening in the game.

Burridge slapped a bouncer right to short. Weed usually stood motionless on the field like a great lizard until a ball hit nearby would send him skittering into action. This time the ball jumped up into Weed's face and Wes easily beat him to second. Everyone was safe.

Weed pressed the fingertips of his right hand to his bald head and closed his browless eyes. " 'Plead my cause, O Lord, with them that strive with me: fight against them that fight against me. Take hold of shield and buckler, and stand up for mine help.' "

Stives rose and, pointing his finger at Weed, cried, "That's my quote!"

Weed looked down his nose. "Satan speaks with the tongue of mine and abuses the Lord's word."

Louis watched at home, waiting to bat. He didn't like all this Bible quoting by Christians; it was like seeing another family living in your home. Willie and Kingsley each got an arm around their respective divinely inspired teammate and counseled understanding, but Louis knew it would be of little use. Battles for the undivided love of an infinite God are never stopped by human kindness.

Young Pitt stole yet another base before order was restored. Standing in, Louis had recovered from his earlier sprint and now felt invigorated by this boy at the start of his life, pushing himself. Even if he had the look of those Jew-hating wolf cubs that had burned down their shop.

Louis's weakening eyes had often made the ball look like a great white blob spinning past him these matches, but as the first pitch came in, he squinted a bit and saw the ball as soon as it left Arlette's hand. It was coming straight, and Louis realized that it was going right into a place he could swing at. He stepped forward onto his left foot and turned his hips perfectly as the ball neared the plate.

The instant he hit it, Louis knew it was gone from the sound, the light feeling of the handle, and his broad, fluid follow-through.

The Rebs didn't contest the home run. It bounced a good twenty yards past Covay, and as Louis began his triumphant trot around the empty haversack bases, he smelled spring; the violets of Pest and the night breeze pushing curtains over his head when he was a child. As he jogged toward first, the years scrolled through his head, and he felt the fullness of his life in this one terrific, and surprising, clout. He saw himself putting his few belongings on a shelf as they moved in with Aunt Marie; asking a question at university, one hand tucked smartly into his vest pocket, the other stretched out in a broad gesture; putting on his new green uniform in 1848; eating goat roasted over coals as an exile in Turkey. At second base, he was in America with Kossuth; meeting Elisabeth at his cousin's home; waiting to hear the cry of a new son in the other room. Rounding third, the opening of his own store; grinding powders to help old women sleep; growing old in this war; then the sound of men clapping like rifle salutes as he came home.

The home run made it 10–3, and Louis was still catching his breath when Karl hit another one with Newt aboard. Another scene came to mind now. He was six or seven, sitting at a long table and wearing his *kippah*. Surprised by this uncommon reminder of the life his family had led before the fire, he searched further in the image and saw the roasted bone on his plate and the three matzos. Words of Hebrew rose in a wary progress, like prisoners released by a mellowing jailer: *"Avadim hayinu"*—"We were Pharaoh's slaves in Egypt." Louis realized he had forgotten Passover.

Tiger stood in, by now fuming and gripping the bat more like a club than the toy it was. A small Rebel rally in the sixth had made it 12–6. Everyone on the field was ready to start the bottom of the inning, save for the pitcher, who hadn't made his way back into his box yet. Tiger saw Arlette on the side, sipping from the canteen. "Would yer Highness be ready?" Then he noticed the *14* painted on its side and there was suddenly no question about who he'd fight or where he'd do it. "Put down our canteen and do yer job!"

Arlette caught his eye, then took another long draft.

"Do yer job, I'm telling you!"

Still staring at Tiger, the pitcher screwed the cap on and dropped the canteen atop his own belongings. He walked to the box, ball now in hand, and asked Tiger if he was ready.

"For the love of Mike, yes I'm ready, as I have . . ."

The ball whipped in high and Tiger ducked just before its intended connection with his head, an impact that would have been as good as a minié for Tiger's health.

"Ye grave-robbing bastard!" Tiger charged the pitcher and the two grappled much as they might have done the night before.

The other men went for their guns, but Micah held up his hands. "It's between them." The men looked around for a moment. When they all seemed to realize that these were two of the least popular men on the field, they put their guns down and formed a circle around the fighters—a prizefight was at least as diverting as a base ball match. Tiger had the size and wanted to throw punches; Arlette was the quicker and he wanted a wrestling match. Each time the Yankee pulled back for a punch, Arlette would step out of his grasp and attack from another side, like a one-man dog pack set upon a bear. A few solid blows were landed, but after three or four minutes Tiger gave up trying to box and the fight devolved to a knot of two bodies, moving only when another grip would tighten it.

Interest in the scrap began to wane with no signs of blood or complete victory. Bits of the circle wandered off, Union with Union, Reb with Reb, but not so far as to break their gathering in the center of the field. Two lines formed now, Union and Reb, and an uncomfortable hush came over them all as even Tiger and Arlette stood and joined them. Lyman finally asked Micah what every Union man was wondering. "So where *did* you get our gear?"

Micah stepped forward. He looked the Union men in the face, then looked back down to his shoes. "The first action we seen was the first action you seen—up at Manassas. 'Cept we didn't get in the battle the way you boys did." He shook his head once, as if regretting something. "You did good."

"How do ye know that?"

" 'Cause we didn't have no fight that day. Our first duty was after the battle—we was sent with the 6th 'Bama ta bury all the boys from yo' regiment." Most men looked to the ground at hearing this, the same way Micah was. "Nobody took nothin' that wasn't U.S. government property. Made sure the graves was deep so no hogs be getting at 'em. Made markers, too." Lyman, Louis, and some of the others began walking back to their side. "First thing we all seen a this war. Mighty sad."

A jay screamed. Every Rebel turned to Brockington, who was lifting his rifle toward the woods.

Strange voices filtered through the pines.

A surge of rustling bushes and branches snapping under feet from the northern trees.

There was no hesitation. Men leaped toward their rifles, loaded quickly, and aimed. Many a Union man knelt side by side with Rebs, barely realizing he was aiming at his own soldiers; others faced enemy lines. A few sights held personal enemies in their cup—enemies of the other side they'd taken a dislike to or enemies they'd marched with and fought beside, waiting for this chance. Death pointed from every man, a fearful geometry of lines.

Burridge called out to all the men, "Hold your fire!" Then he went forward to intercept the intruders. His barked orders echoed back—"We're on picket here! Who are you with? Answer me." The voice that answered was deep and indistinct. "When are they coming?" Another undecipherable answer. "Well, move along farther east; this area is secured."

He returned in a moment, shaking his head. "Colored troops," he explained. "Some new pickets coming through here in forty-five minutes or so."

Sights were lowered, caps removed to mop brows. Tiger spat as the men dropped their guns. Many Union men threw theirs down in disgust, mumbling angrily as if all their concern had been for nothing. Tiger shook his head. "Fucking niggers are prancing about Brooklyn and New York, and, God take 'em, now they're doing it here." Teddy chimed in as well and once they were done, they shut up and waited to hear from the Rebs.

After a moment Arlette growled back, "You'd prance, too, if you finally got the chains off your ankles and was paid for your work."

"What's that I hear? Yer a-loving the nigger, are ye? And yer a Rebel? Yer a breed I haven't seen."

"I got no call against niggers. Only one here with any slaves is Mink. I'm lucky I got me a hog."

Deal had inched up closer to the infield. "I say go ahead and let 'em go free, but you folks up North gotta take care of 'em. No ways we should be losing all our jobs. Even your big abolitionists don't want 'em up there and that's the bull. By the way, Albert, what happened to Cham's tribe and all of Weed's crap?"

Arlette was clearly embarrassed. He spoke into his shoulder. "Never read that part."

Tiger was confused. "So if none of ye wants to keep slavery, what the hell are ye fighting for?"

Deal looked straight at him. " 'Cause *yo'* here. On our land."

Deal had a leathery face, darkened by days in the sun and his Indian blood. Newt found him the most intimidating of all the Rebs, with his looming power and exotic face, but now Newt had nothing to lose. "Are you men really against slavery?"

The dark eyes showed more fatigue now than malice, and his constant talking made him seem familiar, even domesticated. "Most, yeah. We's just as many white men a-working fields as black. Even talk of turning north 'Bamy free oncet. I don't love the nigger, see. Reckon he gots a raht to live the way he see fit, though. Man's a man."

Newt didn't know what to say at first, then blurted, "I think that's mostly right." He was fascinated by the irony and cheered by his visceral agreement with Deal. His own regiment, the 14th Brooklyn, had nearly pulled out of the war en masse after the Emancipation Proclamation. He was surrounded by Yankees who at best didn't care about Africans, fighting against abolitionist Rebs. He considered the possibility that he had joined the wrong army, but the thought of Nathan Bedford Forrest and Fort Pillow smothered the joke. At least some of his guilt was assuaged after this conversation; he thanked God that he hadn't killed any of *these* men.

He caught himself smiling. The bishop's face appeared to him and he bit his cheek to force the smile away, like some flagellating Catholic. He'd always been repelled by their cruel ways of penitence, yet now, thinking of all his transgressions—his cowardice, his hypocrisy, his lies—Newt realized that he would have to pay somehow for the sins of who he'd been until now.

"One more frame, gentlemen?" To the surprise of everyone but Burridge, Mink wanted to play on. "Take your swings. If we can't best you then, we'll call it a match." Though the memory of who'd pointed guns at whom was still fresh, no one was quite ready to quit. The match needed to end when they decided it would. There'd be one more chance for each side.

The Union seventh saw Burridge reach on a clean single to center, Wes tearing open the long back seam of his jacket as he scored. On first, Mink set right to the job of scraping what he called Ewell's intended position into the dirt. Though the lieutenant watched intently, he was more curious about the discussion that had just taken place. "These aren't the common Southern man, are they? What could they know of the colored that you don't?"

Mink checked to see if anyone was listening. "A field of niggers eats like a plague of locusts. They'll do no more than a lick of work and you must beat them to get that much. They're a burden that we carry out of our goodness; but our civilizing efforts have been, I'm sorry to say, quite futile. I say ship them back to Africa. It remains the only answer. Niggers and whites were quite simply not meant to live in any proximity."

The answer—at least the part about Africa—cheered Burridge; Mink and Mr. Lincoln were not so far apart, really. Burridge had seen slaves during his years. Some had horrible tracks of scars and seemed little more than bones, but the others appeared well fed and content, the newly freed happy to eat U.S. government rations and sit idly by while white men chopped wood and loaded wagons—work Burridge felt they should have been eager to do. He pictured the fat mammies and the boys always dancing no matter what time of day it was. Burridge ceded expertise in this issue to Mink, someone who actually owned slaves—who would better know what the true nature of the Negro was and what should be his fate? Certainly not a Brooklyn lawyer. Besides, the Greeks and Romans had owned slaves and that settled it for him. In the two minutes it had taken Louis to run up a count of two balls and a strike, Mink's cold black eyes and Southern rhetoric had allowed Burridge to forget the white-haired old African he'd seen still chained up at Cattlett's Station, the children dressed in rags, weeping, and the proud, resolute faces of the colored troops.

Mink nudged him. *"Ecce."* On the ground was another rough map— thin lines to represent the roads and thicker ones for what had by now become entrenchments. One shaky line stretched across the road, then bulged out in the shape of a horseshoe. Mink said, *"Nostri,"* then corrected himself. *"Scilicet, sui."* He stubbed his toe into three spots along the line and on the bulge, one on the left side and two near its top. "This is where they're weakest. Walker and Hayes, especially."

Burridge smiled. These were real battle plans; weak spots to hit in the Rebel lines, the extra bit of knowledge that can win wars. Burridge had one more question. "Did our last game have anything to do with . . ." He waved his hands around. "You know. With what happened last night?"

Before Mink could answer, the Hungarian singled and Burridge had to leave.

The Rebels accomplished little in their last at bat, save a single by Mink. Burridge scoured the trees for the intruders, but all he saw were their men. Pitt was trying to imitate Haddon's eagle screech, and doing a fair job of it. Willie and the Reb cook were sharing a smoke. Teddy was telling a dirty joke to the one in the straw hat while Huey and some boyish Reb scoured the ground. Mink shifted his eyes back and forth. "Animals. You must *always* stay in charge. Have I made that point clear to you?"

The lieutenant shrank at this first admonition from his idol. Burridge recalled the accusatory tone Arlette and the Indian had when speaking of Mink. Sidney was in charge, but there was risk on his side, too. Not everyone thought well of him, for reasons that probably had little to do with the war. These two groups of men had forged an unlikely bond in the risk of their hours spent together, but it could not go any further than that. The two sides had to remain enemies. It was too easy for Mink and himself to become the targets if they all became friends.

The match ended with an easy fly out to Louis. Unlike the first match, which had ended with querulous feelings of whether or not they'd done the right thing, this morning caps and straw hats were doffed as the men gathered up their belongings. The risks returned to mind, and they were scared and thrilled at once at what they'd done again.

	1	2	3	4	5	6	7	8	9	R	H	E
CONFEDERATES	2	0	1	0	0	3	0	X	X	6	8	2
UNION	3	2	0	?	5	1	X	X	X	13	19	4

Huey and Cowles had been unsuccessful in their hunt for treasure, but as Huey was saying good-bye to Lou, the bird fluttered down off Cowles's shoulder again and squatted over a large rock in the grass.

In a wispy voice, Cowles said, "I'll be damned if Lou don't believe that he a hen." The two started laughing, and then Huey had the thought that any man who could make people think some old colored woman was President Washington's nurse could do big business with a crazy rooster that thought it was a hen.

Huey tugged at Arlette's arm. "Hey, Albert? Could I have Lou?"

"What the hell for?"

The insanity of the idea crossed Huey's mind, but the improbability was exactly what would make Mr. Barnum leap out of his chair and shake Huey's hand. "Well, Lou's trying to hatch a rock right now, and I thought he'd make a fine exhibit for Mr. Barnum's museum."

"Boy, lemme explain something. Lou be four pounds of *working* bird. We set him free near farms, see? Lou attracts some chickens, seeing how's he so perfect. He kills the birds and we eat 'em. See? Lou's probably a little tired and hungry and he not in his right mind, is all. Ain't no reason to go putting him on a box for New York sorts."

Huey looked downcast. "I been looking since day one for something to bring back home and I ain't found nothin' yet and we're done here in a couple weeks."

"A couple weeks?"

"Twelve days."

"Fuck. Jesus. Then ye go home?"

"Yeah."

Arlette's face loosened, as if he were sitting on his own porch, minding his own business, thinking about dinner, then it instantly tightened again. "Well, I'm sorry to say that your lacking a proper souvenir ain't exactly mah problem. We still gonna have to eat while yer sucking down oysters back in Brooklyn, son." Huey kicked a rock aside like a disappointed child. "Listen here. I think about it."

"How do you know we'll see each other again?"

"We'll bump inna you boys again. Now git."

Jauntily flipping the ball from hand to hand, shifting shoulders, and flexing arms as though they were stiff, Lyman relished his first victory, abbreviated as it was, and waited for someone else to call him that glorious name— "winning pitcher." Eager to talk more about the match, the sport, anything to keep the feeling of victory alive, he asked Breese, Mink, and the others standing around exactly how they would go about having a series. For a moment Breese opened his mouth as he had earlier and was about to speak when a glare from Mink cut him off. He said he left that sort of thing up to the lieutenant. Mink looked right at Burridge. "You only have a handful of days before you go back to your homes, so shall we play three more? Best of five wins."

Burridge nodded, but Lyman was skeptical. "How will we meet?"

"Volunteer for picket, sir. We'll find you."

Lyman had another thought. "Nines usually play for a trophy."

Micah pointed toward Lyman's hands. "The ball."

Lyman held out his hand, the rock-hard ball lightly cupped within. "It's just a base ball. You can buy 'em anywhere."

Micah shook his head, as he often did, like a bull shaking off a fly; slow at first, then a snap at the end. "That one has a story."

The thought of surrendering Ernie's ball stuck in Lyman's throat. "My son sent it to me," he said.

"It's a fine ball. Be proud to have it if we win."

Lyman nodded, stuffed the ball into his pack, and got the men into order.

Willie stood over Burridge as the lieutenant shoved a copy of the *Thoughts* of M. Aurelius Antoninus into his knapsack. "What's that?"

Burridge nearly leaped out of his skin. "A book!" He realized that he sounded as though he'd been caught with some contraband material, when in fact this gift was one of the few benign exchanges he had made with Mink. "A book. A, um, Roman emperor. And philosopher."

"You got it from Mink. I saw ye. Is it a code book; some kind a message?"

How could he know? Burridge's mind sprinted toward panic until he detected a slight grin on the cook's face. "No. That would be helpful, wouldn't it?"

"You trade for it?"

Burridge knew a good cover story when he heard one. "Um, yes. Yes, I did."

"What did ye give him?"

What had he given Mink, Burridge thought. For all that the spy had given him, he had offered nothing in return. He resolved to find an appropriate gift for the book, and for everything else. "Uh, tack. I gave him some hardtack."

"Yep. Man cannot live on bread alone, but he needs to have that bread."

Felix Cawthorne had spent the entire match searching for something he could call proof, but his efforts had yielded little more than a rising panic. He had considered absconding with the ball or the bat, certain proof in his mind of what he had been watching, until he imagined the consequences to him physically—at the very least a beating of the most severe sort; the worst unthinkable. There was nothing else to take away from the experience. Then he saw the Worms looking over a piece of paper. He edged close to them and saw a list of every man and, it seemed, how he had performed in the match's activities. It was perfect.

Pindar folded up the sheet and began tucking it into his knapsack. Cawthorne grabbed a corner and tugged. Pindar tugged back, most out of character with the man he'd once been. "What exactly do you think you're doing, Felix? Get your hands off of this!"

Cawthorne stiffened and stroked his side chops. "I'll have that, Worm."

Pindar laughed. "Like hell you will. You think we don't know you're up to something?"

It was time for a performance. Cawthorne assumed the injured expression of a young maiden whose purity had been assailed by the foul claims of a dastardly landlord. "Truly, I wish a keepsake of these matches."

Worm shoved the paper deeply into his knapsack. "Felix, I have no recollection of where I live, what my wife looks like, or what foods I prefer. I suggest you cherish your memories and allow *me* to keep the proof of them."

Cawthorne clenched his teeth and walked away.

CHAPTER
10

I N THE EARLY AFTERNOON, ANOTHER LINE OF PICKETS RELIEVED
Company L. Burridge was surprised to see how crisply his men fell
in, how solid their faces looked when days ago they appeared to be
hollow, played-out skins. As he strode now through the constant activity of the army's rear toward his meeting with Captain Henry, he
ascribed some of their renewed vigor to the base ball matches and
some to his recent hearty leadership, which he owed to Sidney Mink.
Another debt to Mink revealed itself as he stepped into the captain's tent.
Burridge had always felt like a poor relation visiting a wealthy cousin, but
now Burridge felt entitled to be among Henry's gold and leather, and he
did not hesitate to touch the things that interested him. The captain walked
in as Burridge held a long-admired ivory brush. "I'm so very glad you've
made yourself at home, lieutenant."

"A lovely article, Captain."

"Yes." Burridge finally felt the cold in Henry's voice and replaced the
brush. "Were you able to meet again?"

The lieutenant sat down uninvited. "Yes, sir. He's quite an unusual
gentleman, sir."

"So I've heard. What do you have to tell me?" Burridge came to the
desk and drew out the various positional maps Mink had laid out in the
dust of the field, showing the Rebel vulnerabilities and strengths along the
line and at the salient. He also had a list of Confederate officers wounded
and killed. After scanning them, Henry said, "This is good. Very good. The
sort of material that will help us break this damned line of Lee's. We've
chosen the right man with you." Henry crinkled an eye toward him. "Some

wanted a man with experience behind Rebel lines. I said I had a man who knew, really knew, how to manage such an intrigue." Burridge humbly nodded in gratitude for the compliment. "When will you next see him?"

"He said that we will rendezvous three more times, I assume on our turns at picket duty."

Henry's mood seemed to sour at the edges. "I'm not, shall we say, comfortable with assumptions, Lieutenant."

Burridge knew he couldn't explain Mink to the captain. Henry was a businessman; how could he know the kind of trust that existed between himself and Mink? How, Burridge wondered, could Henry even understand the quality of man that Mink represented? "I say that because I believe their line is stretched quite thin, sir. They . . . he is often out on picket. He is also quite observant, sir. A brilliant man and . . ." Burridge stopped before publicly claiming Mink as a friend.

"And?"

"And he has shown himself quite adept at finding me, sir." Henry's silence signaled an acceptance of the situation, at least for now. If the captain had had enough, though, Burridge's curiosity about Mink had not. "Do you know anything about him?" he asked. "He seems a decent fellow."

Henry tugged the gloves he was already wearing more tightly onto his hands. "Let me warn you of something, if I may, Lieutenant. You are performing a tremendous service to your nation, a service that will most certainly not go unrewarded. I will see to that personally. But I hope you keep in mind"—Henry smoothed the two sides of his mustache—"that your contact is a spy." Burridge cocked his head. "Though he is ostensibly assisting our cause, you must not lose sight of the fact that he is still a leader in the Confederate army and continues to take actions that imperil our Union."

Burridge shook his head with a passionate vigor. "But surely not by choice."

"Whether or not it is by choice is immaterial. You've led me to believe that you're a student of such matters. Therefore, I've given you complete freedom to operate as you see fit, yet you must be vigilant. Your job is to receive information *from* him, not to exchange information *with* him. He might be forced into a position of revealing any information he might know by the Confederates. Have you thought of that?" Burridge recalled his disclosure of the Union positions and Mink's thoughts on slavery, but he shook his head again. *He* was the spy in this tent. He knew Mink as no one else in this army did. They were kindred spirits. He no longer envied Alder, Quigley, and the other rough sorts; instead Burridge had risen to enjoy the position that he saw now as his entitlement, a legacy of his intelligence and breeding.

Captain Henry pulled his attention back. "I trust you have revealed nothing and that he has not asked. Yet if any of the contact's actions are unusual, if any event takes place that you deem out of the ordinary considering the extraordinary circumstances, you must notify me."

So far, Burridge thought, every moment had been unusual, but how else was the job to be done? "Of course, sir."

"I'll take this information to those who must see it. Following your 'assumption,' you will know when your next assignation is to take place when you are sent out on picket duty." Henry opened the tent flap. "Thank you, Lieutenant."

Burridge headed back to the company, reviewing the hand. He decided that the game was too far along to do anything other than play it out.

THE
THIRD
MATCH

CHAPTER

11

B UNCHED IN TIGHT CIRCLES AROUND FIRES HEATING COFFEE and fat bacon, the men felt more at risk than they had in the field. General Sedgwick had been shot that morning by a sharpshooter near where they now sat, in a sparsely wooded section not too far behind the front lines. To the south was the patch of forest, ridden with sharpshooters, that they had marched through to reach battle and game. Today had been called a day of rest for all troops, and now with the general's death, it had become a day of mourning, especially here with the Sixth Corps. Soldiers wept openly as they wandered the back lines. An old private with a dozen dogs on ropes —all mutts, but well fed, their tails wagging—trotted up to a knot of downcast men and offered his charges out for temporary petting duty. The soldiers paid their dimes and spent ten minutes hugging the dogs and romping with them until the Dog Father—that was his name around camp—said time was up and moved them on.

Huey said, "I'd like me some a that."

Teddy, who was standing and practicing his swing with Newt's bat, said, "You already got that chicken Lou to play with."

Lyman snapped at him. "Sit down and shut the fuck up!"

"You think you got yourself a little chicken, too. Right? Right, Wes?"

"I said, 'Sit down and shut the fuck up.' "

"Easy, brother. Easy. You sound like that bastard booze merchant I had to take out for Callicot last year." With a great show of reluctance, Teddy took a spot around Willie's fire. Stives was there, underlining passages in the Bible with the stub of a pencil and remaining blessedly quiet, along with

Del Rio and Tice, who were discussing Grant's performance as lieutenant general so far. Newt sat by himself, writing a letter.

Louis, Karl, and Von Schenk were also considering the campaign so far on a rough map the last had carefully drawn on a piece of paper. The Prussian was the most vehement in arguing his position. "This is madness. This Grant will kill us all. We fight in the trees like animals! There is no strategy!"

Louis nodded his head. "Of course there is. Every other general tried to get past Lee, but Lee is too smart. His army *is* the Confederacy now. To win this war we must beat Lee's army. Grant is a bastard, but..."

Von Schenk held up the map and drove his finger on one point as though he were hammering in a nail. "Richmond! We must move on to Richmond!"

Horace Worm said, "Somebody told me Butler's down there now."

Tice hawked. "Then Jeff Davis don't got anything to worry about."

The whole company laughed.

Karl took a sip of coffee, then said, "Richmond falls, Lee falls. Lee stands, Richmond stands. Louis is right. We see Lee, we hit him." Karl watched a line of wagons full of ammunition and entrenching tools head east. Earlier he and Louis had figured the line went for a mile to either side, and a Connecticut boy had told them that the Rebs had a big bulge at their right flank, as if they were building a fortress. "We see him digging in over there..." He pointed into the eastern trees where the wagons were headed. "So we make like we hit him there, then..." He pointed to the west and the direction of Warren's corps on the other side of the Brock Road. "Then we flank him. That's what I think we do tomorrow."

Tice stood up, then squatted into a knee bend. "What I wanna know is when are we going back to the 14th?"

"I do not know. Ask Porridge."

Wes stopped practicing his eagle call to put in his two cents. "Maybe we're some kind of special force."

Teddy said, "Like the three of us back in Brooklyn, right, my friend?" He gave Wes a significant wink, meant for all to see.

Wes agreed with a limp "Yeah."

Willie said, "I heared Longstreet went up. That's a bit a good news."

Tice kept on his favorite subject. "Even so, it'd be nice to get back to the 14th."

Tice and Del Rio grumbled. Lyman had his own thoughts on strategy, but he sat back and watched the men talk, something simple they'd taken for granted until they'd spent a few days hearing little other than shells bursting. In itself, the talking meant little. Lyman knew that men will talk about themselves down to their last breath and they'll gasp for more air just to talk some more. Something had changed, though; they were listening to each other. Seeing the company talk this way—and about tactics yet!—gave Lyman some hope that they could still get out of these twelve days alive as long as their chatter did not include mention of the series.

Cawthorne joined in from where he'd been hovering. "I'm certain that Captain Henry and Lieutenant Stewart have our best interests in mind. Which is more than I can say of you so-called sportsmen." Just hearing Cawthorne's voice made Lyman tense; there were so many risks and so many ways they could be discovered.

Wes waved him away. "We gotta do for ourselves."

Tice said, "Well, I joined the 14th Brooklyn, not some detachment."

Lyman held up his hand. "Listen. Enough puking about goin' back to the 14th. We *are* the 14th. Wherever we go, we bring the 14th with us and wherever they are, they're takin' us. Even if we never get back to them, I'm goin' out as hard as I can these last twelve days because I'm proud of that regiment, and anybody else who wants can come with me."

He expected a cheer. Instead, Tice pulled the spoon out of his mouth. "That's pretty talk, Alder, but what the hell does it matter? Grant's just running us through the grinder. They don't want us at home 'cause they all turned fucking secesh. The captain won't even be seen with us, and we're pals with a bunch a Rebs I personally ain't interested in killing. I can't figure why I'm here anymore. So, Glory fucking Hallelujah."

Del Rio spat. "He's right. Lincoln will lose in November and the war will be over anyway and we go back to being friends with the South. I don't wanna have to kill any of those Rebels we playing. They seem OK by me."

Teddy said, "Hear, hear."

Lyman felt as though he'd been kicked in the gut. He couldn't refute Tice and Del Rio. Though he could feel the heat of the cause and call it

"Union," he couldn't fully recall its features, and, like Tice, Lyman wasn't thrilled about killing those boys. He wanted them on his side. But was it really worth it? The fleeting joys of a base ball match stacked up poorly against a prison sentence. As he began to slip down toward a sullen mood imagining what would happen to Victoria and Ernie if he was caught, he realized that they wouldn't be much worse off than they were now.

Louis shook his head. "Those good men are doing a job just like you, and you respect them as soldiers because of it. But that doesn't mean you stop fighting. We have come too far. We have killed too many men. We have given too many of our own. Quit now and all those dead mean nothing and you will stand with the mark of Cain on your head when the time comes."

Lyman turned his head. He'd never heard him talk this way. Louis bowed his head in what seemed embarrassment after his oration and took a long drink of coffee.

Wes screeched out a perfect eagle, breaking the brief silence. "So when are we gonna get the third match?"

Teddy said, "Yeah, I'm gonna masticate that ball like the Dutchman over there."

Lyman raised his can of coffee. "I say here's to Louis for that home run."

Horace said, "Here's a song for Louie. You old Republican." He broke into an impromptu riff on "The Red, White and Blue."

> Oh we're going back to our Brooklyn,
> but no one we know will meet us there.
> They'll be off selling bullets to the Rebels.
> I hope at least my wife and kids'll care.
> White feathers will fly from the porches
> alongside Dixie's Bonnie Blue flag.
> Though copperheads will tell us—vote McClellan,
> We'll stay loyal to the Red, White and Blue!

If they didn't know what or why they were all still fighting, at least, Lyman thought, they were fighting it together.

———

Newt had his travel desk opened and was wrestling with his own words.

Dearest Wife,
Please Forgive the <u>Passion</u> of what follows, for I have been <u>mightily</u> tossed
by the seas of Jonah and have been much Afraid and Silent <u>too long</u>.

Too alarming, Newt thought. He scratched them out.

I take pen in hand this afternoon to share with you some Observations
I have made regarding the nature of my Duty as a <u>fighting man</u> and a
<u>Christian</u>.

That sounded like an article in the *Southern Methodist Quarterly*. He
tried again.

In the wilder tides of war, we are sometimes faced with the Truest
Vision of ourselves emerging from the fog. For those Blessed to be <u>heroes</u>,

Before he could get any further, a thick hand snatched the paper off
his lap and an Irish brogue began reading aloud as though reciting from the
stage. Newt made no attempt to pull it away from Tiger, who, when he
reached the word "heroes," wadded up the letter and tossed it into the trees.
A roar of Union artillery just to their left shook the woods. The Rebels
answered immediately and a throbbing duel of cannons began.

Tiger stood over Newt and pointed down at him, yelling over the guns.
"Yer a worthless coward. Yer all worthless cowards. And *you*." He looked at
Fry as another volley of Union artillery rocked the trees. "Yer the worst of
the whole worthless lot because yer a fucking nigger lover and ye don't got
the balls to *say* it. That's the worst part—a man can say anything about
niggers and ye just sit there with yer thumb up yer arsehole." Tiger folded
his arms and leaned his face close into Newt's. "So I'd beat the shit out a
ye. So what? So ye bleed a little. I'd respect ye as a man and if I respected
ye as a man, I'd maybe listen to what ye had to say for oncet, though that's
not bloody likely, I'll tell ye." He let that hang for a second amid the cannon
thunder above them, then continued. "And ye think the Rebs think well of
ye for not shooting yer gun, eh?" His shame exposed, Newt reddened and

began to shake. "Oh, surprised, eh? Think I didn't notice? Well, if they knew, they'd say yer an arsehole and they'd thank ye for it."

Another pound of cannons kept Newt from responding, so Tiger went on. "Do ye think the world would end if you went up? Eh? Ye puppy!"

This was the all-out confrontation Newt had been fearing for years. It had come when he finally had sunk below the surface and now his toe desperately searched for the bottom. Would Tiger finally tell Lyman about Gettysburg? Newt faced Tiger head on, hoping to set him off the track. "And you're such a hero that you almost took some of our men into our own guns!"

Now Quigley began to shake. "I should've finished the job!"

"You're just as bad a soldier as you are a man. What would your wife think?"

"Don't ye mention Mary! I'll fucking kill ye!"

"She'd be ashamed to call you her husband."

"It's yer fucking niggers' fault! Don't ye see that? No one told me I'd be fighting for them! I left me wife and she died and it's their fucking fault! Some nigger got her money and her food and she's dead!"

"That's the bull, you fucking copperhead! What are *you* so afraid of? If you're so bloody great a housepainter, what have you got to be afraid of? And if you're not so bloody great, shut up! You Irishmen string them up from trees and kill them on the docks as soon as *you* have to work hard for a living. Why is that some African's fault? I don't shoot my gun. You have me there, Quigley. But the Rebs are laughing at *you*, too. You're all the same. You're afraid of yourselves, not the Africans. You march around talking about being 'white men,' but what you mean is, 'Well, I can't feed my family and all I want is booze, but I'm white!' And one day 'white' means Irish. Then it means Irish and German, but not Italians or Poles, please. And then it means the Poles, too, but no Portuguese. And in your whole life, none of you 'white men' has ever shown a fraction of the bravery any slave shows every day of the week. God forgive me, I may be a coward, but at least *I* know it."

Tiger and Newt stomped off in opposite directions to nurse their wounds. Teddy whooped and called it a whopper of a row, while the other men, men who'd known Tiger and Newt—slept with them, ate with them, fought with them for three years—shook their heads and recounted the argument in hushed tones. The artillery duel eased off and the usual sounds of men and mules and creaking wagons returned to the lines.

Lyman had stood up when the yelling started, ready to intervene if things took a rough turn, and now wondered if there was something he could have, or *should* have, done to prevent the argument. The ground gets shakier, he thought, the higher one goes.

To be fair to himself, he had been waiting for this to happen. Tiger's dislike for blacks and Newt's hesitance in battle, written off by Lyman as proof of Newt's gentler nature, were a dangerous combination among men. He'd been surprised it hadn't come earlier. It had been clear on the train ride down that Newt and Tiger stood on very different sides of the slavery issue, and the fact was, most men were closer to Pete's mind. There weren't too many abolitionists in the regiment; no one had made much of a fuss when they'd had to return three runaway slaves who'd come to them for protection while they were doing guard duty in Washington. Some of the boys were even glad, saying it proved that they were fighting for the Union, not the niggers. After the Proclamation came out, men in the 14th—Tiger among them—planned mass desertions because they wouldn't fight "the Negro's war."

To Lyman, such posturing was for fools. Every man in the regiment had grown up with slavery as the most discussed, fought over, killed over topic for two decades; he'd always believed that anyone who had joined up thinking that this war was about something else was a damned stupid man. As he stood on the cuff of the road watching the wagons roll by, Lyman recalled the political life during his thirty-odd years, and every one of import had revolved around slavery. From the end of the Mexican War and the Wilmot Proviso when he was all of fourteen until now, the United States had talked about little other than slavery and sectionalism. His father had used their kitchen to host a meeting of some other men with mild Barnburner leanings back in '48. Lyman remembered it well, as he'd smoked a pipe with Alder Senior's permission and gotten good and sick afterward.

Everyone thought the Compromise in '50 was the end, but he'd learned the meat business by wrapping chops in newspapers full of tales of tortured slaves and Southern hubris, and when Douglas ended whatever peace there'd been with the Kansas-Nebraska Act in '54, the cards started to fall.

Lyman had gone to a rally with Danny that spring. Victoria hadn't wanted him to go because the new baby had a cough, but he'd gone anyway. Three years later was the *Dred Scott* case, and by then it was becoming hard to remember that North and South had ever been one country since Lyman had spent his life watching them come apart. The blood flowed in Kansas as Lyman's mother slowly died of a brain fever, and Victoria made Ernie practice his reading on the daily reports of the Lecompton situation. Alder Senior bought a new grinder around then. Victoria lost the second baby the next spring, and she wasn't able to get out of bed for three months. All she did was read Mrs. Stowe and *Godey's Lady's Book* and the Book of Common Prayer. Lyman pictured the way she used to laugh before those weeks, her eyes disappearing between cheeks and eyebrows. The night he heard about John Brown he was buying drinks at Piggy's off the first bet he'd ever won in his life—ten dollars on an Irish boy Tiger knew.

Every one of those moments had to do with slaves; invisible black faces that explained the progress of this country with their mute suffering. But like most men in the Union army, Lyman hadn't signed up to free them. On that April day that he had gotten in line with Danny and Tiger, dragging his new friend Newt along, to join Henry's company, he'd considered the real point of the war the rights of the states versus those of the federal government; an abstract argument at the core of this nation that needed an issue to embody all its complexities, and slavery was right there to turn a theory into something that men died to save and died to end. If the slaves had never been brought over from Africa, he'd thought, and no man or woman had ever felt the weight of chains on their wrists, something else would have caused this crisis. As it stood that first day, Lyman had believed that freeing the slaves would be a troublesome but necessary result of the final settlement.

Aside from the exchanges he'd had about slavery over pints of beer for the last fifteen years, though, Lyman hadn't thought too much about blacks. The real lives of slaves rarely entered those discussions, and if a man mentioned the ugly details, he was clumped with Phillips, Garrison, and the worst of the abolitionists, who most of his fellow drinkers said started this whole thing. In Brooklyn, the slaves who had been freed in the '30s had built their little villages in Carrville and Weeksville and mostly stayed down there. Some worked at the Lorillard and Watson tobacco factories, and there was always Happy Jack Camble pushing his cart around but, for the most part, Brooklyn, for all of the thousands streaming in to hear Henry Ward Beecher, had never been a pleasant place for blacks to live, and since the riots it was even less so.

Lyman went back to the fire and sat down. The fight had left the men quiet again, and he decided that was probably best. He took out his greasy handkerchief and started to shine up the buttons on his jacket. He asked himself if he had ever really spoken with a Negro before he joined up, and the answer was no. He'd never had to until the thousands of contrabands attached themselves to the army. The first time he came up close to them was at Cattlett's Station in '62—one of the few times they saw any slaves. He'd expected them all to be a certain way; all angry or grateful or all lazy bastards, but they were like any other group of people. There were old folks singing; angry, sullen young men and others happy to be free; fat women and thin women and hundreds of children behaving every possible way people could behave. There were people he could be friends with and people he could hate. Lyman had felt stupid, and still did, that he had ever thought that it would be any different. At Cattlett's slavery took on a disfigured human face, clambering over the fence rails, crying in joy for the sight of freedom and cheering these men who claimed not to care. Though it may have been used as a political tool for both sides of the issue, slavery had shown itself, to Lyman at least, heartily deserving of its end.

Lyman wondered if other men had been affected the same way. In Fredericksburg, around the same time, the 14th's favorite man in town had been a member of General Augur's staff—Major Halstead—famous for his efforts to bring in slaves and send them North to freedom. The sympathy and admiration many men had for him balanced some of the hate-mongering that had affected the regiment. Though there'd been a fight, the 14th had held together after the Proclamation. Lyman remembered the stricken looks on the faces of those three slaves they'd sent back—furious, frightened faces that resembled many he'd seen on battlefields these three years. Those blacks had been fighting a war of their own or, he considered, the same war on a different front. He could only hope the 14th had done enough to help them win.

Lyman shined up the *14* on his cap.

––––––––

Another hot night fell, pasting wool trousers to legs. Men scratched feverishly at their whiskers, now at the crucial and itchy moment when they became beards. Cards were shuffled. Horace tried to get Newt interested in a song, and Karl threatened to kill Wes if he did his eagle screech one more time. Burridge read a book at his own fire, and Stives continued to make notes in his Bible, looking up with his eyes closed every once in a while, as if memorizing new lines.

Returning from the bushes, a little disappointed that he still had the quickstep when Pitt appeared to have finished with his and resolved not to be abandoned at some death-house camp hospital, Slipper Feeney got turned around. He was sure that his knapsack and blanket were nearby on the left, but now that he was standing where he thought his belongings were, it didn't look right. The fire had sunk low and no one had put another log in, so he also couldn't tell if that snoring hulk next to the empty blanket was Teddy Finn. Someone hurried by; Slipper thought it was Cawthorne, but who could tell? He bent over and picked up the sack to check if it was his.

As he opened it, a German voice bellowed from the trees, apparently on the same kind of journey Slipper had just been. "Put that down, you son of bitch Feeney!"

Slipper had never been caught filching, so he certainly wasn't about to be caught now that he was innocent. He scooted off into the dark and Karl called after him. "If anything is missing, you are dead man!"

Pete held the locket close to his face so he could look at her, wearing the dress she'd worn the day he first saw her at Easter Sunday Mass. Her black hair had given meaning to the white that filled the church; as her hair shone forth with the glory of this world, it made the lilies and the vestments and the altar truly of another. She was proof of God on earth.

He stared harder at her likeness. Her lips were rose and eyes as green as a dewy field in Cork. He'd told her that many times and every time she'd kissed him. To come home sweated and speckled with paint after a day in the sun and see her smile was to lie back into a pool of fresh water. She'd kept some innocence about her for all the death she'd seen, still wanted his protection, was surprised by simple things. A trembling began in Tiger's hands and he could feel the pressure behind his eyes. He imagined the gauzy wrapping that a drink or two would give him; she would understand, given what had happened.

And what *had* happened? That was the worst part. All Tiger knew was that she had died of a choler, hungry and pregnant in their bed. His soldier's pay hadn't been enough. The Dillons above had looked in often and had even posted him once to let him know of her illness, but the letter bearing the news of her passing did not say if she had wept, if she'd been in pain, if she had found peace or had wrestled some with death before she'd gone. Had she asked for him? Had she forgiven him for abandoning her? Abandoning her to the one fate they'd both felt sure they'd escaped?

He'd tried to leave. He'd begged and swore and foamed; he'd even deserted once, but he'd known the provost guard who'd caught him. Instead of feeding his wife and having a son, he was fighting for niggers. Lincoln should have worried about Mary before he let the niggers loose. This wasn't his army anymore. And it wasn't his country. His hands were shaking, desperate for whiskey. The locket slipped out. He dug his fingers into the earth.

———————

Teddy woke up with a pecker as stiff as the rod of his musket. The young day and Finn were both still less than fully awake; the light off in the east hadn't pushed away the four A.M. dark, and Teddy's first conscious thought was to continue along the dream he'd been having. The fat girl in Caleb's photograph had just bent over the arm of the couch and Teddy had his trousers down over his ankles. What followed would demand more than just thought.

He opened his eyes a crack, enough to see if anyone else was awake. A wagon rolled by, clanking cans off its side, and a few straggling soldiers shuffled past in the dark. A soft, idle snore merged with the evening's last crickets. That was it. All was quiet. He checked left, then pretended to shift in his sleep and checked right. Everyone was still asleep.

Teddy reached under the blanket and pushed his trousers down over his rear, then he licked the palm of his hand. He decided to start from the beginning. It had been such a long time that he wanted it to be worth the risk. He closed his eyes and floated back into the soft-edged musky world he'd been torn from. He's having a beer at Kit's—no, she'd never be there. Pat's Hell was more like it. He's having a beer at Pat's Hell and she comes in with that bastard Gill from the Heights. Her tits are pushing out of the top of her dress and her feet look tiny in her boots. All the while she's looking at him and licking her lips like a cat with milk on its whiskers. Teddy licked his palm again. Gill doesn't like her looking at him so the bastard gets up and Teddy just decks him. He grabs Sally's hand and takes her up the stairs to one of the rooms and she's still licking her lips. They get inside and right off have a big kiss with her legs wrapped around his knee and he can feel her rubbing herself up and down...

Suddenly Teddy's balls started to itch. The scene began to fade away as he scratched, and it faded further away as he chased the itch into his hair. One hand wasn't enough. He figured he needed a wash soon. Teddy stuck the other one down and now he had both hands feverishly scratching at his crotch, but to no avail. Then something skittered across his hand and his hands began to itch.

He pulled them out. Little black dots scampered in his palms, angry to have been roused from their warm nests. Shaking, Teddy took a close look and saw tiny legs and jaws, some swollen with what could only be his blood. His mouth dropped open—he was a clean man, one who'd always made an effort, and now bugs were sucking on his jewels.

Teddy kicked off his blanket and with his pants around his knees went hopping off into the forest to a panicked whisper of "Oh fuck! Oh fuck! Oh fuck!"

Del Rio sniggered and said to anyone else awake, "You theenk hees pecker was gone?"

Lyman said, "Shit, I wish I still felt like doing that."

The morning brought better news for the company. Though heavy skirmishing was going on along the entire front and artillery duels sent thick clouds of smoke rising into the hazy skies, Burridge told the men that they were being held in reserve here with General Smith's brigade and that he expected no action. Eleven days remained, and at least one of them seemed to be safe. Willie went to work at sewing up tears and ripped seams of jackets and pants. Long overdue letters were written to family and friends, and the appearance of Clipper Mike, a sharp-faced black Irishman from the 9th Massachusetts, gave those who wanted a chance for a trim and a shave. The greatest difficulty on such a day of leisure was restraining the impulse to talk about the matches. Instead, they played catch and surreptitiously practiced, returning the ball to Lyman with some reverence when unused. Otherwise the day was theirs.

Throughout the afternoon, the sounds of battle rolled in from the right side of the line. On this windless day, another hot, dry summer's day, the smoke formed false clouds that tempted even those who'd marched through too much mud into wishing for a storm.

A thin white candle stood in a mess plate, surrounded by Lyman and the three b'hoys. Bare-legged, each man worked his fingers through the red wool trousers lying in his lap, Wes furrowing his brow in desperate concentration.

"You're never gonna get fully rid of all of them," said Lyman, "but at least picking at them makes you feel better. The less on your balls, the better you feel. They like the seams." He nabbed a louse out of the fabric. "When you get 'em, just pop 'em in the fire." A quick sizzle and it was gone. "That's it."

Wes looked distraught. "That's it? I been doing that all day."

"So you're a natural."

"There's nothing else we can do?"

"Nope. Anybody can kill a man, but to have lice, too—now that takes a soldier." He slapped Wesley's arm. "I guess you three are now full-blown lousy sons a bitches like the rest of us." Lyman waved over at Horace. "Mr. Worm, the bug song, if you please."

Horace warned Pindar to keep an eye on Felix Cawthorne, who was hovering close to his bag. Turning his attention to his audience, he bowed, then lit into song, to the tune of "The Bonnie Blue Flag":

A thousand Rebel fighters invaded my blue shirt,
They're just like any butternut—they're mean and they eat dirt.
I didn't mind them there that much until this morning fair,
When I reached up beneath my cap and found 'em in my hair.

The bugs! The bugs! These blasted Rebel bugs!
I haven't worn a short in years that wasn't hot with bugs.

The lice sure like to bite you; mosquitoes suck you dry.
Weevils in the hardtack make it taste like mincemeat pie.
The captain didn't tell me, when he signed up my mug,
That I'd be fightin' Bobby Lee and his old pal Marse Bug.

Wes set to the task at hand with a queasy smile, but it was a smile, nonetheless, and it soon eased into the smile he'd had after hitting that home run in the first match. He felt free here. Brooklyn had been small boys playing deadly games, forcing each other to heights of murderous, meaningless fun that left their lives as sad as ever. Here he was tested, and for a cause, even if he wasn't entirely sure what that cause was, or whether he was for it. He saw his company—*his* company—all dressed in their uniforms. Strong men laughing and proving things to each other without knives or fists. Wes ran his finger along the split seams of his jacket. He felt like some schoolboy who'd just shit his trousers; the way he'd felt the day the firemen had pulled him out of the alley and brought him over to Teddy. He squeezed a louse. "What's with these red pants, anyways? Are we supposed to be some kind of Zouaves like them turban boys?"

Lyman stopped, and all the veterans stopped their grooming, as well. "We ain't no goddamned Zouaves. These are special from France." His diction became slow and precise, as if he were reading a sign from a long distance. "*Chasseur à pied*. Light infantry, see? City of Brooklyn gave 'em to us—don't you forget it."

A roar of laughter burst from three men standing close to Lyman in an unusual group—Burridge, Tiger, and the heretofore reticent Pindar Worm. Lyman wondered what they could be up to as his fingers scrabbled after a retreating bug until it was finally cornered near a button. Lyman held up the louse in triumph. "You gotta remember with this getup that people see you. You botch up or get caught doing something, everybody knows where you're from and we all look bad." He stared at Feeney, then flicked the louse into the flame. Then he gave a quick glance to Burridge and Tiger, who was broadly imitating Newt's swing and braying. "We don't like that. On the other hand, anything good, we all get a piece of it." He pointed at

Wesley's pants. "Those red trousers make us special. You gotta take care of 'em, not just pick the nits out." Something silver flashed between Burridge and Tiger. Lyman squinted, but he couldn't make out what it was. A bayonet?

Wes poked his finger through the hole in his jacket. "What was the hottest scrap you seen?"

The other men sat silently, picturing their dead friends and all the moments of terror and mourning they'd shared these three years. Lyman realized that Burridge had just handed Tiger a flask. He fixed his eyes on the red field of wool in his lap.

Teddy rolled his eyes and made his voice high. "Tell me a story, Daddy."

"Fuck you."

Finn glared at Pitt, who was cowed by the look.

Willie said, "Go ahead. Tell 'em."

Wesley's rapt expression made Lyman expansive, despite just seeing Tiger preparing to break his pledge. He wished he had tales of his own heroism, the kind old soldiers spun out of remembered cannon smoke. But there were just facts and the responsibility of telling them. As they prepared to leave so many dead behind in the Southern fields, the 14th's fiery years were becoming history and an album of missing faces. There was Billy Egolf, playing with his dog Leo; Alfred Posen cracking open oysters with the butt of his musket; Beaver Peter Ulster dancing a jig the day before Gettysburg, the last day he'd ever walk; Danny Anson's head exploding. The war Lyman would carry home had too many stories for entertainment on a snowy evening. He could never convey the goodness of the men he'd fought with, their bad jokes and honesty and courage; not to someone who'd remained safe and untouched in a Brooklyn parlor.

Lyman hauled himself up and tugged his pants back on. "Well, it would have to be Gettysburg."

Gettysburg was his story; his and Tiger's and Newt's. It was the one thing the three of them never discussed, the thing that they would always hold together. He looked for Tiger but he and Burridge were gone. Lyman took off his cap, felt the hole Clipper Mike had left in his hair, then lightly ran his finger over the cut in his forehead. The whole circle now looked up at Lyman. "The first thing you gotta know is we walked 239 miles to get there. The second thing is, we saved that first day. See, we was up early, some of the first boys in down by the Lutheran Seminary." He scraped a map in the dust with his toe and recounted the positions of all engaged troops that hot July morning. Then he told the story all the veterans were preparing to tell when they got home: how they'd stepped in at the railroad cut and captured Davis's entire Mississippi regiment. "What a goddamn ruckus that was. All our boys are shooting or clubbing Rebs with their muskets. Whatever it took." The moments returned; legs spread and tensed, arms swinging, he could feel in his body that other day. "I'm next to Newt."

He reached down and dragged up Fry, who'd been sitting outside of the circle with his face in his hands. Newt stared at the ground. "We were all together, see. I get off two shots and then this big son of a bitch comes straight at me, bayonet sticking out, and he aims right at my head." Newt closed his eyes. "I hear Newt take him out, but the Reb still got off his shot and the minié plugs me right in the shoulder."

Lyman twitched as though hit again.

"So now I'm laying there on the ground, bleeding like a pig, and there's Tiger and Newt again, standing over me. Tiger wraps something around my shoulder. What the hell was that, Newt?"

Newt shrugged and shook his head, not saying a word.

"Well, the two of them try to sop up the bleeding, and everything after that is blurry because that bastard minié felt like someone had stuck their hand into my shoulder and just starting mashing things around. That was Gettysburg for me.

"The other boys here had a rougher go. Ask 'em." There was a quiet moment before he spoke again. "We should have ended it right then. Meade should've gone right after 'em. Would've been done without all this ..." Lyman wondered for a second if Micah had been there, too, wondered if the world would have changed quite as much if the war had ended before Grant had the job, while men still had faces. He fixed Wes in his gaze. "If you're looking for things to fight for, son, you don't have to look any farther than this circle of men and that uniform."

Wesley nodded, fingering the tear in his jacket.

For the thousandth time, Newt watched the same scene unfold. The Rebs come crashing into them; more than he ever imagined existed. The smoke and the flames and the noise confuse him, and he's shaking like a newborn puppy as the bullets grind through them, and suddenly one Reb is standing right in front of them, aiming at Lyman. Newt hadn't fired at the attacker, like Lyman had said. He'd frozen, and Tiger had seen Newt freeze. He was the one who'd shot the Reb. Newt had shot his gun straight into the air. Lyman was writhing on the ground and Tiger had to tear open Newt's blanket and pack it on the wound as Newt crouched low and prayed not to be hit.

Newt was afraid to touch him, afraid to be infected with death. Tiger had done everything, which included keeping his mouth shut whenever Lyman mentioned Gettysburg. And why did he, Newt wondered. Why hadn't he ever told Lyman the truth? The answer came whenever Newt admitted to himself that in Tiger's shoes he would've set the record straight right off. No matter if it meant telling Lyman that his dear friend had let him be shot, had been ready to leave him bleeding on the Pennsylvania grass. Newt began a letter to Mrs. Fry, but he found he had nothing to say.

CHAPTER
12

WHEN CALLED TO BE SO, LINDEN STEWART WAS EX-
tremely entertaining. He was well-read, and his countless an-
ecdotes about the rich and the famous combined his talent
for telling a story with a sly sense of humor. His face—usually
a pallid, waxy mask covered in a light sheen of sweat that
made it seem as if it were melting—would lose its indolent
expression of disdain at such times and his eyes would show
an engaging spark. Linden Stewart could perform with brilliance and verve,
if he chose to. He was imaginative and had the mind of a true strategist;
his reputation as a lawyer was well established. Any endeavor that demanded
a public face could be entrusted with this increasingly important figure within
Brooklyn's legal circles. Yet none of these were the reasons that Schuyler
Henry had formed such a dependence on the man now sprawled across a
cot greedily slurping down the contents of a can of smoked oysters.

Those who worked with or, more to the point, under him knew his
greatest talent was being a sneak. He padded about the camp at night,
listening in the shadows for any snippet of conversation that could be reported back to Captain Henry. If no one was looking, he felt free to examine
the belongings of a soldier and even read his letters, though he did stop
himself short of theft. He eagerly performed any distasteful duty which
Henry lacked the courage or will to perform. He engaged men in friendly
conversation and drew out information that would be helpful to him and
Henry, no matter the harm to the naive source. He was brutal to subordinates, unctuous to superiors, and consumed by an insatiable hunger for

power. He was also a tremendous coward. Captain Henry found these the most impressive and most useful aspects of Linden Stewart.

As he waited for Henry to return to his tent, Stewart opened another can of oysters. Stewart's wife, Phyllis, sent monthly crates of such treats to her husband, though he considered it more as a fulfillment of marital obligations than a sign of care. A heavy cannonade began on the right and for a moment Stewart held a forkful in midair, listening to the distant throb of another attack he would not see. Many men would feel guilt at such a thought, but Stewart simply felt that he served in another fashion. He had helped to add laurels to Henry's name and to his own with the kind of work that one had to be born to—pulling wires, twisting arms, and the like. Any fool could soldier. Stewart swallowed the oysters and considered his brother Miles, rotting in his grave at Gettysburg. The men may still have admired him, but Stewart preferred an intact body to the respect of a rabble of hod carriers and meat cutters.

He tilted his head back and took the remaining half of a can of oysters into his mouth. He chomped slowly, breathing through his nose, awash in the briny smell, happy at the thought of resuming his law practice and taking the next strides down his road to the governor's office. On the other hand, he did not look forward to resuming his life with Phyllis, a sour woman whose early coltish good looks had turned horsey. Her hair had shaded white before he had left, and her letters were now endless screeds on her troubles, her sacrifices, her late nights in service to the Temperance Group, the Sanitary Commission, and various other relief societies. The daughter of a minister, Phyllis sadly had none of the spit that those ladies sometimes had; instead, she shared her father's barren heart. Those who knew the Stewarts considered them exceptionally well met, and Linden had to agree that they had formed an efficient partnership based on the furtherance of his career. He swallowed, then chased the oysters with a glass of milk. In that respect she had performed well and he had no complaints, but as a wife, she was a harridan of the worst sort, unwilling to act as such yet also unable to accept an arrangement that would satisfy his needs and save her the shame.

The snap of Henry's tent flap and a crisp order given to Pompey reminded Stewart of a nagging worry. Lately the business between Burridge and Henry had increased, and Cawthorne had made some quite bizarre references to fraternization between the company and the Rebels. Though he believed nothing the repellent play actor had to say, the men *were* behaving in an odd manner. The *Richmond Examiner* he had confiscated could easily have been found on the field, so that was no proof. He'd charged Cawthorne to scare up some kind of evidence that would help him clear the issue, but he had little faith in the play actor's abilities. What bothered Stewart the most was not the possibility that the men were fraternizing; it was the chance that something was going on between Henry and Burridge that he had nothing to do with. So far Burridge had parried his attempts to learn anything. Now it was Henry's turn.

Stewart ambled into Henry's tent, hands in pockets, as though he had just been strolling by. Accustomed to Stewart's unannounced entries, Henry didn't bother to welcome him. The number of unsavory secrets shared by the two men made formality unnecessary. "So how was your interview with Fowler?"

"The plan, such as it is, has been made. The right side went in an hour ago, including the 14th, to soften up the Rebel front. No one expects much from that besides control of the rifle pits. The real game will come later at four. Warren will go full guns on the right, as will Crawford. At five Mott will go, and then at six they're letting Upton try his scheme on one of the vulnerable spots we've found in the Rebel bulge."

Stewart turned up his nose at the mention of Emory Upton. "Upton's a boy. I'm shocked that they're listening to him. I've heard some less than complimentary things regarding him, you know."

Henry shrugged. "Only Grant could love the idea of sending two columns of uncapped men straight into one spot." They exchanged sneers. Stewart plopped into Henry's chair and draped his arms over the back, letting his stomach stick out. Henry called out to Pompey for some tea and shuffled some papers on his desk, not wholly engaging in the conversation.

Stewart got to his purpose. "Let me ask you something. What do you think of Burridge's recent performance?"

The captain paused for a beat, then shuffled more papers. "Why do you ask?"

"I've had reports that his men are out of control and that he's making little effort to remedy the situation." He folded his arms and let his fingers rest on his red lieutenant's bars.

"You know as well as I do that Burridge has never had full control of them," Henry said stiffly. "I would be very surprised if it was anything other than the usual squabbles. Who reported this to you?"

"Sergeant Cawthorne. He mentions extensive fraternization with Rebel troops. I've seen some suspicious behavior myself that lends the accusation some credence. They have tobacco, for one. I also confiscated a Richmond paper."

Henry drummed his gloved fingers on the desk, a very nervous sound to Stewart's ears. "Considering Burridge made Cawthorne sergeant, I'm surprised he's making this report. He's an extreme fellow, this Cawthorne. Certainly not the most reliable. Don't forget he was returned to ranks, Linden. It would clearly be in his interest if Burridge was to be taken off the line."

Stewart held up his hands. Usually Henry was as eager to do in a man as he was. "I simply mention it for your information. If you're not concerned..."

"No, no. Of course I'm concerned, but in this case I would need more than Cawthorne's word. I would need physical proof. At the end of the day, I trust Burridge much more than a play actor turned soldier." He turned to the lieutenant. "Don't you?"

Stewart caught the sincerity of Henry's final question and let the sweet power of Henry's dependence wash over him. "Schuyler, I only hope we can." Pompey entered with the tea tray. "Oh, is it that time already?" Unasked, Stewart popped a small scone into his mouth and readied another. Hunger did not distract him from his real concern, though. Something big was afoot.

———

The trees stood between the men and the battle like the backdrop of a stage. In support, they waited patiently, unable to see the action but listening intently for a cue as materials and men rushed back and forth. Warren's attack at four had been a brisk taste of what was to follow and sure to whet the appetite of any bloodthirsty man, with cannons on both sides and the shrieks of thousands running into fire. At five Mott went in for a brief skirmish. He was repelled, but soon the guns were back, farther to the company's left. The men exchanged opinions as to whether this was building to a climax or just the loud finish of a less than successful attack.

And then a silence. Shoulders shrugged and heads inclined, trying to hear more. Many felt the battle was finished. It was ten after six. Orders came for the company to drop packs and move forward toward the front. In a minute they were in the trees, drawing nearer to the battle, listening for the fight that seemed to have ended. A heavy rustle, the sound of thousands of marching men, came from the far left until that rustle exploded into a jolt of screams and gunfire. Cannons opened fire over the entire line and the pause ended.

After twenty minutes or so, the men were sent back to their place and the battle continued without them. Colonel Smith called them forward again at seven to reinforce another attack on the left, and again Company L could only hear it reach a crescendo. Percussive cannons drove the action while a smooth and constant flow of rifles sounded almost mellow in the golden tones of evening, and, piercing all, the screams and cries for comfort. A fire began in the dry clearings and forest underbrush, and once again the men were ordered back, the attacks ending all as failures. Darkness came and the battle was closed. Only the single cannon or blare of musket cut the night, now passing to the slow requiem dirge of dying voices calling out from the black.

Wes and Teddy struck out first on the ten-minute walk through the trees, but they soon lost contact and Wes found himself back at an empty camp, glad he was alone. A couple weeks, hell, a couple days ago he'd set his watch by Teddy and Slipper, but now he hoped they would simply fade into the fog of war. Their presence reminded him too much of the alleyways and sewers they had seen together, the crimes committed, and he could not be generous when a better life appeared possible. Boyish arrogance, impor-tant in the streets but worthless in a war, separated them from this group of men otherwise bound by the frailties they had all seen in themselves and the high standards expected. Wes felt the tear in his jacket like a wound. He shouldn't have tossed his housewife.

As he was about to light a fire, Wes realized again that he was sur-rounded by unguarded knapsacks. He had at least two minutes until Teddy burst in; time enough to rob the queen of England blind. Limbering his fingers, Wes dashed to a well-kept knapsack and stuck his hand in, confident that Lyman would understand this final crime.

The fires were lit and coffee boiled. Karl had stowed his knife in his knapsack and now that the battle was over, he wanted to do some carving since they were not due on burial detail until later in the night. He rooted through his pack and came up with his knife, but he had the sense that something was different. He paused for a moment, then emptied his pack, where a quick scan confirmed his suspicions: Something *was* missing. His housewife was gone and there was only one suspect.

Karl went to Feeney, who was lying on his back scratching, and picked him up by the collar. "I told you if anything missing I kill you! I warned you!" He began shaking Slipper as a prelude to throwing him down and beating the life out of him.

Slipper swore at the German, but when his words had no effect, he switched to the whimpering he had employed to little effect during the battle a few nights ago. Never firmly muscled, Slipper's limbs hung down and shook now as though unboned. Teddy stood up. Before he laid into the German, he hesitated and gave him an opportunity to drop Feeney. "I don't wanna have to pugilize ye, Dutchman. Put 'em down. He didn't hook nothing a yours."

"You know nothing about this. I saw him taking from me last night."

"Feeney wouldn't filch from one of his boys."

Karl stopped shaking Slipper and now just held him in midair. "One of his boys? You making joke, *ja?*"

"No, you're one of the boys. We'll tell the fellas in the Party to take ye under custody, ye know? Take care a ye. Set ye up with a situation. Any pal of mine is OK with the Party and ye can bank that, Dutchman. I'm gonna be mayor, remember?"

Karl dropped Slipper, who quickly scrabbled off to safety. He had four inches on Finn, and as he stared down at the stocky Irishman, he made the short distance seem long and icy. "You are stupid."

Teddy hadn't really wanted a confrontation here, but he was ready for it. He balled up his fists and began working his jaw. "Oh yeah?"

"*Ja.* No one wants to tell you one thing."

"Yeah? What's that?"

Karl smiled. "Democrats sent you here to be killed." His smile dimmed with pity. "You see that? They don't want you come back."

"That's bullshit, ye Dutch bastard! I sup wit Boss McLaughlin and the Front Street Boys all the time and I know Tweed, to boot. They hear about my exploitations out here an' I'll be on the Mutuals *and* running Brooklyn. I'll be the ball-playin' man a the people, ya fuckin' hunky carpenter!"

"If I lie, why they not just give you job, eh? Why Democrats have you go to war they try to stop?"

Teddy was steaming, but starting to get confused because it made some sense. The Party boys hadn't asked him to do much after the brawl in the Eastern District and he'd wondered about their sudden coldness. The other men in the company wouldn't look at him; they showed their agreement with the German by silently puffing on pipes, writing their letters by firelight, or napping. After another day of Confederate repulses, no one had much of a taste for this intramural scrap. Teddy snapped, "You're stuffed full a shit, Dutchman," but the vigor of his protests waned. Suddenly he understood the deceptive look on McLaughlin's face when the boss had told him the plan. He'd known that something was up, but he didn't want to question the one group of people he could consider his family.

"You talk too much. You tell secrets."

Teddy mustered a few weak "Bullshit"s, then turned away. Karl didn't go after him. The small fire Teddy had built shot off a spray of sparks and wheezed. A thin stream of smoke rapidly guttered. Maybe it was the dirty truth: He was simply another expendable thug pulled out of the slums of Williamsburg to serve the Democrats' messy needs. He broke noses and limbs, even went further when he had to, but the reality was that they never consulted him about anything, never pretended to ask his opinion. When they called, he came and they'd toss the scrap of a promise if he stayed around long enough drooling at the crystal decanters full of brandy and their gold watches.

Karl pointed at Slipper. "I give you one day. If housewife not back, I take care you good. *Und* no party boys save you."

In a small and plaintive voice, Slipper said to no one in particular, "Honest. I didn't take nothing."

The Worms checked their sacks; each still had a score sheet. They glared at Cawthorne, who merely shrugged his shoulders.

———

When the messenger came, Burridge was glad for an excuse to put down Aurelius. The order was for picket duty tomorrow morning. Burridge leaned back against his pack and lightly pressed his fingertips together, congratulating himself. Getting what you want, Burridge reflected, was the true sign of manhood.

Burridge recalled that afternoon's conversation with Tiger. He had expected difficulty at first and had received it; he had never believed that the moment they'd shared frightening Cawthorne days earlier had cemented a friendship. Tiger had been his usual insolent self, lobbing an allegedly accidental glob of spit onto his shoe by way of greeting. The lieutenant had pulled the top few inches of his flask out of his pocket and gestured that it was Tiger's for the taking. At first the Irishman gave him a suspicious sneer, which hardened to anger at the insult. But Burridge had faced him down. Tiger's eyes had remained focused on the flask for a long time until they finally melted. It was embarrassing how easily the Irishman had not only surrendered but truly offered himself up, laughing at his jokes and playing the fool to guarantee his reward. Burridge had walked through enough captured Rebel towns to know that it was all a performance, yet he considered it well worth the price of a flask to have Tiger Quigley dancing to his tune. It was a more exquisite punishment than any other he'd imagined for him. He was only sorry he hadn't thought of it earlier.

His accomplishment here, though, only served a larger goal. He had pulled the conversation toward what the Irishman thought of the Rebs, as if he hadn't known, but he had been surprised at just how much Quigley hated them. The drunkard had appeared quite willing to make these matches something other than sporting contests. All the lieutenant would have to do tomorrow was say the word and Quigley would unknowingly apply his considerable strength to the greater efforts involved in winning the war. It was remarkable to Burridge how easily Quigley had come to his side. Every man has a price, he thought sadly.

Burridge opened Aurelius again. He was on Book Three.

Never value anything as profitable to thyself which shall compel thee to break thy promise, to lose thy self-respect, to hate any man, to suspect, to curse, to act the hypocrite, to desire anything which needs walls and curtains. . . .

The lieutenant felt a slight jab. He was playing with these men's minds and lives and hopes. They thought these matches were spontaneous, a deadly risk they were willing to take, yet they took place only to serve his needs and the needs of the Union. Then Burridge pictured Quigley with a mouthful of whiskey and salt pork, heard a field full of men laughing at him after his fall at the plate, and his mind cleared of sentiment. In the end, he decided, they were animals. Their greatest cares were eating and finding a warm place to relieve themselves, and they were lucky to be deceived in such a pleasant way. He took a deep breath and relaxed, remembering the handsome reward waiting for him once this cruel war was over.

————

The dead were pulled from the closest edges of the Union lines, as details dug graves under the midnight stars. Smoky campfires still burned to light the rapid work of interment and the countless sad and filthy faces singing choruses of "Home, Sweet Home." Today's standoff had done little to buoy the spirits of Union men, whose eagerness to press forward a few days ago had given way to familiar doubts about their officers' competence and the possibility of breaking through the Rebels. A fresh gust of failure's sour scent wafted over the Union lines, the scent of friends rotting in the heat.

Across the way, the Rebs had fires of their own and sang the same songs. Carried on the lighter air of night, "Nearer My God to Thee" floated over the field, played by a Confederate band. Movement stopped on both sides as men listened. When the song was finished, a Union band responded with the "Dead March" from *Saul.* With sadness for the dead of both sides established, the Rebels let a minute pass, then raised the ante with a chorus of "The Bonnie Blue Flag," which the Rebel troops topped with a hearty yell in case the Yankees had forgotten them. A few seconds of quiet passed.

The Union boys wondered if their musical defenders had surrendered after only one tune, rebuffed as they had been by the Confederates, but the stately notes of the "Star-Spangled Banner" finally rolled through the night in reply and the Yankee cheering more than equaled that of the Rebs. The Confederates came back with a sweet and gentle version of "Home, Sweet Home" that hung in the air as a blanket pulled over all the men; it was a mother's touch, a wife's caress, a good-night kiss from a child. Once the last notes flickered out like the final twinkles of a large and sparkling firework, a massive cheer went up from North and South and briefly united both armies in the one urge every man among them shared.

CHAPTER
13

—

T HIS WAS WHERE HE BELONGED. HE SHOULD BE DEAD, LIKE this one. Even at two A.M. Newt could see the maggots wriggling in the flesh, clumping together in some places like chunks of fat and streaking other spots so the human meat looked like a well-aged steak. Up until now he had successfully avoided burial duty through a long series of conveniently timed illnesses and errands, but there were no longer enough men in the company to disguise his unwillingness to face the dead. As did most of the others, he had a handkerchief tied over his mouth and nose to screen the fetid air and keep the flies out. He wished he could pull it over his eyes and return to a rest more final than the nap from which he'd just been roused.

Usually waking chilled and hungry on hard ground was enough to make Newt forget any glum thoughts he'd had before falling asleep, but not tonight. When he had opened his eyes, it was still dark. Out in the black, the dead had called and the time had finally come to answer them. He was not meant to be immortal; in fact, circling this rotting corpse, he felt himself a worthless husk, lucky to be around this long, whose only purpose was to lay across the altar of Abraham.

Del Rio was down at the feet of this body, once a sergeant from Massachusetts. A shell had torn much of his left side apart and now it appeared as if that whole area of his body was covered in a fine, shiny mail. Newt tried to avoid looking into the body's empty eyes. Del Rio pointed toward the head. "You get that end, OK? I get feet."

As Del Rio grabbed on to the body, the dark mail rose up into a great swarm of buzzing flies, revealing more of the sergeant's raw flesh. Newt swatted the flies near his own head, then watched them settle back onto the massive wound. Del Rio shook them off again, more, it seemed, out of interest in the habits of the flies than for any concern he had for the body. So far Newt had battled off the queasiness he felt from the sight of these high mounds of bodies reeking in the heat, but the flies and Del Rio's perverse pleasure sent him over the edge. He crouched over and vomited.

"What? You never seen dead man before?"

Newt heaved again, then slowly wiped his mouth on his sleeve. "Of course I have, but this is . . ."

Del Rio let the dead man's feet fall down, which shook the flies up once again. "Yeah, dis is deesgusting. Look at all de bugs."

"I'd rather not."

The two took a silent break. Now that he had resigned himself, Newt wondered what he would do until he died. He couldn't kill himself; the Lord would appoint the time. What would Mrs. Fry say? Or Bishop Joycelin and the fur-collared residents of the church's front pews? Newt, who'd always preferred the reliable, found the answer oddly satisfying: Nothing was expected of the dead. It didn't matter anymore what people thought of him or what was proper or how much money he had saved in Henry's bank. Newt resolved that until called to his pending death, he would do the things he knew were necessary and right, whatever they happened to be.

Del Rio reminded him that they had more bodies to bury that night. Newt stood up, suddenly bolstered with a martyr's resolve. Del Rio took hold of the feet one last time and Newt slipped his hands under the shoulders. They had a ten-yard walk to the pit and they trotted over as quickly as they could manage. The man's head lolled back, the eyes staring directly at Newt with a look that he first thought was thanks, but then seemed more of a warning. They quickly reached the rim of the pit, halfway filled with bodies coated in a dusting of lime that looked like snow in the dark, then swung the corpse back a bit to get some momentum as Del Rio counted out, *"Um, dios, tres."* At *tres,* they let go and the body of this nameless sergeant flopped onto the pile facedown, his right arm flung over the shoulder of the man next to him as though consoling his comrade.

While Del Rio added an abbreviated sign of the cross to the one administered by the chaplain standing by, Newt imagined his body crumpled in a corner of the pit, frosted with white, and turned away. As much as he pretended that the sacrifice he was preparing to make was correct and glorious, his death would have the same value as that of any man he buried tonight.

Del Rio wanted to race him back to the bodies. Newt looked at the blood on his shirt and wondered if he would ever be able to get it off.

———————

Company L was relieved from burial duty around six. As they headed back through the lines, tired and smelling of death, Burridge caught up to Lyman and pulled him aside. He'd just had an idea, he told Lyman, and he shared it in conspiratorial tones. "The morning pickets have not yet gone out. What do you think of our volunteering?" Lyman was wary of Burridge, but thrilled to be consulted on this sort of decision, so he tilted his head in closer, not knowing that the move had already been ordered. "It would give us another chance to play the Rebels."

Lyman had thought about base ball most of the time he was lugging dead bodies around during the night, and he had overheard more than one whispered conversation between other men of the company about getting a good swing against Arlette or shading one way or another on a particular Reb batter. "I'll see what the boys think."

"We'll have to decide. Soon. Why not just tell them we're doing it and I'll go to General Smith."

Lyman stopped. "Like I said, I'll ask the boys."

Burridge seemed flustered. Having stood the lieutenant down, Lyman decided to go further. "Lemme ask you a question. What were you doing with Tiger yesterday?"

Burridge was about to tell him the truth when he remembered that he didn't have to say anything—*he* was the officer. "I believe a commanding officer has the prerogative of communicating with his subordinates without questions."

Lyman smirked. Without another word to Burridge, he gathered the men together for a quick discussion of a base ball match this morning. Newt and Louis were tired but game, despite the increasing risk of discovery as the lines were drawn closer and more clear. Teddy and Slipper had spent the entire evening in a sullen fog resulting from Karl's claims of the night before. Having seen a rapid diminution in the clout they supposed they had brought to this company, they agreed because it seemed the popular thing to do. Wes was all for it, as was Karl, and Tiger said he was in, too. Those not playing welcomed the chance to rest if they could find the 12th Alabama.

When Lyman told Burridge, he expected the lieutenant would dash ahead to pass the word, but Burridge just walked back in with the company, in no apparent rush. An ugly thought hit Lyman's mind, flickered like a lick of fire: Something strange was going on. And whatever it was, it was probably not good. Fate was rarely kind.

The thought unsettled Lyman. As much as he enjoyed leading these men, he commanded none of the forces of war pounding on around them. His confidence was wavering, shaking as a man's arms do when he lifts too great a weight. Another match would be that many more safe hours with friends.

————

Once back to camp, the men loaded up their muskets and strapped on their knapsacks. The long stream of ambulances that rolled on through the night had given way to groups of officers and their staffs quickly riding back and forth between their positions and Meade's headquarters near the Confederate bulge to the northeast. Wagons filled with ammunition creaked on in that direction as well. Last evening's standoff had driven the anticipation up for the battle that would either send the Union army through to Richmond or back up to Washington. Such close proximity to the enemy was winding both armies up to a pitch of frustration, where men were ready to fling themselves at the wall as many times as needed to bring it down.

A few minutes later the company was trudging back out into the woods. After a week of sunny skies—some days blue, others a milky white—a bank of dense gray clouds along the horizon finally threatened rain later that day. The soft, wet breeze warned that a storm was on its way, but that it was coming at its own pace. There was time, it appeared, to play.

The company had left from nearly the same spot as on their last picket duty, so they were aimed toward the clearing once again. Lyman thought it was merely military coincidence, but Louis thought differently. As he walked, or limped, next to Lyman—the night duty had worn him out— Louis aired his own suspicions. "Do you wonder how it is that the Rebels always find us?"

Lyman shook his head. He'd seen so many unusual things during the war that he'd written off the splendid unlikelihood of these encounters to fate. They'd fought each other more than once—the 12th Alabama had even buried their dead; the sad and ferocious nature of their previous meetings were what gave these matches an unspoken importance. It *had* to be fate.

"Or do you wonder why we are playing these matches? It all seems so, how do you say, convenient. Like it was planned. Have you thought about this?"

Lyman shook his head again.

"There is a flower in the tropics, a very lovely flower, very colorful, that attracts flies to itself and offers them nectar." Louis cupped one palm like the bowl of a flower. "The fly comes down and fills itself with the wonderful sweet nectar. He is so busy having his treat that he does not notice the flower closing in on him until the bloom clamps shut like a pair of jaws." Louis snapped his hand shut. "We should be careful."

Lyman tried to picture Micah scheming some awful deception to capture this meager Union company. It just didn't seem possible. "Aw, those Rebels are just..."

"I think there is some other thing happening. A messenger came last night for Burridge; I had to point out the lieutenant for him. He said he had orders for him, but I have heard no orders today." Lyman pursed his lips. "Curious, yes?"

"But it wouldn't do him any good to turn us in; he was all for it since day one."

Louis threw up his hands. "I do not know what the plan is. I am just saying that I think there is one, and if we want to leave here alive in ten days, it would be to our benefit to find out what it is. Don't you agree?"

Lyman took a look at Wes, who gave him a crisp mock salute. One side of the boy's mouth was swollen and bruised. Lyman recognized that he hadn't accepted responsibility for the kid; he'd claimed it. The stakes were awfully high. "You're right. Let's keep our eyes open."

Burridge walked along, happy that he had found an entry last night in Aurelius worthy of remembering. "That which is not good for the swarm, neither is it good for the bees." And, the lieutenant thought to himself, "That which is good for the swarm is good for the bees"—a corollary that captured his thoughts perfectly. Alder and Quigley were now both in play, and he considered how he would manipulate these two bees into working for the swarm. Alder would keep the matches going and Quigley would keep them from getting too friendly; he and Mink would continue to exchange information. Meanwhile, the threat of Cawthorne had diminished; Stewart would have taken some action by now if Cawthorne's word had any value, and his fear of the other men would prevent him from pushing it too far. Mink would be proud of him.

CHAPTER 14

―――――

LYMAN, LOUIS, AND WES TOOK TENTATIVE STEPS INTO THE clearing. Burridge strode ahead and waved at his men to follow, but saw only the grays and browns of the forest wall. Their guns swung before them in an arc and behind them now as well, in case word had leaked out. A minute passed as the rest of the men filtered in through the pines, then another that filled the stillness with imagined prisons and firing squads. Wesley broke the silence with an eagle screech. Something shook in the trees ahead. Hands reached to triggers. Suddenly the dull colors of the trees became liquid and re-formed into the men they knew, wearing the same browns and grays as the forest.

Mink had been the first to pull forward. He looked highly animated this morning to Burridge's eyes, calling men of both sides by their first names in a pointed manner that had a strong tang of plantation roots, as though it were harvesttime and he wanted to guarantee the maximum out of his hands by speaking to them for once as men.

His appearance, however, and that of his Confederate companions indicated that they had barely survived another long night. The bandage around Haddon's head, at this point hard and crusted brown, had been joined by a new one on his upper left arm. Wes noticed that the bottoms of all their trousers were shredded and torn and seemed almost decoratively fringed as they rippled along with the men's movements. If it was possible, their jackets and shirts were even dirtier and more ragged than they had been two days ago. Buttons held loose flaps of fabric together; wide stains of sweat and blood spread over what surfaces remained untorn. Most were barefoot, though Brockington still had on his high boots. Weed's bald scalp, usually clean and shiny, had a large bruise and a pair of ragged cuts; even Deal had been nicked in the side. Arlette tried to mask a limp as he hobbled to Denton Cowles and handed over Lou. Wes pitied the Rebs their poor condition, but he could tell from their eyes that the last thing they would ever want would be pity. He kicked a rock and suggested they get going before the rain started.

The two groups of men shifted into action as though this match were another of their regular duties. As some men laid out the bases, other men from both sides worked together to clear the field of the few dead bodies that still lay strewn across it. Union corpses went toward the north edge of the clearing, Rebels to the south. No one spoke as this duty was carried out, but caps were removed and Stives and Weed stood on opposite sides, mouthing competing prayers to the same God.

Off to the west, the clouds continued to pile and darken, the gray threat of rain stacking higher into the sky. Players of both sides chatted with each other, and if the Rebs were downcast or exhausted, they didn't show it. As he limbered up for his at bat, Newt watched them whip the ball around the infield a few times, clapping and displaying their intensity and good hands, lively despite ragged appearances. They looked like a hospital ward come to play; rude bandages fluttering, bruises and red, bloody gashes could be seen on their flesh. Arlette had given blood the last two days, too; there was a ragged tear fringed red on the leg he was favoring. Newt felt his own hands resting on places where the other men were wounded.

His first swing sent the ball rolling slowly between Haddon and Weed, neither of whom could react quickly enough to reach it. He stood at first now, more and more embarrassed by his good health before all these damaged men—Union and Reb. He had often tried to imagine the pain of a bullet but had always stopped short. Staring at Weed's mottled skull, he tried again and a faint queasiness spread out from his stomach. He turned his thoughts back to the game: In the course of a few minutes he took second and third on long sacrifice flies and scored on Tiger's double. With a tick of the bat his only effort, Newt had come all the way around.

Another run scored in the first before the teams traded sides. With one out in the Rebel first, Covay doubled into the right-field corner, putting him next to Newt. Though his hat was now a dingy shade of gray, crushed on one side and less a jaunty prop at this point than a sad reminder of the dandy he once had been, Mansfield Covay still had an icy pride. Newt thought back to the conversations in the last game about slavery and Deal's distaste for it. How could they keep fighting for an institution they didn't believe in? He edged closer to second. "If you don't mind my asking..." Covay didn't reply, so he forged ahead. "Are you and Deal... Do you both stand the same way on the slavery issue?"

The Indian lofted a fly to center. Covay hedged off the base, waiting to see if he could tag up, but the ball was too shallow. He didn't respond to Newt's question and Fry decided that he'd gone too far until Covay spat and said, "Well, guess I do, for the most part. It's an *ugly* thing." Weed, the next batter, whiffed on a snap. "Kept us a *back*wuds land." Covay scratched at his hand, the bandage dirty and torn, while Weed took strike two.

"So then why are you here?"

"Like Harlan sayed. 'Cause yo' here, mostly. Ye know there's a goodly number of us who think there's more to the South than chaining up Africans. We ain't all like that Mink. Caleb there mostly just wanted to see if the world was made of anything other than piney woods."

Weed missed strike three, and Covay tipped his ruined hat to Newt as he walked out to left. Such a sacrifice they were making for something they didn't believe in. And he was afraid of making one for something he *did*. Newt considered trying to convince them they were wrong about the Confederacy, but the words sounded weak even before he let them out. His thoughts, his words, the things he believed in; they may have once echoed like bells in his mind, but they had been swamped by the sounds of action around him. His intentions meant nothing, even his intention to die. What did intentions matter in a war? It was what a man did. The Rebels did the wrong thing and he did nothing.

As Pindar Worm scribbled down the results of the last play, Felix Cawthorne stationed himself over his shoulder. He'd been unable to get his hands on one of the score sheets, but he'd had a blessed idea on the way in. He could not put his hands on the real thing, so he would make up his own. "Sergeant, please step from my light."

"With pleasure." Cawthorne stepped to the side and began to teach himself how to keep score.

	1	2	3	4	5	6	7	8	9	R	H	E
UNION	2									2	3	1
CONFEDERATES	0									0	1	0

Burridge planned to leave nothing to chance in this match. He swung late on Arlette's first pitch of the second inning and sent an easy bouncer toward Mink, who stumbled over it so obviously that there was an uncomfortable silence from his teammates. Mink held out his hands and said loudly, "My apologies, friends." Then he glared at Burridge. *"Visne ut interficiamur?"*

Burridge shook his head dumbly. No, he did not want to get them killed. Mink got straight to work, sketching out the salient, while Burridge watched the field. From right field, Deal called in, "Could be time for the lieutenant to give Micah there a try at first."

Mink suddenly had the startled look of a deer who has just smelled a bear nearby. He peered up from the dirt map and mumbled to Burridge, *"Melius nobis faciendum est."*—"We must make this look better." Burridge was startled by his idol's nervous grin as Mink cheered on his pitcher for the rest of the inning and ignored Burridge. The rough plan of the salient remained untouched on the ground. Once Lyman grounded out to third to close the inning, Mink made a vague motion toward the map and said, "Next inning."

Burridge stayed at his position on first. Mink led off the bottom of the second with a looping single near the Hungarian, much like the one the Rebel right fielder had sent there in the first. The Hungarian half jogged, half limped over to the ball; he even bent over and pretended to be winded. Burridge shook his head and said to Mink, "He's faking."

"I would hardly be surprised. *Mea turba ignavi cinaedi sunt. Stupentes, rudesque cinaedi"* Burridge was impressed to hear the Latin for "lazy," "stupid," "uncouth," and "bastards," and reassured to see Mink regain some of the arrogant composure he had before the game started. If Mink's uniform was not a dented coat of armor, still the man shone with the light of civility and honor. The bearded second baseman took a wide and clumsy swing at a slow pitch from Lyman, popping the ball to Newt for an easy out. Burridge set back to deciphering the basic Latin vocabulary Mink used to explain the lines of defenses drawn in the dirt.

The Rebs scored two in the second. A home run by Karl gave the Union a lead again, but Lyman knew it wouldn't be for long. Today these two nines were like a couple of dogs both pulling at the same piece of meat, yielding a foot, then taking it right back. Maybe it was just a need to fight. Lyman wished he could say that he'd done well as the air thickened and the pressure increased, yet the second inning saw him offer so many bad tosses to Micah that the Rebel was awarded his first base, and now Arlette had one strike on him and two pitches way outside.

Lyman was losing control. Instead of pitching, he began trying to throw strikes. No matter how long he concentrated on each pitch, though, it left his hand with something undone or done poorly; a bad grip, misexecuted spin. Four scattered throws later, Arlette took first on a free pass and the match began to whirl around Lyman. He no longer felt like the man who started each action; he was simply pulled along by the tides. As he mulled, Arlette broke for second. Wesley was up and throwing immediately, catching the opposing pitcher with time to spare. Lyman met Pitt halfway between home and the box to give him a solid pat. As he did so, he noticed something different about his back. He held his hand on Wes for a moment, trying to figure out what had changed. There were the same broad shoulders, the same uniform. But the tear down the seam of Wesley's jacket opened in the last match was now sewn up. Wes didn't have a housewife; Lyman had seen him throw it away on the first day of the march in. That meant that Wesley, not Slipper, had stolen Karl's housewife the night before.

But there was no time to think about that. Not yet. The Indian reached with a double. One out and a man at second now. Weed called on Scripture to deliver strength to his own marginal batting prowess. " 'O turn unto me,' " he said, " 'and have mercy upon me; give thy strength unto thy servant, and save the son of thine handmaid.' "

Stives leaped up, pointing at Lyman. " 'He will surely violently turn and toss thee like a ball into a large country' "—he pointed toward the outfield—" 'there shalt thou die, and there the chariots of thy glory shall be the shame of thy lord's house!' "

Weed rubbed a hand over his bald head. "We'll see about that."

Lyman gave him a snap ball, and before it could float wide, Weed slapped the ball into left. Deal took off for home, and when Louis's throw sailed over Wesley's head, he scored easily. Weed took third.

The score was tied again at 3–3.

Weed lifted his head and called out, " 'The righteous shall inherit the land, and dwell therein for ever.' "

The Rebel lieutenant followed with another tough ground ball at Burridge, who had proven as ineffective at first base as he had been at home. Lyman winced as Weed scored from third, and he expected to see Mink on first when he turned around, but Mink was trotting back to his side, glaring all the while at Burridge. Arlette, Deal, and Weed squabbled endlessly during play and between innings. In the fourth, Louis limped over to Burridge and asked to trade positions, to which Burridge just sneered. Wes singled to start the inning and Burridge reached on his own hit, but he did not take an extra base when Deal bobbled the ball, so the Rebs yelled at Deal and the Yanks yelled at Burridge. Every action seemed a cause for anger.

Wes scored on a sacrifice to make it four all and then, one out later, Lyman was up. The skies were a sickly yellow. Breese touched the brim of his cap. "Heard you only got ten days to go."

"Yep."

"Good for you. Mister Wade said there's some tall buildings in that Brooklyn of yours."

Arlette missed wide. "Five, six stories. All brick. Hundreds of people living on a block smaller than this field."

"Must be something." Micah caught strike one on a bounce and threw it back. "Like to see that sometime."

Lyman's first impulse was to invite him up, this man he knew nothing about, and show him the store, his house, his family, but a memory of their most recent action a few days ago cast a shadow. Lyman answered as ball two went low. "Well, I heard your part of the country is fine, too."

Breese threw the ball back to Arlette. "It's pretty, for certain. Not like some of the places we been since we left. Shenandoahs. Lord, they beautiful." He shrugged. "Don't imagine He embarrassed of what He done by us, though. You'd like it."

"We got a beautiful country, don't we?"

Without a thought Micah answered yes, but then he saw what he'd just agreed to and gave Lyman a wry smile.

"Y'all nearly had us yesterday at the horseshoe. Another one like that and you're like to have us."

"Didn't see that, I'm happy to say."

"Lotta our boys goin' over there again. You fixing another try?"

Lyman shrugged. "Just about every gun we got's over there, too." Arlette missed high.

"What tricks you planning this time?"

"Well, we got a new kind of cannon headed that way."

Micah rose out of his crouch. "How's that?"

"Called a coehorn mortar. Shell goes straight up in the air, then comes down on your head. Pretty, huh? Seems to me the only way to protect yourself is keep pulling back or pushing forward so the gunners can't get a fix." Suddenly Lyman realized that an enemy soldier had just pulled information about a new weapon out of him; the same enemy who had gotten troops movements from him last match. An enemy that had stopped shooting so he could retrieve Danny's body. An enemy who happened to be his friend.

Micah nodded his head. "Thanks for the tip." Then his voice dropped. "Listen, take it easy in that pitcher's box. This supposed to be fun, hey?" Lyman steadied himself for Arlette's next throw. "And keep your elbow in on your delivery—it's goin' wide and so's your pitches."

Lyman saw his ball coming in and lined it into left.

Lyman felt the surge back to the Union side now. Newt poked another roller between Weed and Kingsley, sending Burridge across for the lead run and bringing up Karl. So far no one had matched the German at the plate, and another big hit from him now could turn the tide of this well-fought match for good.

He took a pitch outside and then a strike. All three outfielders stepped backward a few more feet.

Arlette paused on the mound.

Karl took a deep breath. The pitcher wound up and delivered a sharp speed ball that the German fought off foul.

Two outs. Two on. One more strike left. Karl swung a few slow warning half-swings. Arlette shook his arm loose, then came in with a ball on the outside of the plate that Karl lunged at. The ball skittered to Kingsley, who tossed to Mink to close the barn door.

Union 5, Rebs 4.

Lyman winked at Micah as they passed between innings. He was just about the only man in the field that he really cared about right now.

Louis was glad when Lyman seemed to calm down in the fourth, holding them scoreless. He needed rest. The scoreless inning put pressure on the Rebs, which that young Pitt screwed tighter when he hit a two-run home run in the Union fifth. Burridge couldn't capitalize with a hit after him, but Louis still sensed a breakthrough. He finally got a good swing at one of Arlette's pitches and lined it into left for a single. After hobbling over to first, he held close to the bag with Feeney at the plate. As he did wherever he went, Louis scanned the ground in search of unusual fauna. The dusty patch of earth around first yielded no living things; just some patches of dried grass and a pebble or two half buried by the dust. Aside from the prints of barefoot Rebs and heel marks from Union brogans, two lines curved parallel through the dirt with *X*'s at a number of places on one of them. Feency tapped a slow roller to Haddon, and the Reb's throw to Mink ended the Union half of the inning. Louis walked out to right, mulling the lines in the dirt.

		1	2	3	4	5	6	7	8	9	R	H	E
UNION		2	0	1	2	2					7	11	2
CONFEDERATES		0	2	2	0						4	5	1

The Rebs mounted a minor threat in the bottom of the fifth, getting a man as far as third, but the inning ended without a Rebel tally and the lead began to seem larger. Willie, Tidrow, and Covay sat sucking on hardtack, silent mostly, but occasionally trading a thought, as there was little else remaining to trade between them. An urgent breeze from the west stirred the grass and rocked the trees, warning of the storm. Willie took in the swirls of green leaves, the men playing, and said, "Shame, all of this."

Tidrow scratched his chin through the dense thatch of beard. "Couldn't be helped."

"Something coulda been worked out. This country's bigger than the parts."

Covay shoved the brim of his battered hat higher up on his brow as he spoke. "See, that's the problem right there."

Willie smiled. "No, that's the beauty." He handed a piece of tack to Covay, who accepted it with a little nod. "My great-grandfather mighta given powder to yourn at Yorktown; mine fought so yourn could live free and yourn did the same for mine. You gotta understand—nobody ever tried this kind a living before and I reckon we should keep trying it. I don't mind if you call New York Harbor yours, 'cause it is. Your kin paid for it with blood like mine did for Richmond."

Before Covay could answer, Oliver Stives bellowed out a quote from Ezekiel, setting off another brief skirmish in his private holy war with Weed. Divided by the diamond, the two called out chapter and verse of divinely inspired Scripture until Willie finally threatened Stives with another punch in the stomach. Newt put down his desk and the letter he was writing in order to help Willie contain Stives's proselytizing urges.

The start of the sixth inning ended the outburst. Lyman met Micah's eyes as he came up to lead off and shook his head. "Those two and their Bibles are more than I can take. That Stives won't do nothing but spew out Scripture, and I'm talking about during a battle."

Micah laughed, and caught the first toss inside. "Naw, I'm not one for all that. I been baptized my share, but I rather go fishing than sit in my Sunday shoes listening to ole Preacher Bate."

"That's the truth." Lyman took a strike. He'd imagined going fishing with Wesley when they were all back in Brooklyn.

"Figure if'n the Lord meant for me to stay inside on the Sabbath, it'd rain like Noah's flood every Sunday. Ye got a better chance at finding him outside than in some meeting hall, I say."

Lyman pictured Micah striding through a field with a fishing pole, peering under rocks in hopes that he could spring on the Lord unawares. Micah's faith remained unsullied by what he'd seen since '61, and Lyman envied him that. Somewhere near Antietam, God had stopped walking alongside Lyman and had taken a seat on His throne far above a world He probably rued. Lead miniés, rifled muskets, and canister shot had supplanted the Lord as the masters of Lyman's fate; he did not know the time of their coming, but he lived as carefully as he could to curry their favor and avoid their wrath. Though Lyman accepted the Lord's absence, men like Arlette and Stives and Weed chased after Him, crying after the god who had left, and making promises, as abandoned children do, to be kinder and to behave well if only they could return to the home they once knew.

Thinking little about the match now, Lyman grounded the next pitch to Kingsley for an out.

During Kingsley's at bat, the two lieutenants quickly finished their business. So far Burridge had, despite a faint throb of conscience and an echo of Henry's voice, given Mink more information on Union positions than he'd learned of the Confederates: He told all that he knew about the failure of Upton's charge, the movement of troops and artillery toward the salient, and Burnside's continued laggardly pace. Mink pointed out a spot at the salient's tip where the Rebels had massed most of their artillery and assured Burridge that those cannons would be pulled back from that position by dawn, leaving the Rebs completely vulnerable. Once Kingsley flew to Quigley for the first out, Mink winked at Burridge, then swept away the map with his foot. It was time for Tiger to do his job.

Lyman and the Union boys had felt secure going into the bottom of the sixth, having scored yet another run in the top half, but the threat of a Southern comeback always lurked in their minds. When Mink singled to start the bottom of the sixth, Union shoulders had tensed up and fielders began nervously jumping on their toes between pitches. Caleb and Teddy exchanged heckles, then the Reb doubled past his friend, scoring Mink. It was just one run, but it brought the Rebs back to within three at 8–5, as the wind continued to pick up. Lemuel was up next, and he drove a speed ball through the hole on the left side of the infield. Caleb took third and now there were two on and two out with the tying run coming up in the person of Mansfield Covay. Lyman tried to calm himself with the thought that Covay was unlikely to tie this match again with one swing. Newt kicked the dirt.

Covay slowly stepped toward the plate and dug in, scraping up dirt with the thin sole of his shoe. The first pitch came in low. Newt and Karl chattered tensely, more to calm themselves than Lyman.

Lyman wound up and delivered the next pitch inside. Covay swung and missed. Everyone let out the breath they were holding. Covay spat, and swung loosely.

Lyman windmilled around and snapped his wrist just as he let go of the third pitch. The ball arced in, then dipped off to the left as it crossed the plate. A beautiful snap ball, but Covay had clearly been guessing snap and he took it the other way. The ball rose and took a high curving path, its majestic swoop to the left making it appear a living being on its own chosen flight. Since he was shaded over toward right, Teddy had a long run to track down the drive. Two more runs scored and Covay reached third.

The score was now Union 8, Rebs 7.

Arlette followed with a pop-fly out. The inning was over, but David was at the gates once more.

	1	2	3	4	5	6	7	8	9	R	H	E
UNION	2	0	1	2	2	1				8	13	2
CONFEDERATES	0	2	2	0	0	3				7	11	1

Top of the seventh and Tiger picked up the bat. He thought of what Burridge had just said about it being time to give the Rebs a little more taste of knuckle and found himself less fully in agreement with the idea than he had been yesterday when they'd struck their deal. He'd spent most of the match looking over toward his knapsack to be sure that no one had snuck out Burridge's flask, and now he stood alone at the plate, facing nine Rebels with only the bat for a weapon, certain that no one stood behind him. He saw Burridge wink at him and, five or six feet away, Lyman with his arms folded; his oldest, last, and now former friend. Burridge believed he could buy Tiger for a drink, and Tiger decided that was probably what he was worth.

He hacked at Arlette's slow pitch, sending a grounder to Kingsley. The second baseman lobbed the ball over to Mink, and Tiger was out before he was halfway down the line, but he kept on coming. It was what he had promised to do. He slammed into Mink, sending him sprawling into the dirt.

All action stopped.

Tiger loomed over Mink, hoping the Rebel would start up the fight Burridge had hinted to him about, waiting for something, anything, to happen. Mink pushed himself up, pinning Quigley with an icy gaze, and brushed off his tattered uniform. Tiger couldn't pull away from the face; hollow eyes behind a human mask too sharp and proud to be a product of God's rough earth. The black eyes told nothing of whatever lived within them. His heart beat faster. If death had a face, this was it.

Mink finally said, "You, sir, simply do not understand your actions." Then he walked away.

Tiger got out a few slurs on the Confederacy before Lyman pulled him aside and got up close into his face. "For chrissakes!"

Tiger jerked free. "Fuck the Rebs and fuck all ye, too."

The Irishman stomped off and Lyman didn't follow.

Burridge lined a clean single into left and trotted to first, afraid of the explanation he'd have to make. Why had the Irishman decided to target Mink, who'd never done a thing to him; who was, in fact, on his side? Burridge had been certain that he'd attack someone else more on his level, a Deal or a Covay. He'd wanted a dogfight, not an assault. Mink was burning cold when he got to the base. Deep thunder growled softly behind them.

Burridge smiled apologetically. "I apologize. That was my idea."

Mink shook his head a bit, as if he hadn't heard. "Pardon?"

"Quigley. All that."

Mink's cold glare focused on him. "What ever for?"

Burridge could never put all of this into Latin, so he made sure no one was looking, then whispered, "Keeps appearances. Don't need this to get too friendly, eh? What's good for the swarm is good for the bees, and all that. I never intended for you to . . ."

Mink leaned in close, his tone that of someone trying very hard to keep his temper in check. "Listen. If we perform our duties properly, all these poor sons of bitches"—the Rebel gestured toward his fellow Southerners— "will be all quite dead in a day or two. Let them have their sport. *Panis et circenses,* eh? We'll be drinking punch in Richmond, and Marmaduke will be deep under the dirt." Mink gave a joyless smile. "Don't have at me, son. I'm your best friend here."

Mink flipped a drooping crescent of his hair back with a snap that Burridge couldn't help but find dashing as Mink's words sank in. All dead in a day or two. Best friend here.

The inning ended with a simple force at second, so the lieutenant took his place back at first. He told himself that Mink's brutal order of execution was only a clear statement of purpose for their actions; the fatal end, part of which they had nearly accomplished on these Rebs two nights earlier at Laurel Hill. Marmaduke winked at him as he ran off the field, and Burridge imagined the boy splayed across a sodden field, death holding the Rebel's eyes half open while he and Sidney exchanged toasts. A chill went through Burridge's shoulders. He considered how little he really knew about Mink. He pictured Feeney dead now, crumpled in a mass of Union rags, and realized from his cool reaction to the thought that he knew more about Mink than words could say; their darkness was their bond. He was his best friend here, wasn't he? That was what he had wanted all along. Burridge saw himself behind the broad, mahogany desk he intended to buy for his new office and once again he felt calm.

Louis limped out to right with a new picture in his mind. He'd wanted another look at the dirt around first base, so as he ran out his grounder, he'd made sure to pause there and look around at the dirt.

But the lines were gone. They had been very intentionally wiped away; not a trace was left. What, he wondered, would someone bother erasing?

	1	2	3	4	5	6	7	8	9	R	H	E
UNION	2	0	1	2	2	1	0			8	14	2
CONFEDERATES	0	2	2	0	0	3				7	11	1

Though the Rebs were down a run, Lyman—and every other Union man, he was sure—couldn't shake the feeling that a tied game was inevitable now, and when that feeling of doom steals into the minds of a team, it's only a matter of time before it becomes true. Singles by Deal and Weed sent Wes out to the pitcher's box to calm Lyman down, but Lyman was in no mood to listen to what he had to say. He could feel the match slipping away, the desperate instinct to tighten his grip only speeding the loss. The hits and runs were not the sum of what moved a match; the force created by their occurrence had to be included as well. The storm would be breaking soon, and holding back the Rebs now would be like trying to hold back that storm. Without a word, he pointed Wesley back to his position behind the plate.

He was not on the Court Street Grounds; he was not wearing the white of the Excelsiors. His family was not watching from the crowd. Lyman was alone, trying to stave off something that felt stronger than him. Micah's presence was not reassuring right now. Lyman held the ball tight, ran his fingers along its seams, across the rough surface where the leather had been scraped. The same ball you tried to hit one minute, you tried to stop another.

Forty-five feet away stood the greasy Reb lieutenant. Instead of his usual motion, Lyman brought the ball up to his eye and stared over its top into Mink's chosen spot. He pulled his arm back and let loose a speed ball that Mink missed badly. Wes yelped when the ball hit the meat of his hands, but he urged Lyman on for another.

Lyman didn't hear him; it was just him and Mink. He took aim again and whipped in the speed ball Wesley had asked for. The Rebel got around late, and popped it to Karl, just barely in fair territory, for the first out. When Deal was caught stealing at second, there were suddenly two outs and an end to the inning on the other side of Kingsley's weak bat. Maybe this was the Rebs' high-water mark, Lyman thought. One more. One more out. One more battle. Ten more days. He served up a pitch weakened by all the hope he'd burdened it with. Kingsley slapped it into left to score Weed and tie the match at eight all. Though Kingsley was caught trying for the extra base, with two innings to go, they were right back where they started and the Rebs had the surge.

	1	2	3	4	5	6	7	8	9	R	H	E
UNION	2	0	1	2	2	1	0			8	15	2
CONFEDERATES	0	2	2	0	0	3	1			8	14	1

The eighth inning passed quickly, as though both sides wanted to get to the ninth as soon as possible and settle it there. No man got past first base. Between innings Albert told Huey that he could have Lou after the fifth match. Huey shook Arlette's hand with all the solemnity of a man being sworn into office. Though Huey reached out for his new charge-to-be, Arlette held on to Lou and stroked his neck until called back to the pitcher's box.

The clouds to the west had mounted while the men played. A

gray-and-yellow mass churned closer every minute, adding another kind of urgency to the tension of this final inning. Brockington knelt in front of the trees on the Southern side. Huey went from man to man, offering free pets of the rooster, but there were no takers; not now. Even Caspar nibbled at a fingernail and, despite himself, Cawthorne watched intently as the heart of the Union lineup prepared to bat.

Going into the ninth, the score remained 8–8.

As Karl went to the plate, Newt reminded him to stay loose and no matter what anybody said, to wait for his pitch—it was Arlette's job to give him what he wanted. The German grunted, then stood in against Arlette and called for a high toss. The first pitch pushed Karl away from the plate.

He glared and edged up closer this time, not intimidated by Arlette's speed. Albert took a deep breath as low thunder rippled nearby. He laid in his next pitch shoulder high, right into Karl's favorite spot, and the German saw it coming. He stepped into it, driving the ball deep to left center.

Deal and Covay converged as Karl sprinted to first and when neither fielder could make the catch, the ball bounced in. By the time Deal touched the ball, Karl had rounded second and now it was a race to third—Karl's pumping legs against Deal's arm. They both hit the bag at the same time, but Karl snuck his foot in first. He was safe.

In his last at bat, Teddy had shown some signs of coming alive. Three of his four at bats today had shown power, and he delivered a fly ball on Arlette's first pitch with a towering shot to center. Deal camped under it and made a strong effort to catch Karl but the throw was too late.

Karl crossed the plate and it was Union 9, Rebels 8.

The Union boys received Karl and Teddy with handshakes and backslaps. Karl put his arm around Finn and said, "Now you finally doing what you talk so much about, *ja?* We don't always need home run; sacrifice is *gut auch.*" As Tiger went up to bat and the cheering subsided, Karl added something to his praise. "Now get me back *mein* housevife, *ja? Bitte?*"

They'd gotten what they needed, which was all that they had left. The Yanks went down easily after that. The one-run lead would have to do.

Covay opened with a grounder to Feeney, who went on to Burridge for the first out.

Lyman clapped his hands, then remembered his sportsman's calm and called, "One out!"—the sound of an Excelsiors crowd building in his ears, Leggett's voice cheering him on. He reminded himself of where he was. Two more outs, he thought, just two more outs and they would squeeze through. As usually happens when a team starts counting the outs remaining before victory, the outs immediately came harder. Arlette slugged the next pitch, a high speed ball, into left for a single. The tying run was on first with one out.

In right field, Louis stared down at a patch of dirt pocked with holes. Ants swarmed across it—black ants and red ants battling for control of this prime square foot of the world. Reds held squirming Blacks in their mandibles and snapped them in half. Packs of Blacks tore at the legs and antennae of cornered Reds. Some paired off and grappled in the dust. Tiny carcasses lay scattered about.

Louis looked up when he heard a cheer. Deal had flown out to Quigley and now there were two outs. He looked back at the battle, wondering if this was their Gettysburg. Three or four Reds mounted an assault on the Blacks' entrance and were bitterly repulsed, one of the bodies ripped apart with what appeared to Louis almost gratuitous violence. He felt pity for the dead ant; a tiny speck on the earth, its meaningless life turned back into carbon. Was there someone still in the heavens watching the battles *he* fought with the same fascination? Were they as removed from the war's purpose as he was from whatever territorial urge or lack of food had caused this war of ants? He'd had another odd dream that night, almost more of a memory from the years before the fire; a peaceful dream of listening to his grandfather tell him stories of King Solomon, whose reign passed without war. Was the God of Solomon staring from above on the miniature armies of the North and South, as they were battling themselves on some tiny plot of dirt?

Louis let his mind fly up to where the Lord would watch the petty wars of man and suddenly realized those scribbles in the dirt were not just scribbles—they were a map of Spotsylvania. Drawn by Burridge.

Two outs and a man on first. E. Simon Weed at the plate.

With thin lips and closed eyes, Weed sent a prayer to the Lord, whom he believed was intently following this match. "The Lord God is *my* strength, and he will make *my* feet like *hinds'* feet, and he will make *me* to walk upon *mine* high places." He gave Stives a smug smile and drilled Lyman's pitch into left field for a single. Arlette had been running on the pitch, so now there were men on first and third, and all the Rebs on the side were standing.

Two on. Two outs. Rebs down by one and Sidney Mink took five long, erect strides to the plate, bat resting lightly on his shoulder. Lyman didn't need the Worms' scorecard to tell him that Mink had done well so far. Mink wasn't a long ball hitter, but he was the kind of striker who controlled the bat and found the gaps. Chances were that he wouldn't hit a home run, but he wouldn't strike out, either. Lyman stared in at Wes, then at Mink with his greasy hair slipping down around the sides of his face. A slippery fellow, Lyman thought. He took a deep breath and stepped into his first pitch, a speed ball that Mink ticked foul before it crossed the inside part of the base.

The foul ball dropped the tension for a few seconds, but once Lyman had the ball back, the pressure began to mount again. Thunder roared only a mile away. The storm would break any second.

Lyman looked in. Mink plucked at his shoulders with his left hand, rocking back and forth on his feet. Lyman wound up and delivered a slow pitch that fooled the Rebel with its change of pace.

Wes jumped up cheering as he tossed the ball back to Lyman. Two strikes. One more and it was over. Lyman tried to clear his head of everything but Mink. He'd come inside once with speed, then changed the pace and gone outside once with the slow ball. Which would Mink be expecting? Lyman decided on the snap. Wes gave him a thumbs-up from behind the plate and Lyman twisted off the pitch.

The ball slipped off his fingers and came in softly, but it dropped off the table and Mink was lucky to get his bat on it, tapping it foul down the right field line.

They'd start over.

More thunder.

Now, Lyman thought, the snap again. He collected himself, wound up, and let go with a fine snap ball that Mink swung at, a high, deep drive to right field. It was catchable if Louis could get there in time.

The crack of the bat brought Louis's attentions away from his terrible realization that Burridge was a spy. As he looked up, he could see every face in the field staring at him and far above a white dot, bright as the moon against the dark thunderclouds hanging over them. The ball had reached the top of its parabola and was beginning to curve down. Louis started toward it but he knew he couldn't reach it. His calculations were instinctive, not mathematical—rapidly falling ball plus slow old man who hadn't been paying attention. Both sides cheered loudly and a peal of thunder shook the field.

Louis limped as quickly as he could, but the ball kept falling: twenty feet, fifteen, five.

Louis dove.

The ball bounced a foot in front of his outstretched hands and rolled past him. Arlette and Weed scored and were mobbed by their teammates as they stepped on Micah's haversack. The final score: Rebs 10, Union 9. The Rebs now led two matches to one.

	1	2	3	4	5	6	7	8	9	R	H	E
UNION	2	0	1	2	2	1	0	0	1	9	17	2
CONFEDERATES	0	2	2	0	0	3	1	0	2	10	17	1

For once thunder sounded like a cannonade along the front, instead of the other way around. The storm would hit any second. Quick good-byes were exchanged; Huey returned Lou, and Caleb waved Teddy over. With a furtive look, Caleb Marmaduke took out his two girlfriends, scanned them quickly, and handed one of them over to Teddy. "Here." He sniggered. "Thought maybe y'all'd like some company, if'n ye know what I mean."

It was Sheba, the one on the couch. Teddy was grateful, but he was never one to be shy. "You know, I like that other one better. Do ye think . . . ?"

Caleb punched him in the shoulder. "You dog. That Cleopatry is trumps, ain't she? Well, I got a liking for her, too, but . . ." He traded cards with Teddy. "She's all yourn."

Teddy shook his hand. "Thanks, brother. Take care a yerself."

Caleb tipped his straw hat.

Haddon went among the Union soldiers, shaking hands. With Newt, Wes, and Lyman, he stopped and pulled a dented locket out of his shirt. Micah stood behind Haddon as the wild-haired Reb opened it to show an enamel likeness of a woman, all of an inch wide and an inch and a half long. The first thing Lyman noticed was her neck: thin, almost swanlike, and circled with a length of velvet. She had blond wavy hair cascading over her shoulders and bordering her face as rays of light surround the sun, a mane much like Haddon's, and Lyman could see even more of the resemblance in the sloe eyes and trim mouth. After expressing his admiration, he gave Micah a questioning look. Breese said, "That's his gran'maw. Least that's what they told him. She got his likeness, so I tend to believe it."

Lyman clapped a hand on Lemuel's shoulder. "She's a beautiful woman, Haddon. Mind you don't lose that."

Haddon shook his head with great vehemence and tucked the locket away. Another clap of thunder rumbled through the field and the trees creaked in the rising wind. Newt tugged Lyman's arm. "We better get going."

The three Yankees waved farewell and joined the rest of the company already heading back into the trees. Lemuel waved back. In his reedy voice he said, "Good-bye, friends." And then the rain came.

GAME POSTPONED

———

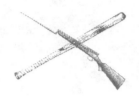

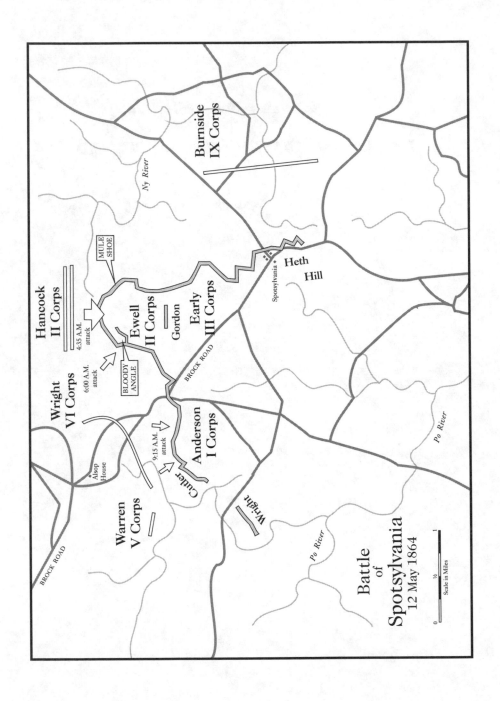

Battle
of
Spotsylvania
12 May 1864

CHAPTER 15

A T FIRST THE RAINDROPS WERE SCATTERED, BOWING INDI-
vidual leaves so that they appeared rung from below like the bells
of a cathedral, but after a few seconds passed, the whole area
around Spotsylvania drooped under the constant press of a long-
deferred storm. Edged out just beyond the tall pines and the false
safety they offered from the lightning, the men of Company L
lay on their stomachs in what was quickly becoming mud and
regretted any prayers they had privately made for rain. The heat and the
dampness turned their woolen uniforms into heavy casings that reeked of
sweat and every other emission the human body, dead or alive, can release.
Tice took out his rubber liner and tented it over his head for protection.
The other men hunched up their shoulders and watched the raindrops bead
and fall off the brims of their caps. Losing the match would have put them
all in a funk on a sunny day; this storm let the defeat seep in and their idle
minds dwelled on all the runs they should have scored or catches they should
have made.

Newt reached over to Karl and patted him on the arm. "You played a
fine match today."

Karl let the hiss of rain fill the silence. He shook his head. "*Nein.* No."
He tapped his considerable nose, pondering. "I cannot be easy with them."

Newt licked away some water that had dripped onto his lips. "They're
all Americans, Dutchie. Just like you and me. They have some misguided
ideas, but not everything those Alabama boys say is wrong. They should be
a part of this country. Sometimes we have to be friendly and try debate and
reason but if that doesn't work..." Newt saw where the logic was taking

him. "If that doesn't work we have to fight. As long as we know when to stop fighting and when to start talking again, we'll be fine."

By now he was looking forward into the gray skies, toward the Rebel lines. Hadn't Samson wielded the jawbone of an ass? Christ himself used violence in the temple. When evil only understood force, then force must be used to fight it. He'd spent his whole life talking; talking after seeing John Brown's body at the Stearns House; talking after a speech by Lincoln at the Cooper Union; talking, talking, talking about how the world should be. It was time to take action. Lying on his belly in the deepening mud of Virginia, Newt ran a finger along the shaft of his rifle and wiped some water off the sight.

Lyman watched the bubbles play atop a small puddle in the mud two feet ahead of him. Smaller bubbles banded together to form larger ones, which then swallowed other larger ones to become single wide bubbles with shimmering surfaces stretched beyond their strength, quickly bursting in the ripples caused by falling drops.

The liquid motion calmed Lyman, whose temper heated every time he thought of Wesley Pitt. There was the anger of deception, that despite all of Lyman's efforts to bring him into the group, the boy had remained a deceitful, thieving bastard; and then there was the anger of failure. Lyman wondered if he bore some of the blame, especially since Ernie had a propensity toward the same sin. A pair of small bubbles bound together and went hunting for more. Though nothing strange had happened during the last match, Lyman was beginning to take Louis's warning more to heart. Were they too good to be true? Tice whispered over to Lyman for what seemed the twentieth time, "When the hell we getting pulled back?"

Lyman told him yet again that he didn't know. "Why don't you ask Burridge?"

Then Willie shared with Lyman the news that he was hungry. Teddy and Wes directed their complaints about the rain toward Lyman, while Von Schenk wanted to know when Grant would do something about the Rebel line. Cawthorne ducked his head even lower into the mud to avoid getting tagged with any of these unanswerable questions and unreasonable requests being fired at Lyman.

Lyman told them what he knew and swore at those left unsatisfied by his answers. He now had to listen to everyone's petty complaints; an endless stream of whining tinged with the unspoken accusation that he could in some way resolve it and had to this point chosen to do nothing. He had to listen to this grousing on top of getting them into battle and out alive. Lyman couldn't recall hearing Danny pecked away at by these men, but he had to admit that he had probably done his share of pecking.

A tightening sense of defeat gripped him and Lyman let his body slough into the mud. For two hours he'd kept himself flexed, hoping not to get entirely soaked through, but it was too late for that. He pictured Louis diving for the last hit of the game. If they'd been playing bounce, he could have trotted over and taken the ball easily for the final out. Lyman had never liked the fly game; he'd thought it was too athletic and unsportsmanlike when he first saw the Excelsiors play that way, but he had to admit now that this all-or-nothing style made the stakes higher and matched the ways of modern life. The old way was the easy way and Lyman had accepted that, but it raised a new question in his mind: If you made one great catch and five errors, were you still a hero? If you saved the lives of men you imperiled, were you a hero? A base ball match was not just about single moments, it was an accumulation of moments and success was based on being consistent.

Lying in his own pool of mud, Burridge was in a much better mood than Lyman. He'd gotten his information, spent time with Mink, and now eagerly anticipated sitting in Henry's dry tent with a shot of whiskey in his hand as the captain thanked him for his selfless duty to country. He imagined Stewart standing outside in the rain, ear pressed to the canvas, hoping to hear some snippet of their conversation. Though he'd only been at it for a week, the lieutenant decided that he had a definite talent for spying. It was a skill that he thought might place him above Stewart in Henry's eyes. If there was more time in their enlistment, Burridge thought, he would have Stewart's job.

––––––––

The men spent two more hours on their bellies before they were finally pulled back behind the Union lines, and there waiting for them as they came in was Lieutenant Linden Stewart, covered in a rubber cloak that made him look like an A-tent or an Indian tepee. Though relatively dry, Stewart still appeared miserable, his bulging eyes mournful. After delivering the long-anticipated orders to rejoin Cutler's division and the 14th for the duration of their enlistment, an announcement that brought sighs of relief and a good number of cheers, Stewart told Burridge to move his men out. As the company made the short journey from General Smith's position on the north side of the Brock Road to the 14th's place with Warren on the south, Stewart remained at Burridge's side. Without looking at him, Stewart said, "Captain Henry requests a council with you immediately upon your arrival, for the usual reasons."

Burridge nearly laughed—"the usual reasons!" A pathetic attempt to lay a trap. But instead of considering the sizable danger Stewart posed, Burridge tramped along next to his superior through the spreading quagmire and compared him to the other lieutenant in his life, Sidney Mink. While Stewart cajoled and demeaned him, Mink spoke to Burridge as an equal. Mink had a classical education, whereas Stewart on more than one occasion had tried to convince Burridge that the dime novels his shrew of a wife sent him were better reading than Caesar or Virgil. Mink knew all the secrets, all the true workings of this war, a knowledge that Stewart only played at.

Burridge smiled to himself as Stewart lumbered on beside him, itching to know what he knew, an urge as natural and unstoppable to Stewart as sniffing other dogs is to a gutter mongrel. Someday Stewart would be wearing a blocky suit with worn elbows, calling on *him* for lunch and a chat about the old days that led up to a twenty lent out and never thought of again. The lieutenant turned back and looked at his men, men he was as ready to dispense with as Mink was his. This ability to see the necessary order was requisite for his acceptance into Mink's delicious realm, and that he felt a twinge of guilt only heightened the pleasure, as he knew from the acquaintances he'd often made in Bowery shadows. Stewart's stubby, boyish fingers began to work around his mouth. Burridge preferred his choice of hero.

After crossing the Brock Road and walking another ten minutes, Burridge saw hundreds of men digging trenches in the mud, dressed just as he and his company were; a cheering sight for even the most cynical and the moment they all had been looking forward to for a week. While this was enough for the rank and file, Burridge's moment came a few minutes later. Pompey showed them both into the captain's quarters, the sound of the rain now a drumming on canvas instead of incessant sibilance, and Henry coughed in surprise as Stewart entered alongside Burridge.

Henry saluted both of them, then extended his hand to Burridge. "Thank you for your experienced work on picket. It is much appreciated by the generals."

Burridge smiled as he often had after a pat on his head from an indulgent master in school. "Thank you, sir."

Henry tugged at the fingers of his gloves in distraction, his brow creased. He was tense about something, and much coughing and shuffling took place during the silence. "Well. Stewart. You're safe and sound. Why don't you have a cup of tea in your tent while I tell Lieutenant Burridge our orders. No need for you to stay. I'll send Pompey around with the tea. Pompey!" Burridge squirmed with glee as a dark look crossed Stewart's face.

Stewart crisply saluted Henry and the second lieutenant, then reluctantly backed out of the tent to let them conduct their business, a medium-size bearded man with much red braid on his shoulders brushing past as he left. He saluted Colonel Fowler in a surprised reflex, but the regiment's commanding officer didn't notice. Lingering outside near the tent flap, Stewart listened as Henry welcomed Fowler and introduced him to Burridge as "that young man I've been telling you so much about."

Pompey tapped the preoccupied Stewart on the shoulder, nearly sending him back into the captain's tent in a leap of fright. "What?" Stewart hissed.

"Want your tea?"

"No!" Stewart recovered himself and added in a calmer tone, "But thank you. That is all."

Pompey did not take the hint to leave or, more properly, he did. He stood at the flap next to Stewart, chattering about the foul weather and destroying any chance Stewart had of eavesdropping. Knowing he'd been defeated, Stewart nodded good-night and shambled off until he was out of Pompey's sight, at which point his steps toward Cawthorne took a decidedly brisker pace.

Alongside Lyman, his head held high, Wesley Pitt reentered the 14th Brooklyn a man much changed from when he left it a week ago. Pitt had departed from Culpeper an overgrown boy and now, just a week later, he was a young man, a killer, a member of this regiment, a defender of city and state who saw the regimental flags sagging in the rain and felt a thrill of pride. Instead of feeling left out by the handshakes and greetings offered to his comrades from the rest of the regiment, he took his share for himself as he tagged behind Lyman, who was wading through the puddles and the knots of smiling Brooklyn men reunited for their final ten days of conflict. In his life, Wes had returned to rat-infested basements, urine-soaked stables, and dozens of other grimy hovels that by dint of the shelter they lent his few belongings had earned the name of "home." Though they kept him dry when it rained, none of them ever provided him with the security he wanted, and today as he walked toward the field of men wearing exactly what he was wearing, all soaked by the downpour and slopping wads of mud and dirt into piles that wouldn't stop a bullet as much as they would smother it, he learned what it really felt like to come home.

After warning them not to say a word about the matches to anyone, Lyman staked out an area for the company on the western edge of the regiment's camp. They set down their knapsacks there and laid out their rubber liners over the muddy ground as soldiers came by to say hello, happy to stop their grimy, thankless labors that bore resemblance to those of the Israelites forced to make bricks without straw. Surrounded by the bored and curious men he took to be Lyman's admirers, Wes didn't notice that Lyman was ignoring him. In his turn, Pitt ignored Teddy and Slipper hanging on the edges. They would never be at home here, but Wesley had made this regiment his family, with Lyman Alder sitting at the head.

As the late afternoon turned to evening, some men tried to light sputtering fires in the rain as others continued digging their damp, shapeless entrenchments with shovels and hands soiled beyond cleaning. Willie pulled some new stocks from the trains and fixed what supper he could under the damp circumstances. He found much to occupy the time and mind of Huey, who was dying to talk about the matches. Karl and Caspar visited with another German from Company B who was trimming down logs to bolster the fortifications, while Del Rio chattered in Portuguese with one of his countrymen. Stives sat motionless in silent prayer, afraid to get his Bible wet. Rumors of battle dominated even the most idle conversations and the newswalkers and stragglers wandering by stoked the speculation with word of troop movements and snatches of military strategy held on the authority of everyone from General Wright's servant boy to Abe Lincoln himself. Much of it conflicted, but the one thing all the gossip agreed on was that the final battle would be tomorrow.

Troops of the Sixth Corps waded through the mud behind them, under a gray sky lit at times by shafts of lightning, heading east toward some unknown place on the Rebel line. The storm above had broken, and now it was time for the tension between these two lines to break as well. Every Sixth Corps man walked with his head bowed by the rain and by the knowledge that he would in some way figure prominently in tomorrow's inevitable attack. Reddish mud had stained their blue pants nearly up to their knees. A recalcitrant mule stuck its heels deep into the mire, refusing to go forward, and each man slogging toward the assault point wished he had that animal's courage. The 14th watched them pass by with few words, wondering when and where they would face the enemy tomorrow.

At every opportunity, Wes placed himself next to Lyman, even though Lyman had said virtually nothing to him since the middle of the last match. Wes wrote it off to fatigue and a desire to talk to some soldiers other than those he had been with the last week, satisfied to listen to Lyman regale men with stories of their fight at Laurel Hill. Sitting beside his friend, distracted from tomorrow's battle by tales of yesterday's, he was content. Lyman had just finished describing the scene of the first Rebel charge; he sat hunched over, about to reenact the surprise second wave. "We were trying to catch our breath..."

Wes broke in, eager to help. "Ye couldn't see a *thing!*"

The men around the fire fell silent when they saw Lyman's annoyed expression, but Wes beamed, looking at an audience he considered his by extension, not knowing he'd made a mistake until Lyman slowly turned and said, "Why don't you go play with your boys over there?" He gestured toward Feeney and Finn as some men from other companies laughed.

Suddenly Wes felt the weight of all the day's insults, the introductions not made, the angry tone and unanswered questions. Puzzled, Pitt splashed over to the distant spot in the trenches where his two old companions huddled under their blankets, shivering in the now chilly air and occasionally bailing out water. Teddy sucked on a damp piece of hardtack, and Slipper shuffled a deck of bent and swollen cards with little enthusiasm. Wes leaned against the trench wall next to them. Finn let a minute pass before he said anything. "So look who's gratiated our presence here, Slipper. It's the hero of the war, Wesley Pitt. Or should I have said Wesley Alder?"

Wes let the water run down the inside of his collar, down his back. "Fuck yerself, Teddy."

"A stirring retorture. Maybe you should run for Congress. What's with you and Alder, anyway? You his chicken? Huh?" That got a laugh from Slipper.

"Fuck you again, Teddy. He was a friend a my, you know, my father. He knew me when I was a kid."

Teddy smiled in a sickly sweet way. "Aw, that's nice." Then his face hardened. "Does he know what you are now? What a thieving little orphan bastard you are now? How ye took that German's sewing kit and now you're blaming yer old boy Feeney here?"

Wes swallowed hard. "You got that wrong, Teddy. That coulda been anybody—Del Rio, Stives."

"Oh sure, a guy spoutin' Bible all day is gonna filch a bag of needles. No, I don't think so. I think the one guy who's sewed up a big hole in his jacket is the one, don't you?" Wesley's denials continued as insistent as the rain and just as unheard.

Stewart avoided being in the sinks when another man was there. Since the long trench was used by thousands of soldiers for relief, Stewart had to visit at odd hours to assure the privacy he required. Tonight's visit, though, was more social in nature. Stives had directed him to the best place to find Felix Cawthorne, and it was there he found him buttoning up his trousers and trying to salute at the same time.

Stewart returned an impatient salute of his own. "Did something happen out there today?"

Shocked not only by Stewart's surprise appearance, but also by where it was taking place, Cawthorne took a moment of blinking and nodding before he answered yes.

"I need proof, Mr. Cawthorne. No more rumors. Proof."

"I've given it my best efforts, sir, but now I can personally guarantee you'll have a score sheet for the next match. We meet them when we're out on picket duty." Stewart considered that such a document, whatever it was, might indeed serve well as evidence for a court-martial, but the word "court-martial" set Cawthorne's guts rumbling so hard he began to creep back toward the sinks. "You mustn't tell anyone, sir! They'll kill me! They'll know who revealed their scheme!"

Stewart forgot Cawthorne's pleas as soon as they were spoken, and he walked away with a mumble of reassurance. Cawthorne trotted back to the sinks.

Before Wesley could get away to talk to Lyman and admit what he had done, Newt Fry came stomping over with Karl in support. He pointed at Slipper. "You stole my desk!"

Slipper shrank further under his blanket, less and less able to face his accusers. "I didn't take nothing! I swears it! I swears it!"

"Then where's my desk? I had it in the field and now I don't have it. You're a motherfucking thief and you better hand our stuff over before we string you up, Feeney."

Wes tried to intervene, pushing himself between Newt and Teddy, who had gotten up ready to fight. Lyman trotted over now and crouched above the trench. Wes called up to him, "Lyman, I gotta talk to ya bad."

Lyman hissed into his ear, "I don't want to see your face." He turned back to the argument about to explode. "Step back, boys. Leave off Feeney there. He didn't steal none a your stuff."

The German put his hands on his hips. "So who did, eh?"

"I know exactly who did it. I'll get both a your things tomorrow. Don't kill our second-base man until tomorrow."

The men faded away and Lyman watched the solid mended back of Wesley Pitt clamber out of the entrenchment and straggle away into the rainy night. Lyman felt the world of the last few confident days about to come apart. The rain came down heavier.

After eleven hours of storm, the Virginia soil had had its fill and now, at midnight, the water began to pool across any flat surface. Though their rubber liners were meant to keep the men dry, they were of little use when they were under inches of water. The temperature fell and damp heavy clothing became clammy and wetter still from the incessant rain. Even so, many slept tucked under their blankets, propped against the walls of the trenches with feet and rifles.

Sitting beneath a blanket reeking as wet wool does, Louis wondered if he should describe the markings in the dust to Lyman. The two had spoken privately that evening. Lyman claimed that he hadn't seen anything strange during the game and claimed it with an insistence that made it clear he did not wish to question this one happy aspect of their increasingly brutal lives. Louis tended to agree, despite what he had seen. The more he thought about his theory of Burridge spying, the sillier it sounded, like the ramblings of an old man in a corner saloon or one of the long-bearded scholars his father made fun of after the fire. He decided he would need one more piece of evidence before he could accuse his commanding officer of being a spy for the Confederate army. If it wasn't Mink and Burridge, who could it be?

A shift in the wind set the rain licking at his face, and he curled up more as he closed his eyes and saw the base ball thud into the ground before him—a brief flash of white. Any man who couldn't make a routine catch like that could hardly be expected to serve well as a soldier; he would cost more lives to his own side than he would take from the Rebs. What, then, he wondered, was this old man's value to the 14th? He squeezed his eyes tighter and again he saw the ball bounce away.

Tiger sat Indian-style on the back rim of a ditch with his head uncovered, hair pasted to his face. Rain thrummed onto him; his eyes were half open as if he were trying to stay awake during a stint of guard duty. If there had ever been a time when it wasn't raining, he could no longer remember. If there had ever been a time when he cared whether he lived or died, he no longer remembered that, either. Tiger only saw blackness; the meaningless crevasse men sink into when they lose their footing on the road. He had tried the last few days to gain a handhold on the slippery sides of his mind, but his grip wasn't strong enough. If there had ever been a day of sun, it was long ago and in a different land.

Tiger hefted the flask; it was still full. That's what his mother's price had been after a year in the poorhouse—a flask of whiskey, good or bad. A year later it was half, and by the time she died, a man could do what he would for a sip. Meeting Lyman and Danny had brought him back to the land of the living. Their war led him back to the grave. He unscrewed the top and took a whiff. He'd promised Mary, promised her and Lyman. He'd taken the pledge. But Mary was dead. And anything between him and Lyman was null and void. His thoughts slipped down the sides.

Tiger put the flask to his lips and tilted his head back. A burst of rain forced Tiger to close his eyes and when it had passed, his eyes were still closed.

CHAPTER
16

THUNDER SHOOK LYMAN'S EYES OPEN. KNEELING IN A FOOT of muddy, stinking water, his face pressed against the slimy wall of the trench, he was alone, wrapped in a thick morning fog and unsure if he was awake or still dreaming. Another burst of thunder forced his eyes open a bit further, and when he realized that it wasn't thunder but a cannonade off to the left, he knew he was awake and wasn't sure if that was good or bad. His greasy, uncomfortable sleep came back to him, a night of half-conscious and unremembered dreams too close to reality for his mind and body to relax. He had dipped in and out of sleep as if he had taken small cups of water from a fetid pool and spat it out each time, the taste too rancid to keep even as memory. The one firm image he had was of Tiger sitting legs crossed, staring off into the dark, and Lyman couldn't say whether or not that had really happened.

He pushed himself away from the slick wall of the entrenchment and tried to peer through the heavy mist. Suddenly a roar from the left crashed over the line and the two forms flanking Lyman stirred in the water. The twelfth of May had started; blood and rain already flowed; the Battle of Spotsylvania had finally begun.

The first hours of the day had been loud. The attack far to the left had brought screams along with the constant rifle fire, while the Rebels opened artillery on the position directly to the north of Cutler and the 14th. The few men with constitutions so hardened or so soft that they could sleep through the battle on the left had awakened at the artillery fire and watched as the cannon flashes ushered in the dreary light of this fog-swaddled dawn. Drenched through and muddy, their thin leather brogans swelling or, in some cases, coming apart from the hours spent in the trough their trenches had become, the men of the 14th now sat sullen and quiet, ordered to remain at the ready for immediate attack. They bailed water, tried to keep their cartridges dry, and prayed, waiting for the call to attention.

Newt and Karl had stayed together through the night and were doing their best to slop as much water as they could out of the trench when Del Rio slipped over to them. "Leesen. I seen Feeney selling something to some-body."

Karl and Newt both shot up erect. The German asked where he'd seen him. "Dee sinks. Where else you see Feeney? Leading a charge?"

Despite Lyman's promise to retrieve their goods, the three caught Feeney returning to their camp with his now-standard expression of cowed apprehension and an erratic gait that showed a week of quickstep was having a mean effect. Heading toward Willie's fire, Slipper Feeney walked along, gazing at something he was holding in his hand. Joaquin and Karl locked into his step and joined their arms into his as though they were three bully friends going for a stroll.

Newt faced Feeney, stepping dangerously backward through the mud as the three walked forward. Newt felt an anger in his gut, a combination of righteous indignation and fear. He had been cooking this brew of hatred all night, stirring in wrongs and churning things up from the bottom, hoping that he could resort to its powers during the fury of battle. Newt had let it run close to boiling all morning and Feeney's apparent lack of remorse set it over the rim. He grabbed at Slipper's hand. "Whaddaya have there, Feeney? Huh?"

Slipper held his fist tight but did not bother to squirm against the grip of his accusers. "I told you that I didn't hook nothing. I swears to God."

"Del Rio here says you were selling the desk and the housewife over at the sinks. Let's see what you got for 'em."

"I traded something." Newt tried to pry open his hand, but years of picking pockets and dealing cards had given Slipper strong fingers. "Leave off me! Just 'cause I took ye at Bluff don't mean I'd steal ye blind out!"

Karl and Joaquin pulled Slipper's arms behind his back, and just as

Newt hauled back to deliver the first punch he had ever thrown in his life, one aimed at a defenseless man, Lyman caught him. "Jesus, I told you he didn't do it!"

Newt seemed to reenter his body. He looked at his hand, balled into a fist and held back at ear level by Lyman, and swallowed, the fury draining from his eyes. He had a calmer tone. "Del Rio caught him selling our things to someone."

"I don't believe it."

Newt pointed at Feeney's hand. "Whatever he got for them, it's in there."

Lyman looked Slipper in the eye. "Show us. Open your hand."

Karl released Feeney, who held out his hand and slowly opened it like a dank, dingy flower to reveal a thin leather cord strung through a small silver cross. A drop of rain splattered onto it. Feeney turned away and meekly said, "I traded him my deck a cards. I don't wanna play cards no more."

Lyman shook his head. "Let him go."

Captain Henry called the company to attention. The men stopped where they were as he reported that the Second Corps under Hancock had attacked the Confederate works with resounding success, capturing an entire division and four generals. Henry allowed a few seconds of cheering, then ordered them to be ready for attack in an hour's time, at eight o'clock. The regiment went back to its business, hearts beating faster with battle coming into clear view. This would be it. If they took Lee here, the battle—hell, the war— could be over. Lyman left Newt and Karl to find Wes.

Officers would not be on horse today; Henry and Stewart would have no choice but to go in with their men. Stewart did not relish the thought, but something else bothered him even more and walking back with Henry to their tents, he finally had the chance to bring it up.

"What did Fowler have to say?"

Henry's voice gave nothing away. "Oh, you saw him?"

"Yes, on my way out."

"It's a shame you missed him, but just as well, really. It was nothing special."

"Burridge stayed?"

"It was tedious business; supplies, if I recall correctly. Thought it would be a good lesson for Burridge. A taste of how humdrum a captain's life can be."

Stewart nodded and worked his thick lips. He was not accustomed to such blatant lies from Henry, but he was learning that he'd better become so.

Lyman knew he didn't have much time before they went in, so he scrambled about in the rain until he finally found Wes toward the back of their position, securing a new load of dry cartridges in his metal box. Wes had the penitent look of a child about to be punished. "Lyman, I can explain."

Lyman stared into his face, wanting to see something deeper in it, and he was disappointed to see nothing but a blur of confusion on the boy's face and a layer of light whiskers catching raindrops. He'd trusted him. "Your father would die a second death if he knew about this."

"I have the housewife in my knapsack. I'll give it back to Karl right now and I'll take whatever licking you boys think is fair."

"And what about the desk? What about the fucking desk? Newt has a wife and a family he writes to and you have no one. What was the fucking point of stealing *that*?"

Wes felt a jab of loneliness. "You gotta believe me, Lyman. I didn't snag that desk. I don't know what happened to it. I took the housewife to sew up my jacket, but I didn't take no desk."

Lyman wouldn't hear him; instead he launched into a sermon on morals, unusual from a man who hadn't seen the inside of a church in years. Wes saw Lyman's face hardening, so he broke in. "It's just a lousy desk. Fry's gonna be out a here in ten days. Who gives a shit about his desk?"

Lyman saw the men of the regiment carefully loading their weapons, trying not to get their cartridges wet in the constant rain. "We better get going."

"Go fuck yourself, Alder. I wouldn't do what you tell me if it would save my life."

Lyman had already started back to his spot in the trench, but he stopped and turned around. "I don't care if you live or die." As soon as he'd said it, Lyman wanted to take it back, but it was much too late.

———

Though it was eight o'clock—midmorning for those who had been shooting since four over near the salient—heavy skies and rain blocked the sun and forced the watery dim blue of the minutes before dawn to serve as light for this battle day. Lined up on the muddy stretch in front of the trenches, Lyman peered into the fog, which the weak light had diluted. A thatch of pines stood before them and off to the left, and ahead were the black remains of a house that Lyman guessed was the one they'd seen burning in the distance when they'd first marched in. That placed them now far on the right of the Union line, behind the two lines of Robinson's brigade in ready for attack.

Newt had been telling himself for days that he could die at any moment, and now the moment had come and he was wavering, pulled by the life he would return to if he lived: playing piano in the parlor, Mrs. Fry's head upon his shoulder when the children were asleep as she read *Godey's Lady's Book*. Would it matter, he wondered, if he killed now? His bullets wouldn't matter, his anger couldn't win the war. He smoothed his mustache, then slid one hand down to the pouch that held his caps. He asked himself, Am I bound to stay the man that I've become?

A screaming charge went up on the left as Warren's attack began. Newt held his hand upon the pouch.

Louis asked himself much the same question: Will I die today? Every other day his beating heart and pride had answered no, but today he heard the bullets of the charge and Providence could make no promise.

Lyman noticed motion ahead in Robinson's line; it was time. He trembled, unusual for him. His men were nervous and he knew he had to do something for them and for himself. "Willie, give us a quote! Give us some God!"

Swords and pistols were raised to send the 14th into the trees behind Robinson's brigade. Willie had to think a second, Lyman urging him on, but then the cook finally screamed out in the loudest voice he had to all the men around him. " 'The shield of his mighty men is made red, the valiant men are in scarlet; the chariots shall be with flaming torches in the day of his preparation, and the fir trees shall be terribly shaken!' " Men looked at their pants and smiled. Some of Robinson's men looked back in amusement, but a thrill rode through the 14th's line.

Newt capped his rifle and the swords came down.

A quick march began into the trees. Wes had been fuming already, burning with shame and a personal anger that he was ready to vent on the Rebels ahead. He marched next to Teddy, who was quiet, too, but not so resolute. Picking through the pines, Teddy no longer thought he was the eye of the storm, nor was he protected by some shield of power; he was one of many, a minion, a drone, and the cracking rifles sounded like his father's oiled belt. He was afraid.

No bullets yet, Burridge thought. They hadn't hit the Rebel pickets yet and he prayed he wouldn't recognize them when the regiment did. Weaving through the trees, he saw Henry and Stewart a line back. Since they'd rejoined the regiment, the two had no place to hide and no excuses, fear painfully evident in their pinched expressions and overstuffed gaits. All morning Stewart had been taking a more active and unwelcome role in the direction of the company, giving orders to men whose names he didn't know and in general behaving as though he had some inkling of what his job entailed, which he most certainly did not. While it was entertaining to see the expressions of hatred on the men's faces, Burridge knew it bode ill.

The officers both caught his eye and stared. Burridge responded by tilting his head up and away. However this scheme might unfold, the lieutenant felt himself secure from enemy attack, be it Rebel or Union; he was, after all, the man who had set all of this glorious pageantry, these banners flying, and the opportunity for brave men to prove themselves, into motion. He straightened his back to provide a model of moral courage for his simple soldiers.

The passage through the maze of pines resembled a milling throng pushing into the doors of a theater, and the confusion gave every man tense thoughts of the Wilderness. During the hour it took to make their way through, the men heard waves of charging Yankees rush on and be scattered upon the firm Rebel works.

Finally the trees broke and the ground sloped down into the bushy ravine. Robinson's brigade held for a second, then plunged down toward the abatis laced across the bottom, with the 14th and the rest of Rice's brigade behind. Rising out of the dirt, the abatis looked like a devilishly uniform sort of underbrush instead of sharpened fortifications.

Rain poured down into the ravine. A massive burst of artillery exploded toward the bottom, spraying mud, water, and bodies of men high into the air. A storm of shells broke, along with the deadly whir of miniés. Yankees rushed toward the abatis and tried to return fire. Others went to their stomachs and shot from there or hid between the tightly wound branches. Near the front of the 14th's line, Newton Fry howled and shot his gun wildly. Every emotion he had went into loading his rifle and firing it toward the Rebel works on the crest. He shot for love; he shot in hatred; for self-pride and for pity; for his regiment and the boys from Alabama. Newt shot, reloaded, then hopped up, sprinting past the limping Louis, and shot again. Given the sword, he dealt mayhem with no thoughts of mercy.

Lyman pushed his way through the vines, over Stives's body—unsure if the baker was dead or alive—past Von Schenk on hands and knees crawling toward the front and moaning. The gunners were getting better range on the field of men pinned down by bullets and shells. He knew they'd never make it up the muddy, overgrown ravine. Again they'd been sent in to distract and die.

A blast shot up a wave of blood and brown water, and the pitch of screaming and shooting increased. Rain held the smoke close to the ground, then pulled it down into greasy puddles and onto the prone bodies of men.

Burridge was out ahead of them all, trotting low to the ground. The miniés came in like hail, or was hail now mixed in, too? Someone next to Lyman clutched his chest and fell onto a bush. A panicked urge to go faster flashed through him. Keep moving, he thought. Just keep moving.

Burridge was tucked down, forcing his way into the bullets and rain. As usual in a charge, he had gone ahead far beyond contact with his men, and he now struggled alone through the thorny underbrush of the ravine. A shell exploded off to the left and more blood-reddened mud splattered across his face. Wincing, he pulled one foot out of the soft muck he'd stepped into, the nature of which he was afraid to check, and ducked the miniés that were beginning to come in stronger.

This is my place, he thought, and no other thought could wedge its way into a mind sparked with battle fire and fear. He surged forward and was about to step over a gutted torso when he felt his leg pulled, as if tugged back by a body he'd just crossed. As he turned around, another shell burst and all Burridge felt was a great blast of white heat and a searing pain in his face.

Ten yards behind, Lyman saw Burridge get caught on the bush and then, at the shell's impact, fall to the ground with a descending cry that sounded as if the lieutenant was tumbling down a flight of stairs. Two more shells hit nearby in close succession and Lyman went to his stomach; there was no question of going forward. The only question was whether he would save Burridge.

The pain was not sharp enough to dull the lieutenant's sensation of being injured and trapped under Rebel guns. Panic made his mind work faster, if not more clearly, and Burridge could not see a way free. Looking forward, he saw the cannons; looking back he saw men in blue running away from him. He could not shake himself free. The blood trickled into his mouth, its rich iron taste coating his tongue. Pulling himself through the mud, he dodged one minié by luck, but he could not dodge them all. Not alone. This was the way he would end, and his mind slipped into the misty land of shadows to prepare him for the light.

Lyman watched as Burridge tried to reach back to free his leg, the uncertain movement appearing like a wave of greeting. Miniés dove into the mud around him as the Rebels took aim, trying to finish the slaughter. Burridge's death would raise all the boats and Lyman saw himself greeted as "Sergeant Alder" on the streets of Williamsburg. If he died, there'd be one less arrogant lawyer, one less slink officer sure that he was better than he was. One less Burridge, who'd passed him over.

Burridge knew whose arms were cradling him. Who else would come find him in the midst of this frenzy? Who else would wipe the blood off his wound, stroke his head, and tell him that he would live? When he'd seen Mink scuttling forward through the smoke, he was surprised that he was wearing blue, but Mink *was* a Union man and that explained it. The last few moments trickled back into Burridge's mind: a white flash, a numbing explosion, then black and the taste of dirt and blood in his mouth. Even with the miniés and heavy shells, he felt calmer now.

Why Burridge was saying Sidney Mink's name over and over Lyman had no idea, but when he had reached his body, he saw that a piece of bone from some other shattered body had sliced the lieutenant's face. Shock and the briars had pulled Burridge down. Seeing the boy's horrified face, Lyman yelled in his ear, "You're not hit! You're not bleeding!" He hunched over the lieutenant, shielding his body.

Why was *he* here? Burridge wondered. This man, of all men, was trying to save his life; a man he had insulted, undermined, and sneered at. It made no sense.

The concussion of a Rebel shell shook them both. As much as he wanted to reestablish his authority, Burridge's mind had not firmed enough to lead and he cast his eyes about for a way out.

The shells came down harder. On the right, a squealing mass of Pennsylvania Reserves ran back to the safety of their lines in a repeat of their sorry performance four nights ago, but up front the men stood firm at the abatis and were cut down by torrents of Rebel fire. The advance was broken. The Yankees could only try to hold until they had orders to retreat.

Lyman pulled the lieutenant to his knees. "Follow me." On all fours, the two crawled back up the Union side of the ravine.

The slaughter continued for another twenty minutes. Despite the sacrificial nature of their position, most men held their ground until the bugle calling retreat cut through the screams and thunder, and Cutler's men crawled back up their side of the ravine and through the woods toward the safety of the Union lines now hidden by smoke and mist. The retreat was done with order.

CHAPTER
17

B ACK IN THEIR ENTRENCHMENTS, THE MEN TOOK ADVAN-
tage of whatever minutes were offered for rest and water before
the next assault. Though taking the Rebel position across the
ravine was impossible, everyone knew that the staggering losses
resulting from its pursuit were very much elements of Grant's
strategy. Every man in Warren's command assumed there'd be
another try at the enemy line, whether in ten minutes or two
hours. The storm had continued during the failed assault, so even with some
hurried bailing upon their return, the men slogged through fetid water now
calf deep and huddled close to the walls for protection against sharpshooters'
bullets and the slanting sheets of rain.

While most sucked greedily at canteens or, if they'd run out, in desperation sipped at the trough they stood in, Lyman made his way down the
line taking a head count. Louis and Karl had propped Caspar against a wall;
the fat Prussian had his eyes closed as his lungs reached for as much air as
they could take. Rain washed the sulfur off his face in streams.

Lyman moved on, stepping over the four legs of the Worm brothers,
who were arguing where the Fifth Corps would go in next, and stopped
near Tice, whose teeth were chattering. Once he was satisfied that Tice
would live to see more fighting, he stood up and bumped into Burridge,
who was performing a similar duty from the other end. Their eyes locked
for a brief uncomfortable moment until Lyman broke away. He had gone
to the aid of many men during this war, as many as had come to his. That
friends would imperil their lives to save yours was a natural, unconsidered
act. To speak of it was to describe your wedding night; the world did not

have words for such moments, and as he stood face-to-face with Burridge, Lyman's greatest fear was that the lieutenant would try to find them. He felt proud and annoyed that he had gone out to him and he wanted it past them.

Burridge blocked his way for a beat, his eyes shooting from corner to corner. He opened his mouth as if to speak. Lyman cringed, but all that came out was "Excuse me" as Burridge pushed past. Lyman exhaled and continued his rounds. He absolved himself of his good intentions by swearing never to help Porridge again.

Slipper Feeney had just emerged from the trees when the troops were ordered back into line by Stewart, swept into the vast momentum of a battle that had swirled out of any one man's control long ago. "Don't leave me here!" he called out to them. Wes gave him his canteen, then Teddy hauled one of Feeney's arms over his broad shoulders and helped the played-out dealer along the road with the 14th and the rest of Cutler's division toward Hancock's position. As ugly and as dangerous as that assault had been, it was just another in the series of jabs and feints the two armies had been making along the line since the eighth, each waiting for an opening to land the knockout blow.

The furious activity on the roads behind the front gave evidence that Hancock might have finally delivered it off to the left. Galloping teams of horses bolted past them pulling wagonloads of ammunition and splashing waves of mud onto the lines of trudging men. Mounted officers cried out orders or conferred with aides; the bewildered and the wounded streamed in both directions. Similar activity had been going on since this line was formed, but it had never reached this pitch of urgency and speed. It appeared that Hancock was fighting the *real* battle of Spotsylvania, the fight they'd all been waiting for that would end this standoff and maybe even the war.

Teddy tried to heft Feeney up just a bit straighter. "Look at this, Slipper! This is gonna be a big one, this is!" Tired and wet and apprehensive as they all were, the same necessary nervous energy that had Teddy twitching surged through the whole regiment and the whole line, an energy masquerading as an eagerness for combat and that, when worn on the faces of thousands of men, helped create that most precious commodity—true courage.

In the flurry of men and horses, no one had noticed something else that had changed, but suddenly a soldier called out, "It ain't raining!" For the briefest second, everyone—officers, infantrymen, mule drivers—stopped and noticed calm on the thousands of puddles. A grateful cheer went up and the column began to buzz, hopeful that the storm was passing, hopeful that they were headed toward a more pliable place on the front. Already revived some by the pause in fighting, Horace Worm tried to blow on the small ember of spirit left unquenched by the rain. He cleared his throat and in a trilling baritone voice sang his own version of "La Marseillaise."

> *Hear the drums, O men of Brooklyn!*
> *Heed the cry of liberty!*
> *The land thy fathers fought and died for*
> *calls again for bravery.*
> *From the Navy Yard to the highest steeple top*
> *let the banner of Union ever furl.*
> *Take arms, you Brooklyn men!*
> *Avenge the blood shed by thy brothers.*
> *Black night approach, evil stretched upon the land.*
> *A darkness spread by rebel hand.*
> *Shall the chains of bondage conquer?*
> *Lay down thy hammer for a sword!*
> *Arise and fight the traitor horde!*
> *Take arms, take arms, valorous art thee*
> *Who die to keep men free!*

The 14th burst into another round of cheers, and many applied their buoyed spirits to heaving a stuck wagon out of a deep wallow of mud.

It was nearing one o'clock when Burridge stopped to watch Lyman and Karl apply their broad backs to the rear of the wagon. The embarrassment of his last encounter with Alder had not yet faded in Burridge's mind. He'd meant to thank the man; grudgingly, he would admit, but it had seemed the only proper thing to do. Then he'd looked Alder in the eye and what he saw was the same disgusted, disapproving expression he'd seen in the whore's face after he thanked her for her patience that first time. Still, the man had had no reason to come to his aid, and what was more puzzling was that he had stayed a few moments even after it was clear that the lieutenant was unhurt. He'd stayed only to comfort him. Burridge watched him smile as they got the wagon loose and granted that these calloused, unschooled men lived with a debased nobility.

Marching along, Burridge listened to the idle nervous conversation between Henry and Stewart ahead of him. They had no such feelings about the company, and they'd shown that by avoiding the contact other commanders considered necessary and correct. Mink, he knew, would laugh or spit if Burridge ever ventured the thought that workingmen had a value beyond their labor. But how, he wondered, would Mink respond to the ministrations of one like Alder? Away from Mink's glowing presence, Burridge saw a man shrouded by secrets and a casual arrogance disguising the cold Caesar's heart. Yet there was glory in the name of Caesar, and surely Caesar was allowed an imperial darkness.

A quick breeze snapped open the Stars and Stripes fluttering at the column's head and Henry's white gloved hand crisply swung in pace. As he marched toward battle and the final nine days of his term, Burridge knew he would continue in the path dictated by his ends, yet he nursed a small ember of his own. Fed by the strength of his men, it was the first sign to him that he could have been one of them.

An hour of marching took them two miles northeast, to an opening in the forest. Drops of rain dripped off the branches of trees, shaken loose by the thunder of guns and the wagons rolling by. The order was to prepare for attack. Motionless, hearts beating, guts churning, the company waited to move. They listened to the sounds of battle and to their own thoughts.

The minutes passed. Heads leaned to the side to catch a glimpse of what lay ahead, but the fight was shrouded in smoke and too far away. The minutes crept by. The tension and high spirits that had straightened spines ebbed into impatience. Teddy began a low chant of "Fuck, fuck, fuck, fuck" that Stives, too scared to respond in a biblical fashion, could only cluck at.

The fire of combat had danced across Newt's skin all morning and now threatened to consume him. Possessed by a passion born too late and therefore oversize, Newt thrust his chest out and rolled a fresh cartridge between his fingers, caressing the chunk of lead inside the paper as if it were a jewel, feeling its curves like cut facets. The pangs of fear each second brought whetted his taste for blood, one which everyone else nearby had sated.

Newt ripped open the cartridge with his teeth, even though there'd been no order to load up, and poured the powder down the muzzle of his gun. He licked his tongue around his mouth to spread the foulness and feel its full effect, then forced the minié down with sharp plunges of the ram. To finish, he stuck a cap onto the hammer. He felt ready now; eager to kill men.

———

They waited for an hour, doused by the showers that had returned in the afternoon. The sounds of rifles never slackened; this was not a battle of attack and counterattack. Lyman pictured the cogs grinding against each other again. Only machines could keep up that kind of constant fire. At three the order finally came—they were to relieve Wheaton's men in the front line.

Flags went up and the column began to move through a dense line of bayoneted provost guards meant to keep any man not crippled in the fight. They went on through the clearing in the trees and down the side of a hill, over once grassy land turned to swamp by the rain and the thousands of men who had crossed it that day. Another hill faced them, and beyond it rose the thick plume of smoke formed from eleven hours of rifle fire. They trudged up and at the crest had their first view of the battle.

There was grass, maybe two hundred yards of a field that slipped into a gully and then back up, turning to reddish gray mud for another two hundred yards until it became the discolored scar of entrenchments, part of which bulged out in a point toward the hill. And there, in the distance, was the fight. A slight circular ridge topped with log walls curved around to both left and right like a low fortress and quivered at two sections with gray and blue figures. Rifle smoke wreathed it, slowly feeding the white pillar they had seen coming in. Even from this distance, it was clear that chaos reigned there and the men avoided each other's eyes.

The greenness of the grass immediately struck Lyman. It shone emerald and sparkled even in the dim light as it rolled down toward the gully and a small run swollen by the two days of rain. The other bank of the run began the gentle slope up to the fight, and it was here that the bodies started as well; a solid blue covering like a lava flow, single dots at the farthest points from the battle, but layered with corpses closer to the top of the rise. Among the dead, debris—knapsacks, canteens, caps, shoes, bandages, blankets—littered the grass and mud. In support of those fighting at the top, lines of living men lay in the muck amid the dead and shot into the Rebel position. The 14th was headed right toward the point of the entrenchments, a sharp angle swarming with men of both armies. Union soldiers and their officers ran back and forth over the green grass, while others hauled away what wounded and dead could be retrieved from the front or brought in fresh ammunition. A line of cannons to the left lobbed balls and canisters into the Rebel emplacements.

As they got closer, Lyman noticed something else. In most battles, men screamed to exhilarate themselves, to relieve tension and convince their eternal souls that they could kill. The noise of Spotsylvania was a churning, a steady buzz more like a building site than any battle Lyman had seen. He knew that this meant those fighting were too tired to yell, though men still shrieked in death. Like drones, the men accomplished their individual murders methodically under the eyes of pitiless foremen; insanity was necessary to perform the job. Lyman, nearly folded by the cramping of fear, his balls shriveled into his guts, wondered how he'd get his men out alive.

The column neared its destination at the front. Though the Rebel fire was directed toward the ongoing assault at the foot of their position and not at the incoming troops, the men stayed low as they waded across the foot of water in the gully. Grunts and moans from the line became distinct. Arching high over them, a shell plunged into the Rebel position twenty yards behind the emplacements with a screech, then a thudding blast. No one had ever seen a shell act like that before. That had to be the mortar. Lyman winced at the explosion and at the fact that he'd told Micah about it. Willie whistled. "That's a new way to kill men," he said, and winked. It looked to Lyman like one of Arlette's slow balls. Could they possibly be there, on the other side? He chose not to think about why Micah and those boys seemed to be everywhere Company L went. That was Louis's job.

The line passed a still body alone on the rise, presumably dead. Karl stopped next to it, despite Stewart's command to keep marching. He was about to make a quick sign of the cross and commend its spirit to heaven, when the corpse shot a hand out and tried to pull itself just another foot closer to the hospital. Karl jumped and Tiger began laughing and high-stepping through the mud until he slipped and fell on his rear end. No one else laughed. They left the wounded man to his own devices. Lyman said nothing to the drunken Tiger. Clearly Burridge had supplied a prisoner of drink with more drink. Lyman hoped Tiger wouldn't die or kill any of their men, but there was no pity for a man who went into a fray chocked full. The scene itself was a hallucination, a smoky, grinding dream of battle that was out of control. Flags swayed as their bearers fell, then rose up over new hands or pulled one way or the other over the entrenchments. Mounds of blue along the trench walls sharpened into focus; they were stacks of bodies, faces carved forever into puzzled expressions. Lyman could only guess what it had been like during the first assault, but thought that it couldn't be much worse than the shapeless slaughter taking place at that moment. Cutler called his troops to a halt. Del Rio crossed himself obsessively, Karl's rosary in his hand, while Caspar shook his head with the same crazed urgency. "This is madness! This is madness!" To the right a number of brigades lay on their bellies in the mud, at some places ten ranks deep, keeping up a regular shower of bullets into the Confederate works until they would join the continuous assault in front of them. To the left another melee roiled at the sharp angle of the salient. Here a line of Union men laid flanking fire into the fray and into the Rebels farther back on the low hill. These men had the protection of a small rise in front of them and the parapet of the Rebel works, which made it difficult for the butternuts to get a good shot at them. The 14th would relieve one of these groups and Lyman prayed it would be the latter. No matter which direction they went, though, he envied the men they were about to replace. At least they were done with this fight.

The column moved again. A brigade of Pennsylvanians went off to the right and the spirits of the 14th got a slight lift. Colonel Fowler waved them to the left, with orders to prevent the Rebels at the rear of the rise from firing or coming out from their works. With the 56th Pennsylvania and the 147th New York behind them, the 14th used their rifles to scale the rise and the knee-deep mud to reach the trench walls. Tice whimpered audibly and at the same time, without consulting each other, both Willie and Stives quoted the same verse—" 'Through thee will we push down our enemies: through thy name will we tread them under that rise up against us!' " They looked at each other, smiled, and said, "Amen."

Horace straightened his brother's cap. "To state the positive, at least we are not expected to attack." He put his hand on Pindar's cheek. "Be careful." Then he rubbed the bristles with a playful vigor and slapped the other Worm's cheek. "Take a shave, Pinney."

Pindar knocked the hand away. "Don't call me 'Pinney.'" He winked at Horace and the two slogged ahead with the line.

Linden Stewart nervously fussed with his nose as he watched Henry and Burridge lean their heads together, each pointing at features of the landscape and battle ahead of them in private conference. A shell slammed down farther back in the Rebel works, but Stewart didn't flinch. The guns did nothing to his nerves; losing his power frightened him more than losing his life.

Louis could tell from the pitch of Tice's whining that the boy was about to burst into tears. The mewling dug its nails into the Hungarian's back, but he tried to ignore it and instead watched the lines of weary men trudging through the mud toward them to exchange positions. Some pulled along their friends, others were too bent and exhausted to help anyone but themselves. Hollow-eyed, wandering, hopeless faces black with powder, they had seen too much, Louis thought. Another mortar shell dove into the earth, searching for the proper range, but it was thirty yards too short and blasted a muddy patch clear of Union soldiers.

A man with empty eyes staggered by, staring far off into the distance. His face was coated black like a minstrel's and with a swollen tongue he begged for "Awta. Awta," in a bland voice that conveyed no hope of receiving a drink in what had become again a driving rain. Louis stopped him with a hand against his chest, then gave him his canteen. Without a word of thanks and with eyes aimed far away, the man tipped back the canteen and poured the water down his throat, splashing and wasting much of it. When it was drained, he dropped it on the mud and walked on.

Louis picked up his canteen. He had seen fields of men reaped clean by bullets, stirring charges withered under guns, but compared to these countless men and their countless torments, this storm of confusion and evil and unrelenting death, he knew that those were the upper circles of hell, where dignity and tragedy still robed the lives of those condemned. This was farther down. His days as the Lion of Comorn now over, a guilty flush rode over Louis as he realized that what he had lauded as a necessary act of man was nothing but the foul core of Dante's journey.

Tice whined again and Louis snapped. He turned and slapped him full and hard across the cheek, then grasped his face between his hands and turned it toward the seething mass of men. *"Ecco Dite!"* he said. Behold Dis, and all the hellish wonders of the Inferno.

Overwhelmed, Tice slipped into the mud. Louis knew that he would be Virgil to this weeping softness at his side who did not know a single line of verse. The love of battle that brought Louis here had also drawn poor boys down to a pit of suffering they should not have to know. Now he had to guide the innocent out. A pair of starlings, black against the sky, wheeled past and Louis cursed them. He pulled up the fallen Tice. "Hold on to my jacket," Louis said, and the two began their journey.

––––––

So the 14th entered the battle, aided by the belief that it would be their last. The men filed up so that the lead company butted against the trench wall and Company L at the end hung off to the right. They quickly fell to their knees or onto their stomachs, yet despite Fowler's command to commence firing, there was a stunned pause as the soldiers made brief and unsuccessful attempts to find some order in all that was happening. A few dozen yards before them, across a thick sea of the dead and mud, Rebels and Union men fought at arm's length over a single four-foot log wall of entrenchment. Shreds and chips of wood shot off by bullets sprinkled everything nearby. A ditch ran along the base of the wall filled with a bright red mud. Virginia mud runs to red, but never as red as this paste of dirt, blood, and rain. A hand held up out of the muck attested to the many bodies that had disappeared into it, drowned first if merely wounded. The stiff bodies still exposed had gathered against the sides of the wall and served as a ramp for the combatants.

Bayonets bristled in each direction. A Yankee held his rifle over the works and plunged it down blindly in hopes of piercing Rebel flesh, but a butternut grabbed the muzzle. Screaming in anger and in pain, his hands burning now from the searing heat of the muzzle, the Rebel pulled the Yankee over the top, and in a moment all that could be seen of the Yank was a hand reaching to the sky. It trembled, then fell, and the Rebel's face reappeared, leering and hungry for his next victim. The pitch of shooting swelled again. The heaps of bodies squirmed with injured men trying to push free of the crushing dead atop them; they could hear growls and barks and individual Yanks cursing individual Rebels. The men peered into the depths of human desperation and slaughter and were struck dumb.

An officer with no lower jaw, just the top portion of his skull pouring blood and saliva onto his blue jacket, leaned against the wall and gestured madly with both hands. Willie nudged Lyman and yelled into his ear through the din, "That fella's a Mason!"

"What?"

"That fellow's a Mason!" The officer kept waving his hands about, even tugging at the trousers of dead men so they would pay attention. "I shouldn't say, but that's the distress signal!"

Lyman's head swam. He looked around at the other men as he reloaded. Wes was nearly on top of Slipper, helping him reload his rifle and howling encouragement into his ear. Tiger was laughing hysterically, singing bits of songs while shooting. Karl and Teddy and the Worms had begun shooting as well, and by the time Lyman had shot again into the Rebels behind the works, the entire company was in action to the best of their abilities. Lyman felt as if he had just been plunged into the cold center of a deep black-watered pond. Would he have enough air to ever come back to the surface? He had to start swimming or drown. Lyman quickly tugged another cartridge out of his box.

———

The clouds and the coming night pressed harder onto the battlefield. The rain had slackened some, and as Burridge settled back onto his stomach, he had a clear look at the melee. A Rebel leaped onto the entrenchment wall and shot down at the Yankees, then tossed his rifle back and took another handed up to him. He got off one more shot before a bullet drove through his neck. Another Rebel took his place. Burridge considered the remarkable courage of the men climbing upon the works for what they, even in their bullet-addled minds, had to know was a suicidal end. Caesar had seen nearly the same action from the men of Vercingetorix in Gaul, who gave their lives one by one to stoke the flames around the ramps of the besieging Romans, and he had had to comment on their heroism, even though they were his foes.

Burridge shot and loaded again by rote, his tongue drying out from the harsh gunpowder. If Caesar could see glory in the acts of a single Gaul, surely these men around him had their glory, too, and their deaths were tragic endings of families and homes where an empty chair beside the fire would remember the men who were missing. What if Alder had died while in his aid?

Yet Caesar, supposed friend to the common man, admirer of their noble deeds, sent droves to their end for his own good. He'd used their lives and watched them die without regrets; the lieutenant had aspired to the same. Burridge shot again and the searing pain he felt as he considered the consequences of every hurtling chunk of lead and stabbing bayonet finally placed him among the thousands. He could not be Caesar; was not meant to be, nor was Mink. Those he fought with were not pieces on a board or toe marks in the dirt around first base. Each was a man, and so was he.

Pressed hard against the earth, Newt couldn't shoot fast enough to satisfy his urge to kill or convince himself that he'd live through this. As the men at the salient had merged into one seething body, so his fear of being shot and his desire to prove his mettle had blended into one inchoate sense that he must shoot and somehow make this stop.

The random design of battle had placed a man, legs curled under his lifeless body, against the mound of fallen. His arms hung down at his sides and his eyes were open and clear and staring right at Newt. As Newt's eyes met his, a bullet crushed into the man's chest, exploding in a red blossom, but not changing the man's expression. Another ripped a chunk off his upper arm.

Newt's hands trembled. He dropped a cartridge, fumbled with the next, all the while panting, each breath accompanied by an urgent whimper. Lyman reached his arm out and put his hand on Newton's shoulder. "Don't waste your fucking cartridges! Pick your shots!"

Lost and deaf to all who'd find him, Newt couldn't answer. He loaded and shot and hoped he'd killed the man who would have killed him. He loaded, shot again, and hit the corpse to make it stop staring, but the eyes remained open.

———

Under clouds of gun smoke and a constant rain, the men of the 14th continued their work. By six o'clock the flashes from their rifles added light to the scene along with color as they watched a necessary truce play out at the angle. So many bodies had piled up at the wall that a break was needed to lever them away and make room for more of the living. Teams of Union soldiers dispensed with any respect due the dead and pushed carcasses aside to carve a space for their next assault; the Rebels did the same on their side. Bodies splashed into the mud, sank into the ditch, or tumbled into new smaller heaps. Mud or the tons of corpses quickly muffled what cries the wounded made as they were shoved about. Union men crammed hardtack into their mouths, crumbs spilling over them, and downed drafts of water brought up by runners during the pause.

The 14th, the 56th, and the 147th provided most of the fire during this break; little more than an annoyance considering the fury of what the angle had seen so far. After ten minutes or so of this relative quiet, the Union men crept back into their position and formed lines. The Rebels snuck back to the transverses and crannies of their works. A Yankee general raised his sword and the charge went in again, met by a volley of Southern bullets. Those who made it through the wave of lead stormed the works, and the confused and gruesome struggle resumed.

Teddy wasn't grinding his teeth as much as he was cracking them together. Wesley did his best to calm him down.

"Just keep shootin', Teddy. They can't get us under here."

"We're never a-leavin' here, Pitt." Teddy bucked and shifted in the mud like a hog who has smelled the blood of the slaughterhouse and knows his fate. "They're leaving us here ta die. I know it."

"Load up and shoot." The same thought had occurred to Wesley during the last three endless hours, but he had fallen into a rhythm, and seeing that no one had been hit in that time despite the healthy volume of miniés aimed their way, he knew that for him, the monotony of killing was the greatest enemy. In every other battle, there had been the frenetic release of a charge, but tonight was different. There was no time when this would be over and he could not run into the fight or away from it.

Teddy watched a Union man booted with mud up to his knees, musket torn from his hands, pull a log from the works and heave it over the top and onto the Rebs. A Yank and a Reb stabbed each other at the same time with bayonets, and though both strikes were true and fatal, neither body would fall. Each propped by the force of the other, they stood until bullets shredded their flesh and toppled them onto the log wall and apart.

Squirming by on his belly, Lyman asked how they were doing on cartridges, every word a scream in the din of shouting and guns. Though he looked worn to Wesley, the boy quashed the urge to volunteer to help and instead stuck out his canteen for Lyman to send back with the cartridge runners.

Amid a carpet of empty paper cartridges, Louis yelled instructions to Jimmy Tice. "You must find a man in your sights and then shoot. There, point at the one holding the flag." The gun slipped off Tice's muddy shoulder as he pulled the trigger, sending another stray bullet into the skies. As Louis taught this innocent to kill, he wondered if he would be damned like Virgil. Any Christian would say he was already. He knocked the wad of mud off Tice's shoulder, his spine cracking as he twisted. A shell burst. Someone's arm flew off and the owner scrabbled over the heap of bodies, retrieved it, and splashed through the mud brandishing the limb. "I got it! I got it!"

Louis got off a shot, feeling his heart harden to the details of slaughter like winter ice on a deep pond. Louis broke the crust and forced himself to see the faces he shot at and the faces that fell, to think of who they were and why they had come to this. To shoot and ignore the consequences was easy and many did it to survive, but if his heart hardened here in the fires of hell, Louis knew that he would truly deserve the damnation he had never believed in.

Karl dropped his rifle into the mud and began cursing. "*Donnervetter! Mein* gun is fouled!"

Del Rio called out that his was fouled, too, and Wesley reported that his was too hot to touch. Lyman was not getting off his usual steady fire, and he fought the inertia of fear by going from man to man and doing what he could to help. When he had collected twelve canteens, he handed them over to Stives with orders to take Del Rio back and collect as much tack, water, and cartridges as possible.

The two crawled away and Lyman asked himself if he had done the right thing. They were two of the least reliable men in the company and he'd sent them for the materials they all needed to stay alive. His stomach flipped. Worse than the bullets was the threat of madness brought on by scene after scene of inhuman destruction. Hope of breaking the Rebel line, of this being their last battle, had long ago sunk under the bloody mire in the ditch, and now they were losing the use of their weapons. What would Danny do here? What would anyone do here, anyone who knew what they were doing?

The Rebels were taking better aim now and miniés splattered into the mud a few feet before them. He would have to act. Lyman had seen men farther back from the front handing up loaded rifles to men at the wall, who then returned them and took another loaded weapon. It was the only way to keep up the fire and make best use of what cartridges they had. Shouting into the storm, Lyman organized the men into teams of four, with the better shots up front and the others behind reloading.

The men began to arrange themselves into fighting units, instinctively understanding the value of cooperation, but all Stewart saw was half the company edging back from the line and not shooting. Eager to reclaim what turf he'd lost to Burridge in this intrigue, Stewart heaved his bulk through the mud and berated those slackers who were now rapidly loading for their fellow soldiers.

In the noise, Burridge could only indicate to Henry that there was a problem. The captain made his way over and tugged at Stewart's sleeve to get his attention. "Let Burridge handle this! Come on!" With only the suggestion of force, Henry dragged Stewart back to their position on the regiment's right flank. "Not your cup of tea, this, eh? More Miles's sort of thing. You'll give your best from here; let them fight it their way." Linden Stewart, a man of black thoughts, began to have some darker than any he'd ever had.

Tiger took another sip from Burridge's flask and felt a warm rush of courage flow through his body. Death after death took place before his eyes and he was not sated. A bayonet flew over the log works and landed in the chest of a bearded Rebel and the roll of gunfire echoed in Tiger's ears. He grinned as a dough-faced Yank stared into a Rebel musket two feet away; burst into a smile as the flash and smoke erupted from the muzzle and the skull and brains splattered onto the men around. He didn't so much recognize the crazed and vacant looks on those in combat as he felt it in his bones, in his whiskeyed blood. Death itself was lost in the sheer frenzy of destruction— the very center of this furious purging of all the world's pain.

The wild fire that had lit his eyes in earlier battles returned and Quigley turned to Teddy Finn, grabbed the lapels of Teddy's jacket, and howled into his face, "They need us up there! They need us!"

The thick hide of Teddy's anxiety had deflected all of Wesley's calming words; he wanted action, craved action, because action was all that Teddy knew. A quick run to the maw of Death would mean he was not just one gun among the thousands. He frantically nodded. Huey heard Tiger's call as well and the three raised themselves up on their knees, quickly sinking down into the mud but holding their weapons high.

Wes threw himself onto Teddy and Huey, knocking the two of them down, and Lyman got a brief grip on Tiger's jacket before it slipped out of his hands. Tiger was now on his feet and taking his first step toward the wall. Splashing into the mud, Lyman tried to get up, but he had no solid surface and fell back down face first.

Two miniés kicked up the mud in front of Tiger. Lyman stretched out his arms in a final desperate reach and hooked three swollen fingers into the small gap between Tiger's leggings and his trousers as Tiger hauled his leg up. He pulled back and Tiger splashed into the mud.

A minié dove into the muck three feet from Tiger's head. Lyman pulled, but Tiger fought, ramming his hand deep into the mire and heaving forward. "Leave off me, goddamn ye! Let me do it!"

Lyman felt the leggings give way. "Wes, help me!" Pitt crawled over the stunned bodies of Finn and Huey and grabbed Tiger's other leg. Screaming and cursing, Tiger was slowly retrieved.

Before Quigley could damn another man to hell or threaten his friend's life, Wesley landed a right to Tiger's jaw and knocked him out cold. Lyman dragged him back from the front of their line, leaving Tiger in Huey's care with instructions to pop his nut if he woke up again.

Wesley's tackle had done the work of smelling salts on Teddy and Huey. Lulled into an act of insanity by the ceaseless rhythm of this battle, they now took rapid stock of where they were and, with sheepish glances to Wesley that served as thanks, they went back to work.

Caspar Von Schenk had not fallen into one of the units Lyman had organized, and it was not because Lyman had failed to include him. Any group would have welcomed his good shot or his Prussian-trained ability to load a gun in seconds. But Caspar choose to fight on his own and confront alone the cruelest battle he, or any man, had ever seen. Von Schenk had been paid all his life to bring the proven methods of European destruction to warring factions throughout the world, but the mad *tableaux vivant* presented to him this day had nothing to do with the limits that civilized men had placed on the ritual exercise of force. The only thing clear to Caspar as he wallowed in the mud was that this battle was madness, a madness shared by both armies of the Americans.

His own madness rose, too, as the bodies piled up. He was alone here; more alone than he'd been in China, or Ghat, or among the Hindoos. The world he knew meant nothing in this field, and seeing this primal slaughter, he sensed that none of it had a meaning anymore. This young and brutal country had tossed off all the bindings reason put on man and loosed the fateful lightning within each human soul that would surely set the world he knew on fire.

Stives was right, he thought. The seals were being opened. No one near enough to stop him, Caspar stood and walked to meet the Horsemen, singing his favorite hymn.

> *Ein feste Burg ist unser Gott,*
> *Ein gute Wehr und Waffen.*
> *Er hilft uns frei aus aller Not,*
> *Die uns jetzt has betroffen.*
> *Der alt böse Feind, . . .*

Von Schenk made it halfway to the churning whirlpool at the wall before an exploding mortar shell lit him in the dusk. A Rebel finally noticed him. The minié slammed into Caspar's stomach, throwing him onto his back, arms spread to welcome the pouring rain and his lonely end.

During the hours spent watching his mute questioner be blown to pieces by miniés from both sides of the wall, Newt constructed an entire life for the fellow. When his arm flew free, Newt gave him a pair of kindly parents; as his legs were shot down to the bone, Newt named his two sisters and three brothers, all faithful correspondents. He became an employee of a fine Boston bank as his body was tossed aside during the six o'clock pause, and the bullet that smashed open his skull and sent parts of his brain sliding down his face earned him a warm friendship with Wendell Phillips. Newt couldn't tell if it was a Union minié or a Reb's that finally knocked the other side of the boy's head off; the darkness had thickened to where the ends were all that were visible.

As Newt squinted into the gloaming for one last sight of the body, a loud whir shot past his left ear. It had finally happened; he'd been shot.

Newt's overactive brain ricocheted off the sensations even as he began sinking into a daze, and everything around him slowed down. The first thought he had was that it did not hurt, and the thought would have set him laughing but for the numbness that had overtaken him. He felt pummeled; weak and tired the way he'd been when he'd had the fever as a boy, the way he'd felt the one and only time he'd drunk whiskey. He just wanted to sleep and never move again. He noticed strange things, such as how Lyman's cleft chin resembled a man's buttocks. Faces floated by, lights, the sounds of explosions in his ears, hands touched him, jostled him; everything happened slowly and Newt was content to let it all happen as he lay in the mud.

He couldn't say how long he lay there, an hour or a minute. Then he felt it, or at least thought he felt it, a small finger probing in his chest. Newt clutched at his breast and the warm ease he'd floated in evaporated. He was hot and dry in this drenched plain of mud. The minié was in him. He felt it. His chest started to burn and the warm blood was a distinct feeling easily separated from the constant moisture of the mud and rain. The initial cushion of shock had worn off, and Newt's scattered thoughts began to gather around the idea that he had been shot in the chest and was soon to die.

The blood pumped faster. He saw Mrs. Fry, the children, the piano in the parlor. This was the moment of death, he thought. The moment he had feared his whole life.

Panic sent a throb of energy through him. He was up and moving as fast as anyone could toward the hospitals in the rear, in search of someone who could return to him the life he was recently so willing to give.

Lyman had seen the bullet drive into Newt's jacket and had immediately torn it open to check the wound, relieved to see it was just an ugly, but relatively harmless, laceration across his chest. Newt was bleeding and knocked out, but he'd be fine. Lyman had left his canteen with him and planned to check on him in a few minutes, but the next thing he knew, Fry had popped up and was wading down the slope behind the two other regiments as though in full retreat.

Lyman called out to him—"You'll be fine!"—but Newt couldn't, or wouldn't, hear and soon merged into one of the long black lines of wounded. Hundreds of thousands of men were swarming right now around a few square miles of Virginia, and his addled friend was about to lose himself among them. Lyman was gripped by a sudden impulse to chase after him, but he'd never find him now. Besides, Newt was the one walking away from the guns; the odds were in his favor now, not Lyman's. The butcher waved once and prayed that they would see each other again before they left for home.

Night had come by eight o'clock. Five hours of lying on their stomachs for the 14th, shooting and loading in a mindless pattern, ticking metronomes keeping up a rhythm for a kind of music no one had ever heard. Other regiments had been in action for seventeen hours as dark smothered the field and there was no sign that this contest would end. There were more pauses to clear aside the dead bodies, but when that work was over, the fighting resumed with as much deadly vigor. Most battles have a climax, a charge or repulse that defines the moment of crisis and decides the victor. After hours, or even days, of swirling and countering, wide swings of fortune and the unexpected come true, a Pickett charges, the English archers release their bows, Napoleon's Imperial Guard turns back, and the day is won or lost in those few minutes. Fighting men may fear the slaughter and defeat implicit in such moments, but they also know that when the tide has reached those heights, it can only ebb and the battle's end will soon emerge from the smoke. Spotsylvania was a methodical frenzy that never built to a climax; instead, each cycle of battle played out its monotonous fury, then turned back on itself and began again. The tide never crested. Wave after wave crashed off the entrenchment walls in the same steady, infinite pattern that creates the sand.

A few dozen Rebs spilled over the wall in what the Yanks around them first took to be a feeble counterattack. After two Rebs fell dead from Union bullets, the rest raised their hands very high and yelled, "We give!" and "You got us!" to prove that they were surrendering. Only a few days earlier Lyman had sneered at some Rebel deserters, even as the evidence had mounted that Grant was making obsolete the codes of honor that men of each side held the same proud way they held the tatters of their flags. Lyman took a sip of warm water from his canteen and thought of Micah and the boys from the 12th. They were more for the Union than half the men up North. Del Rio prodded him with another loaded rifle. Lyman grabbed it and took careful aim at darkness.

Tiger had woken up not long after Lyman punched him, but much to Huey's relief, Quigley showed no interest in dashing off into the battle again. Instead, he remained contented to nip at Burridge's flask, sing insulting ditties about his fellow soldiers and blacks, and sink further into an alcoholic mire that rivaled the Virginia mud for the tenacity of its grip. Lying on his back, Tiger now sipped down the last of the whiskey and dedicated another song to the clouds.

> *Newton Fry signed up to fight*
> *Because he loves the nigger.*
> *Too bad he didn't tell a soul*
> *He couldn't pull the trigger.*

His own version of "Yankee Doodle" finished, Tiger belched once, then finally dropped his head unconscious in the mud.

Huey tugged at Lyman's leg and called up to him. "Lyman, he's out again!"

Lyman shot, then edged back to Huey beside Tiger's large and motionless body. "Good." He pointed at Willie. "You and Huey take him to the hospital, then bring some cartridges on the way back. Two trips was enough for Stives and Del Rio."

Willie grinned and shook his head. "Them guards ain't gonna let him through. He ain't got no blood on him."

Huey nodded. "He's right."

Lyman scratched his chin, wincing as a mortar shell shrieked overhead. He wanted Tiger out of the way, but he also wanted him safe. If anything happened to threaten this position, every man would have enough of a job protecting himself, let alone worrying about a drunk and abusive Irishman. Lyman tore open Tiger's jacket and ripped open his long johns to reveal the hairy chest. Then he pulled the bayonet off his rifle.

Huey looked alarmed. "What are ye doing? Don't kill 'im!"

Lyman pressed the muddy bayonet against Tiger's chest. A round bead of blood appeared. Like the butcher he was, Lyman pulled the blunt iron point down Tiger's chest, drawing a red line that broke the skin and nothing else. Blood welled up along the line and Lyman worked the cut so that it would flow and seep into his uniform. "There, he won't die from that. Tell 'em some Reb got him with a bayonet."

Willie winked at him. "You're a bright one, Lyman." He crouched over Tiger's head. "Take ahold of his feet, there, son." Huey got a hand on each ankle and the two began an unsteady descent down the slope.

Lyman called after Willie, "See if there's any news of Newt!" Willie nodded. "Hurry back!"

Willie pretended not to hear that.

CHAPTER
18

EWT HADN'T INTENDED TO JOIN THE LONG LINE OF wounded men making their way to the rear. He knew the direction to head in and struck out that way down the hill, slipping a few times in the mud and noticing the dark figures shuffling alongside him only as another obstacle to be avoided. Though men with one good leg and one ragged, bleeding stump hobbled by, men with hands and ears missing, jaws blown off, men carried off in litters, screaming and weeping, Newt could not fathom the possibility that any of their pains and torments surpassed the grave nature of his own. With Divine Providence, good fortune, and rapid medical attention quickly brought to bear, Newt felt his life could be saved, so he tromped past the line on a parallel course.

Those who could grabbed at him as he passed, but their cries and weak hands were no match against his crusade. The thousands of wounded straggling through the rain were only lesser characters in the great drama of Newton's injury. He splashed on ten yards before the mud began to pull at him and the steps became harder. He could feel his heart beating. A man with his jacket tented over his head like the Reaper's hood reached out to Newt to either stop him or ask him for help, but Newt shoved him away. The exhaustion and pain began to wear on him. The mud sucked him down more and more so that no matter how hard he tried, his pace could only match that of the column next to him. He started to think that he would die right there in the mud.

As he leaned far over to haul a foot out of the muck, a boy dragging one leg, limping along with his rifle as a crutch, put his arm around Newt's neck and pulled him in to his side. The boy was no more than eighteen, with stringy wet hair hanging down to his shoulders and a wispy goatee. He could see the panicked expression of disgust on Newt's face. "Sorry, friend, but I need some help here and you don't 'pear to be gettin' anywheres faster than me." Newt looked the boy up and down. "It's my leg. Don't worry; I ain't gonna bleed on ya, if that's yer fuss."

Pulled into the line, Newt now heard the pained exhalations, the groans and cries of the men he was marching with. He asked the boy what his name was.

"Carlton Soame. Fourth Maine Volunteers. You?"

"Newton Fry. Fourteenth Brooklyn."

"One a them red legs, eh? Hear you're a fine parcel a men."

"Well, we heard that of you, too." Newt had heard no such thing but thought it was the only response under the circumstances. Pain flickered across Soame's face and both fell silent as they lumbered along in the mud toward the black line of provost guards. The world was now in two colors: dark gray and black. Thousands of black forms lay still on the gray mud. Black treetops lined the gray clouded sky. Black wagons and other lines of the wounded and straggling plodded on across the field of mud. The din of the battle grew more distant behind them.

It took them until nearly nine to reach the line of provost cavalry guards and the throng of men milling around them in the clearing they'd come through this morning. Mangled limbs, spilling entrails, and spouts of blood all had to be offered one by one to the guards for permission to proceed on to the hospital. Bright dots of light marked where the guards stood, using lanterns to examine the soldiers. Those being carried or missing limbs were passed through without question and usually evidence of blood was enough to get a man through as well, but not tonight. Upon the orders of the generals, the guards demanded debilitating, life-threatening wounds, while their horses nosed through the mud for stray blades of grass.

As word spread to the back that only serious wounds would be passed, Newt touched his hand to his breast; the first time he'd touched the wound. He immediately got dizzy from the thought of what was in there. A bullet wending its way to the heart was certainly life threatening enough, he decided, and he gave full rein to his fatigue, and by the time he was face-to-face with the bayonet of a provost guard, he and his companion, Soame, both appeared to be near their ends. The short, mustached guard raised a lantern in one hand and looked them over, keeping a small pipe clenched between his teeth as he pointed his rifle at Soame with the other hand. His voice was deep. "Yer laig?"

"Yes, sir."

The rifle went to Newt. "And you?"

"Chest." Newt pulled his jacket open wider to show the blood.

"If you had a chest wound, you'd be dead by now, soldier." The guard used the point of the bayonet to push aside the fabric and take a closer look at the broad red line that had torn and stained Newt's underclothes and jacket. "Damn bloody, I'll give ye that." The guard took a weary and con-templative suck of air, as though the burden of deciding these things wore heavily on his soul. "Right, then. That's a hog full a blood there. G'wan." He waved them through. "Next!"

––––––––––

At the front, the battle continued. Burridge watched with increasing horror as Union men pounded into Rebel positions, exacted what destruction they could, then fell back for a brief respite before another charge and melee. A white light now burned at the wall, a flickering but persistent light from the uninterrupted shooting that looked like the inside of a furnace. The men around it fed the flames, and Burridge caught quick images of their faces in the glow before they fell; a final expression of fury or fear preserved in his mind by the flash, as though photographed.

Burridge had circulated among Alder's teams more freely than he ever had during these hours and was about to check on them again when Captain Henry crawled over to him. Propping himself up by his elbow, Henry saluted. Burridge returned the salute, noticing that Henry's gloves were now the same dark gray as the mud and the column of smoke rising over the battlefront. The roar of shooting made it necessary for the captain to lean into Burridge's ear and yell directly into it. "You're to be con-gratulated!"

Burridge signaled his confusion with a hunch of his shoulders.

Henry pointed to the fire and the screaming and the dark mounds of bodies at the line. "For this! Your friend's bit of knowledge about the Rebel cannons in the horseshoe made this battle finally possible!"

Burridge turned to the fight. His friend. A black figure in a rain cape leaped onto the wall of the entrenchments and spread his arms wide, seeming to exult at this peak of battle. The details of his face and dress were not visible, only the silhouette of this dark creature, who was now tilting his head back and laughing. Whomever, whatever, it was, Burridge had helped to put it there. He remembered Mink's words—"All quite dead in a day or two." His spying with Mink was not an abstract exercise or lines on a map. It was not a game. It cost men their lives. His eyes welled with tears as he faced his role in creating this slaughter, and he wiped them clear for another look at the demon on the works. It was gone.

Burridge wept openly now, and Henry tentatively patted him once or twice on the shoulder. "Yes, it's a strong moment. This may win the war for us." The lieutenant didn't respond, so Henry coughed self-consciously and made his way down the line.

Wesley did not look for faces in the mass of men or any other signs of life. He helped Slipper load a rifle whenever the dealer's fear got the best of him, exchanged foul jokes with Teddy to keep his spirits up, and the rest of the time shot, his mind free to explore the wonderful memories of his parents and that past life finally dredged up by the pressure of battle. His father's smoky breath, reading him poems about krakens and King Arthur's death; building a fort of snow with Edward that they topped with a muslin flag donated by their mother; the Easter Day he was allowed to sit at the adult table. He mumbled two lines of a poem that simply came to mind—"For I dipt into the future, far as human eye could see, / Saw the Vision of the world, and all the wonder that would be . . ."

Teddy called over to him and the poem, the Easter ham, the lace table-cloth and silver all drifted apart like blown smoke. "I just remembered one! Dukey'll love it!

> *A girl born and raised in the South*
> *Could do devilish tricks with her mouth.*
> *With a lisp she would crack*
> *To all Yanks near her shack,*
> *'Feel free to come inthide my houth!'*

Wes laughed to cheer Teddy up, then tried to paste together the bits of memory, a few more—"Where in wild Mahratta-battle fell my father evil-starr'd— / I was left a trampled orphan, and a selfish uncle's ward."

A few miniés hit close to their line and Wes had to fight down a rise of fear, disappointed that he could still be scared. He shot and watched Lyman pat Karl on the back, listened to Henry's hollow exhortations, and saw every other man around him being tested. He wondered if there'd ever be an end to the challenges, but at eighteen, he was beginning to understand that a man's life consists of little else.

Stewart tore open a cartridge and remembered the sour taste of the powder as soon as it hit his tongue. His moves were clumsy, spilling as much powder as he got into the muzzle and coaxing the minié down with light taps of the ram. To him, slavery and the Union were terms idiot newspapermen and Republicans employed to convince the unwashed of their war's importance, yet despite his moral apathy, he'd needed no convincing to put on an officer's bars or take leave of Phyllis. The purpose of his war was advancement; it was a sterling opportunity for him to add a rank and some powerful new friends to his growing inventory of possessions. The Rebs had never been his enemies. His enemies were competing with him for promotion. Like John Burridge.

Stewart pointed the gun forward, closed his eyes, and pulled the trigger, the butt slamming into his shoulder. He groaned from the force. The thought of aiming, of actually hitting a Rebel, never crossed his mind. Instead, he rubbed his collarbone and plotted against his foes.

Louis's body had given out. His arms were too heavy to lift; he had a bleeding sore on his trigger finger and a weariness that felt like a cold pain in his bones. Atop the wall, a large soldier pulled a smaller one up out of the fray and tossed him back down onto his comrades. The men had become ants and it was time for Louis to hand over his weapon. If the walls of Jericho were to fall, it would not be from the force of his feet marching. Tice handed up a reloaded rifle, but Louis pulled Tice up instead. "You must take over for me. I will load for you."

Tice blanched, his eyes wide. "I-I-I can't..."

Louis would accept no excuses. "You must, or we will all die." He knew he was overstating the situation, but Tice worked on high emotions. "Come along now. You did well before." The two shifted positions in the mud and Louis held his breath, waiting for Tice to shoot.

An anonymous cackle of mad laughter echoed over the field and Tice pulled the trigger. Relieved yet saddened that Tice was finally becoming a soldier with nine days left in his enlistment, Louis poured some muddy water over the hot shaft of his musket. The laughter turned into a long scream of death. An insanity had been loosed upon the world, Louis thought, a butchery made possible only by an age of gas lamps and locomotives. As war became less necessary, it grew more abominable; man became more of an animal the further he progressed. He rammed a minié down the muzzle of a rifle, damning all wars and all battles, and prayed for a peaceful God to deliver them.

————

It was on to ten when Newt and Soame entered the rim of a broad field where thousands of men lay in the grass, weeping, moaning, begging for death or water, cursing their lives and deaths, some writhing, others immobile. Five large white tents stood amid the haphazard rows of patients, the candlelight inside throwing off a warm glow onto both those who could be saved and those simply brought here to die among friends. But the warmth was deceptive. Oddly shaped mounds rose next to each tent, and the screams from inside them had the terror of pain induced with calculation. Two-wheel and four-wheel ambulances rolled in and out, depositing their hopeless freight and going for more.

Soame dropped his head, then lifted it up and slurred into Newt's ear, "I loved my mother. I did." Soame's body had gotten progressively heavier during the journey, and Newt was much relieved by the prospect of getting him into a doctor's hands. Passing stretcher bearers—brightly dressed and turbaned members of a divisional band forced against their will into duties beyond playing the tuba—sullenly directed them to the first pair of tents.

They slogged past a headless man holding a spray of dogwood blossoms, past a chaplain stuttering "...g-g-g-give us th-th-th-this d-day..." for a motley band of men showing no sign of interest, into the reeking field with its harvest of bodies. When they reached the tents, Newt took a close look at the flesh-colored piles next to them and saw that they were heaps of limbs: arms, legs, feet, hands, the ragged-edged bloody remains of the amputees. He couldn't look away. One hand was balled into a fist, while another was splayed out as if warding off a blow. Flies swarmed over the piles and the stink was tremendous. Legs cut midthigh appeared to be in stride, arms reached out to touch, hands curled around phantom pencils. Pools of bloody rainwater had formed around each pile like a moat. Newt's stomach heaved.

An old surgeon with huge white bushy eyebrows and the jowls of a bulldog stood between the two tents pointing the line toward the back of the field as if parking carriages at the track. From the chest down, his apron was covered in blood and yellow blotches of pus. Blood had splashed onto his face as well. He put a poorly washed hand to his mouth and dragged on a cigarette. He seemed bored, idly kicking aside a foot that had tumbled off a pile as he directed traffic.

Certain that Soame was about to die, Newt stepped out of line with his charge and asked for help. The surgeon tapped ash off his thin cigarette and looked Soame over. "He's got an hour or two." He pointed to an area already covered in bodies where orderlies picked their way through, offering beef broth and water to groaning, cursing men. "Drop 'im there." Then the doctor turned an eye on Newt. "And what's *your* problem?"

Newt bristled at the doctor's brogue. "Chest, sir." The doctor leaned forward and poked his finger into Newt's wound, running down its length. Newt howled in pain and swirled into a dizziness that finally eased into a deep throb when the finger was removed.

The doctor's boredom flared into an Irish fury. "How the hell did ye get back here? That's a goddamn flesh wound. I ought to have ye arrested." Newt tried to describe the bullet creeping toward his heart and the unpleasant sensation he had there, but the doctor would not listen. "Spent minié; there's no bloody finger in ye chest. Yer going ta work here." He ordered Newt to drop Soame, then dragged him into a hospital tent. Soame called after him once, and that was the last Newt heard of him.

———

Bearing an unconscious man who was bleeding from the chest, Willie and Huey were quickly allowed through by the provost guards and soon came upon the field hospital. They watched the scene for a minute, nearly as hellish as the front with its screaming and the intensity of its pain, then set Tiger against a tree to decide their course of action. Huey was nervous that someone would discover that Quigley wasn't seriously injured, which would then get them all arrested for straggling. Willie wasn't as concerned, but to keep the boy happy he said they'd just haul Tiger in and drop him off without a word to anyone.

Willie looked down at Tiger's body, the head twisted to the side, mouth open in imitation of a moan but actually snoring. If one didn't know he was just sleeping it off, he appeared mortally injured. Willie shook his head and said, "Maybe they'll ampahtate that hollow leg a his." The two went to find the 14th, hoping the company wouldn't be where they left it.

At ten o'clock, at the western angle of the bulge, a terrible cracking rent the air. Bullet after bullet, both Union and Rebel, had dug its small divot out of the two-foot trunk of a tall oak that stood next to the wall, as though two woodsmen were chopping from opposite sides, and now, cut through, the tree crashed down upon the entrenchments and the men fighting there, crushing some underneath.

Both sides stopped shooting. The mounds of bodies hadn't made the enormity of what was happening comprehensible. Nor had the rivers of blood, the tons of bullets, the hours of screams. No one had had a way to measure the fire and the uncertainly of fate until the tree fell and each man could imagine how many bullets had flown into those two feet of the line and what a miracle it was that he was still alive. A collective breath was taken, and then men rushed to pull those trapped from beneath the trunk and branches, searching in the moonless dark to find the victims of this accident. Death by bullet or shell was to be expected, but this kind of killing was unintended and its victims deserved rescue.

The pause was brief. As soon as the bodies were moved to the side, the winds of battle rose up again and the tree became just another obstacle. The bullets clicked off the branches and twigs flew through the air, putting eyes out and adding another gruesome detail to a scene that already had too many.

Lyman had to piss, had had to piss for at least an hour, and while no one would ever know, or even care, he was ashamed to lie in the mud and relieve himself. He'd had to do it other times, in other battles, and each time he'd promised that if he could help it, it would be his last. But this time, again, he couldn't help it. He pictured Ernie in his cloths, looking embarrassed even as a baby that he'd dirtied himself. What would he think of his father pissing in his pants? Lyman took a deep breath and resolved to hold it in for however long it took.

The light of a shell burst glinted off Von Schenk's bayonet. Lyman considered what he could have done to save him. He should have had Louis or Karl talk to him. He should have run after Newt. He could have worked harder to keep Tiger from drinking; he should have kept a better eye on Wesley. His tenure so far was a sorry list of actions not taken, but in the end, as he lay there trying very hard not to piss, he saw that there was a limit to what he could do for these men. Louis loaded rifles with weary deliberation, looking damp and spent—Lyman couldn't make him young again. He couldn't give Slipper, now mewling in the mud, a dose of courage, couldn't make Wesley any less of a thief and a thug. He couldn't change any of these men. The things he could have done wouldn't have mattered. One home run, one suicidal charge on a stallion could make a man memorable, but it guaranteed little else. Greater forces obliterate the efforts of single men, especially when that one man was Lyman Alder.

Lyman reached back into his pack and touched his base ball. The mortar hadn't seemed to make any difference in this battle. He wondered again, as he had when he'd first seen the gun work that afternoon, whether Micah was over there. Whether what he had told him had saved Micah's life; saved Micah's life and hundreds more in order to kill Union men. Was Louis right about the spying? Was it really Mink and Burridge, as the Hungarian thought. There was one other possibility. Micah was some Rebel spy, playing him for information. Lyman still wasn't convinced.

A sharp pang from his bladder made him wince. There was no point in holding it in any longer. Lyman let go and the warmth spread across his groin with embarrassing comfort. He saw himself sinking into the mud, unable to move, welcoming the Rebels coming toward him.

———

Though he had become accustomed over the course of the night to Soame and the pathetic cries of the injured, Newt entered the hospital tent with reluctance. Lit by wax candles, the operating tent was a place of concentrated suffering, where great pain was inflicted with the purpose of alleviating other great pains. About fourteen feet square, its canvas top was splatted with blood and its sides were a solid red to waist level. Two operating tables stood at opposite ends, surrounded with smaller tables bearing basins and boxes of instruments. A few of the wounded waiting for attention lay along the sides or against the poles holding up the tent. At the first table, two assistant surgeons tried to hold down a screaming young soldier whose struggles sent sprays of blood from the handless stumps of his arms. One of them called over to the doctor, who had a firm grasp on Newt's upper arm. "Dr. Boyle, we're ready!"

"Chloroform the sorry son of a bitch! I can do nothing with this orang-utan until ye stop him stroogling!" He shoved Newt toward the other table. "G'wan and give Dr. Prine there a hand. We're short. And I'll fucking kill ye if ye try ta get out."

At the end of the other table, a steward held a paper cone over the mouth of a trembling man. Newt judged Prine to be in his midthirties; clean-shaven, but with an unruly mass of brown hair topping his thin patrician face. He had a knife in his mouth and with one hand he smoothed the sweaty hair of his patient. The doctor looked up and motioned Newt to come over.

An enormous hiss and a piercing scream came from Boyle's table. Newt looked back and saw Boyle applying a hot iron to the bleeding stumps. The man's face expressed a pain beyond comprehension. Newt took a step toward Prine while still watching the cauterization, splashing into a deep pool of blood. Prine called to him, the exasperation clear in his tone. "For God's sake, come here!"

Shook awake by the blood and Prine's voice, Newt stepped over to the table. Prine pointed at the man's leg. "He's almost anesthetized. That has to come off."

The soldier appeared to have drifted into sleep, but Prine did not want to take chances, directing Newt to take hold of the man's foot. The patient was twenty at the most, a burly man with a rich beard. Lint and gauze had been packed into the massive wound below his left knee. Prine turned to the steward. "Had he rallied?"

The steward, a stout fellow with bushy sideburns that stopped just short of his chin, nodded as he spoke. "Yes, sir." He pushed small gold spectacles back up the bridge of his nose.

"Then let's begin." Prine pulled off the lint, tossing it in a basin of rose-colored water to be rinsed out and used again. Already woozy, Newt had no choice but to look at the wound. Like an exotic flower, meaty petals of flesh spread open to show the white bone sticking up in the center. Bits of bone, leather, cloth, dirt, and other debris blown into the flesh by the bullet spotted the gore. Newt began breathing heavily, drawing Prine's gaze. "Steady, man." Blood began welling up in the wound and Prine called for some persulfate of iron to stop the bleeding. He plucked away what debris he could with forceps, then, bloody knife still in his mouth, he began probing into the wound with his finger for the bullet.

Newt winced, but the harsh look on Prine's face conveyed more malice toward the minié than it did toward the patient. The soldier squirmed some and Boyle yelled out, "Next!" at the other table, and the smell of rotting flesh and pus rose up into Fry's nose. As the soldier squirmed more and someone outside cried in pain and a chaplain began murmuring prayers and some blood slid onto Newt's hand, tent, table, doctor began to float away.

Through clenched teeth, Prine addressed Newt in a loud voice, louder than the screams coming from Boyle's table and the curses Boyle returned to his patient. "Were you up at the salient?"

Eyelids fluttering, unable to speak, Newt only nodded at first, but then he felt his pride stirring and his stomach settling down. Yes, he'd been there, and done his duty as a soldier. "Hell of a fight. I must've gotten off a couple hundred miniés before I got hit."

The knife in his mouth pulled Prine's mouth into an involuntary grin, but his eyes darkened as Newt spoke. "There you are, bastard." He shoved a pair of forceps into the meat of the man's thigh and slowly removed a formless lump of lead. He waved it in front of Newt's eyes. "Well, this is what happens to your miniés when they go into a man's leg."

Newt didn't know what to say to that. Prine tossed the lead onto the ground, then took a cloth out of a basin sloshing with more reddened water and cleaned off the wound. The gash now presumed to be clean, he took the knife from his mouth and sliced the flesh six inches above the wound, leaving a flap on the other side of the bone. However deeply the patient had been under, it wasn't deep enough and he began to squirm and whine. Newt's eyes fluttered again.

"If you're going to vomit, vomit. But you cannot faint." Prine's voice softened a bit for the next sentence. "We need you."

Prine put down the knife and picked up a bloody saw, which he laid into the kerf of the knife cut. The saw teeth growled against the bone and the patient began to kick with both legs, the cut only a quarter of the way through. Newt couldn't control him. Prine shouted, "Hold his legs! For chrissakes, hold his legs!"

Newt had the strength to restrain a chloroformed man, but the nausea and disgust were making him useless.

Prine held the saw under Newt's nose, his eyes bloodshot and puffy. "You've killed enough men today! Help me save one!"

Newt pressed his eyes shut and held tightly on to the man's shin as the saw worked through the bone. The patient had gone unconscious again, this time from the trauma of the surgery. A full minute after the cutting stopped, Newt released his grip on the leg and opened his eyes to see Prine sewing ligatures on the severed arteries now spouting blood. The leg had become an object in his hand. Prine gave him a quick look. "Go put that on the pile and then come right back. We'll need your help to move him."

Fry grabbed the ankle and walked past Boyle's table, where the doctor was trying to push a man's intestines back into his abdominal cavity. He burst gasping out of the tent flap and into the rain to find the air only slightly less redolent of chemicals and putrefaction than it was inside. Before him a field of men squirmed in pain, unprotected from the rain; next to him a heap of limbs buzzed with flies despite the downpour. No moon. Steady gunfire still filtered through the trees. He was exhausted, but he was glad to be out of the rain and the bullets. Newt carefully placed the hairy leg, complete with sock and brogan, onto the pile, noticing that the heel was worn on the outer edge. He took another breath, then turned and went back inside.

CHAPTER 19

TIGER DIDN'T SO MUCH WAKE UP AS COME TO. THE CONSTANT rain drilling onto his face and the ravings of the man lying next to him had hauled him out of his stupor and left him gasping on the shores of a mad place he did not know. He sat up and tried to make sense of his surroundings. It was dark and it was raining. There were big tents, sputtering fires, and a huge number of men on the ground making noise. There were no guns and no shooting nearby, so he knew that he was not in a battle. The man on his left rolled from side to side, whipping his arms back and forth and saying the name Jane in rhythm with his motion. To Tiger's right, another soldier silently stared into the rain with his mouth open, a large patch of red staining the midsection of his uniform.

Tiger leaned toward the silent one and said, "Lad." A sudden urge to fall back asleep came over him, but he squeezed his eyes shut and shook it away, his brain sloshing painfully in his skull. He poked the man. "Say, laddie. Where do ye reckon we are, eh?"

A deep chorus of moans and cries and names called out in vain rose up from the field of men, but Tiger's companion did not answer.

Another poke. More silence.

Annoyed by such an unbrotherly attitude, Quigley bent over the man and saw raindrops splashing into the water pooled in his mouth. Tiger's drunk burned off in a flash. He remembered death. He knew he was in a hospital and he remembered marching up to the front, laughing and falling in the mud. His mind held only snatches of what came after. Out of habit, Tiger wondered where Lyman and the rest of the regiment were, but the thought of them brought up a heat of anger that made him recall that he was on the outs with that whole outfit and especially their self-appointed leader.

He closed the dead man's mouth. Water brimmed out of the corners of the lips. Tiger closed the eyes as well. He was not dead and he thanked God for that. He didn't want to spend another minute in this stinking field full of wounded men.

He stood up, the rattle of the ambulances, the screaming, and the low moaning echoing inside a mean headache. Before him were five tents, easily identified as the hospital tents from the unearthly yowling coming from inside, and behind was a wall of trees. The choice was simple. Tiger turned his back on the tents and began stepping over bodies. Most were awake. Those with enough strength used their arms to shield their eyes from the rain. Sad, desperate pleas for water, mothers, and wives went up to him as he passed, some voices manly and deep and others just changing. He had to shake his leg loose more than once from clutching hands. Nearing the edge of the trees and the end of this All Souls' Day scene, the words of a prayer emerged from the din, spoken in the sweet tones of an Irish boy. "Holy Mary, mother of God, pray for us sinners, now, and at the hour of our death. Amen."

Tiger took a few steps into the solitude of the woods. The darkness quickly enveloped him and he was alone with no particular goal, stumbling into trees and trying to keep his head as steady as possible so his brain wouldn't ache too much. He had no interest in returning to the 14th.

And then the name Mary made her face appear. He collided with the reasons for his anger as he was continually colliding with the pines in this dense forest. Tiger pictured himself alone on second base, alone in the mud, alone in center field; alone in this forest, alone at Gettysburg, alone back in Brooklyn in an empty room. A wife dead and backs turned to him. Alone on a bar stool.

Sobering up, Tiger now had two goals: The first was to find a little hair of the dog, and if that failed, he would get lost beyond finding in this maze of trees.

———

Though the bullets had slackened in many parts of the line and the twenty hours of surflike pounding on the entrenchments had ended as a stalemate, the absence of attack by other Union regiments made the 14th's position a focus for the Rebels. Mad laughter and screaming had stopped; no mortar shells traced through the sky. This battle had finally ended, but the fighting could not stop. The bursts of firing guns snuck closer to the 14th's position. The men expected to be pulled back at any minute, but the bullets kept splashing into the mud and bodies before them and they remained on their stomachs, wondering how long they would have to stay there, alone as the rest of the Union army recovered from its day.

Cheek pressed into the mud, Slipper Feeney tried to remember the words to a prayer. Any prayer. In his time of need, Slipper had no words to offer the Almighty. He could offer strength of emotion; his fingers clenched the silver cross so tightly that his palm was bleeding. He could offer a soul stripped of pride; he'd soiled himself more times than he could count these endless hours. And he could offer a heart boiled free of violence. Slipper had seen so much blood in nine days that he could no longer stand to even touch a rifle.

Karl kicked back at him, narrowly missing his head. "*Was ist los?* Give me another gun, you thief bastard pig!"

When Slipper didn't move, Karl kicked at him again. "Give me another fucking gun!"

Feeney made no effort to load another rifle. Instead, he tentatively reached an arm out toward Wesley and tugged the hem of his trousers, his voice plaintive. "Wes."

Working on reflex, Wes shook Feeney's hand away. "Yeah."

"Wes, I gotta have a prayer. Gimme a prayer."

Karl bellowed back to him. "*Ich muss ein* fucking gun *haben!* Gimme a fucking gun, you stealing pig!"

"Let 'im alone!" Wes tossed his rifle over to Karl. "Here! Can't you see he's played out!"

"In *neun* days he's played out? Fuck him!"

Feeney pulled at Wesley's leg again, so Pitt crept back a few feet from the front to look at the dealer. "OK, Slipper. How's about 'Our Father.' That's a good one, huh?" Slipper gave a series of quick small nods, like a child shy in accepting a gift that he desperately wants. Wes had to think for a second himself, but once he recalled the first line, the rest came tumbling out. He put his arm around Feeney and the two recited together.

———

Dr. Boyle stood between Prine and his next patient, shouting into the young doctor's face. "I will not have ye saving the life a some Rebel bastard when there's a hunnert Union boys awaiting the knife!" Only the crimson bloat of Boyle's stomach kept his nose from butting into Prine's.

Prine called over to his steward. "Gullman, get us more candles, would you please?" The portly steward scuttled off and Prine turned back to Boyle, who had kept his pasty face wrinkled into a scowl until Prine's attention returned to him and the officer's gold on his shoulders. "I won't have this insubordination again from ye, Prine! Every battle...!" Before the captain could continue his tirade, his assistant surgeons called for his help in performing a resection. "Prine, I'm a-warnin' ye! Don't touch him! I'll have yer knives if ye do!" Then he waddled off to the unnecessary torture taking place under his name.

Gullman had placed new candles in the holders and Newt got his first good look at the Rebel lying on the table. The patient was long and dark-skinned, near olive in complexion, with very black hair and deep-set eyes. Newt's heart leaped when he thought he recognized Harlan Deal, but this soldier had on a gray army uniform and a jagged scar playing along the line of his jaw. There was also a hole on the lower left side of his chest; a wound not as bloody as it was full of creamy white and yellow pus. Newt could see colors other than red in there as well, the dark browns and pinks of organs he could not identify. Prine ordered Gullman to bring him some hot water. The screams continued from Boyle's table and others filtered in through the canvas.

Given that this was not a Union man, nor a friend, Newt raised his lip in a disdainful sneer that he intended to show his fighting mettle. Prine was picking bits of debris out of the wound and plopping dollops of pus into the washbasin, but he did notice Newt's expression of contempt. He gave a snort through his thin nose. "Remarkable, isn't it?"

Newt wasn't sure what he meant. In the last few hours, he had watched Prine poke his fingers into wounds of such magnitude that by now only the most horrible forced Newt to do anything more than take some deep breaths or a whiff of salts, and this wound, ugly as it was, failed to turn his stomach. He shrugged his shoulders. "I don't understand, sir."

Gullman handed Prine a pot of boiling water, which the doctor proceeded to pour into the wound. "What I mean is, you enjoy killing them and I enjoy saving their lives."

Newt wrinkled his brow, still holding on to the chloroformed soldier's shoulders. In a near-whisper, he said, "I don't fancy killing them."

Prine looked under the table and saw the water flowing through the wound, trickling onto the floor. He raised an eyebrow at Newt. "It certainly appeared as though you did."

Without further comment, Prine set to work repairing what he could of the Rebel's shredded organs, but his accusation grated on Newt's pride. It seemed too easy to work behind the lines and never face the personal and moral dilemma that Newt had wrestled with for three years. He mustered up the courage to call Prine's disdain. "Have you ever shot a man?"

Gullman's eyes went from Prine to Newt and back. Prine cleared his throat, but he did not look up. "No. No, I have not." He leaned closer to the patient, appearing to want a better look, but more to disguise his interest in the answer to his next question. "What is the sensation?"

Newt heard the sincere interest in his voice and instead of delivering a cant response, he thought for a minute, eyes lifted toward the drumming canvas roof and memories of the battlefield. "It's the most satisfying thing I've ever done and the very worst. But I had to do it. I believe in this war and a man has to do what he believes in."

Though Newt thought he had reached an understanding with Prine, his answer pulled the doctor's hair trigger. He looked up with an acid glare. "Oh really? And what is that you *believe* in?"

Newt paused a moment to give a dignity to his response. "Freeing the African."

Prine's face brightened, as though he were entertained by what Newt said. "Well, we don't hear that very often, do we, Gullman?" Gullman shook his head, but retreated a step from the table to stay out of the fight. Prine pointed to the Rebel. "Is this an evil slaveholder? Can you tell?"

Newt looked at the body in the flickering candlelight. Just another tired, hungry, courageous Reb. "No. It's not."

"How can you tell?"

Newt shrugged his shoulders. "He just isn't."

"Just a body to you, eh? A piece of meat."

Newt had had enough. He'd tortured himself for years, cut through twisted moral arguments and his own cowardice until he could finally act on what he believed. "I didn't come here to kill men!"

"Why else do you go to war?"

"To win! Do you cut men's legs off to hear them scream or to save their lives?"

Prine's hand made a quick movement in the Rebel's stomach, as if it had slipped. The patient shook and whimpered, able to feel the pain through the chloroform. Prine swore at himself. Finally he looked at Newt. "Why don't you see if Dr. Boyle needs your help."

———

Lyman took a shot and listened, waiting with the slight hope that it would be his last in this battle. His last for good. He strained to hear word of retreat from either side, the words "truce" or "cease firing," but the Rebel bullets kept coming, a little closer every minute. A man to their right, from the 56th or the 147th, let out a scream and was promptly followed into death by another of his regiment. More exposed, the men of those two units were beginning to take casualties, and their cries were added to the rifles and the supplications of the wounded. The pace of the shooting muskets didn't rival the constant fire that had illuminated the field earlier, so night made its presence felt, further stranding the men still out in the mud.

Stives returned from an ammunition run with the bad news that what they had in their pockets and boxes was all that was left. Teddy began swearing again. "Wes, I told ya! They're leavin' us here!"

Lyman, Karl, and every other man was thinking the same thing. Another Union man went up with a howl. They looked to Burridge, who looked farther up the line, but there was no sign of retreat. The three regiments would stay out there.

As he lay on his side, methodically loading another rifle, Louis felt a slap on his back. He turned around and made out Burridge's face in the gloom.

"Hurry up!"

A man whose martial instincts and abilities had needed cooling, not fuel, Louis gritted his teeth. He had done his best to avoid this confrontation with Burridge, but since they'd left Culpeper, and especially since the Wilderness, the lieutenant seemed to appear with no warning, bearing these uncalled-for intimations of cowardice. Louis was insulted and tired, and it was time for it to stop. While it was no secret that Louis had gotten too old for battle, Burridge did not know that the Hungarian had a secret about him. He had seen that map of Spotsylvania in the dirt around first base; maybe not enough proof to have Burridge court-martialed, but suspicion enough to make a battlefield claim. Before he said anything, though, Louis thought of an even better wrinkle.

He spat out the accusation. "You spy!"

Burridge's jaw dropped in surprise, his eyes widened, and everything else about him froze in obvious panic. The lieutenant could not formulate a response beyond pants of breath that he tried to pass off as speechless fury. Louis knew better. His suspicions about Burridge's activities with Mink confirmed, he stepped in with the rest of what he planned to say. "Tice was just giving me a rest and you are spying on us!"

The relief on Burridge's face only further reinforced Louis's theory. The lieutenant swallowed and told the Hungarian to continue what he was doing.

———

Dr. Boyle poked at the wound in front of him as if checking a steak, and with each new pressure, the soldier yelped a bit more. The assistant surgeon, a long-headed man with closely cropped brown hair and a thin mustache over pursed lips, asked if he should apply more chloroform.

"Whatever for?" The stink of whiskey and tobacco blasted out of Boyle's mouth and nearly knocked Newt to the floor as he helped to restrain the patient. "I think I've found it."

Boyle rammed his finger deeply into the man's upper arm, which brought a blood-chilling scream out of the man on the table. Watching the finger root around in the flesh, Newt couldn't help but remember the sensation of Boyle's finger in his own wound, prodding about for the bullet that wasn't there. Newt winced as the tear across his chest began to ache.

"And what's *yer* gripe, missy? Too hard for ye? Ye must get the bad humors out." Boyle stuck his tongue out of the side of his mouth as he concentrated. "Ye can stop yer crying; this one'll live." He grinned. "Maybe he won't be so pretty, but he'll live. I'll have the saw." The assistant handed Boyle the saw and Newt held tight, knowing that the soldier would feel every cut of the blade. The doctor stroked through the arm, blood spewing over them all.

Boyle yelled into Newt's face, pointing into the wound, "Put yer bloody fingers on this vein and plug it tight!" Silently apologizing for the pain he was causing, Newt clamped the vein shut with his fingertips, knowing that the man would live. And that he would, too. Both damaged and having known pain, they would live.

————

Colonel Fowler ordered the regiment's flags to the back. Any second the Rebs could burst through.

Lyman checked his cartridge box. He had two left. He loaded and shot one of them toward the counterattack. The tension along the line was growing as the miniés whipped in faster, and Lyman could think of nothing he could do to defuse it. It was up to the officers. His fighting units had broken apart as the ammunition dried up, and no one wanted a pat on the back or a song or a full canteen. Lyman crawled over to Burridge. "When the hell are we pulling out?"

"I don't know."

"Whaddya mean, you don't know? The Rebs are coming! Get us the fuck out of here! Ask Henry!"

But Henry had no answer for Burridge. Henry answered to Fowler, who answered to Cutler, who answered to Warren, who answered to Meade, who answered to Grant, who answered to Lincoln. And none of them would give the word that would allow the 14th Brooklyn to pull out from the front. Burridge returned to his place in the line, blinking away tears of frustration.

Lyman shot his last cartridge, then hugged the ground, silent and unable to help his men, maybe even responsible for the bullets coming at them. He was drowning only inches from the surface.

————

Near three A.M. the orders came, and after twelve hours the men of the 14th starting crawling out of the mud, believing that they had seen their last action.

Louis looked up. A small patch of the night sky appeared within a crack in the blanket of clouds. He saw the stars, their steady glow like those of candles. As easily as he took a breath, he silently recited the prayer he hadn't said since larger flames of evil, also lit because they were the Chosen, brought their lives as Jews and peaceful people to an end. *"Baruch ata adonai..."* The battle of Spotsylvania was over.

TRAVEL DATE

———

CHAPTER

20

THE NIGHT PULLED BACK WITH THE GRUDGING HESITANCE of a man removing a bandage; just a corner at first, then one edge, until finally the whole wound was revealed. No one expected it to have healed since the weak light of dusk, but the devastation was still shocking. Blue bodies covered the field of red mud. Those longest dead had begun to swell and blacken in the heat and the rain, which had not yet ended. Black stumps of trees stood among vivid red pools on the earth too saturated to accept any more blood. Living men tried to move beneath piles of the dead. Teams went out to find those who could stand the journey to a hospital, adding to the growing flood of stretchers and mule-driven ambulances flowing to the back. The stench was overwhelming. Union soldiers climbed over the works and found them abandoned; apparently the Rebs had pulled back during the night's darkest hours. Those who examined the trenches would not speak of what they found.

———

At six A.M., slapping wads of mud onto works, the men of the 14th were stunned and exhausted. As each man dug, he recalled a different act that frightened him either because he had seen it or because he had performed it himself. These brief, harrowing trips to the past became minutes of standing still in the mud, eyes locked on something far away. Lyman's eyes, though, were searching for a missing face. Newt should have been back by now; his wound was more of a scratch than an injury. Had he been impressed into some duty? His injury was slight enough that arrest for desertion was a possibility. But what if he had been hit again? Lyman told himself that he should have grabbed him back at the angle and not let him run off alone. If—when—he saw Newt again, it would be the first thing he'd say to him.

Next to him in the trench, Burridge listlessly helped Karl prop a log up against a slimy wall of mud. Since last night, everything he saw seemed his responsibility. The mowed trees, the legless men, the vacant stares: He had created them all with his arrogant treacheries at first base. In Company L alone, five men were dead or missing. Mud kept slipping off the sides of the shovel blade, so he tossed the tool aside and began heaping the muck up with his hands as if building sandcastles at the beach. There was little talking among the men, only the patter of raindrops on capes and liners and mud, so everyone heard Lyman. "I'm going to see after Newt."

Burridge caught his shoulder as Lyman tried to pass. "You can't go."

Lyman slowly turned to Burridge. Though mostly black with a paste of powder and mud, the soldier's face was mottled where rain had cleaned it and every wrinkle stood out clear. His eyelids wavered with exhaustion, the sides of his mouth drooped. The wound on his forehead had scabbed over with festering greens and browns, and beneath his cheeks, the jaws clenched and unclenched with anger. There were other hard fighters here now and other good men, but none of them matched Lyman Alder. Burridge couldn't risk losing him. "We need you here, Lyman."

The butcher was about to push past him when Lyman realized that everyone was watching. No slaps of mud on mud, no tired chatter; only the dappled sound of rain hitting mud and puddles and heads. Twelve men stared, every inch of every one of them covered in the reddish gray mud, sagging under the rain. Faces as black and as haggard as his, mouths pulled into weary frowns. Wes, Finn, and Feeney all faced the ground, but looked up from beneath their eyebrows, Pitt's mouth bleeding a bit again. The expressions on the faces of Karl and Louis challenged him. Though using a rifle as a crutch, the Hungarian looked at least six feet tall. The others appeared small and dirty and nearly helpless in the storm.

Lyman saw the red trousers beneath the mud and knew he had to stay and help them, even if he could not bear them across on his shoulders.

———

By seven the activity behind the lines had increased enough that Tiger could come out of the trees and travel the muddy roads wherever they led him. He had spent the night wandering, wondering which direction offered the most promise of liquor, and he had not been alone. Through the dark and into the morning, he passed men sitting in the shadows or shuffling by, asking things like, "Where's the 3rd Michigan?" or "You seen the hunnert an' eleven New York?" Tiger would say no, then ask if they'd seen the 14th. He didn't really want to know where his regiment was, but very few of them wanted to know, either; they'd simply exchange nods and move on. Tiger figured that the stragglers were those who hid the embers of their pipes while the men just brazenly walking by were really lost or totally played out and beyond caring if they'd be arrested. Now he faced the murky morning after along with the thousands only now seeing the damage they'd wrought the night before. Weary men with minds as blank as the gray sky trudged through the mud in a muffled confusion, their voices low and movements heavy with a lethargy born of the realization that the night's endless terrors had produced no victory.

Tiger, with every man in the Union army, pondered the next move. Some thought about military strategy, others their injuries or the injuries of others. But Tiger Quigley was now thinking about food. He smelled beans cooking in a clearing off the road where a large group of men were gathered around a wagon. An aproned cook doled out the grub and knots of soldiers were lying in the mud, slopping beans into their mouths. There was a risk that he could be turned away, but Tiger decided that the mud caked onto his uniform and the general apathy of the morning provided enough of a cover for him to fold into the unit unquestioned. He merged into the group and kept his head down.

The line moved slowly and a few provost guards strolled through the field, looking, it seemed, for no one in particular. Tiger hunched his shoulders until he reached the vat of beans and received a borrowed bowlful along with a handful of coffee offered by a Sanitary Commission member who also gave him a tract on Christian Temperance. Tiger accepted the pamphlet so as not to arouse any suspicions and now stood, bowl in one hand, can of coffee and tract in the other, looking for a group of men with a fire big enough to accommodate him.

Small smoky fires made of damp wood burned throughout the field, each surrounded by a tight ring of men who knew each other. Even though the mud tempered the bright colors of his uniform, Tiger was an obvious outsider here. There were no fires open, except the one nearest to him, which boiled the coffee of ten or twelve Negro soldiers talking low among themselves. Tiger had chewed coffee grounds in his life and he would do it again before he would sit down there. He considered how long it would take to gather up some twigs of his own. A grating voice said into his ear, "And what outfit are *you* with?"

Tiger's head shot around to see a regular army sergeant scanning him from head to toe, clearly weighing whether Tiger was just a straggler or an out-and-out deserter from the ranks. Though he had no future plans, one thing Tiger had ruled out was a stretch in a military prison, so he swallowed and began working his mouth while his startled mind fumbled about for an explanation. It did not come quickly. The sergeant's eyes peered out from beneath the brim of his cap. He had a thick beard that rimmed his face but no mustache and he was now drumming his fingers on folded arms. "Well?" A grin crept across his face, the grin a man has when the fish on his line begins to tire.

As Tiger was about to get reeled in, another voice—a black man's voice—said casually, "Oh, he with us, sir."

Tiger was lucky that the sergeant turned immediately to the voice because his jaw dropped at the statement. The sergeant pulled the corner of his mouth up in a sneer that even those in the cheap seats could have appreciated. "What in hell would a white man be doing with you niggers? Hmm?"

Among the black men sipping coffee and eating beans was one with his cap tilted way back on his head, pointing with a fork at Tiger. A couple of the men were older, but most appeared to be in their late teens and early twenties, like the rest of the army, and this one was probably not too much younger than Tiger himself. He loaded in another forkful of beans, then said with his mouth full, "He with us on burial duties." He locked on to Quigley's eyes. "Ain'cha?" The rest of the soldiers kept on calmly eating.

The sergeant turned back to Tiger, whose immediate thought was to give the officer a friendly punch in the arm and a look that would say, "I wouldn't go near no niggers if you paid me." The choice between being arrested and keeping a firm grip on his pride was not an easy one.

"Well? You with these niggers?"

Tiger felt as though the breath had been knocked out of him. The man who had spoken had returned to his beans. He'd thrown the wood into the water; now it was up to Tiger to swim toward it. Quigley saw himself in prison, then saw himself eating beans next to a black man. He waved good-bye to what was once a very important part of himself. "Uh, yeah. Yessir. I am."

"Oh, you're Irish. I guess you're in the right place, then." The sergeant laughed, gave them all a parting sneer, and walked away.

A spot had opened at the fire beside the man who had covered for Tiger. As long as the sergeant was in the field, Quigley figured he had to play along, so he took the spot and stuck his coffee into the fire without a thank you, his face flushed in anger. He could feel the man looking at him, laughing at him, waiting for the acknowledgment Tiger would not give. The man finally put down his plate and stuck a hand in front of Tiger meant for shaking. "I'm Hayes Nelson."

Ten black faces stared at Tiger. Some of the younger ones seemed tense and exhausted, like Finn and Feeney; others kept eating as though they'd seen it all. None of them were singing or dancing or cutting jokes. They looked like soldiers. Ten large soldiers. He shook the proffered hand out of what he considered self-protection. Though these men had confounded his expectations already by acting like any other hungry, tired fighters in the rain, he clutched his notions tightly and still thought them a threat. "Quigley."

Nelson smiled and nodded. A few men removed their caps and said quiet hellos, but most said nothing. The silence mounted against the sea of questions waiting to be asked. Tiger jiggled his can of coffee to speed it toward boiling, sneaking looks at Nelson as he did. At first Tiger had considered the tilted cap a sign of youthful rascality, but the hardness of this man's eyes proved that he was not a child. He seemed tired, and not just from the soldier's life. Nelson wiped a long hand across his brow, then back over his short black hair. "That's one stupid sergeant."

A few men snickered. Nelson gestured with his head at Tiger's trousers. "You one a them Brooklyn mens, ain'cha?"

It was pointless to deny it. "Yep."

"I got kin there."

Tiger pulled his coffee from the fire, took a sip, then said, "Well, Brooklyn's always been kind to the Negroes."

There were more snickers around the fire and Tiger caught men looking at each other with wide eyes, doing their best to hold in their laughter. A couple others were not amused. Suddenly a black soldier a few yards away called over to them to prepare to move out and the men began packing up.

Tiger looked around. At first it appeared that the sergeant had left, but Tiger saw him standing over another group of men asking questions. Nelson leaned over Quigley's shoulder. "Come with us."

"Not on yer life."

"Man gonna git ye then. Y'all just straggling anyways. Got no place special you going; that's all over your face."

"Go ta hell."

Nelson turned toward the man who had ordered them to pack up. "Sergeant! 'Scuse me! Sergeant!"

At Nelson's call, the man began to walk toward them. Tiger gritted his teeth and growled, "Have it your way!"

By now the black sergeant was in front of them and giving Tiger an odd look. Nelson started to fidget and jump up and down a bit. "Sergeant, do I gots time to take a piss?"

The sergeant paused, then said yes, walking away. Hayes winked at Tiger.

———

Newt propped a soldier up with one hand and tipped the cup of broth to the boy's lips. He was twenty at the most; pale, soaked, and shaking like a kitten hauled out of a well. He had no hands. All around them, acres of men still groaned and cried as they had been doing for more than a day, though their sounds and movements were less intense now than they had been when Newt entered the clearing last night. Hour after hour of rain had beaten the rows of dying men into a more quiet acceptance of their fate, and the field was again just a field. What screams remained came from the operating tents and the ambulances beginning their bumpy rides to Fredericksburg.

The boy lapped at the broth and Newt had to pull it away, afraid he would choke. "Easy, son." The boy panted, his eyes focused on the cup.

Though hoisted on his elbows, the handless boy hadn't made even a grunt of pain. Newt thought of him standing in a wheat field, watching another man work his horses through the rows, or in a factory, peering over the shoulder of the man who had his seat. He saw the brave look on the sweetheart's face as she tried to hide her desire to be touched.

Newt was roused by the boy's tired voice. "Can I have more?"

He was about to place the cup on the boy's lips when the soldier turned his head to the side and stared at Newt. "Damn minié went through both of 'em." The boy looked down at his bandaged stumps with a cool expression that Newt figured was shock. "Could've happened on the farm just as easy. My uncle lost a leg 'neath a horse, see, but he can't say it was for anything other than clearing a patch a land. Leastwise I got a good reason here."

The boy turned back to the cup. At first Newt pitied him, but then he looked up and saw a freed African helping a one-legged man along. Beyond them was a flag with a star for every state in the nation drooping on a pole. Those were Newt's reasons and they seemed good enough for the boy as well. Who was Newt to judge the cost too high? Some people, like Prine, could further their cause and preserve their conscience at the same time, but most had nothing to give but their lives and their souls, and men of both sides gave them willingly in the thousands now, knowing the risks. All Newt could give was himself and his passion, the way Lyman had throughout these three years, and he'd have to if he was to live with himself. Only God could judge these issues; not Prine and certainly not Newt. Newt's place was to add weight to one pan of the scale and trust that he was right.

A steward came by, examined the boy's bandages, then told him to head toward the ambulances. Newt encouraged him with a smile and a jaunty twist of his mustache. "Off to F'burg and a clean, dry bed. I envy you, son."

The boy raised an eyebrow. "Oh yeah?"

Newt winced, but the boy let his bitter smile and lined forehead melt into a warm calm. They locked eyes and realized in the silence that they shared the need to fix a point of justice amid the confusion. Newt's wound suddenly ached and he felt terrible and good all at once, with a pain that seemed necessary, like the pains he'd had in his legs as a boy. They saluted each other, hand and stump, and the boy moved on to the ambulance train.

Bucket in hand, Newt began looking for the olive-skinned Rebel among the hundreds of bodies, the one gray uniform in this field of blue. He wandered up and down the rows for an hour or so, giving out broth when asked yet always craning his head for a sight of the Reb until he finally admitted the futility of his search. He was making a trip back to the fire when he saw a flash of gray in one of the four-wheel ambulances about to leave for Fredericksburg. Newt ducked his head into the wagon and saw a Rebel on the lower right-hand berth out of six stretchers, all suspended by leather straps that supposedly offered some cushion from the jolts of the road. Newt trotted around to the outside and looked in through the gap between slats of wood. It was the Rebel that Prine had operated on, his eyes fluttering and occasionally popping open at loud sounds, as though he were dipping in and out of sleep.

"Say, Johnny." Newt reached in and shook his shoulder just enough for the Reb to wake a bit and look at him. The Rebel said nothing. Newt leaned closer to the slats and took in the man's ashen face. He would die soon. "I did what I had to do. I'm sorry."

The Rebel made an attempt to swallow and shifted his lips as if to speak, but he could only manage to close his eyes and nod once, very slowly. A freedman cracked his whip and a team of shaggy mules pulled the ambulance away. Newt wanted to find the 14th now. He wanted to go home.

CHAPTER

21

ACROSS THE BATTLEFIELD, ON THE OTHER SIDE OF THE SA-
lient, Tiger put both hands on his lower back, stretched, and
cursed whoever told him that the colored man was lazy. Since
breakfast they'd done nothing but dig graves and tip bodies into
them, one after the other, at the same pace they'd started hours
before. Tiger would pitch headlong into the work for half an
hour, just to prove what a white man could accomplish in that
time, then stop for a rest and the colored men would keep on working; not
as fast as him, but steadily. He'd pick up the shovel again and they'd still be
working and they'd be going when he took his next rest, too. If their spirits
flagged, the tall, bony one they called Oryel Goody would up and start
moaning something that sounded to Tiger's Irish ears like the wind in a
snowstorm, and they'd all toss in a word or two to cheer him on. It didn't
make them work any faster; it just kept them working.

Tiger bent over and his back gave off a series of little cracks. He would
have kissed one of his fellow grave diggers for a drink. Hayes Nelson, who
was already standing next to another body, leaned onto his shovel and looked
at Tiger the way he would at a little boy in the field for the first time. "Lord,
y'all having yourself another rest? Shee-it!"

Quigley swore under his breath and walked the few feet to Nelson. The
body between them had the same mottled purple face that all the bodies
had, the same leathery white skin, sunken eyes, stiff limbs. Nelson took pity
on Tiger and did most of the digging, which left Tiger to slip his shovel
underneath the body and tip it into the shallow grave. The blood had drained
out of the higher sections and pooled close to the ground, turning the body

a deep purple where it met the earth. Tiger pushed up the handle and the corpse flopped into the hole. It gave off a ripe stench, but nothing near what it would've been without the rain.

Nelson waved a hand in front of his nose. "Lord Jesus, he stink!"

"Stop yer acting and have an ounce of respect for the dead." Tiger affected the serious mien of a parish priest, even making a crisp sign of the cross. Nelson smirked.

A tiny bald-headed man called Marl hollered out, a dash of surprise in his voice, "This one look like Marse George!"

Nelson went over to Marl and laughed. "So he do! See this one, Hollis!" Hollis was extremely dark; Tiger judged him the most African of them all. He gave the body a serious appraising look, nodded, then went back to his work. Nelson stayed, though, fascinated by the resemblance, his laugh petering into long, deep breaths. Soon he was running the sharp edge of his shovel along the hardened neck of the corpse, his arms tensing, pressing the edge down harder, his pink tongue playing on his black lips.

Marl gently blocked the path of Nelson's shovel with the handle of his own. "What's dead is dead and you just gotta bury it. Go on back to you own work."

Nelson returned to Tiger's side and the two started on another grave.

A new conversation cropped up a bit later between two of the younger men—Isaac and Albert—regarding what exactly they would do to General Forrest and Robert E. Lee when they caught them. Isaac favored whipping and then a long sentence involving fieldwork on his farm while Albert wanted his vengeance to be quick, bloody, and fatal.

None of the men had ever seen combat, not even yesterday, but most of them had enough sense to know that the assembled powers of the Confederacy would not be facing them in battle whenever they were finally called. They shook their heads and kept on at their work, waiting for their chance. Marl tried to shush the boys, leaning toward Tiger as a reminder that they had an outsider among them, someone they should be wary of and impress at the same time. Isaac understood and shrank into his shoulders.

Albert understood, too, but his reaction was the opposite. "Oh, what he gonna do? Tell Robert E. Lee I'se comin'? I wish he would. They friends, most likely."

Tiger had been quiet most of the day, partly out of fear and partly out of arrogance, but he couldn't keep still now. The boy reminded him of Teddy Finn. So much about these men reminded him of Company L—the recklessness of Isaac and Albert, the hard faces of Hollis and Louis, the small groups they broke into. He'd almost begun to feel comfortable. "Ye stupid little nigger. Ye've not seen a bullet and yet yer telling me something about this war. Lemme say I seen heads blown clear off. Yes, I have. And friends killed you wouldn't believe how many times over. Yer sort won't make it in battle and everyone knows it."

Albert spit in the dirt. "I seen my daddy sold down the Mississippi and overseer take my mama 'fore my eyes. You seen anything like *that*?" His face had contorted with rage. "I been whooped with a branch about as thick as your thumb. You seen *that, Massa*? I didn't think so. *No,* sir. You ain't seen *nothing* like that in *your* time!"

Oryel cried out, "*No* sir!"

Nelson smirked again. "What exactly did y'all do with your yesterday, Brooklyns? Straggling around the back roads mostly, I guess, eh?"

"I was at the wall, laddie. At the wall, fighting to free yer ass against me will and better judgment!"

Instead of attacking Tiger, Nelson asked, "What kind job you got in Brooklyns?"

Marl jumped in. "What kind a home you got? Big ole thing?"

Oryel's baritone voice rumbled in. "Little ones. I bet you got all kind of little ones and a wife."

The questions came in a charge, much too fast for Tiger to answer and they weren't meant to be answered anyway. Though he had no more than a poor man's job and a seedy room beneath a cigar store, Tiger never thought to admit the truth. Raising his hands to silence their questions, he disguised his own hunger as homesickness and fought back by showing them the life they could never have; the life any white man walking the streets of Brooklyn could have if he did something with himself and his advantages; the life he himself would only dream of now, with a whiskey in his hand. Tiger sketched at great length the comforts and warmth of his big house, the power of his important job, his sweet, devout Mary, and the baby in its crib. Some watched the ground and scowled, others looked off into the sky, but they all listened smoldering with rightful anger, self-pity, and greed that Tiger happily stoked with more lies. Albert was as taken as the rest, requesting details about the garden and the paper in the dining room.

Finally Marl said it had to stop. Oryel lowed the first notes of a new tune and the men walked back in pairs to whatever body they'd been burying in the mud, peeking over their shoulders for another look at Tiger.

Isaac stopped in front of Tiger as he passed by, shaking his head. "All I wants is a wife, a job, a house, and some babies. That's all." Now somewhere between their hatred and their envy, Tiger picked up his shovel and began a new grave.

Nelson stood next to him, looking at the body of a Union soldier twisted for eternity by rigor mortis. After a minute he said, "That's a good story, if it's true."

The sun had to set before the burial detail would sit for a piece of salt pork, and by that time Tiger was ready for a nip and a good night's sleep. He'd worked silently next to Nelson all afternoon, though he had nearly asked once what had caused the thick black swelling around Nelson's brown wrists. When he recognized the work of chains, he was glad he'd kept his mouth shut. As fires sprang throughout the woods around them, the men now fried a little meat, Oryel hummed, and Tiger got thirsty.

Nelson offered him some pork and hardtack out of his sack, a gift Quigley initially refused on the grounds that he was not hungry. Tiger's stomach turned traitor, though; it growled at the sight of food and the Irishman delicately plucked a slice of greenish pork off the black man's hand as though it were a specimen for Louis's collection. The stomach noticed no difference between the foul taste of this pork and any other.

Now Tiger wanted that drink and he considered a band of coloreds a fine bet. He leaned back and casually said, "A shot of whiskey would be sweet indeed." Nelson did not respond one way or the other, so Tiger decided that he was being too subtle. He tried again. "Ach, I'd give anything I had fer a lick of whiskey," he said, directing a meaningful look at Nelson.

Nelson pointed at himself. "Me? No sir. Never liked the liquor. Ask Hollis; he known to sip."

The lure of a drink destroyed any pride Tiger might have had. He shot right up and went straight to Hollis's side. "I hear ye might have some of the knockum."

Hollis sighed and rubbed his broad nose. "Wisht I did. I really do." Tiger seemed to deflate. "Oh ho, I know that feelin'. I do. We's all gone dry here." Tiger saw no reason to get up; they'd be back at work in a few minutes anyway, so he remained next to Hollis and soon felt him staring at him. "What that little one of yours call again?"

They had decided on Emmitt for a boy and Kathleen for a girl. "Emmitt."

"Fine name." He nodded, clasping his large hands together. Tiger figured him for fifty. "I gots a little one, too. We called her Sarah." Hollis smiled at the thought. "Like a sunny day in May, that one. I was a free man then, before they took back the law. Sent her and her mama North and I picked me a new massa. Glory days. Warn't so bad, the massa, but I, I was a *slave* again after being a free mans." A harder look came into his eyes. "Every time I wants a drink I say, 'Hollis, you ain't gonna be nobody's slave *no* more.' Been slave to too many mens and too many sins. Starting over *every* day! Amen." As suddenly as he'd began, Hollis went quiet. Tiger stayed next to him.

CHAPTER

22

———

UGLY AS THE WORK HAD BEEN THESE SIX HOURS, MOST MEN of Company L did not welcome Henry's order to leave the trenches they had been digging. The exception was the usually pessimistic Del Rio, who this morning felt convinced that moving back to Warren and the Fifth Corps meant that they'd be pulled out of active duty. He rubbed his hands and chattered about going home for much of the arduous march through two miles of knee-deep mud and muddled troops trying to recover from the day before. The others tasted futility in the gunpowder still clinging to their lips and in the blood they'd licked off fresh wounds or ones reopened. They saw it on the road they were traveling for the second time in as many days; heard it in the guns throbbing again along the whole line and the hiss of the rain. They felt the futility as they formed into part of Warren's second line of battle and waited in support of another failed Union foray, their hopes of lighter duty postponed. They'd given many lives in three years and it appeared they were to give more. Even Del Rio quieted when the shovels were handed out and they began digging new breastworks in the same mud they'd slept in two nights before. Disgust and anger began to brew.

One of the few conversations that day came when Tice, slopping a healthy mound of mud onto a wall of logs, stopped and said, "What about Von Schenk?"

A second passed before Louis said, "What about him?"

"Some fella ought to write his kin."

Eager to perform a service, Burridge piped in. "Yes, that would be the proper thing to do. Karl, do you know if he had any family?"

Karl didn't bother to look at Burridge. Instead, he brought his foot down on the flat edge of his small shovel and pried up a load of mud. He patted it around the logs, then finally said in gray tones, "*Er hat niemand. Keine Frau. Mutter,* father..." He shrugged. "I do not know."

The men continued their tedious muddy work in silence, Von Schenk's lonely passing a reminder of last night. Constant artillery gave notice that this battle, which only hours before had seemed at its end, would continue its bloody progress. This war was nowhere near finished, and while the night at the angle had convinced many, and rightly so, that the war had changed, the infuriating sameness of their actions and surroundings proved that this was still the war they had entered three years before, only larger and more fearsome.

Burridge replaced the paper he'd taken out to write Mrs. Von Schenk. The German would simply bloat in the heat now, unremembered to anyone who might care. The world had not ended last night, he told himself. He and Mink had not brought on the Apocalypse; they'd only helped to birth a new kind of terror. Burridge picked up his shovel and drove it in. Mink now held all of his secrets, as well as secrets of the Union, and though he'd always believed in Mink's reliability, Burridge decided that his men's lives were not worth the risk. Though it was impossible to know for whom Mink sold his trust, he was a traitor to one side or the other and Burridge no longer cared which one. He hoped never to see Mink again. He already had too much to atone for. He couldn't be like Mink, nor could he ever be one of these simple men. He would have to finish this war by himself. " 'The eye sees not itself, but by reflection, by some other things.' " He checked to see where Lyman was, then went back to his digging.

––––––––––

It surprised no one in the 14th that a short march to support one section of the line resulted in nothing more than four hours of standing in the mud and rain with no sleep or hot food. Nor were they surprised when orders came for the entire corps to march seven miles for a four A.M. attack on the eastern side of the Rebel mule shoe. The idea was absurd; any man who'd just tried to slog the last half-mile with them would have known that no troops, even ones that had been fed and rested, could make it to their as-signed position in time at anything near full strength. The men accepted the order with little fuss because they had no intention of trying to accomplish it. They would do their best.

At ten P.M. they set off at the same molasses pace they'd made earlier that evening, and in a short time it became evident that the company could not stay together. They'd dug too many trenches, fired too many bullets, missed too many nights of sleep for them to make it through the muck as a unit. Burridge and Alder both tried to exhort their men forward as one, but finally gave in to the pull of the mud. Each step was an effort. Each man would do what he could on his own.

So Company L disintegrated, as the regiment had, as the whole Fifth Corps had. Wes and Teddy dragged along the shell of Slipper Feeney, who'd given up the night before and now only moved when moved by others. They were the first to fall out of line, joining the thousands of strays and stragglers defeated by the combination of fatigue, hunger, and mud. They set Feeney against the wheel of a wagon long abandoned to the grip of the road and caught their breath. Four other men lay snoring underneath the wagon. Wesley noticed a man walking by who had his eyes closed, still marching in his sleep.

Before half a mile, the movement became merely a migration of soldiers. Men cursed the mud that sucked the shoes off their feet and the generals who drove them through it; they cursed their bodies, too weak and too tired to go on. Past Finn and Pitt, the Worms marched together, as did Louis, Karl, and Tice a dozen yards farther. Stewart and Henry had set off at the head with Cawthorne in tow, but these three had slowed and were now passed by men of other companies and regiments. Stives and Del Rio lumbered along as an unlikely pair and everyone else in the company was gone, which left Burridge and Lyman next to each other. Lyman thought to walk past him, but it would be a long march. Better an enemy for company than no company at all.

They watched sadly as the unit crumbled into twos and threes. Just when the company had finally pulled together, it seemed to be pulled apart now by common mud. Lyman tried to distract himself with thoughts of base ball, but when he noticed Louis limping ahead, he wished he could forget the suspicions and possibilities Louis and his own mind had raised, the guilt that could be involved, the friendship he still wanted to maintain. He asked Burridge a question before he could decide whether or not he wanted to know the answer. "Was there any, you know, anything odd about them matches?"

Burridge had been waiting for this question, and after Louis's surprise accusation at the front, he'd developed more of a bluff face. He looked at Alder and easily read in his tilted eyebrows and hesitant expression that the man really didn't want to know the truth. With all of Lyman's friends gone, Burridge considered it a favor to spare him. "No. They were straight."

"We're almost done here, so don't hand me the bull. We ain't gonna see those boys again."

Burridge watched the raindrops bounce off Lyman's face. "On the level. I'd stand to lose much more than anyone else if we were found out."

Lyman thought that over for a second, then crinkled the corners of his eyes in as much of a smile as he'd allow himself today. Burridge knew he'd done the right thing. "Can't imagine us ever seeing them again."

"I'm not sure I'd want to." Burridge waved his hand around. "Not after this."

"Nope."

Neither man's tone was convincing.

Now that night had fallen, Tiger saw no reason to stay with the black soldiers. He and Nelson were working near the edge of a clearing, and while small fires and lanterns lit the area, the darkness of the trees called Tiger. Once they'd tamped mud down over the grave, he looked into the woods and said, "Ye wouldn't rat me out if I took me leave, would ye?"

Nelson broke ground for the next grave with a few spadefuls of mud. "I don't even know your name. How I gonna rat you out?" Tiger took a wary scan around, but didn't move. "G'wan." Nelson sounded impatient. "Nobody gonna stop you."

Tiger drove his shovel deep into the mud so its handle stood upright, tipped his cap to Nelson, and began walking into the trees with the deliberate nonchalance of a man obviously hiding something. He was a stride or two from disappearing when he heard Nelson calling, "Hold up, mister!"

He froze. He could hear quick steps slapping the mud behind him. The last thing he wanted was a colored man trying to run off with him. Tiger turned and there was Nelson, his eyes as hard as ever. "Wait up. I gotta make one statement before you go. Now you ain't so fond a us and truth is, we warn't so thrilled to have you around, neither."

"I don't have to listen to yer . . ."

"Wait. Your kind and my kind may never gets along ever in this place, but I gots to say one thing. I'm grateful you fighting for us. Even if'n it's against your will."

Tiger scratched his neck and mumbled something indecipherable in an irritated tone. There were other things to be said, but Tiger couldn't say them. He turned back around and entered the dark forest of lost shades.

————

During his day at the hospital, Newt had been able to sneak a couple hours of sleep by hiding among the rows of wounded and pulling his jacket up over his head, but as he watched Dr. Prine pour some kerosene on a head wound seething with maggots, he realized that Prine had not sat down once in the time he'd been there. Prine's fingers were swollen, red, and puckered by their constant immersion in liquids and they shook some when he began plucking the remaining maggots off with a pair of forceps. His face drooped and black circles ringed the eyes. "Gullman, please bring me some tea."

Gullman nodded and silently waddled away. Though the men condemned to Boyle's table still gave off rending screams when the doctor set to work, the most common sound now in the tent was a piteous whimper. The wounded who were reaching the table only at this point had endured hours of agony under a pounding rainstorm. Their cases had been considered less promising and so they brought worse wounds that had progressed further into rot and hemorrhage; most had already yielded to insanity and despair. Boyle and Prine had held some patients back from the table so their wounds could rot a bit more and develop the laudable pus that indicated the release of bad humors, yet even these men, their prognoses deemed excellent by the doctors, floated off to the safe place in the mind where pain cannot go and where men rarely return from sane.

Prine asked Newt for some lint, then proceeded to swab as much blood as he could from the patient's shattered brain cavity. As much to himself as to Newt, he said, "God of mercy, take this one." Not willing to enter into another philosophical discussion with Prine, Newt said nothing. Aside from calling him over to help with this operation, Prine had not spoken to Newt since that morning and Newt still felt the tension. The doctor flipped a chunk of lint into his basin, by now filled with more blood than water. "More lint, please."

Newt squeezed a wad dry and handed it to Prine, who took a few dabs at the brain before throwing up his hands and running them through his hair to calm himself. He stared at Newt. "I apologize for what I said earlier. You really must excuse me." Unexpected as the apology was, Newt did not react. Prine reached for a wide cloth bandage and began winding it around the patient's head. "I have seen so many boys and they all kill for what they believe in and die for it." Despite his swollen fingers, Prine used his hands with care and gentleness. "They all ask for their mothers. Have you noticed that? Their mothers." He looked over Newt's shoulder, through the canvas of the tent, and into the distance, still winding the bandage, then faced him again. "The fact is, I enlisted for the very same reasons you did. It's not your fault I'm homesick and tired."

Prine finished a tight knot on the bandage just as Boyle howled into his ear, "Get a move on it, Prrrine! Ye got another gaping head right behind ye a-waiting yer special touch!" Boyle strode off while a pair of orderlies took the patient away for his trip to Fredericksburg, followed by a Washington hospital or a cemetery.

Prine gave Newt a weak smile. "I admire men like you. Your decision to enlist was a difficult one and from what I've seen I would guess that you've adhered to the terms you've made for yourself." Orderlies placed another body on the table, this time a reedy youngster with the very crown of his skull shot away. Gullman brought the tea and Prine stood back for a moment so he could take a brief sip.

Newt peered into the basin of bloody water next to him and saw the reflection of a man with a dense beard and a handlebar mustache that needed trimming. There was nothing happy about the face, nor was there anything especially sad. The face belonged to a soldier, a man who acted on his beliefs, a man who took responsibility for his actions, a man who accepted pain and offered succor to others. A killer, a nurse, a father, a son, and a husband. It was the face he'd always hoped to see when he looked into a mirror. He had the face, and now he felt he could live up to it. He plunged his hand into the basin. "Lint, doctor?"

Prine held his hand out. "Please."

———

Alone in the woods, Tiger weaved among the tree trunks, haunted by the faces of that day's dead. Hairless boys in pools of blood, the shit leaking out of their assholes; men stiff and contorted into positions of submission they would hold until bugs ate them and they rotted. Stinking masses of flesh, organs torn from open stomachs, vermin chewing on limbs and extremities—he'd seen it all before; here, in Brooklyn, and in Cork. Each time he'd pledged it was his last communication with the dead, yet more and more it seemed that death was his companion, not his fate. He began to tremble in the rain and the urge to sip whiskey seeped down through his body.

He picked his way through the trees until the blackness turned to gray and he could see a clearing ahead covered in white. Tiger drew closer and saw they were shelter tents. Row after row, the tents stood in textbook military order; a captain's dream, the canvas taut and the lines all straight. No one had lit a fire, nor was there a sound in the air other than the distant movements of wagons and men. Only a small path ran alongside this clearing. No guards had been put in place, no horses. There was no sign even of which army this bivouac belonged to.

Warily, Tiger came out of the trees and entered the encampment. No snores, no burning candles or games of Bluff. No smell of coffee. Just tent after white tent, thrumming in the rain. He told himself that it had been abandoned; that whichever regiment this was had been called into battle before they could pack. But there were no packs lying about, no smoldering fires with beans cooking over them.

Goose bumps rose on his arms and neck. Tiger had the feeling that something was wrong here, that he was walking someplace he shouldn't walk, that he was disturbing something. Men were in these tents; he could sense them.

He took a few more steps, listened to his own cautious breathing. Tiger snapped open a tent flap and saw a pair of eyes wide open and staring at him, the mouth agape in a silent eternal scream. He dropped it shut. In a frenzy, he raced from tent to tent, the pairs of bodies lying still within them.

It was a bivouac of the dead, bodies stored here until they could be buried. A whole regiment of the dead, awaiting the blast of a horn that Tiger did not want to hear. He fancied he heard them call to him from the jaws death had fused open and he fell to the mud, to his knees, then face-down, covering his ears to block out the silence.

It was still dark when Tiger came to, but he couldn't say how long he'd been out. Remembering where he was, he took a deep breath and told himself that they were just dead bodies. One of which might have a flask of whiskey.

Armed with the calm reason of self-interest and chuckling at his loss of nerve, Tiger got up and casually strolled down the rows, gingerly entered tents, and patted down the inhabitants for any illegal hooch they might have. The tents had four men each, stacked atop each other. Because they'd been kept out of the rain, the bodies were even riper than those he'd been burying today, but he was not deterred. Occasionally he would open a wallet or read a letter while sharing their dry tent, chatting with the dead as though he were mayor of the camp. He twined rosaries around fingers, closed eyes when possible, and had no luck at all in finding booze.

He entered a tent with one colored soldier in it. Tiger figured that whoever had made this camp had felt it necessary to insult this man even in death. He had a *23* on his cap, which meant he was from Nelson's regiment, the 23rd U.S. Colored Troops. The large bullet wound in the man's chest had obviously caused his death, but Nelson had said the regiment hadn't seen combat yet. Tiger assumed the boy had been trying to desert and a provost guard took him out or he sassed some antsy sergeant. Death had locked the man's jaw closed and clenched his fists into balls.

Tiger sat down next to the body and patted the pockets. Two shiny pebbles in one trouser pocket, a piece of Confederate scrip in the other. A small pipe rested in a jacket pocket and that was that, unless his fists concealed something else. Quigley pried open the man's left hand.

One gold button embossed with the letters "CSA" sat in the pink palm, attached to a swatch of gray uniform fabric. It looked as though it had been ripped off a Rebel's body. Tiger immediately judged the man a grave robber, but then he checked his lips. Though the man had dark skin, it was easy to see a heavy black film of gunpowder over his face and around his mouth. A man could only earn a mask like that by loading and reloading a rifle. This man hadn't died running away from anyone; he'd been going forward, into the Rebel guns, onto the Rebel works. This separate tent was probably an honor, not a slur.

Tiger forced open the other hand to reveal a gold locket. Two well-rendered drawings took the place of photographs inside: one was of a striking colored woman in a simple homespun dress and the other was of a young boy, smiling shyly at whoever had made the sketch, a finger to his lips and a stick held behind his back.

Tiger felt tears running down his cheeks. Life had been wonderful with Mary, wonderful as this man's life must have been the day he was set free to live as he wanted with his family. A family like the one Tiger would have had. A man like the one Tiger would have liked to have been. A colored man.

Tiger wanted to live again. Not the lies he'd told Nelson and the others; just a way to make a living and a reason to wake up in the morning. Tiger filled his lungs with the smell of decay in the field and gulped for more between sobs. It was time to find the 14th.

CHAPTER

23

———

WHERE DO YE THINK THEM TORCHES EVACULATED TO?"
Early in the march, the light haze over the column's front from the sputtering, smoky torches of guides had reassured Teddy, but they'd long ago lost that cheering glow and Teddy was concerned. He and Pitt, bearing Feeney in between, had made poor progress. Now their only guides were the hulks before them and hundreds of men sleeping along the sides of the path. Wesley grunted, pulling one of Feeney's legs out of the mud and planting it farther ahead. "Teddy, would ye mind givin' me a fuckin' hand here with Slipper?" Feeney's head lolled onto Wesley's shoulder, eyes half closed, body and soul reliant on the man who'd let him take the heat for a crime he hadn't committed.

Teddy considered Feeney's sorry state partially Wesley's fault; he couldn't blame him for the quickstep, but the wrongful accusation was certainly all his doing, and Teddy had lost more in the last few days than his illusions of power.

Wesley's eyes flared. "Fer chrissakes, Teddy!"

All together too much sass coming out of Pitt now, Teddy decided Seven or eight years ago the party boys had plucked Wesley out of a rag pile, reeking of horse shit, and gave him to Teddy for grooming. Teddy had shown him all the ropes, but instead of loyalty he got orders. The thought soured in his stomach. Finn began to work his jaw, the blood pumping a bit, nostrils flaring with his sharp breath.

He glowered and flexed his arms. Usually Pitt dropped tail at that, but tonight he balled his fists and leaned across Feeney to stick his face into

Finn's. "I saved your life last night. And Feeney's. And you know it. The German's right—it's time for ya ta clamp that gob a yers and do something. If you want a piece a me, come on and get it, my friend. Otherwise, shut up and help me." Wesley leaned back.

Teddy's heart fired at the challenge. He sized up his opponent as he reached for the straps of his knapsack. No one had ever spoken to Teddy Finn like that and lived.

Until tonight. Teddy consoled himself that he'd taught Pitt well. He stuck an arm under Feeney and took his share of the load. After a few slow steps as hard on his spirit as they were on his legs, Teddy brightened. If nothing else a practical man, he was glad to know that *someone* was in charge. He let the new order of things sink in for a few yards, then, pride swallowed, order preserved, and a leader crowned, Teddy assumed his role with the effusive grace of a good party hack. He winked at Wes. "Oh, when we get back to Brooklyn, we'll have the yarns fer 'em, I'll tell ya. This'll be one of them." The patronizing smear in Wes's answer was familiar. Teddy had used it himself.

"Teddy, we ain't leaving here with the rest of the boys when their three years are over." Wes looked over at him and smiled. "The three of us is here till the end of the war."

Teddy thought he could see the torches glow ahead; he fixed his eyes on them. "Don't I know that, Wesley. Don't I know."

Wes and Teddy didn't notice that Slipper had gone limp. All his life Slipper Feeney had tried very hard to keep up. While Teddy chided him for being slow, he'd always waited for him and that, more than any reflected glory or physical threat, had kept Feeney loyal. Slipper knew he should have gone to the hospital a week ago to stop the quickstep and now he felt a coldness in his bones, a slow hardening. It was too late. Feeney slipped his tongue through his lips and tried to wet them. In a hoarse whisper, he said, "Stop."

They stopped. Wesley shook his head. "We just had ourselves a rest, Arch."

Arms over his friends' shoulders, Arch Feeney let his head hang down, his chin resting on his chest. Teddy and Wes met eyes over his bent head. Teddy grimaced and Wes made a slight gesture with his head over to the side of the road, whispering into Slipper's ear, "I guess we can set another minute."

Wes spread the liner out again and Teddy laid Feeney across it. Feeney tucked his knees up and curled over them like a baby as the other two, anxious to move, rocked in the mud. After a minute spent listening to the moans and splashes from the road, Wes clapped his hands and stood up. "Catch a few winks there, Slipper?"

The cold had stolen through Feeney's arms and legs and as it crept nearer to his heart, he relaxed into the soft mud as though it were a feather mattress. "Leave me."

Both Teddy and Wes grabbed at his arms and started to haul him up, but Feeney mustered what strength he had remaining and let out a plaintive "Noooo." The hollow, otherworldly sound of Feeney's voice froze them and out of kindness and a speck of fear for what they'd just heard, they set him back down. "An ambulance will get me," he whispered, and closed his eyes.

No ambulances would be coming along here; they all knew that. Wes and Teddy heard the request for death in Slipper's voice. Wesley made a small protest, but Slipper had known his end was coming and had prepared in what ways he could. He clutched the cross around his neck. "G'wan. 's OK." He stretched out a closed hand toward Wes. "Here."

Wes felt the damp metal of Feeney's lucky dollar fall into his palm. "Slipper..."

" 's OK. Take it."

Wes took his blanket out of his pack and covered Slipper. "You'll be fine. Have a few winks and the doc will be by when you wake up."

Teddy stammered as Wes began to pull him away. "T-t-take care a yourself there, Feeney. You'll catch up with us."

Slipper didn't move. He kept his eyes closed until the splashing of their boots merged into the other damp noises around him, then briefly opened them to see the familiar backs getting farther and farther away. He closed them again, snuggled into his mattress, and listened to the distant sounds of passing armies rise to his attic from downstairs.

The mud was littered with abandoned goods, and it was among such a pile of souvenirs, loose clothing, canned goods, and cooking paraphernalia that

Linden Stewart discovered a cheap edition of Hugo's *Les Misérables*. The book had been printed by a Southern firm, so this particular copy had probably come off a dead Rebel somewhere in the Wilderness. Sitting on a forgotten blanket, he flipped through the pages. Phyllis had sent an edition to him months earlier, which he had voraciously read and discarded. Often he would offer books to Burridge, but Stewart recalled that he hadn't given him the Hugo and as he remembered the plot, he decided that the omission had been providential. It would make a perfect gift for his own Valjean. He took out a pencil and scribbled a dedication in the dark.

The line of march took the troops across the outskirts of the field surrounding the salient, around the house that had served as a headquarters and then back into the forest until they hit the Ni River. Hundreds of feet, hooves, and wheels had whipped the muddy banks of this slow-moving river into a frothy muck that thinned as one got closer to the water. A group of men tried to shove a cannon up the far side. Torches glimmered in the shattered surface.

Lyman pointed to the sky before he stepped in. "What time do ya have?"

Burridge flipped open his watch. "Half past three."

"You and me ain't gonna be in any four o'clock attack, I can tell you that."

Burridge looked both ways for other officers. "Good."

"Seven more days," Lyman said. "Seven more days."

No one attacked at four. First light revealed that only a few hundred men of the corps' thousands had completed the march by the designated time, and now, at daybreak, the head of the column was brought to a halt about three-quarters of a mile from Spotsylvania Court House. Griffin's men were sent into the fields on the left of the Fredericksburg Road to face south and southwest, while Cutler and the 14th went off to the right, facing due west. Officers tried to get the few available men into a line of battle, but those present had spent themselves on the march; at best, they could boil coffee and sleep.

For the next couple of hours, men trickled into Warren's camp, found their regiments, and collapsed into the mud. Henry, Stewart, and Cawthorne had hitched a ride on a passing wagon, their combined rank dismissing the objections of the driver to their combined weight, and they waited in the intermittent showers for the company to arrive, savoring the stunned expressions of their men, who had assumed they were behind them. Louis, Karl, and Tice were the first soldiers to reach camp. They had had no difficulties fording Madison Creek and the final mile on the Fredericksburg Road proved less traveled, and therefore less swampy, than many of the roads they had followed. Burridge and Lyman were next at around 5:30. Teddy and Wes made it by six.

By 7:30 the artillery had arrived and about thirteen hundred of Cutler's men, twenty-five hundred of Griffin's. No sign yet of Crawford from behind. Union cannons boomed as a small force went in against a hill about a mile and a half away from the 14th, off to the southeast, but no one in the company paid attention. Exhaustion numbed them. Artillery throbbed throughout the day. Louis and Karl slept sprawled on the mud as Tice gnawed on a piece of salt pork. Lyman sipped a second cup of coffee and watched the rear, hoping that more of theirs would wander in, hoping this company would leave as more than this handful of men. He waved to a few Brooklyn men from other companies, but no faces from L.

Wes and Teddy sat ten feet away silently staring in the same direction as Lyman, waiting for a face they knew they wouldn't see.

Burridge was standing next to Henry, discussing the foul weather, when Stewart came by wearing a treacly smile. He held a book out to Burridge. "A gift for you, Lieutenant. I came across it and thought it might be a volume you would appreciate."

John took the thick book with the tips of his fingers and returned a faint smile for the captain's benefit. He read the title—*Les Misérables*. The smile hardened. "How thoughtful of you."

Stewart bore his eyes into Burridge. "Have you read this yet?" A streak of venom shot through his words. "Say you haven't."

"In fact I have, but I greatly admire Hugo . . ."

A fat hand settled onto Burridge's arm, then squeezed it with just slightly more strength than necessary. "Then accept it as a memento; a presentation copy, if you will." Stewart squeezed again. "I've written a dedication. Do read it."

Burridge opened the book.

Henry smiled, pleased to see his staff getting along. "So, then. Enjoy your book. Men, our orders are to build breastworks along this line..." Henry explained the orders at great length, but Stewart and Burridge heard very little of them.

———————

Newt had been helping to load men into ambulances when the Fifth Corps passed by. The torches' glow had crept slowly toward them like the advancing front of a forest fire, and soon the brays and whinnies of stuck livestock and the curses of stuck men filtered through the trees. Through the night, exhausted soldiers stumbled into the hospital begging rest and a warm drink, their legs wrapped in thick boots of mud. Newt continued his duties, but he kept an ear open to what information the marchers had, and when he learned this was the Fifth Corps, he began to actively search for the red trousers of the 14th. Past dawn and into the early morning, the stragglers plodded by, hunched, their eyelids drooping, arms swinging and barely in control. Newt watched and while he felt the value of the service he had been impressed into, he knew that with only seven days left, he should be with his regiment, and with Lyman. He needed to talk to his old friend, to tell him some true things about Gettysburg and Tiger Quigley.

He found Boyle standing in the same place he had met him, puffing a cigarette next to a heap of amputated limbs. The only differences were that the pile had grown considerably larger and Boyle's apron, then mottled red, was now wholly saturated with blood and shined like oiled leather.

Newt presented himself to the doctor. "Sir, if I may, sir, I would like to rejoin my regiment." He swatted at a few flies on leave from the pile, buzzing around his head.

Boyle squinted at him. "Who ahr ye an' what do I care?"

The cigarette smoke warded away the flies, but Boyle paid for that comfort with a hacking fit. Not wanting to believe that he could have left at any time, that his servitude had been essentially voluntary, Newt intended to wait out the coughing so he could explain. He began to unbutton his jacket in order to refresh Boyle's memory when he realized that an explanation was not only unnecessary, but foolish. Newt refastened his top buttons and was walking away when he heard Boyle launch a wad of phlegm, then call after him, "And good riddance to ye, I say!"

He had one more stop to make. Newt slipped into the operating tent and stepped over a few bodies propped up against the support poles, reaching Prine just as the doctor pulled his hands out of a man's chest. Newt announced himself to Prine and Gullman. "I wanted to say good-bye, sir."

Prine turned to Newt, his eyes blinking rapidly, then settling down once he saw who it was. He weaved a bit as he spoke. "Leaving us?"

"Yes, sir. I only have seven days until we're mustered out."

"That's splendid. Good for you. Where will you go then?"

"Back to Brooklyn, sir."

"Bully. Bully." They stood nodding at each other for a few seconds. "Well, that's it then." Prine held out a bloody hand, which Newt shook. "Good luck to you."

Newt felt the blood on his hand. "Good luck to you, sir."

With a nod to Gullman, Newt turned and left the tent, heading off in a direction that greatly differed from the one he had come in from.

CHAPTER

24

———

LYMAN SCANNED THE GRAY SKIES IN HOPES THAT A SMALL crack would open in the heavy cloud cover. Their duties for the day were to build breastworks and rest, in that order, so as Karl and Tice went out into the ash-brown pines and occasional greens of the forest in search of wood, Lyman began yet another entrenchment in yet another patch of muddy ground.

The mud was soft, like snow; and, like snow, it was very heavy. The rain kept falling and the water collected in the trench, each shovelful of mud removed only let it sink deeper. Another shovel of mud, another inch of rain. On and on it went. The soggy rhythm of his labors mixed with the patter of rain made him stop and take some very deep, easy breaths. He was bone tired.

A man nearby from Company K began to sing what felt like a lullaby to the melody of "Maryland, My Maryland":

A pisspot feels upon me poured;
Rain again. It's rain again.
With Southern rain I am so bored.
Rain again. It's rain again.

Seven, eight, or is it more,
Inches of rain on my trench floor.
I'd trade my rifle for an oar.
Rain again. It's rain again.

Lyman had closed his eyes. Only the shovel kept him vertical. A gust of wind shook the pines and he took another slow, deep breath. Then a piercing whistle that only a steam locomotive could match for intensity and volume pierced through his slumbering mind. He jolted upright and took a groggy look behind him in the direction of the sound, swearing like a sailor out of instinct. Willie Winston, with his whistling fingers still in his mouth, was back, with Huey Van Dueven behind him, waving like a maniac.

And Tiger. Not the Tiger he'd cut, but the Pete Quigley who stood next to him at his wedding, jaunty, gruff, smiling. Tiger let loose a great laugh. "We're back, laddies! Ye can't lose us that easy! We found each other in the woods, fancy that!"

Quigley stood there, waiting for Lyman to speak. "Lad. It's the old Tiger." Lyman looked him up and down, nodded a few times, gave him one grunt, and went back to work.

Tiger straightened and put his arm around Huey. "Come on, Hugh. A can of coffee will do ye wonders and make me a smarter man. Willie, will ye fix us a few cans a the mud?" Willie was already scrounging dry wood from a neighboring mess a few feet away. "See, me boy? Everything's going to be fine."

Tiger and Lyman managed to avoid each other for the balance of the morning. Since Henry and his lieutenants had the good sense to let their men rest and work on an easy schedule, Tiger could nap while Lyman dug and vice versa. Within a few hours, it seemed as if Willie, Huey, and Tiger had never left the company. A greater surprise came around noon. The possibility of Del Rio and Stives ever coming back had seemed remote at best until this pair strolled into camp, well rested and full of news from the stragglers' line. The welcome proved a good reason for everyone to stop working and lounge some more; Lyman even found himself shaking Stives's hand and staring at the baker's long teeth, unusually exposed in a gaping smile.

The rain let up briefly around three. Lyman was standing against the back wall of his trench, facing out toward the west and the Rebels, when he felt a tap on his shoulder. It was Tiger, lying on the ground over him. He seemed subdued. "Have a catch with me, Lyman?" He made a small throwing gesture. "Rain stopped."

Lyman was pleased by Tiger's way of apologizing, but he didn't plan to make it easy for him. He took off his cap and scratched his scalp. "I don't think so; ball'll get wrecked in all this mud."

"Don't think I can hold on to the bean, do ye?"

Lyman wanted this to be hard for Tiger, but he didn't want to start another fight. He said quickly, "No, no, that's not what I'm saying."

"Aye, I'm just pullin' a saw on ye, laddie." He reached out and patted Lyman on the shoulder. Tiger let the hand rest there. "Just pullin' a saw."

They said nothing for a minute, listening to the world without rain, wondering what would come next. Tiger took his hand away. They both shifted a bit, wishing their strength could squeeze the contents of their hearts into words. Then as the silence grew, they tried to communicate without them, as they had countless times in their lives. They could sit or walk or work silently together, their bodies in one place but each mind wandering everywhere in the world with confidence that the other man was guarding him from dangers both without and within and would always be there to do it. They hadn't done that in a long while. There'd been much too much noise of late. Moment after silent moment passed, yet instead of bonding them, it increased the discomfort. Their silence grew heavy and threatened to fall. Tiger steeled himself. "Lyman, I just wanna..."

Lyman waved him off. The intention was enough for him. "No. You don't have to say..."

"Yes, I do. I, I'm sorry I been such a bloody arsehole to ye." They stared in separate directions. "I just wanna get home now. Get on with me life. Eat that steak you're gonna hand over to me the second we put a foot back in Brooklyn." He gave Lyman a gentle smack on the shoulder.

Lyman smiled, then let his smile sag. "Yeah, get on with it. That's right." He coughed. "It'll be odd without Danny around, though."

"Much has changed, laddie. No man can tell ye that more."

"It's all different. Your Mary's gone. Ernie's grown. I think Victoria..."

"Bah! Stop all your thinking." Tiger scowled. "It makes ye more of a fool than a wise man. You *got* your family, lad. They're not a bloody bunch a horses, so don't ye go betting on 'em. Things change for the better, too, eh? Think a *that* for once."

Lyman nodded and the two sat quietly for a few seconds, testing their weight on the bridge of silence, gratified that it held now. "How's your chest?"

Pete put his hand to the cut. "Don't hurt, but I don't remember getting hit."

"I cut you so the guards would pass you through."

"Ach, so I got you to thank. What about Newt?"

Lyman gave him a suspicious look. "Since when is that a concern of yours?"

"A man can change, I tell ye." Tiger spit casually into the mud. "Besides, there's somethin' to be said for a man who won't hurt another."

Lyman creased his forehead into even deeper furrows. "Have you . . . ?"

Tiger shook his head slowly. "Dry as a bone."

Lyman made a small *hmph* and the two settled back into silence.

Down the trench, Burridge sat and flipped through the pages of *Les Misérables*. He had lied to Stewart; he'd never read the book, though he knew well enough what it was about and which character Stewart surely empathized with. Burridge looked again at the dedication written in Stewart's loopy, boyish handwriting, an odd script for one as powerful as he was back in Brooklyn—"Your innings are over."

As the lieutenant closed the book, he noticed a heat settling onto the back of his neck. It was not a pleasant warmth; Burridge felt he was being watched. He resisted the urge to duck his head down into his collar. It would be a challenge to escape with his life, and an even greater one to escape a free man. Sitting in the mud, he decided that these seven days promised to be extremely long. And extremely dangerous.

———

Night began to steal across the field. By six o'clock the wet wood of campfires hissed and sparked under a steady light rain and the ending of the artillery gave a kind of peace to the land. Willie had drawn meat for the company, freshly culled from the large herd of beefs the Union army brought along south, and Huey was making some biscuits as Lyman sat next to his fire, occasionally staring back toward the Fredericksburg Road. After a day of light work, he was beginning to feel better, at least physically. He was sore, but aching arms or legs could be rubbed down or rested; the pain he felt at Newt's absence deepened with the steely dusk.

Lyman pulled a stick through the mud, then tossed it into the flames. He pictured what Mrs. Fry would do when he told her. She was not one to scream, but she *would* faint. The children weeping. It would be a horrible scene. They'd lose the house. He put his face into his hands.

"Quit yer blubbering, missy." Newt stood on the other side of the fire, his face lit from below. "Time to get into your work."

Lyman grinned. "You son of a bitch. You lousy son of a bitch."

"Heard Willie got his hands on some steaks, so I decided to come back."

By now Lyman had sufficiently recovered from the shock to stand up. They shook hands, but hands could not say enough tonight. Lyman pulled him into an embrace and they thumped each other's backs.

"You son of a bitch. You got hit bad there, Newton. Are you . . . ?"

"Like hell I got hit bad. Flesh wound, is all."

"Still . . ."

Newt rolled his eyes. "Been hurt worse stacking cans."

Lyman had not anticipated this Newt, jauntily tossing aside the injury, and he was pleased by the surprise. He put his arm around Newt's shoulder. Though he felt the urge to give his friend's cheeks a paternal squeeze, he settled for knocking Newt's cap off with a flip of his hand. "Come on, boy. Some folks here'll be glad to see you."

The smell of frying beef rose from the fire where Louis, Karl, Tice, Teddy, and Wes were swearing about the rain and impatiently wagging sticks over the flames. A chunk of meat pierced by a bayonet jutted off the end of each stick and coffee boiled below, the cans catching occasional droplets of hot fat. Lyman pulled Newt to the outskirts of the ring and said, "Guess who made it back."

Teddy and Wes almost dropped their meat into the fire. They snapped around, but when they saw Newt walk into the light, their faces fell and their welcome was restrained. For the others, the warmth of the handshakes had more to do with the sense of pride at reassembling the unit than with any particular joy at seeing Newt. Stives and Del Rio came by from the other fire, while Karl shifted over on his rubber liner to make room for Newt. Lyman called over to Willie for another steak and the men caught Newt up on what he had missed. Newt stuck his steak into the fire and asked if anyone still hadn't returned.

Del Rio said, "Dose Werms. Dey coming back, I tink."

"What about Feeney?" Newt looked at Wes, who was checking to see if his steak was well-done yet. None of the men could swallow meat that had even a hint of pink at the center.

"We left him with an ambulance. Too much a that quickstep, I'd say."

"That's a shame."

Wes laughed. "You hated him." He took his steak in his hands and bit into it. No one bothered to use a knife and fork much anymore.

"I never handed money to a better card player."

His mouth full, Wes said, "He cheated."

"Probably so, but he was a good cheat."

Karl ripped off a large hunk of meat with his teeth and talked excitedly about how Slipper had asked Wes to return the stolen housewife. As the grease shone off Karl's lips, Newt leaned back a bit and turned to the other fire twenty feet away. One figure sat in front of it, a black shape now tilting its head back and tugging at a tough strip of beef.

Newt spoke into Lyman's ear. "I see Quigley made it through."

Lyman poked a bayonet through his steak. "He's acting mighty strange. Son of a bitch was so drunk we had to knock him out. Willie and Huey took him to the back. Hasn't told me what happened at the hospital, but I expect he saw something or other. You run into him back there?"

Newt squeezed his steak and found it still too rubbery for his tastes. "If he was at the hospital, I didn't see him." He watched Tiger's black form take a sip of water. "There must've been a thousand men."

Karl's voice broke into their conversation. "I am saying to you, Lyman, what do you think we do now?"

"I don't know."

"We should be pulled off the line before the next battle. We moving just like when we leave the Wilderness: like a crab, *ja*. Sideways. This is Grant's way."

Louis gnawed the last bit of meat off a bone, then tossed it into the fire. "So *when* are they taking us out, Lyman? Hmm? This is enough; we have done our part." He stretched out his leg, which snapped like a dry twig.

Karl said, "*Ja. Das stimmt.*"

Surprised by the Hungarian's sudden change of attitude, Lyman responded cautiously. "I don't know anything more than you know, Louis." He looked him in the eye. "Probably a good deal less."

Louis was not satisfied. "Look at us. We have survived every obstacle they have put in front of us." Heads nodded; Karl added his own *"ja, ja"*s to punctuate the point. "They could not break us. No. They could not. We have done our part and now it is time for us to go! Our war is over!" He slammed his fist down onto his open palm, a gesture he had last performed in 1848, on a street corner in Pest. It had had its effect then and it had its effect now, but Louis saw only a glimpse of that moment before he imagined himself in a new position; *kippah* on his head, he was expounding on midrash to a yeshiva room full of boys. He took his place as Karl and others gave their own concurring speeches and strayed close to the fringes of mutiny.

Lyman was more amused than concerned. Two weeks ago this little rebellion could never have taken place. None of them cared enough then, but they *had* made it through everything since—and their survival came in some measure because of the matches, because they could turn a double play even if they didn't like who they were throwing to. Even if there was something fishy going on around them, the matches had given them a reason to press on. Louis and Karl had become loud voices in the group. The Irish were even talking to the Dutchman; Wes, though still a thief, was a tough fighter; Teddy had learned his place. And, most of all, they stuck together. He couldn't change them, but whatever else he'd done, he'd done what he could to bring them to a place where they could do it themselves.

Wes sucked one of his fingers. "I'll tell ye what. I'd like another whack at those Rebs."

Louis tossed his bayonet into the mud. "You haven't had enough? You want more blood?"

"No." Wes wiped his hands on his muddy pants. "We said five matches, and I want five matches."

Lyman smiled. The fact was, they hadn't gotten home just yet. A lot could happen in seven days, and he didn't know for certain that Micah was a spy, or that anyone was. He would ask him to desert; a spy would not, but given their sympathies, Micah and the boys would come over if they were on the up and up. They were better Union men than most Union men. That would settle it for him. Lyman wanted to play again.

No one said anything for a minute. Karl wiped his mouth off with the sleeve of his jacket. "*Ja*, well it would be good, but it is dangerous. We made it this far without breaking *und* we should be happy to get out *und* not go looking for no more base ball games."

The scraps of a regimental band—a bowlegged shoulder horn player, two piccolos, one tall and one short, a bald clarinetist, and a pot-bellied bass drum—began a sporting rendition of "The Girl I Left Behind Me," which roused men within earshot to clap along. A day of rest had done everyone much good. Partners were taken for the next number and soon dancers skimmed across the mud in the firelight; a few pairs of bearded veterans plodded through a lively *schottische* with more spirit than rhythm, applauding its finish and demanding more.

Distracted for a moment, Karl turned back to the fire. "*Ja*, we are all together. They must pull us off. That is all that matters."

Louis heard the German's voice droop a little, so he bolstered it with a vigorous "Yes, that is exactly right," directed at Lyman.

Across the fire, Lyman nodded. "We *should* be pulled off—we've earned that. Now, I'm just one man here, but I think there's something left to do and I'm surprised Pitt is the only one to say so. None of us, 'cept for maybe Pitt and Finn here, is gonna see Bobby Lee hand over his sword. I mean *we* did not win this war." Looking at the faces staring from the fire, Lyman knew he was the leader here; nothing could change that now. Ordinary as he was, the mantle was his. "All we got to look forward to is what our peace is gonna be like, and for me, I wanna go home with something to be proud of. I wanna *win* something. I'm with Pitt there." He caught Wesley's eye. "I wanna stay on the line until we can see those Alabama bastards, beat 'em three out of five, then shake their hands and invite 'em home for supper."

Wes said, "That's right!"

"Besides, what's *your* plan? Shoot Captain Henry? Desert? You got a wcok left; which one a you is gonna desert? We all want to get back at those sons a bitches, who don't send us out there to win, but just to kill men and die. This is the only way to get 'em. They don't care how you kill the Rebs—with a gun or your hands or you can bite their fucking heads off for all U. S. Grant cares—but what they don't want is for you to be friends with them." He remembered Micah's face flickering in the flames of the clearing—one moment shooting, another smiling, calling a truce. "Now, you and me know those Rebs are men, but I wonder sometimes what I am. When I walk by a man bleeding to death and I'm thinking about eating beans, I have to wonder if all this business has made us plain killers. You know that's what the generals want. They don't want soldiers anymore; they want killers. But we made it through as *soldiers*. That's what we came here as and we held together through this war. Let's *leave* as soldiers, as men who can be as good with peace as we were with war."

Hour by hour resolve firmly, like a Roman and a man, to do what comes to hand with correct and natural dignity, and with humanity, independence, and justice. Allow your mind freedom from all other considerations. This you can do, if you will approach each action as though it were your last, dismissing the wayward thought, the emotional recoil from the commands of reason, the desire to create an impression, the admiration of self, the discontent with your lot.

How ironic, thought Burridge, that this came from Mink's own book. As he watched a few dozen smelly, battle-hardened soldiers prance about the mud to a polka, he decided that grabbing a man's hand to dance demanded more natural dignity than anything he, or Mink, had ever done. The dignity, he thought, came in carrying others. Burridge cringed as he remembered agreeing with so much that Mink had offered as truth; Aurelius was a harder master than the pleasing Mink.

Burridge looked over at his own men. They sat about quietly, writing letters or finishing their steaks, oddly subdued as a waltz began and the dancing caught fire throughout the camp. Though he'd lied to them, put them in peril beyond what their duties demanded, Burridge resolved now to protect his men this last week. Only he should have to suffer for his dreams to come true.

The dance went on spreading and more couples joined in, spinning past fires and then spinning back into the dark, those who were waltzing remembering life as it was in the towns that they came from, as it might have been through the years they had missed. Tiger dragged on his pipe. He knew Fry was above him; anyone else would have spoken by now. Newt finally reached down and tapped him. "Pete. Wanna dance?"

Quigley let out a cloud of smoke, then spat. He squinted ahead toward the dancers, his mouth pursed as if considering a large-scale attack against some difficult enemy position, then slowly turned up to Newt to ask the question that needed to be asked. "Who's gonna lead?"

Newt folded his arms and returned Tiger's pensive glare. "Well, if the next one's a waltz—I will. If it's a polka"—he pointed at Pete—"you do it."

Tiger considered the terms of their peace. He picked a dot of tobacco off his tongue and stared at it as the song ran down. The dancers clapped and now waited for the next one. Tiger flicked the tobacco away. "Fair enough."

Both men avoided looking at each other until the music resumed. "Listen to the Mocking Bird"—a polka. Tiger leaned his head toward the dancers in as much of an invitation as Newton would get. They stepped onto the muddy dance floor, assumed their positions, and began.

Their first steps were tentative and showed more concern by each for their toes than their style, but a few injury-free measures passed and they soon relaxed. Newt responded perfectly to the clear directions Tiger gave with a push on the back or a lead with the extended hand, and, for his part, Newt steered Tiger around the more menacing puddles during spins. Halfway into the song, they were cruising through the mass of dancers with a grace neither had suspected possible. Tiger upped the ante, doubling his steps as a test for Newt and Newt kept up, which both pleased his partner and annoyed him. Tiger wasn't sure whether he wanted Newt to succeed or to crumble, but friendly competitors never do, and at the end Tiger tried Newt on a few fancy spins that other pairs stopped to applaud. The number finished with a flourish on the clarinet and Tiger on one knee, presenting Newt to the cheering crowd.

The two bowed and walked off to calls for more. Tiger spat again, then looked Newt in the eye. "Me friend, yer an arsehole of the greatest sort."

Newt held the stare without blinking. "The feeling's mutual."

They broke off, then took a few more steps before Tiger said, "But you're a fucking good dancer."

THE
FOURTH
MATCH

———

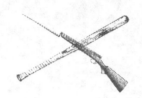

CHAPTER 25

BURRIDGE COULD TELL FROM HENRY'S LOW TONES WHY HE had been called into the captain's tent. "Recent desertions have given us some valuable information. It seems your friend has moved his company in reaction to our march. The Rebels have their own intelligence capabilities and apparently he has the power and independence to avail himself of them. Of course, it could also indicate that he is having some difficulties. Anyway, he is reported to be with his company now on this side of the Confederate line." Captain Henry gave each knuckle of one white-gloved hand a precise crack; two pure, soft hands that gave no evidence of what they had recently touched. "There is one other explanation possible for the spy's uncanny familiarity with our whereabouts." The captain inclined his head toward the lieutenant.

"Sir?"

"I've asked you this once before, but I feel compelled to request an answer once again. Have you given this spy any extraordinary knowledge of this army's movements?"

Burridge lied easily. "No sir! I assure you."

The captain held up his hand. "I trust your word. It is why I intend to introduce you in Brooklyn. You do what you say." He picked up a decanter of brandy. "You will go out for picket duty in the late afternoon."

Burridge folded his hands in his lap, sitting upright and stiff. "Do you think this is wise, sir?"

Henry had begun pouring the brandy into a crystal glass, but stopped at this. "Why ever not?"

The crystal, the gold, the fine woods; today they reminded Burridge of the offices of some old Manhattan lawyers he'd visited. Stacks of books and papers, objects, most of little practical value, lying about untouched for years. Rooms full of things whose only true purpose was to confirm the owner's ability to own them. He saw himself behind the broad mahogany desk he would buy when he returned. "I think the danger in this situation has increased tremendously, sir."

Henry put the decanter down with a thud. "What do you think 'danger' means now, Lieutenant? What do you think that word means a few days after what we saw at the salient? Is there a duty more dangerous than that which thousands of men performed at the wall; a duty that we were, thanks be, spared?" Henry let that settle onto Burridge until he saw the lieutenant focus on the ground before him. "This is a mission to which you agreed. I did not impress you into this service, nor did I cajole you or in any way keep you in anything less than full knowledge of its considerable risks and its equally considerable rewards." The captain poured his drink, then looked again at Burridge. "You have done a masterful job to this point and I do understand your reluctance. I must say that in some ways I even find your concern for the men commendable. But this is your duty to complete. This is not a time for your heart to go slack."

Burridge's "Yes, sir" was barely audible.

The captain let him sit for a moment. "One more thing I must mention, Lieutenant. I have had a report—an odd report, I grant you, but one I must pay some heed to—that you and your men have been fraternizing with the enemy, I would assume as part of this mission." He took a slow sip of his brandy, not looking at Burridge's stricken expression. "Apparently you were playing . . . base ball?"

"No sir! That is false. I would never . . ."

Henry tapped a white finger to his lip. "A shame. I thought it a novel idea. At this stage I believe it could only help draw some deserters over and some such. But your word is proof enough for me."

Burridge sat motionless in the chair. He'd lied to the one man who could save him, lied irrevocably. He'd chosen escape and found himself trapped. Whatever happened from this point on, Burridge could not tell the truth. He had turned his success from a thing of brilliance into a lie and a crime. Now his cell was dark; he would have to feel his way about alone.

CHAPTER 26

Lieutenant Burridge did not share the orders with his men until the middle of the afternoon. As he'd gone about his business this morning, he'd overheard a number of them grousing about their position on active duty and gleaned that an enthusiastic presentation of the news would be impolitic. Instead, he let them wallow in this tense and sluggish day of waiting. There was a bit of excitement when Newt asked Wesley for the return of his desk, which had gone missing in a manner suspiciously like Karl's housewife. Pitt claimed no knowledge of its whereabouts and Newt came close to starting a row. Cooler heads sent each man on his way, though. Otherwise, the men wrote their letters, bailed their trenches, smoked, ate, drank coffee, fiddled with their guns, and tried to stay dry. He knew that he couldn't risk an attempt to pass this duty off as something they could volunteer for, so when he finally did break the news to them at four that they would be detached for picket duty, he delivered it as the order that it was.

Confirmed now in his belief, Louis objected. "This is a trap. We will go to prison."

"No. How could it be?" Burridge had lied twice already that day and now he could see it wouldn't end. "We've moved to the other side of the front; we'll never run into Mink and those men. Personally I would have liked another go at them, but I see no way to effect such a meeting." He placed another lie on top to help weigh the others down. "The truth is that this is my fault. The other duties had been assigned by the time I reached the captain's tent. We'll be joining some other picket companies and stepping off at five."

Burridge walked away before any more questions could come up, leaving the men to debate this development. Louis remained skeptical, his cynical ears itching at the lieutenant's unnecessary disclaimer of wrongdoing. Karl was his only outspoken ally. "If there is no hope of seeing them *und* playing, I have no desire to picket." Tiger lit his pipe and reminded him that he didn't have much of a choice. Unless they were interested in deserting or mutiny, they could either picket and complain or picket and hope the Alabama boys really were out there.

Lyman stood on the side with a puzzled look. There was a logic behind the lieutenant's assertion that he would stand to lose the most from any revelation of their meetings, an argument that in Lyman's mind went a little distance in ruling out any larger machinations. It was also true that, despite Lyman's desire to find Micah and the others, the odds were quite long for such an encounter. Without real hope of seeing the Rebs, picket duty now was stupidly hazardous. If such a hope existed, it was worth the risk; he wanted to see his friend again and know once and for all what he was. Of course if they did see the Rebs again, somebody had to be planning it. He bit his lip and as he hesitated, Wes looked at him, then said to the group, "Sometimes ya just gotta trust the right thing'll happen. If they're out there, we'll play 'em and beat 'em. If they're not, we've lived through worse than some goddamn picket duty."

Louis drummed his fingers on his folded arms. "And what if we are caught in the act of playing?"

Tiger let a big cloud of smoke roll out of his mouth. "Wouldn't go any worse fer us now than it would've a week ago. Ye were bluff enough then, soldier. Besides..." He bit down on the pipe stem. "What choice do ye have?"

The truth of that point resigned them all to the inescapable duty, and at five that evening, as scheduled, Company L moved out on picket alongside other companies from Cutler's brigade. As the lines were constructed, Cutler's trenches ran almost perfectly north and south, with Burnside's lines running toward them broadside bearing south-southeast. Burnside's trenches did not intersect with Cutler's; there was a gap of about a quarter-mile between them, and it was into this gap that the picket proceeded, veering sharply left. A wall of trees loomed a half-mile ahead, hiding the Rebel line to the west. It then curved east at its north end to obstruct Burnside's left flank, now facing south. To the company's left were a few thick patches of woods on a north-northeast diagonal that would provide some cover from the Union lines and also from the other pickets in case there actually was a match. If the Rebs were out there, they would be somewhere in that small protected area. Since he'd been put in charge of the detail, Burridge sent the other three companies straight ahead toward the line of trees with orders to halt before they reached a swollen run that bisected the field. He told them he'd check on them in a few hours, then he led his men away.

The rain had softened to a fine drizzle that verged on mist. This area had seen little action during the salient attack. The ground was heavy and wet; grass and weeds held the soil together, and while their feet left deep prints in the mud, the men were able to make reasonable progress along the line of trees.

Burridge scanned the area with military calm. Forced to maintain his indifferent pose, he listened for Haddon's birdcall and hoped not to hear it. Lyman, too, looked into the tops of the pines and strained his ears for something other than the squish of brogans in mud and random skirmishing farther north. He was nervous, hoping they were all still alive, hoping to see Micah again, but if they did show, he would be forced to ask how they got there and how they knew to get there. The company stopped for a few minutes but heard nothing; an occasional shift in the breeze set a tree creaking back and forth, and the crows called out to them the unremarkable news that it was still raining. At one point, Teddy mistook a caw for Haddon until Louis pointed to the fat black bird making the sound on its branch. After half an hour, shoulders shrugged and whispers began.

Having viewed the area earlier, Burridge knew that if the Rebs were out here, they were on the other side of the trees to the company's left. That was why he had not led them through, but by now Lyman had looked the area over as well and Burridge knew he would come to the same conclusion. Pointing at the trees, Lyman stepped in. Burridge let Alder bear the weight of the inevitable; he followed Lyman and the rest of the men into the thatch.

They all stopped inside the trees. Wes screeched a few times hoping for a response, but there was nothing. He tried it again, and still only the creaking pines and the crows and the bullets could be heard, so they pushed through to the other side and into a clearing that was more loosely boxed than others they'd come to, but that could still serve as a protected ball field.

The men crouched low as Wes screeched, then screeched again.

They held still.

There was silence for a minute, until Lyman pointed off toward the western wall of trees. A couple of city blocks away, gray forms slowly pulled free of the mud and came toward them with stiff, weary steps that reminded Louis of the golem. Like the golem, this Southern army, gray and muddy from head to toe, had been created to protect, and Louis thought it was now time for someone to speak the word that would let them return to their soil and rest. Only one man among them seemed to move quickly, his head turning from side to side.

It was, of course, Sidney Mink.

As the Rebels drew closer, Lyman's first reaction was to note their wounds and bandages and to take stock of who was there and who was gone. Most had survived the last battle: Arlette, his shoulders rounded and strangely empty without Lou; Weed's venomous face and bald head coated in mud; and the long, stoic gaze of the Indian, Deal. Tidrow, Kingsley, and Cowles were there, too, and Micah, whose eyes rose from the ground until they met Lyman's and told him some of what they'd seen with a hard blink.

Teddy scanned these faces, then asked, "Where's ole Dukey?"

Mink, who had already grabbed Burridge's shoulder and was trying unsuccessfully to pull him aside, answered over his shoulder. "Gave his life for the cause, sir. A good man; seed of the Confederacy."

Micah looked up and gave his head a slight shake as if apologizing for him to the heavens. Lyman and the rest hadn't even turned toward Mink; instead, they looked at Micah for answers. Lyman wiped his nose with a finger, rubbed his hairy cheeks a bit, fidgeting until he could work up the courage, but Micah took the step first. "They gone. Lem and Dukey and Mansfield. Gone up ta Jesus." Karl and Del Rio crossed themselves. Tiger spit. "You missing some a yourn boys, too."

Lyman nodded. "Von Schenk."

"That fat Dutchman?"

"Yeah, and Feeney and the twins."

Despite the gloom, Mink skittered about the Union line and greeted men with a pugnacious enthusiasm suited more for Charleston in '60 than

Spotsylvania in '64. The two groups of soldiers stood silently while Mink patted backs and told the Yankees how hard the Rebs would be to bust. It was unclear which side he was out to impress, and it was obvious to Burridge that he was in trouble. His eyes had sunk back into his face so that the outlines of his skull were visible and the dingy black of exhaustion ringed the sockets. The men of both armies ignored Mink's frantic energy and Burridge, embarrassed by this pathetic display, wished he could ignore him, too.

Lyman rearranged his cap. "Well, seeing how you lost some a your players, some of our boys could go over and..."

Micah held up a hand. "Naw. We got enough for a nine. Guess they'll just be some new players. Y'all think the field'll work?"

"Got a better one?"

The two exchanged bitter smiles and turned to assemble their new nines as the bases were laid out. Every Union man who had played before was in for this match, except for Louis. Del Rio volunteered for his role, which left Slipper's spot on the infield to be filled. Willie and Huey would not answer the call and Cawthorne was out of the question, so it was Stives to whom Lyman and Newt pleaded and it was Stives who shook his head in refusal, the long locks and beard swaying in time. Every offer and threat failed until Newt stood up straight and said in a loud voice, "Arise, go unto Ninevah!" pointing off toward the field. Stives jumped and his eyes peeked from side to side as though he didn't know that it was Newt who had spoken. He looked down at his hands, nodding intently in what appeared response to a voice only he could hear. After a final series of rapid nods, he stood up and bellowed, "I will!"

Felix Cawthorne put down his liner and took a seat on the side. Then he pulled his desk out of his haversack, removed a piece of paper, and draped his jacket over his lap. Underneath, where it was dry and dark, he began to imitate what he'd seen the Worms do in the third match.

For the first inning, Lyman searched for signs that either Louis was right and these matches were sham, or that this was all on the straight, as he had hoped. Eyes peeled for winks and nods and signs of collusion by anyone else, he only saw a field of muddy grass and men weary of this war, going about this match with the same vacant effort they'd been making every day in battle. The play was sloppy, as it had to be. The ball got stuck in mud and slipped through wet hands; men slid about. Raw players like Stives muffed plays. They had to win this one to keep alive in the series, so Lyman bore down, knowing that offense would have as hard a time as defense in this mud. His aim was true and the Rebs only scored twice in their at bat.

Lyman went to the side, still wondering whether he should ask Micah about deserting to see how he'd respond. Surely this match had become more a duty than a pleasure, yet all the surviving Rebs were here, with some new men in the field as the Yanks came to the plate in the bottom half. Behind Arlette, a fellow named Emmitt Welch with a squash for a nose had taken over Haddon's place at third; Denton Cowles, his pale white skin flushed and his eyebrows raised in expectation of disaster, stood in left; and Curtis Tidrow, the cook, scratched his beard as he manned right.

Arlette began the inning with a quick strikeout of Newt, but then Karl slapped a catchable liner past Welch into left, where Cowles picked up the ball and walked it in to Weed, allowing Karl to reach second. The veteran Reb players grumbled; Arlette slapped his forehead. Why would they still be playing if they were spies? Why not just have a quiet truce with coffee and swapped stories for an hour or two? This had to be about base ball, not him giving Micah secrets.

A double by Teddy and a dropped fly by Cowles tied the score. Burridge then stepped into a high pitch, lining the ball again toward Cowles. Tiger scored. The Yankees were up 3–2.

	1	2	3	4	5	6	7	8	9	R	H	E
CONFEDERATES	2									2	2	0
UNION	3									3	3	1

Taking the box, Lyman tried to shake some of the mud off the ball. While he was able to get the biggest clumps off, the slimy coating was now permanent, the mud seeping through cuts in the leather. Off on one side he could hear Arlette explaining to Huey how Lou had met his inevitable fate; on the other, Teddy and Deal exchanged a few sad words about Marmaduke. How could any of these men be spies?

The Rebels opened the second with the three new players at bat. Tidrow squeezed the bat like an ax handle and sent Lyman's second pitch skimming along the third base line for a double. The light gloss of water on the surface let it slip like a skimmed rock on a lake, and Teddy nearly fell twice trying to stop it. Welch struck out quickly, but Cowles, more turtlelike than any Worm brother, stretched his thin neck forward and got enough bat on a slow pitch to roll it between Karl and Lyman. It stopped dead there, held by its muddy weight, and left men on first and third with one out.

The scattered cracks of Rebel applause were music to Lyman. Weak as they were, it meant they cared; that this was real. As Arlette came to the plate, Lyman decided that Burridge—pompous ass that he was—had been right.

Off in right field, Joaquin Del Rio had spent the first inning jabbering away, the only man on the Union nine to display what could be called spirit. While others had been pointing fingers and murmuring curses during the messy play, the fishmonger had only encouragement for his teammates. When Arlette lofted a pop fly toward him, he heard no similar chatter, so he provided it for himself, yelling, "I got it! It's coming right at me!" Burridge blushed to be on the same field as this man.

The ball was not hard to pick up. White against blue on a good day, today it was dark reddish gray against the enervating sky of pale clouds. Del Rio was perfectly placed, but still he dropped the ball. Welch scored to tie the match at three, Cowles made it to second, but Arlette got caught between first and second, to bring up Mink.

Sidney winked at Burridge as he stood in and swung late on Lyman's first pitch. The ball came toward first. The lieutenant had resolved that Mink would have to earn his way on base today. Moving to his right, he reminded himself to bend his knees and keep his hands low, but the flat soles of his brogans lost whatever grip they had, sending the lieutenant sprawling onto his face. When he stood back up, Cowles had third and Mink waved from first. Burridge tried to dry his face and hands, but every spot of him seemed already wet or muddy. Mink silently shadowed him, offering meaningful glances from the corners of his eyes. Burridge decided that his only choice now, forced as he was to follow this terrible course, was to ignore Mink. He would have to stand next to this tempter and not renew the bond. A sheen of sweat glowed dimly on Mink's face and Burridge winced, turning away as the Rebel leaned in close to whisper in his ear, "I had no expectation of being here—we were pulled off the salient. I thought by now every one of these bastards would have been buried." Burridge imagined the winged beast at the salient. All dead in a day or two. His stomach turned. *"Auxilium mihi terre debes ad me eiciendum!"*

Mink wanted to escape, and he was not asking for Burridge's help; he was demanding it. Burridge figured that the Rebels were probably on to him; if not his officers, then his own men had seen through the pose. He clenched his teeth, fighting an urge to respond with anger, with sympathy. He pretended not to hear Mink as Deal swung and missed a snap ball.

"Quod tibi dolet? Mihi dic!"

Mink wanted to know what was wrong with him and demanded that he speak. The Rebel's voice was pitched higher than Burridge recalled. Crouching over, hands on knees, Burridge watched Lyman work and tried to convince himself that Mink must never have his help, no matter how desperately the spy might need it.

Louis noticed the fevered expression on Mink's face as the Rebel stood at first, so he casually limped over to listen. Burridge said not a word and Louis was not able to get close enough to make out Mink's hissing voice before the end of the Confederate half of the inning. His curiosity piqued, the Hungarian sat down a few yards from the base and looked forward to the next at bat for either lieutenant.

	1	2	3	4	5	6	7	8	9	R	H	E
CONFEDERATES	2	1								3	4	0
UNION	3									3	3	3

The Union second began with a three-pitch strikeout of Stives.

As Lyman came up, he exchanged a short nod with Breese. The dour look on Micah's face reminded Lyman of the sad and quiet man he'd watched the first match. Arlette came inside and Lyman stepped out. He looked at Micah again, who was fishing the ball out of a puddle behind them. "I'm sorry about Haddon."

Micah tossed the ball back to Arlette. He shrugged. "Nobody's fault. I mean it's *somebody's* fault, but not yourn. He liked ya'll."

Lyman took a strike. "A good boy."

"Yeah." Breese crouched. "He was an ever'day ord'nary boy. Liked them birds."

Lyman took another ball down low, then glanced back at Micah, whose forehead rippled under the strain of sadness. To Micah, "ord'nary" was the taste of warm corn bread made with corn he'd grown; "ord'nary" was the sun and mounds of clouds and folks who bound together so all would have enough, who let each other worship God as they saw fit. "Ordinary" in Lyman's Brooklyn life had become canned corn and excuses; Irish hating Germans hating Jews hating Poles and all hating Africans; weakness and fear offered to explain failure and evil...

Something whizzed by, then splashed.

"That was a good pitch, Lyman."

Two strikes now. Arlette stepped out of the pitcher's box and tried to wipe some mud off the ball, while Lyman sank back into his thoughts. Lyman realized that he liked Micah because he was so very ordinary.

He heard Micah's voice, as if very far away. "You awake?"

"Ordinary," thought Lyman, was the stuff that all men were made of, the original goodness and strength. The ordinary man was the world's finest creation. But those who used the word "ordinary" to identify the acceptance of failure and agreement to run in a herd, those who dressed up stupidity and cowardice as essential human nature, were part of the new type of evil waiting in factories back home.

"You better do something here."

Lyman was positive that unless something unusual happened, there was no reason to ask Micah to desert. What was done was done. This was a good man. He stroked the next pitch into left for a single.

The Rebels took a 6–4 lead into the bottom of the third, but their faces remained as drawn as those of the Union men. Runs had been scored today, but rather than competing with each other, the two sides seemed to be playing the elements. The field would only get harder to play on, their shoes would only get heavier with mud.

Burridge came up in the third with men on first and second and one out. He looked over at Mink, who was clapping his hands and saying, "Hit it here, son!" His eyes gleamed with flecks of anger and fear, and the fierce stare he gave Burridge stopped just shy of a verbal order. "I defy you!" Burridge knocked some mud off his shoes and then pulled the ball at Welch, who tagged Tiger for the second out.

Burridge ran to first grinding his teeth, angry for making the out, but even more that another conversation with Mink was unavoidable. As Del Rio came to the plate and got into his crouch, waving circles in the air with his bat, Mink approached Burridge. The Rebel's eyes flared and a thin smile like a razor cut sliced the area beneath his sharp cheekbones. In that fire and that smile were no emotions Burridge could even call human; the fire burned unnatural and cold, and Burridge wondered what he had ever admired about this man. Dignity, wealth, land, status, intelligence—this unshaven man in soiled tatters who'd been leering at him and hissing entreaties in Latin appeared to have none of that. Burridge had given over Union information that was heard by God knows which Rebel officers, and caused battles to happen, battles he'd led his own men into. He'd lied to Alder. Killed Von Schenk. Given Union secrets to the Rebs. Put Tiger back on the bottle. Helped Mink try to get his own men killed . . .

Burridge cringed at the amiability of Mink's voice, a lulling whisper with a praline drawl; evidence that he had divined his accomplice's change in attitude. "Are you well? I don't find you angry with Friend Mink now, do I?"

Del Rio took a strike. Mink's tone began to weaken Burridge's resolve. "Have I done something?" He looked Burridge in the eye and spoke with the concern of a friend; he did not sound at all now like a spy. These were the secret whispers he had imagined that first match. "I *val*ue our friendship, John. You *must* help." Burridge swallowed. "Hell, I have some business schemes and I had thought after the war, we . . ."

Just as Mink was about to paint a portrait of a peacetime partnership—an idea that Burridge found deeply fascinating and revolting—Del Rio swatted a triple to left center that scored Wes and Burridge. The score was tied, and when the Portuguese came screaming and diving into home between pitches—a play that Alder confirmed as a perfectly legal move called a "slide"—the Yanks were up 7–6.

Inspired, Stives held his hands above his head, gripping the bat, and said, " 'I have raised up one from the north, and he shall come: from the rising of the sun shall he call upon my name: and he shall come upon princes as upon mortar, and as the potter treadeth clay!' Isaiah 41, verse 25!"

	1	2	3	4	5	6	7	8	9	R	H	E
CONFEDERATES	2	1	3							6	5	1
UNION	3	1	3							7	7	6

Long ago in his entomological rovings, Louis had made the observation that rain brought out in creatures an interesting variety of behaviors not usually seen on sunny days, and this afternoon he was learning that this held true for his newest subject of study as well. Sitting within earshot of the base, Louis had been patient as the first few meetings of Mink and Burridge went by with only some urgent and incomprehensible whispering by Mink. But the student of nature knows that patience is usually rewarded. The top of the fourth began with Mink reaching first on a slow tap to Karl. Louis edged closer to the base. Despite a cross expression that Louis immediately took for dissimulation, Mink then launched into a tirade of beautifully constructed Latin. The druggist was pleased to find another use for his language skills beyond reading labels on bottles and decoding Linnaeus; he translated to himself as Mink went on—"I want them ambushed. I want them dead. And I must know where the Fifth Corps is headed!" And then Burridge responded, "Yes, yes, I'll tell you."

That was enough for Louis; he didn't have to hear the details. He had his proof—Burridge was a spy, and he was about to have Company L ambushed.

Burridge closed his eyes. Mink wanted one more match, after which his men would be ambushed. Then he would desert. If Burridge didn't help, people would hear about it. Important people. As Mink's insistence had grown, the lieutenant could only think of one way to quiet him and that was with lies. Arranging to ambush these Rebels was so beyond Burridge's desire or power that he could lie brazenly, but Mink wanted an answer now on the point of desertion. There was no way to draw a map in this mud; Burridge had to pass the information verbally. In his mind, he ran though the names of places farther south on the map and chose Snell's Bridge as the spot where Mink would be able to meet the Fifth Corps when he wanted to desert. As Burridge had no clue which way the corps was headed, come the time Mink would likely find himself alone on a road, prey to whatever side would have the most fun with him and out of Burridge's reach and temptation. When Harlan Deal hit a smash to short, Mink thanked Burridge and sprinted off through the swamp to second, reaching safely before Newt could tag the base.

As his pre–at bat prayer, Weed delivered a quote from Jeremiah— " 'Outa the *north* an e-e-e-evil shall break forth upon all the 'habitants of the land' "—then promptly popped out to Pitt. Over the last few innings, the swirling mist had clotted into full drops of rain and new puddles began to collect around the field. Water filled the base paths, which now resembled the trenches they had all lately escaped for this match. Uniforms meant little now; teammates were identified by their faces. The Rebs scored twice, edging back into the lead. Lifting his face to the rain, Weed offered a Biblical cheer—"I will say to the north, 'Give up'; and to the south, 'Keep not back!' "

	1	2	3	4	5	6	7	8	9	R	H	E
CONFEDERATES	2	1	3	2						8	7	1
UNION	3	1	3							7	7	7

Lyman watched Micah and Arlette toss the ball to each other on this slippery gray field, beneath a gray sky starting to slump into evening. More rain was threatening; they'd have to play six innings for this match to count in his mind.

Micah nodded to Lyman as a neighbor nodded to a neighbor encountered in a crowd. Lyman returned the greeting.

"Hey now, you awake this time?"

Lyman loosened up with a couple swings. "I'm into my work now." He took a pitch low.

"Good eye." Micah bent over for the ball. "Long days we all had."

Whatever the Reb wanted to chat about was fine by Lyman, as long as it wasn't about troops and positions and battles. Before he could say anything else, Lyman jumped in. "What's he throwing next?"

"Something fast, I reckon." The pitch slipped in low. "I was surprised we got moved this-a-way. You got any more secret tricks coming up like that mortar gun?"

"Aw, who knows anymore. Let's just think about this match."

"Wisht we could." Lyman swung and missed on a slow ball. "Where you boys a-heading now? 'Cause we just gonna probably slide along 'sides you, maybe make a stand at the North Anna River."

Lyman wanted to stop his ears, but it was too late: He would have to ask Micah to desert, have to ask him to prove himself. "Micah, right now I'm just going where they send me."

He lofted a fly to deep left, high over the fielder's head. Lyman saw Denton doing a dance of small steps trying to find the right position, but Cowles let the ball bounce off his outstretched hands for another run. Lyman took second.

Newt and Karl failed to move Lyman along, but Teddy knotted the game again with a double to right. A wild attempt at a pickoff let Teddy reach third, then Arlette dropped a pop by Tiger to make it first and third with two outs. Arlette grit his teeth and muttered. Wes dug into the mud. The result of the showdown was a grounder that slithered through Kingsley's hands for a 9–8 Union lead.

	1	2	3	4	5	6	7	8	9	R	H	E
CONFEDERATES	2	1	3	2						8	7	3
UNION	3	1	3	2						9	9	7

Joaquin Del Rio loved water. He would sit for hours watching a river go by, swim until the tips of his toes puckered, and open his arms to the skies on these gray days of Southern rain. He had been raised on the sea, his youth spent on fishing boats off the coast of Portugal, where he repaired nets under the spray and his father's eye. As the rain picked up in the top of the fifth and a heavier pall sank over the field, Del Rio found himself in an increasingly better humor. A leadoff single by the Rebel third baseman was cause for him to call in some encouragement to Lyman, as were the two strikeouts that followed. The Reb lieutenant was up next. Out in right, Del Rio ventured a few practice cuts with Mink's style and considered trying it when he came up again; it was a very dapper move, with its little snap when the bat hit the ball. Though he booed to show his displeasure when Mink reached first on a throwing error by the German, Del Rio was secretly satisfied with another victory by the forces of flamboyance and the rain.

There were two runners on now and two outs as the strange Weed stood in. A Catholic, Del Rio had never heard much of the Bible, though a leather-bound copy had sat upon his kitchen table since the day he was married, so Weed's quotations fascinated him like fragments from an exotic land. This time it was " 'I will *remove* far off from you the northern army, and will *drive* him into a land *barren* and desolate, with his face toward the east sea, and his hinder part toward the utmost sea, and his *stink* shall come up, and his ill savor shall come up!' Joel, chaptuh 2!"

"Stink!" "Hinder part!" These words were in the Bible? As he imagined Jesus saying "hinder part," Del Rio realized that bat had just cracked against ball and he didn't know where the ball was. His eyes cast about desperately until he saw it peaking over his head, the Rebs already cheering for Weed's certain home run.

He ran backward, chasing after the ball. It seemed impossible. He could never reach it, not through this mud, not on a dry field, even. But pumping his arms and legs, Del Rio kept his eyes on the ball as it was falling twenty-five, twenty, fifteen feet in front of him.

The mud was pooling with water, like a shore moments after the tide had pulled out. He had to do it now.

He dove, a full-body stretch, fingers out as far as they'd go, headfirst, blinded by the muck; mud in his eyes, up his nose, in his mouth.

And the ball in his hands.

No one had ever seen a catch like that; not here, not in Brooklyn. The Yanks came at Joaquin, who started at first when he saw them, accustomed as he was to sneers from most men rather than smiles, but in a few seconds he was already telling the story of how he had performed such a miracle.

Stives bellowed out to Weed, "You left out the rest, brother! 'Because he hath done great things.' That's the balance of the Scripture!" He slapped his knee, laughing, and Weed scowled.

It was as though the match had been restarted. Men clapped and cheered now, despite the increasing rain; acrobatics in the mud became the norm for fielders and decorum was buried. The Yanks went down in order in the fifth, on wonderful mud-splattered catches by the Rebs; Rebels were stomping up waves of mud trying to run the bases in the sixth, and Union men were diving and wallowing. Though he knew the truth about these matches, Louis watched, amused and even a bit envious as Stives and Newt turned a perfect little double play in the top of the sixth and Curtis made a leaping catch off the German in the bottom half. Burridge had joined in with the rest of the players, happily splashing through the mud, much to Louis's disgust. When Mink grabbed the sleeve of the lieutenant's jacket and pulled him to his face, Louis leaned in to hear. "It's unseemly," Mink said. "You said yourself they should not be too friendly. *Quibus rebus factis, hoc est injustum? Tu ipse dixit felicitam hominibus licere antequam eos morire!*"

Burridge responded in Latin. Louis quickly made out the words: No, Burridge did not find this wrong, not after what they, the lieutenants, had done. Mink had told him to allow the men happiness before they died. Louis sensed that Burridge knew he was listening, so he looked everywhere but at the two lieutenants; still Burridge didn't seem to care. As Del Rio struck out, Burridge pulled a small volume out of his pocket and handed it to Mink, saying that the Rebel needed it more than he did. Louis wondered what it was; the insulted expression on Mink's face proved that whatever it was, Burridge had scored a point. The last snip of conversation between them intrigued Louis, abbreviated as it was by Stives's strikeout. Mink said something quickly—too fast for Louis—about another attack tomorrow or the next day. The Rebels would be held back. They'd stage the last match, then afterward the ambush. Remember this, Mink said. You're not the only man I know. My order for this ambush will go through regardless of your opinion, so I advise your complete cooperation. For your own good.

A great bolt of lightning sliced into the field not fifty yards away with a blinding flash, as if the world had taken their likeness, as if the knife had missed its mark. Not a second later the thunder followed, scattering everyone in the field as a cloudburst swept through. Louis's ears rung. He thought he heard a bell.

	1	2	3	4	5	6	7	8	9	R	H	E
CONFEDERATES	2	1	3	2	0	0	X	X	X	8	11	4
UNION	3	1	3	2	0	0	X	X	X	9	10	8

The men scrambled to gather their things. Micah was picking up home base and trying to change it back into his haversack by dumping out some mud when Lyman grabbed his arm. "Say, Micah." Lyman had never touched Micah before and he was surprised by the softness of the arm; he'd expected rock. Micah turned around, still crouched over his sack. "You boys ever give thought to taking the oath?"

Micah straightened up and despite the urgency everyone felt to get out of this exposed field and the rain, he sighed. At once his eyes were tempered hard and wistful, warm thoughts of home mingling with the sharper truth of war the way the waters swirl when a fresh river meets sea. Lyman could see the battle on Micah's face. The soldier in him felt embarrassed for mentioning desertion, but Micah's lack of anger gave him hope. It showed that he had thought of it before, maybe on some rainy night or after another tearful letter from his wife and a handful of parched corn meant to last two days.

Micah affected a low tone and he tried to glare. "How do ye know I wouldn't kill a man for saying something like that? Asking me to *dee-sert*..."

Lyman tried to be bluff, pushing harder. "Micah, I like these matches fine, but I'd rather you was on our side, and the fact is, you and me and all the boys in this field are." He imagined them all in white, throwing the ball around the grounds on Court Street, Ernie serving up the lemonade. He prayed Micah would just say yes.

"Hell, I wish you was with us, too." Micah snorted. "We all thought you might come over to *our* side the first day."

They both smiled at that idea, then Lyman said, "Well, we *are* with you. We're all goddamn Americans." Lyman ventured a hand onto Micah's shoulder. "We get mustered out in six days. Come over, take the oath, and you can come up to Brooklyn with us. Mrs. Alder makes a fine pie..."

Micah took his cap off and held his face up to the rain as if cooling off, then turned back to Lyman, the water running down his cheeks. "You look like you 'spect I'm gonna come a-running right now." Lyman's face dropped some. "Men got families. 'Sides, you know by now what I'll do."

Lyman was afraid of that. "No, I don't."

"Well, can't just go a-running off without giving those things a full think, Lyman. Would you?" Lyman had no answer at all for that. " 'Sides, what about the last match?"

"To hell with that. I'd rather you..."

Micah held up his hand to stop Lyman from saying anything more. "We got ourselves one more match. Man's gotta finish what he fixing to do. If we's coming over, we'll do it then and not 'til."

He hadn't said no. Lyman held on to that one small hope. "Good enough. Next match."

They shook hands. "Right, then." Micah touched his forehead and blinked once. "Almost forgot." He reached into his pocket and pulled out Newt's missing desk. "Lem found it after last match. He wanted to make sure y'all got it back."

Mink slid up next to Burridge and dug his fingers into the lieutenant's upper arm, his mask of kindness left behind in the mud. "We *must* see each other again. There's more." He dug in again and Burridge let out an involuntary hiss of pain. "We *must*. For your own good, if you have no interest in mine. And don't let yourself think that ball was truly out of my reach."

The spy released him and slid away.

Teddy caught Harlan Deal just as the Rebs had begun walking back to their lines. "Hold up, there! I'm retaining something here's that orter be returned." He held out the photograph of Cleopatra. "Belonged to Marmaduke and..."

Deal sniffed as he looked it over. "She's a big 'un."

"Yeah, he bestowed it at me and it should go..."

"You keep it. Don't think his family's gonna want that much. His maw. See what I'm saying? To be true, I don't 'spect Dukey was ever sure what to do with that there pitcher." Deal winked at Teddy. "Somehow I think *you* do, though. See ya." Teddy gave Deal a limp wave good-bye, then joined up with the company. The series was tied at two matches each.

CHAPTER
2 7

T HE RAIN TAPERED BACK TO DRIZZLE LATER THAT NIGHT, and the fires they had lit upon their return from picket duty pushed higher into the dark without challenge. Louis felt it was time to tell Lyman the truth. He waited until Lyman got up to visit the sinks, then waylaid him.

"I have something to tell you."

"I have to piss. Whaddya want?"

"There is no longer any doubt. Burridge is a spy. I know."

Lyman tried to hide his eagerness. "How do you know?"

Louis ticked them off on his fingers. "First, I have told you about the map on the ground, yes?" The butcher nodded. "Second. During the battle he confronted me and I called him a spy." Lyman raised a suspicious eyebrow. "He reacted as though he had been found out!"

"That means nothing."

"Yes, it does! But you will believe me *now*. During the match I sat near first base. When he and Mink were together, Porridge told him secrets in Latin."

"How the hell do you know he was passing secrets?"

"I am a druggist, Lyman." Louis recounted what he had overheard. Burridge and Mink were spies and there was to be an ambush next match.

It sounded real to Lyman—Burridge and Mink had created the matches to pass messages. But was Micah in on it? He *had* put off deciding about the oath until after the final match. The scattered bits of information took form in Lyman's mind, shattering the one true thing he had done. The matches had given his war meaning, had held the few scraps of meaning left in his life. He saw himself sitting silently in the parlor, newspaper in his lap, as Ernie gets up and leaves the room and Victoria pushes aside the lace curtains for a glimpse of something—someone?—passing by of much greater interest. The clock ticks. He is returned to his place in a world gone past him. A common man in all the ways that he hated, he had tried his best and been defeated. His service had been to fill a place in the line, as his life merely filled a space, took a job another would have taken, married a woman another would have surely wed.

Louis stared at him as the butcher wrestled for a long silent minute with what he wanted to be true and what the truth seemed to be until Lyman came to like oil springing to flame. He jogged off toward Henry's tent and though Louis called after him, Lyman had gone too far.

While Louis and Lyman conducted their hushed conference near the sinks, a thin voice wandered through the 14th's camp singing a foul shanty called "The Lady from Ghent" accompanied by an identical voice that asked all those it passed in a worried tone where Company L had laid out. The lewd song attracted more hisses and thrown shoes than it did assistance, so Horace spent a frustrating half an hour visiting the fires of the regiment in search of theirs and apologizing for his brother at each. The final insult came when they arrived home. The brothers stood behind a fire and silently presented themselves, waiting for embraces and questions as to their whereabouts, but after a minute of wary glances, Horace realized that no one recognized them.

From his side of the fire, Wes saw two men with bruised faces and black eyes who appeared to have survived a saloon brawl. Newt thought they were newswalkers and pulled his knapsack closer. Only when one of them began speaking could the men tell who they were. "It's us. The Worms. I'm Horace." Pindar launched into another verse of "The Lady from Ghent" and the company rose up to offer the handshakes and greetings that Horace had expected from the first. Coffee boiled, meat fried, and the Worms were bidden to tell their story, a tale that involved a nap in the mud and a game of Bluff with stakes much higher than Pindar was able to produce. Though he had tried to keep his brother out of the game, another in a growing string of necessary interventions since Pindar's drastic change, Horace had been forced to accept the same punishment as Pindar, namely a thrashing at the hands of the winners. Administered by a trio of massive Irish stevedores, the beatings had broken no crucial bones and, after the battle at the salient, had actually seemed less frightening than what they would have had in a Brooklyn barroom. Pindar sat next to Horace throughout the retelling with a sheepish expression, but one still less repentant than his brother would have liked.

Their tale told, the Worms asked after the company, and following a description of the last match, they requested a look at the score sheet. Newt and just about every other man shrugged his shoulders. "I don't believe anyone did it," Newt said, then Del Rio leaned in. "Feelix did. I saw him."

A quick scan around the fire did not reveal the play actor turned sergeant. "And where is our own Booth?" Newt asked.

Del Rio held up his palms as if to prove he wasn't concealing Cawthorne in them. "I do not know. He snuck away, like little rat."

Tiger spat. "I have a ken where the slick bastard is if no one else here is bothering to think. He's with Stewart."

The men hissed curses, but a few of them saw beyond the anger to the threat, and Newt was one of them. He put his head in his hands briefly, then raised it up and took a sharp breath through his clenched teeth. "We're in for it, boys."

"Are you listening to me, Lieutenant?" Burridge snapped his head up. He'd missed the question a second time. "I will not repeat this question. Is the scout in good health? Is he safe?"

The polished surroundings of Henry's tent had never seemed so inviting, so golden and calm. Burridge fixed on a shiny brass knob of the washstand and pictured his father, a great spot of grease on his vest, the edges of his lapels fraying, as he extended his hand to another wealthy, well-groomed former student come to pay a charitable call on their kindly and envious old master. "I did not find him, sir. I believe our contact has come to an end."

"You followed the procedures you had established with him?"

Did Henry know he was lying? Did he know about the ambush order? Burridge had no way of knowing. "Yes, sir." Something rustled outside and Pompey could be heard asking if someone was out there. Both Henry and Burridge turned toward the canvas wall and held silent, waiting to hear more. A moment passed. The captain formed a steeple with his hands, pressing his fingertips together. "This is unexpected." He tapped his index fingers against each other. "You are completely certain there is nothing more to relate?"

Could Henry hear his heart beating? Burridge wanted to place his hand over his chest in hopes that it would muffle the sound. "Yes, sir."

"And you maintain that throughout you have passed no secret information . . ."

What he'd told Mink was no secret; men throughout the Union side knew of it. That which was privy measured to little. The lieutenant leaped in with emphasis. "No sir!"

"No information at all . . ."

The window slammed shut again. Burridge shook his head. "No, sir."

"Do you recall what I said to you about trust, Lieutenant? I said your word was proof enough for me. There is a reward for that trust, as I have described to you often these weeks, but there is a punishment if it is betrayed. You see, there is my word, and there is your word; consider it as though we have traded hostages, our dearest beloved exchanged and held bond in the other's home. That is how seriously I consider this issue." This was the Captain Henry that Burridge had known before. The lieutenant kept fixed on the knob. "If you lie to me, Lieutenant, we shall have to exchange pawns, as it were. Your word against mine. And so 'exchange' is hardly the correct term, is it? They shall be weighed and one shall be deemed of lesser value than the other." Henry leaned toward Burridge. "Do you understand me, Lieutenant? Do you understand my, shall we say, appreciation of honesty?"

Burridge stared at the floor. "Yes, sir."

"Good. Now tell me something true."

Burridge could not think of one true thing, save maybe one. "Our job is finished."

"Hmm." The captain tapped his chin. "You recommend . . . ?"

"I believe some reward should be paid to the men for the great risk they have taken. I recommend the company is pulled from the line; tend the beefs, guard the ammunition, and the like." Burridge straightened in his seat. "The spy has moved on."

"Yes, you've said this. But how can you be certain?"

"His unit had already sustained heavy casualties by our last meeting. I imagine our most recent action decimated what remained. They were already close to their end." Burridge saw his broad mahogany desk floating away as if borne by seas.

"How did you know the condition of his unit? I thought there had been no fraternization?"

Burridge cursed at himself. He felt like a prizefighter who'd let down his guard for a second, only to find himself well tagged in that open instant. "He had offered it as intelligence, sir."

"Hmm." Henry smoothed his eyebrows with gloved fingers, brought the brows together once in a pensive crease, then released them. "I will take your request under advisement."

Burridge nodded. "That is the most I can ask of you, sir."

CHAPTER

28

LYMAN HAD STOLEN AWAY FROM HENRY'S TENT AS SOON AS he had heard that it was Mink who was the spy. The Rebs were the target of the ambush, not Company L. But where did that leave Micah? Was he a Union spy like Mink, preparing to betray his friends? Or was he a Rebel spy? Neither thought was pleasant. He wanted Micah to be a man who would bring all his men over because they'd changed their minds about the Confederacy. He sat on the damp ground back in the woods dragging loose sticks through the mud, disconsolate and considering whether or not he should tell the men, unsure as to what he would tell them if he did.

He had dug a miniature trench in the mud and was starting to support it with twigs when he heard two sets of steps coming toward him. Not in the mood for explaining his presence to anyone, Lyman got up and slipped away to brood alone. He did not notice that the steps belonged to Linden Stewart and Felix Cawthorne.

"One would have to be an owl to see us now, Sergeant, so if you'd please..." Stewart stuck out an impatient hand, wriggling its fingers.

Cawthorne slid a piece of paper out of his pocket and began to unfold it. "You see, each Rebel name is on the left and..."

Stewart plucked the score sheet away from Cawthorne. "Nicely done." He dropped a hand on the sergeant's shoulder, tilting Cawthorne to one side, then delicately removing it when he realized that he'd actually touched the man. What this piece of paper was exactly, he couldn't tell. "Is this in your hand?"

"Yes, sir."

It was worthless, even if it was some record of a sort. Who would believe evidence created by a witness such as Cawthorne? A play actor. Still, Stewart considered that his own word did have value. "When I catch them, you will not be arrested or in any way harmed if gunfire is necessary."

Cawthorne winced. "Gunfire? You never mentioned any..."

"Your friends may have been having a sporting time of it, but this is war."

"But I must have that back! They'll search me. If I don't have it, they'll kill me!"

Stewart looked at the paper, then at Cawthorne, weighing their relative value. A difficult choice, but the sergeant had the benefit of a new strategy; the lieutenant was losing interest in a court-martial in favor of a more permanent sort of punishment. Cawthorne had not yet outlived his usefulness. Stewart neatly folded the paper again and handed it back. "Here. Keep it safe. I may have need of it." Stewart walked away before Cawthorne could salute him.

Lieutenant Burridge stayed on with Captain Henry long enough to share a brandy toast offered with the minimum of kindness required between gentlemen. He was focusing on the regiment's fires ahead, sloshing on toward the company, when a strong tug spun him around. "Why did you lie to me? Tell me! Why did you lie?"

Burridge looked Lyman in the face. The last time he'd looked at him so, Lyman had been saving his life. It was time to be honest. "You wanted me to."

Burridge had never seen a man drown, but he thought that if he ever saw one, it would likely resemble Lyman at this moment—panicked, desperate, angry, and, most of all, helpless. "I did it for you. For the things you believe in. The Union." He'd lied enough the last few days that one or two more out of kindness would mean nothing, so he spoke to keep Lyman afloat. "At least the matches were real. When we played, we played fair and square."

Burridge expected thanks, but Lyman still struggled, as though deaf to the sound of someone calling to him, someone pointing the way to the shallows and safety. "The matches *weren't* real." Lyman began saying it over and over, as much to himself as to Burridge.

Burridge grabbed Alder's jacket front and shook him. "Listen to me! You want miracles, don't you? Well, getting out of here alive will be a hell of a miracle! Ask one of the dead bodies around here if that would be a miracle. I apologize if your base ball fantasy had a more temporal cause, but for chrissakes, Alder—be glad for what you have! We're in trouble. Stewart is on to us!" Lyman imagined the court-martial; he'd never see Victoria again. "And Mink wants the Rebs ambushed."

"I know." Burridge looked startled. "We're not all as stupid as you think. Listen. Is Breese in on this?"

"I doubt it, but I don't know."

He pictured Micah sitting quietly, smiling as Haddon whistled like a morning thrush. Suddenly Lyman didn't care which side Micah was on. There were so many possibilities and explanations that none of them mattered anymore. Just one thing mattered. "We have to save them."

"It's too late. Mink passed the order on over my head through another channel. And we would most certainly face a firing squad if we were caught. At least we can avoid Stewart for the last week and get home alive. He has no proof."

Lyman seemed as if he hadn't heard a word. "We have to save them from Mink."

"Don't tell the men. We can't go out again. We'll be lucky to save ourselves."

Lyman pushed past Burridge and headed toward the lights.

In his acting career, Felix Cawthorne had accepted the challenge of many difficult roles—Brutolf in *The Red Mask, or, the Wolf of Bohemia;* Chowles in *Linda, the Segar Girl;* and, of course, his triumph as Wallop the schoolmaster in *Take Care of Dawb,* to name a few. But even with the kind of viciously critical audiences he played to in Brooklyn, none had ever threatened failure with death as this current one did. Surrounded by Quigley, the German, Pitt, and Finn, Felix felt a bayonet blade prod the soft spot under his chin as the Irishman repeated the question. "I said, where ye been, laddie?"

Cawthorne's bowels released and the stink provided him with an answer that he offered in panicked breaths. "The sinks. See. Quickstep. The sinks. I just did it again."

But the bayonet and the man holding it were not convinced. "I wouldn't put it past ye to shit yer britches fer an excuse. It don't prove a thing."

Another bayonet poked his side. "*Ja. Das stimmt.* You were *mit* Stewart, *ja?*"

"The sinks! For the love of God, I was in the sinks!"

Pitt and Finn circled around Cawthorne's back and prodded him from there. Wesley reached into the sergeant's pocket and began rummaging around. "You know what we want. Hand it over."

"*Ja. Und* if you don't have it, is not *gut.*"

Cawthorne sagged in relief. "Is this what you want?" He took a few rapid breaths as he dug into the pocket Wesley hadn't gotten to, then produced the score sheet.

Tiger tore it out of his hand and the four men looked it over to make sure it was the real thing. Once satisfied, Quigley folded it up and put it in his own pocket. "We'll keep this, if ye please."

"Fine! That's fine!"

The bayonet skipped over the veins of Cawthorne's throat once again. "Ye have two strikes on ye, laddie. We know ye saw Stewart, shit or no shit, score sheet or no score sheet, so lemme put it to ye this way. Whatever happens to us, happens to you." Felix felt something warm trickle down his throat, but he couldn't tell if it was tears or blood. "If I'm going up fer twenty years, I may as well go fer life. I don't care much, see, so it'd behoove ye to be our friend. Not our enemy."

Cawthorne whimpered assent and the four men left him alone.

CHAPTER 29

T HE NIGHT CREPT ON AND LOUIS KEPT HIS WATCH. TO THE
west, darkness and the Rebel line; to the east, a lighter blue that
signaled day. The rain had stopped. Louis added another log and
another can of coffee to the fire. The base ball sat on a special
perch near the flames—a log set on its end like a post—on display
to all as it dried out. The Hungarian spread some of his wet
clothes nearby and settled back to look off into the east, the direction from which Lyman would have to come. He stared at the same dark
blur of trees and bushes and wagons he'd been staring at all night, damning
his own poor eyesight. Tugging the corners of his eyes, Louis tried to bring
any distant movements into focus, but all that registered was how unsuited
he was to be a watchman. If their camp had been in a precarious place, his
bad eyes would have doomed them, but tonight he was only looking for one
man and that man finally appeared as a shape drawing near in that faint
blue of coming light.

Louis pulled his eyes into focus to make sure the shambling figure with
its hands in its pockets, slightly hunched but its head held erect, was definitely Lyman. Louis got up and greeted him before he reached the camp.
"What did you find out?"

Lyman had the expression he often had after a battle: faraway gaze,
slack face, sorry eyes. He didn't look at Louis as he spoke, instead he kept
his eyes focused on an empty spot ahead. "It's more complicated..."

"We discovered that Cawthorne has told Stewart."

Lyman nodded. "Yes, I know." He walked on toward the open area with his pack, Louis alongside. "Mink and Burridge are Union. The ambush is for the Rebs."

"Thank God. We're still in danger, though."

Lyman glared at Louis. "Yes. We're *all* still in danger."

"It has gone too far, Lyman. They are men. They can take care of themselves."

Lyman sat down, then looked up at Louis. "They're being set up to be killed, Louis. We know these men." Louis had not yet melted, so Lyman shrugged his shoulders and stretched out. "We'll let ours decide. In the meantime, let me know if you see Stewart sniffing around. I don't want to be executed any more than you do."

Louis felt old, as he had for weeks. But now he also felt afraid and not with the reasonable fear of a man under fire; it was timorous, the kind of exposed and helpless fear he'd had before he'd picked up that stick from the smoldering remains of their house and resolved to never feel that way again. The fear made his bones feel lighter and more brittle.

———

The weather held through the early morning, and by eleven, as a group of skirmishers were being formed off to their left and the clouds cracked open to reveal a blue sky, the men of Company L had spread out as much clothing as they could to benefit from the nearly forgotten sun. The same milky light that had welcomed them to the Wilderness seeped again through the trees and over Virginia, and while this midsummer light and drying ground certainly cheered the men, two problems remained. First, there was Lieutenant Stewart. As much as they hoped that morning would present a way to escape court-martial in these final five days, no solutions resulted from the anxious conversations held over coffee and in the trenches throughout the company's camp. Around ten, Stewart had walked slowly by the men with a pleasant smile that everyone knew hid poison, and while they each held their breath, he did not sweep down on them with a band of guards; rather, he toyed with them, talking politely and with enough typical Stewart spite that it came very close to a sincere visit. He stood next to the fire most of the time, allowing no one to stash the prominent base ball into a sack. Instead it remained atop its log, the center of all attention and pointedly ignored by

Stewart until the very end of his visit when he took it in his hand and examined it, as though seeing a ball for the first time. Some men expected it to go into a pocket and end the series, others just hoped it would, but Stewart knocked off a dried bit of mud, carefully replaced it, and said, smiling, "Carry on."

The second problem was talk of an attack that afternoon. Burridge had made no mention so far, but men from other units were speaking freely about it and the soldiers of Company L, like soldiers anywhere, were as disturbed by what they didn't know about their fates as they were by battle itself. Would they be arrested, or would they be fighting again?

CHAPTER

30

———

THE TENSION ROSE AS TWO O'CLOCK CAME CLOSER. Though everyone knew that the campaign would grind ahead now to another major conflict, bloodshed was still inevitable here, as the generals fought the endgame of another stalemate. Burridge, who was waiting for Henry to show up with the happy news, had not told the men yet that they were off active duty, and he began to wonder whether the captain was good for his word. The murmur of men anticipating battle, chattering nervously or complaining, scurrying about to get more cartridges, hoofbeats pounding back and forth behind them, and orders barked by officers hiding their weariness behind ferocity; each sound, each tremor from a cannon urgently pulled by, reminded them of past action and what they might still have to do to earn their return home. Newt and Karl fought back their nerves by taking the ball off display and tossing it around the trenches. Preparations continued. The lieutenant's skittish behavior combined with Lyman's unusual quiet kept the fear of battle smoldering.

While the first lines of battle were being formed, newspapers came and the company had a few minutes to be reminded of what they had missed and where they'd be going if they could live through these final five days. Presented with fresh evidence in the pages of the *New York Tribune* and *Times* that their homes were still waiting, the men cursed as Burridge ordered them to put away their papers and fall in.

As the men had been reading, Burridge had received orders to pull the company back in support of the attack. Maybe Henry had agreed to his request. Unless Henry knew of the order, in which case maybe they were just being held back until then, until they could be arrested in the act. Burridge had no choice now but to live by the minute. Every minute that he kept these men away from the front, out of fire, safe from Mink and Stewart, brought them closer to home. Time was too short for the large plans that had always governed his life. Action was all that was left.

The entire regiment moved back and waited in support of another attack that never took place. Union artillery batteries exchanged fire with Rebel cannons and skirmishers from Burnside's corps traded some brisk fire with Rebs on the eastern side of the salient, but there was no advance by any of Warren's troops.

At dusk regiments of Ayres and Bartlett retook the hill off to the 14th's left, a solid strategic point that no one in the regiment cared much about. They had lived through another day free of bullets and arrest and now got to work on their supper, one of the last they would eat under Rebel stars.

Back at Captain Henry's tent, Lieutenant Stewart and the captain sucked the last bits off the bones of a chicken Pompey had roasted for them. Grease smeared around his mouth, Stewart had to remind himself to place the clean bones onto the china plate rather than toss them into a corner. Indulging his slovenly ways had been one of Stewart's greatest joys in this war, and he knew that he would miss this freedom once he was confined to the office and Phyllis's dictatorial housekeeping.

But eating had not been Stewart's real purpose in coming to this tent tonight. With only five days to go, events had conspired to prevent him from setting the proper trap for his company, and he had sat down to the customary shared supper with Henry in need of an answer. Stewart placed his silver fork on the plate and wiped his mouth. "Will we be following our brutal Mr. Grant any farther south, do you think?"

Henry dabbed at the corners of his lips with his linen napkin. "No. Not unless there's a very rapid movement in the next few days, and I have no knowledge of such. Fowler tells me we'll be pulled from the lines on the twenty-first, if not sooner."

Stewart raised an eyebrow. Was it too late? "So the regiment is off active duty?"

"Oh no! The 14th will do its duty to the end. Wouldn't be seemly otherwise. The regiment will move to the right in the morning and then Fowler will be adding a few companies to the afternoon pickets." He draped the napkin over his finished meal. "There's another order as well. Interesting, I think. There's to be skirmishers after the pickets. Give them two hours lead, then go in. A scout tells us that there may be a Rebel incursion in the area during these pickets."

The lieutenant kept an even face, but inside a thread of happy evil danced like rising smoke. "Will we be among them?"

Henry called Pompey in, asked for coffee, then sent him away. "Will we be among whom? The pickets? No, I don't think that's necessary, do you? The men have served well, done much extra duty. Lieutenant Burridge feels they've seen quite enough." He peered at Stewart. "Don't you?"

Stewart paused briefly before answering. "They've seen no more or less than their share."

"Still, I'm inclined..."

Stewart had one more card. "What if the men were to volunteer?"

Henry pulled on a pair of white gloves. "I'm chilled. Where is Pompey with the coffee? Pompey!" The captain yelled for Pompey once again before he addressed the question. "If they were to volunteer?"

"Yes."

"I lumm." With a white finger, Henry stroked his mustache in contemplation. "Well, if they felt strongly, I would allow it. Yes, I would. I would feel compelled. Who am I to prevent glory?" Stewart caught the small smile on Henry's face, forming like an early frost. Pompey popped his head in the flap. "There you are! We would like our coffee now, if you please."

"Sir, the water gots to boil and I was a-getting thats to happen when you was a-calling me. Now I can go backs and makes the water boil, or I can stands here a-chattering with you. Tell me which one you wants."

"Well, yes. Go. But it seems so slow."

"That's nature for you. Can't go no faster 'less you with the devil." Pompey pulled his head out of the tent and could be heard muttering to himself outside.

"Been with the family for decades. I could find better, but the children would howl."

Stewart did not want to discuss domestic help. "So there would be no obstacle if they were to volunteer?"

"Again, no. Let me just say that it would be a most, well, pleasant surprise."

They exchanged a very familiar glance. "I'd be very interested in leading those skirmishers."

Captain Henry smiled. "See a final bit of action before we go, hmm?" Henry nodded his approval. "You *are* certain, now?"

"Of course."

The captain looked down only long enough to jot a brief note. "Consider it done. As I said, who am I to prevent glory, hmm?"

"Thank you, Schuyler." The lieutenant enjoyed another long half-hour of coffee and chatter, relishing his return to position, before he dashed out in search of Felix Cawthorne and a wager on the company's misguided sense of fair play.

CHAPTER
31

THIS NIGHT THE COMPANY SAT TOGETHER, THEIR CANS OF coffee and sticks of meat all sharing the same flames of a huge bonfire Karl and Newt had lit. Only Burridge had removed himself. His small fire a few yards away seemed a moon to their glowing sun and the light breeze that pushed his flames in their direction also drew theirs away in an endless chase.

The lieutenant had just taken out the *Commentaries* when Cawthorne appeared out of the dark and delivered the news that there was a picket duty tomorrow afternoon for which they could volunteer. The sergeant simply dropped the fact at Burridge's feet, then moved to the other fire and relayed the news there before Burridge could respond. His impulse was to jump right into their circle and tell them all he knew, but the large fire and deep voices around it belonged to a council he did not lead, and he stood in the shadows intent on listening first, waiting until they might grill him on what he knew.

A week ago Lyman would have been the first to speak, but tonight he, too, sat back and listened. Tonight they would decide themselves. After all the scowling and commotion today about having to just line up in support of the afternoon movements and given that Stewart was on to them, Lyman believed that the men would greet Cawthorne's offer to go out on picket with hoots and curses; it had to be a trap. Instead, there was a moment of silence, filled with the wheeze of smoking logs and a crackling knot. The ball sat back on its place of honor near the flames. Then Karl cracked his knuckles, a sound that Lyman thought at first came from the fire, and said, "I want them. I want to beat them."

Newt grinned. "Yeah. Me, too. We know they're out there."

Tiger peered into the dark outside of the fire's range. "Say, Burridge, come here and take a seat." The lieutenant stepped into the light with an embarrassed expression, partly from being caught and partly from the un-accustomed pleasure at being asked to join their group. "That's right. Shove over and let a man sit. Here, lad. How's that?" Quigley's pleasant tone, at first honey to Burridge, began to make him suspicious and rightly so, as it became harder and the smile on the Irishman's face disappeared. "Now tell us what ye know."

Surrounded by his men, the meanest now glowering at him, Burridge had a quick pulse of fear. His instinct was to lie, say he knew nothing, say anything to keep them from going out and mostly to keep them from know-ing he was involved. He decided to tell them the end result of this unusual duty, and he expected cheers for it, though it was only a fraction of the story. "I have asked that we be taken off active duty. We will be pulled off the line probably tomorrow, though I can't be sure. I hope very much that Company L of the 14th Brooklyn has seen its last battle."

A deep, relieved breath seemed to rise and fall in every chest. Men exchanged gratified smiles and winks, but no loud cheers or back-slapping at the news. Instead, they accepted their possible release from the army's edicts with calm and moved ahead to the larger decision presented. They were free men again, and around this fire they would now choose how they would finish their time in the War of the Rebellion.

"Is that all, Lieutenant?" A voice emerged from the dark beyond the fire opposite Burridge. Lyman took a step into the ring of light, arms folded, eyes a bit too righteous for Burridge's pleasure. "In the interests of an in-formed electorate, sir, I think you best tell all."

Burridge saw only one course of action and it was the one he really wanted to take anyway. He would tell the truth. A surety came over him, a release as if the chambers of a lock had finally slipped into place and a door stood ready to be opened. He lifted his chin and answered. "The matches were a setup." From silence, curses now buzzed among the men. "They allowed Mink to pass Rebel information on to me, which I passed on to Captain Henry."

"And?"

There was no reason to stop now. "And Mink has ordered an ambush of the Rebs after our last match, which we can have tomorrow if you choose to volunteer for picket duty."

The group sat quietly, piecing it all together. Del Rio scratched his head. "So if we want to save their lives, we should stay back, yes? So dey don't come out and get the ambush."

Newt shook his head. "What if Mink pulls them forward anyways? This is his idea; you have to guess he'll do anything to see it out. We gotta save those boys from Mink."

A billow of smoke rose from Tiger's mouth as he tapped the bowl of his pipe. "There's something else we best remember, lads—Stewart's on to us." He pulled a small stick from the fire and relit his pipe. "Stewart's setting a trap, he is. Ain't I right, Feeelix? This deal smells ripe as your britches."

Cawthorne could still feel the blade of Tiger's bayonet twinge against his throat and the memory made him stutter, a grave shame for a play actor. "I-I-I d-d-d-don't know."

"Don't go shitting 'em again, laddie."

"The lu-lu-lieutenant told me nothing. I know nothing. Just what I've told you."

Newt grabbed the base ball and flipped it from hand to hand. "We know it's a trap for the Rebs, but we don't know if it's one for us, too. Stewart could get us anytime he wants. He's got the proof and the witness right there, right, Cawthorne?" He held on to the ball and looked around the fire. "Listen, here's what I say. I say Stewart can get himself fucked. That's what I say. In for a penny, in for a pound. We haven't come all this way to go home with nothing in our hands. I know it's risky, but we have to help those Rebs. Hey, Finn." He tossed the ball at Teddy, who made the catch. "You think Slipper woulda taken the last card here?"

Teddy was stretched out with his feet nearly in the fire, one arm propping up his fighter's bulk, the other holding the ball. "That boy mighta been awfully deficacious and the bullets made him tense, but he did relish a turn a the dice. He'd a given Stewart what for right in his soppy fat mug and he'd a taken his cuts against that Arlette..."

Lyman broke in. "Before you get all riled up, you gotta know there won't be time for another match tomorrow. Ambushers ain't gonna pay ten cents and watch us play." Everyone went silent again. "If we want to save them—and us—there's just enough time to convince them to come over to our side and get out. Hell, they're more Union than we are!" A few men laughed. "If Micah and the boys are in our guns, no one will shoot anyone and we'll all be better than safe."

Burridge rubbed his eyes as if he were very tired. "If we lay low for five days, we're safe. We'll be headed north by then. Stewart's proof is weak. We'd only be giving him more, and an excuse as well."

Fire was the only sound now, as the men considered this match. Finally, Tiger spat a chunk of tobacco off his tongue. "Lyman is right. We can't quit now, even if 'tis a trap. But we can't play, either. We can just save them. Finn! You lads are in for the run; is this what ye want? It's a gamble and for no winner."

Teddy flipped the ball at Wesley. "The right thing to do is to smackify that Arlette back to South Carolina. But if we can't do that, we'll save his Reb arse."

"Wesley?"

"We gotta. Say, Bibleman!" Wesley tossed the ball to Stives. "Don't you got some Scripture that'll tell you what to do right about now?"

Stives bobbled the ball but did hold on. He stretched out his arms, shadows deepening within the crags of his face. " 'Son of man, set thy face toward the south!' "

"We'll take that as a yes to picket duty. Whaddaya say, Willie?"

"I say, Amen."

"Willie says amen. Huey?"

Unused to being asked his opinion, Huey ducked his head back and forth a bit until a mutter from Tiger's direction got him going. "Like to see them again. Yeah, sure."

Newt wasn't giving the whole meeting up to Wesley, so he continued the roll call. "What about you, Tice?"

"I wanna get home."

"So do I, but what do you want to do tomorrow?"

Tice slowly shifted his face into a sneer and said, "I don't think it's worth it."

Louis pushed himself up, firelight caught deep in his black eyes. He took the ball away from Stives and stuck one hand in a pocket. "Soldiers *know* that they may have to die. They do not complain unless they are made to die for no reason." He began a short pace. "When you decide there is a time you can stop fighting for justice and freedom, yes, you will have peace." He looked at Tice. "And you will have fear. And you will have slavery. And *you* will be the slaves." Tice looked away. "This duty is not pleasant, but I do not believe God was happy to kill Pharaoh's army in the Red Sea. Some things simply *must* happen." Louis handed the ball to Karl. "I ask nothing I will not do myself. We should do what we have to until the very end— play *or* fight."

Tice shook Louis's hand as the Hungarian sat and now Karl took the floor. "There is one last reason you cannot deny." He gripped his jacket and held the fabric out for all to see. "This regiment." Karl pointed west, toward the Rebel lines. "*Und* that regiment are *Bruders*. We must save life of Americans."

The Worms said, "Hear! Hear!" in one voice and Tiger turned to Lyman. "So ye know how we stand. What do you think, Lyman?"

Karl pushed the ball into Lyman's hands. Lyman stared at the graying leather and the seams. The ball had taken a beating. It bulged in some spots; seams frayed in others. In about inning five of another match, it would have burst apart. "I'm not embarrassed by a draw with those men." He placed the ball back on its pedestal, then stood up straight and turned to Burridge. "Lieutenant? Company L of the 14th Brooklyn regiment requests the honor of picket duty tomorrow afternoon."

Burridge looked at all his fellow men around the fire. Did Tiger really want to die before a firing squad? Did Lyman understand he was choosing to stand humiliated before the ranks of the Fifth Corps? They were walking away from hope. But, he reminded himself, his own will had only gotten them lost. Maybe theirs could lead them out. He saluted Lyman. "Request granted."

———————

A draw was fine. Respectable, gentlemanly, and a cricket finish. Not a base ball finish, but cricket. Too many lives are lost when there has to be a winner. Lyman pressed his eyes closed, but in a second they sprung open again and focused right on the ball, glowing in the last blue and orange of the fire. This would make a good story, he thought. Ernie sitting by the fireplace, even Alder Senior forced to admit that he'd done something wonderful, that he'd saved lives and helped the cause. There'd be a moment of respectful silence, Victoria beaming, and then Ernie would say, "You mean nobody won?"

He squeezed his eyes shut, hoping the ball would just go away. Tomorrow would come and they'd save those Rebs and who knew—maybe they'd settle it all back in Brooklyn. A grand match for all the stakes. Ernie would have his winner then. He saw himself making a crisp, hard swing and lining a hard shot into left center that just kept rising as it went past the boundary.

One question remained. Where did Micah stand?

Lyman's eyes popped open. After a check for snores and closed eyes, Lyman crept over and grabbed his base ball, finally falling asleep with it in his hand.

THE
LAST
MEETING

———

CHAPTER

32

S PRING WAS NO LONGER EMERGENT IN VIRGINIA; FIVE DAYS and nights of rain had replaced the soft wash of green and the scattered patches of dogwood and violets with a wealth of color and dense bunches of leaves that added their languorous swish to the heat, portending another humid Southern summer. This morning's early light came in strong beams glinting through treetops and warmed the men of Company L faster than their campfires boiled the coffee.

The talk at those fires was of home; jobs to resume; children to meet; whether or not they were turning their backs on it all when they were so close. Tempting thoughts of what they'd soon see mingled with pangs of remorse much like those had on their train ride down three years ago.

Burridge walked through the camp preparing as much as his distracted men and his own distracted mind would let him for their eight o'clock move to the right.

As he went from man to man, telling them they had half an hour to go before they all moved out, he wondered what he could do to stop this, and with each "Yes, sir" he heard from one of his soldiers he heard an echoing "Nothing!" in his head. He had destroyed their one chance at protection from Stewart by lying to Henry. He could grovel before the captain, offer himself up for charges if only the men would be physically removed from the line. Yet, the excitement around the fire this morning proved beyond any doubt just how badly the men wanted to do this. Starting up this series and all he had done through it was betrayal enough; to now stop the men from exercising their free will, to hold them back for what he thought was their own good, would further complicate his traitorous actions. He helped Huey douse the fire, then went on toward the Worms, always keeping an eye out for Stewart, a shadow across the bright sun. Burridge did not know the hour of his coming or how, but Stewart's malevolent air was already drifting this way, and at times he found it difficult to breathe. He continued to the Worms, where they discussed whether they'd take a train or a steamboat back North and tried to ignore the pressing knowledge that something bad was going to happen today.

Burridge returned to his small fire and began stuffing his few utensils back into his knapsack when the *Commentaries* fell out. He leafed through the pages, picking out lines he'd underscored over the years by dim firelight. The Roman certainty of Caesar told him that the men had made a mistake. After all, he thought, they really were just a rabble of workingmen who, for all their admirable intentions here, were asking to walk into a trap. If he chose, he could still reverse the request; an unusual and maybe even unseemly thing to do, but the wisest course he could see for them; the only course that did not imperil lives.

Burridge closed the book, then reopened it to the engraving of Caesar on the frontispiece and tried to divine what he would have done in this situation. As the lieutenant stared at the prow of a nose and the determined imperial eyes, light, formless notes of piping music floated toward him. Turning, he saw a single soldier strolling along and idly running his fingers over a tin whistle. When he noticed Burridge, he stopped for a second to tip his cap, then walked on piping as Horace whistled a few notes of brief harmony. Burridge tossed his book into the smoldering fire and took the base ball to Lyman. The die was cast.

A few feet away, Louis sprinkled some salt into his canteen and set it down next to the weeds he had collected and the three squares of hardtack. Under the circumstances, this was as close as Louis could come to a seder, and he sorted through the memories of four decades for the prayers; a futile effort considering that he didn't even remember if he ate the bitter herbs first or the matzoh. Humbled by his ignorance, he asked for forgiveness and poured a bit of the salt water onto a few of the weeds, then leaned back and put them into his mouth.

He could hear Tice next to him, mumbling to himself as he finished packing. "What are we here for?"

Louis answered in his mind as he swallowed the bitter leaves. *"Avadim hayinu."*

Tice stared over now at Louis. "What are you doing?"

In the Wilderness, Louis thought, two questions were as good as four. "Here, take a piece of bread and I'll tell you."

CHAPTER
33

S THE LINE MOVED OUT AT EIGHT, NO ONE NOTICED THE small arrow of twigs Cawthorne had laid out on the ground. The sergeant didn't know if there'd be provost guards or skirmishers; all he knew was what Stewart had told him—that he should hit the ground as soon as Stewart appeared.

The march was a short one and by 12:30 they had dug passable trenches to return to after picket. Burridge had encouraged their hard work as a way to burn off some of the rising anticipation, but when they went forward at one and then bore left, they were still as jumpy as a group of schoolchildren. Lyman and Burridge both had to warn them repeatedly to keep quiet, warnings that had little effect until they reached the thatch of trees. Here, silence took over, save for the sound of Cawthorne rustling in the bushes, where he was supposedly relieving himself. Though he continually shook the bush to prove he was there, he was able to tie a handsome bow facing the direction they had left.

They crept through the woods, then poked their heads out into the clearing they had played in two days before, bordered on both sides by trees and angled so that only troops stationed directly in the space between would be able to see them play. The rain after the last match had leveled the ground, hardened nicely by the sun. The patches of grass that they had not stomped apart were a brilliant green.

Wes screeched. Newt closed his eyes, hoping to hear a response, but there was nothing.

Wes tried again. Lyman pushed them all the way through, into the clearing, where they lay down in the grass and waited for an answer.

Wes screeched a third time. No motion in the distance; no other birds save a hawk floating on the currents of hot air above them.

A minute passed, and then another and another. Lyman squinted off toward the trees to the west. Had they deserted already? Were they caught by their own? Del Rio began to whisper that it was a trap, his whisper becoming more shrill every time he said it until Lyman angrily hushed him and waved over at Wesley to try it again.

Wes screeched.

An arm waved across the field and heads appeared up from the ground. Teddy got to his knees, but Lyman motioned him back down. He wanted the men across the way to come closer. In twenty yards they finally came into focus.

The first thing Burridge noticed was the revolver on Mink's hip. Until then, Mink had carried a rifle like the others, but today the ivory handle of the silver sidearm and the black leather straps of the holster made him stand out even more from his men than usual. Seeing the usually slicked hair on Mink's head uncombed and his eyes shifting back and forth reminded Burridge that he could not simply ignore this foe. Mink was at a desperate point. His conviction that he had passed his last secret and aided his final slaughter steeled him against the spy's advance. "Glad to see your friends, Lieutenant?"

Burridge said nothing, letting the others greet the friends they had made. Mink sneered. "Not talking, Lieutenant Burridge?" He rubbed his hand on the revolver. "I expect you might later." Then he walked away.

Burridge put his pack down and leaned his rifle on top of it. He had loaded the gun before they left and now he placed a cap next to the hammer. The lieutenant planned to go out fighting.

Micah's expression held many signals for Lyman, and reading it was like trying to read tracks in the litter of an autumn forest floor. At once the crinkled eyes appeared cheerful and wincing, the genuine, warm smile set hard in his face. Seeing him made the thought of treachery on the Reb's part hard to believe, but Lyman's mind told him that he could not discount anything. Not yet.

Micah held out a big paw, which Lyman shook. "Not much time today."

Lyman shook his head. "Nope. Not much." He looked down, scuffed his foot once or twice. There was no reason to put this off; speed was the whole point. "Listen, you boys better come over right now. There's..."

"We staying." Micah scratched his nose for a second.

"You don't understand. You have to come now. We don't have time to play. There's..."

"I understand more than you know." Lyman made a move to protest, but Micah held up his hand. "Don't need ya making this any harder." He scratched his nose again. "We'd all like this war over. It's over for you, and I say thank the Lord, but we"—he spread his arms toward the men out in the field—"we gotta stay." Micah bent over and picked up a handful of dirt. "It's our land. When ye shove all the things we agree about off on the side, there's still this." The dirt tumbled through his fingers as he rolled them. "You boys say it's everybody's; we say it's ourn."

This wasn't what Lyman had expected. A refusal based on principle cheered the soldier in him, but Lyman found himself wondering if it was true. Breese filled in the silence. "Fact is, if'n we *was* to bolt, boys'd head on back ta their families before they'd go up by *New* York."

Lyman nodded. With Grant driving the army farther south and these barefoot Rebs grateful for whatever food Willie could spare, the bleak consequences of their choice did not need comment. He saw the starvation ahead, the burnt fields, the dwindling ranks as these boys stood fast until the nearing end. "I understand. You got your family, and your boy."

Micah shook his head sadly. "No, don't got no son. No wife, neither, if yer gonna ask. Just me and my dawg and a stretch of pine trees. Arlette there's the one with five boys and a daughter and a wife." Another picture dissolved in Lyman's mind and Micah saw the confusion on his face. "See, we ain't so alike, you and me. You was thinking we was the same man, weren't ya? Just wearing different clothes?"

Once Lyman had believed that something either was or wasn't—be it good or bad, North or South, success or failure—but nothing was that simple anymore and maybe it never had been. Lyman looked at Micah and saw only his friend. There was just one way to settle this, as gentlemen and as soldiers. "We'll play you for it."

"What?"

"We'll all play the fifth match. If we win, you boys desert. You win, you stay."

"So we play for our freedom?"

"No, we play to keep you as our brothers."

"Goddamn." Micah smiled at the wonder of the idea. "Goddamn. Where'd you get that?" A shrug was all he could answer with. "We don't got much time... Seems right though, don't it?" Lyman held his breath. "I'll ask my boys. They's more than a few gamblers."

Lyman exhaled, then went back to his men with the plan. It was madness, but everything about this war had become so. And at least someone could go home the winner of something.

Newt twirled one tip of his mustache. "I thought you said we didn't have time."

"The more time we yammer, the less we got to find ourselves a winner and get those boys over. We're either in or out right now."

Tiger took off his jacket and cracked his knuckles. The rest came in behind him and the Union nine was ready.

Micah met Lyman halfway between the two groups of men. "Well, you got yourselfs a wager."

"We've each been home nine twice. What say we flip for it?"

"Sounds fair. Got a coin?"

Lyman patted his pockets for a moment until Wesley handed him Slipper's dollar. Alder tossed it up in the air.

Micah called tails.

It fell heads. The Yankees would have the last raps.

Micah growled, "Let's play ball."

Arlette, the leadoff man, welcomed the Worms back with a gruff smile. "Thought you sons of bitches was dead."

Pindar licked the tip of his pencil. "Hell, no! Not the Worm boys! You didn't tell anything to Cawthorne here, did ya?" Cawthorne sat unhappily at their side, with Jimmy Tice's rifle pointed at his head. Arlette said no and stepped in to start the fifth match.

As he had before the first match, Lyman stood on the mound and took in the scene; today he knew that whether he liked it or not, he would never forget what would happen here. The men of both sides talked and joked with each other, and the real stakes drove a current of tension beneath it all. Even Brockington, who'd lurked back in the trees through each match, set down his rifle momentarily so he could take off his boots and air his toes. The sun powered down from near its zenith in a blue sky and drew more jackets off before the match even started. There was no time to waste. Burridge guessed they had two hours, which left no margins for bad pitches, foul balls, or chatter. Each man had loaded his rifle and laid it atop his pack. Those on the sides kept their guns in hand and waited for the inevitable intruders.

The Rebels pounced on Lyman for a quick run, but there were two out by the time Micah Breese hefted Newt's bat. From the pitcher's box, Lyman watched Micah have some warm-up cuts and he saw many things. He saw Micah back on the Excelsiors' grounds, tossing balls with him; he saw Micah throwing a ball to Haddon in the Alabama hills; Micah aiming at his head; Micah dead on the ground. Drifting among these images, Lyman finally heard Wes yelling out to him to wake up.

Lyman's mind suddenly rushed back into his body. He had to push all that aside and do his job right. As it had in that first match, Lyman's body tried to remember what it felt like to pitch well. He knew the motions and so now he concentrated on performing them perfectly against Breese. It was in his power to save their lives.

The result of all this remembering and concentration was a fat lob that Breese slapped over Newt's head, and now there were men on first and third. Kingsley gave the Rebels a two-run lead when he poked a slow pitch into right to score Deal.

Wesley's expletives bounced off Lyman. Continuing to force the play, he missed badly on three pitches, time enough under these limits to get people grumbling. He stepped out before the next and tried to clear his mind of anything that wasn't base ball, but base ball was what it had all come down to, and the game, its moments and every detail, haunted him now. He yawned once, then set for the pitch. Tidrow jumped on it and only missed a home run by an inch on the bat.

The Union side was lucky to escape only two down.

	1	2	3	4	5	6	7	8	9	R	H	E
CONFEDERATES	2									2	3	0
UNION										0	0	0

Eight minutes. Burridge slipped the watch he had borrowed from the German back into his pocket. Eight times 18 was 144 minutes, a good half an hour too long. If the whole match moved at this rate, sometime during the seventh or eighth inning a squad of Union men would burst into this clearing and probably start shooting at everyone in sight. The lieutenant put his hand back into his pocket and rubbed the soft gold of the timepiece—an heirloom, the German had cautioned. From his father. He'd gone along with this last match, but that couldn't keep him from wishing it were already over. His impatience grew as Newt pawed around at home and took three pitches to ground out to second. The match had to move faster. Arlette did his best, throwing strikes most of the time; Tiger and Teddy were the ones not helping with their scratch singles. As Tidrow caught a pop fly for the third out, Burridge pulled out the watch. Sixteen minutes for the first inning.

He trotted out to first, heart beating as quickly as Karl's watch. Mink would probably be up this inning. Burridge wondered what he would say. Though he might have discovered the false desertion point, on the other hand, Burridge had indeed delivered his lambs and the fifth match was taking place. Two quick outs gave the lieutenant a short burst of hope—that would surely help speed things—but the comfort didn't last. Arlette extended his arms, turned his hips, and stroked a lovely hit that caught Finn and Quigley unawares. Only a nice leaping grab to his left by Teddy kept it a double.

And now Mink was up.

Burridge screwed his toes in a bit, ready to move as Lyman laid in an easy pitch. The lieutenant tightened up his muscles, his body just waiting to be told where to go. Mink uncoiled, springing at the ball and sending it sharply along the first base line.

Burridge didn't even have to think "left" for his body to dart into the ball's path—it bounced once at his feet before he grabbed it and stepped on the base.

He snuck a look at the watch. Four minutes.

And one less visit with Mink.

He was leading off the Union second, so Burridge concentrated between innings on the ways to avoid Mink. One was to strike out on purpose; the other, to get at least a double. One was easy; guaranteed, in fact. And safe. And weak. The lieutenant picked up the bat, well dinged in spots and grimy at the handle. It was heavy for him and always had been, but all the men had been using the same one. One does what one must, he thought.

He looked toward first and there was Mink shifting from one foot to the other in a nervous rhythm. Burridge squeezed the bat, felt the strength in his arms, and decided to swing for the boundary. Arlette's first pitch was high, and though he knew he should be patient, before the ball had left the pitcher's hand again, Burridge had resolved to swing. It was low, and the lieutenant took a late swoop that dumped the ball into shallow left, leaving him just where he did not want to be.

Mink smiled a hostile smile, like a dog baring its fangs. Burridge tried to ignore him as Del Rio came up. He leaned off the base, away from Mink, but a cold whisper followed him. *"Tabulam geographicam aspexi. Tuus locus conglobandi intra nostras lineas est."*

He had discovered the lie. He'd checked a map and found the spot inside the Rebel lines. Burridge felt a hand touch lightly on his wrist. *"Et tu, Brute?"*

Burridge took off for second and stole the base, leaving Mink behind.

Del Rio, Stives, and Lyman went down in order and under five minutes. Twenty-five for two innings. Burridge kept playing with the numbers, distracting himself from what felt like a scald on his wrist.

	1	2	3	4	5	6	7	8	9	R	H	E
CONFEDERATES	2	0								2	4	0
UNION	0	0								0	3	0

Had this really been worth it, Lyman asked himself. Every few minutes Burridge pulled the German's watch out of his pocket and a stricken look would cross his face. As best as Lyman could guess, a good half an hour had passed and they were only one out into the fourth inning. The men on first and third were thanks to back-to-back errors by Stives; the two balls to Denton Cowles, the batter, thanks to Lyman, whose mind was wandering the streets of Brooklyn with Micah, or examining every aspect of his delivery, or seeing himself dead. He didn't feel a part of this match; it was as if he was operating on a different rhythm than everyone else. Though he couldn't see him, he was certain Burridge had his hand on the watch, fretting.

Still down by two and without a tally, Lyman knew they couldn't afford to give up anything here. Arlette looked unstoppable so far; his pitches were fast and true. He took a deep breath and entered his motion: Present the ball with both hands; lift left foot as you pull back right arm; step forward as you release. Just at that moment, when the ball was about to leave his hand, as his plan became his execution, he thought he heard a rustle off in the trees. Were they here already? Was it time? He held the ball for just a beat longer than usual, hoping to hear what his future would be. With only silence behind him, he looped it in over the outside corner.

What timing Cowles may have had was ruined by Lyman's hesitation; he swung and missed badly. Twice more Lyman heard a sound as he was about to release, and twice more his little pause threw off Cowles for the strikeout.

Newt trotted out to him and slapped his shoulder. "Bully pitch! There's your third, brother!"

"How's that?"

"That pitch. Just keep doing it."

There were now two outs, though Lyman could hear the Rebs grumbling about some new trick pitch. He held the ball, listening for whatever was there, but all he heard now was Burridge urging him to get on with it. Arlette was up and he'd doubled twice already. Another here would clear the bases and stretch the lead, possibly beyond reach. The voice in Lyman's head became louder. Was the ambush in place? Had no one else heard that? He ignored Wesley's motion for a speed ball and threw a snap.

Arlette knocked a clean single over Newt's head. Tidrow scored and Welch took third. It was 3–0, Rebels.

The damage done, Mink lined out to Stives to end the inning.

Lyman thought he saw Micah clapping, but he couldn't be sure.

	1	2	3	4	5	6	7	8	9	R	H	E
CONFEDERATES	2	0	0	1						3	7	0
UNION	0	0	0							0	4	1

As Burridge walked in from first, Mink hissed at him, "*Mihi egrediendum est! Intellegunt!*"

Translating had always been difficult work for Burridge, so he didn't bother now. "I quit."

"*Nihil deficiendum!*"

"This land doesn't need a Caesar, Sidney."

"I'm no Caesar, and neither are you, John, but we have our roles to play. We are Brutus and Cassius to..."

"No! This isn't Rome! Don't you see that? The sort of republic you want has nothing to do with these men."

Mink rolled his eyes. "I could be well moved, if I were as you, and I thank God I'm not. Who said I wanted a republic, anyways? There's a tide in the affairs of men, and it usually runs gold. You, son, are set to drown in it, but I know better than to fight the tide."

Burridge glared at him. "You'll be fortunate to live."

Mink composed himself, flattening out his hair as he took his base. "I believe I've taught you a few things." He touched his revolver. "But we'll see who's alive at the end of this day." Burridge checked the watch. Forty-three minutes gone.

Wesley decided that something had to be done. The Union side was getting edgy, down 3–0 and yet to mount a serious threat. He lumbered up to the plate and without knocking the dirt from his shoes or adjusting his cap, without even a practice swing, he strode into Arlette's first pitch and watched it as it kept heading up, even as it was in the outfield. Denton trotted back to retrieve the ball and Wesley ran the bases. The lead was back to two and though Burridge, Del Rio, and Stives went down in order after that, the blow had been struck. Arlette was not invincible.

	1	2	3	4	5	6	7	8	9	R	H	E
CONFEDERATES	2	0	0	1						3	7	0
UNION	0	0	0	1						1	5	1

Newt scuffed around some dirt behind second base, waiting for Harlan Deal to bat. As the minutes went by and the ambush approached, Newt had to question the sense of all this. He'd become a different man and he couldn't wait to present himself to his wife and all of Brooklyn. There was work to be done; he was eager to begin his share of it and playing for human stakes right now seemed to be a detour before those tasks. Besides, he'd never played for stakes much beyond a tureen of chowder.

Deal took a sharp cut at one of Lyman's mediocre snap balls. Newt wasn't surprised to see the pitch lined into left center well over his head and before Tiger. He watched Deal lope toward first, admiring the natural stride. Suddenly, about three feet beyond the base, Deal's eyes opened wide. He sprinted to second. Newt raced to the base and turned back to the outfield where Tiger was just going into the motion. The Indian reached easily and without recourse to Del Rio's "slide."

Newt nodded to Deal and Deal, as tall and chiseled as ever despite his torn homespun shirt and lack of shoes, returned it. They exchanged no words of greeting though, and after a few seconds the simple circumstance of neither man talking became their recognized condition. While Weed got set at the plate, they enjoyed a silent and amicable appreciation that they were in the same place at the same time.

They maintained their reserve through two failed examples of Lyman's new timing pitch, but then a foul ball by Weed brought on a pause during which it would have been pure rudeness not to speak. Newt rubbed his hands together and decided to take a fearless approach. "So, how do you think you'll like life up North?"

"Only the fifth inning, friend." Harlan smirked, but then the reality of the question seemed to sink in. "I guess I'd like it awlraht, 'cept for all that business about coloreds."

"How so?"

The question hung in the air as Lyman wound up. Weed swung and dribbled the ball foul again. "If'n you win this here war..." Harlan pointed a finger at Newt. "And I ain't saying ya will—you gonna have ta do something—and I mean *do* somethin' to help 'em."

"Brooklyn's full of organizations that will..."

Deal cut him off with a wave and a scowl. "Tha's all horse shit. Makes people feel better but it won't help no coloreds. What are *you* gonna do? Gonna give 'em jobs? Gonna rent 'em rooms in your house?"

"Well, we would certainly help them..."

"If'n you been telling the coloreds that y'all come down here to save 'em, and then you don't wanna have nothing to do with 'em, you're as bad as some damn slave owner. Problem's only half about slavery, hear me? You gonna free 'em, then you gotta let 'em live with ye, too, and let 'em work and live like any white man, but all we hear is, 'You Southern bastards let 'em go and you take care of 'em!' like you folks never made a penny off they black backs yourselfs. This is everybody's problem, son. Don't just be telling us what to do and then lock your own doors. Them abbylishers don't want no black men next to their house, neither, but somehow that don't come up in your polite talk. If'n you win this war, you gonna have a bigguh problem if you don't learn to live with the black mens." He saw the guilty look on Newt's face. "Maybe *you'll* do something, friend."

Harlan took third on a ground out by Weed, and Newt could only watch as he scored on a Breese single into the gap between him and Karl.

Was that all that he could ever do—stand and watch? Newt told himself he might have gotten there with a stretch or a leap. He could have tried, at least. He felt as if he had climbed a mountain and upon reaching the summit, he'd looked over and realized that his mountain was only a foothill. A whole range lay beyond him. He would never achieve that ultimate state of Christian purity of which the bishop spoke; the point was not simply to climb Sinai and Calvary. A man was to climb them, then continue the journey, each step demanding his full effort. A man could never let go of the mountain.

Newt dashed to his left, snared a one-hopper by Kingsley, and stepped on second for the final out of the inning.

	1	2	3	4	5	6	7	8	9	R	H	E
CONFEDERATES	2	0	0	1	1					4	10	0
UNION	0	0	0	1						1	5	1

No one expected Arlette to completely shut down the Union side. When Newt opened the Yankee fifth with a hard double to left, it was as though the first small pebbles were rolling down the hill, warning of an avalanche. Karl's double pushed Newt across to make it 4–2, and suddenly Rebs were pawing the grass. Teddy sliced another double and the lead was down to one.

Huey met Arlette as the pitcher came to the side. "I wanna give ya something," he said. "Something..." He shrugged. "I don't know." Huey pulled a small mass of paper out of his pocket and handed it to Arlette. "It ain't Lou, but it's something."

Arlette peeled the scraps apart and saw pictures of a giraffe, some piglike creature, an elephant, and more. The edges were worn and many were ripped, but each square of newsprint had been neatly torn and clearly cared for by Huey. "Uh, son, what are these?"

Thrilled by Arlette's question, Huey went picture by picture, explaining all about Van Amburgh's Menagerie, pointing out his favorites and asking Albert questions about the animals and their foreign homes. Albert had never seen anything stranger than a possum and never been twenty miles from his home until the war, but while he had no use for the clippings, he saw the generous pride in Huey's skewed and wandering eyes, and the conviction behind his sacrifice shouting down his reluctance to part with them. He stacked them up and tucked them into a pocket. "Huey, them's fine. I'm gonna treasure 'em. Thank ye."

Huey waved a hand. "It was nothing."

	1	2	3	4	5	6	7	8	9	R	H	E
CONFEDERATES	2	0	0	1	1					4	10	0
UNION	0	0	0	1	2					3	8	1

Cowles opened the Rebel sixth by squibbing a ball at Stives, who bobbled it but was still able to catch Denton at first. Arlette then took a ball low and a strike before flying out to Tiger in medium center. The hands seemed to be falling faster to Burridge, but now Mink was up. Nearly vibrating at the plate, he hit a clean single to left on the first pitch and trotted to his base, where he immediately turned on him. "Your men know and they're telling mine." In a hoarse whisper, he added, "We will both be killed!" The spy's face was red as he spoke—"I should have seen you for the vulgar being that you are."

Deal hit a grounder to Burridge, who stepped on the base.

He had one thing to thank Mink for now—he *had* taught him how to win, even if the methods had been rough. Burridge had the taste for victory in this match now and a need to see justice triumph. He looked at the watch—one hour and thirty minutes gone. They'd never make it. He reminded himself that he had yet to cap his gun.

There were two outs in the Union sixth and Stives was on first when Lyman came up again. He tipped his cap to Micah, cleared his throat, and stepped in.

"You boys 'spect to see any more action?"

Lyman froze.

"Still looks like the North Anna for us."

Lyman still hadn't moved, hadn't turned back toward Micah.

The Rebel sighed. "You still wondering, ain'cha?"

The first pitch came in high. Lyman slipped out of his stance.

"Yep, still thinking. I like that about you, Lyman, but do ye really wanna know?"

Lyman took a hard swing at a good pitch, but he couldn't escape the truth; the ball looped foul. He yawned.

"I know you got it all planned out, but how do you know what side I'd be a-scouting for? Hell, Mink be as much a dirty slaveholding, Union-hating bastard as I's ever seen, and he passing on to your side. Then again, maybe we just needed a rest. What difference do that make? What's the worst you done? Save a few Rebel lives? I thought you said we was all Americans? Maybe I asked you all that so's we'd not have to fight each other. Think of that?"

Lyman lofted Arlette's outside pitch high but shallow and Tidrow took it to end the inning.

Dispirited, he wandered back toward the box. Once Wes took his place behind the plate, he tossed a few lame pitches toward him that bounced in the dirt.

Wes walked the ball back to Lyman. "What's the problem? This is the match that'll decide the whole thing and you're throwing shit at me all afternoon. Why don't ya just hand 'em your fucking ball right now, because if you keep playing like such a fucking muffin, we're gonna lose, brother."

"I think Breese may have been..."

"Aw, cap it, Lyman. We come out here to save his life and you're mooning. I can't figger you."

Lyman looked over to the Rebel side. Micah was staring at him, smiling indulgently as if he were a sweet, foolish child, a younger brother who'd just learned a hard lesson. The Rebel swept the cap off his head. For some reason Lyman expected some grand, dramatic gesture, but Micah simply wiped his brow and stuck the cap back onto his thatch of black hair. An ordinary man. Lyman smiled back, shaking his head, finally in on the joke. The truth was not a chunk of gold buried somewhere in this field; you pieced together what you knew and that was when faith came in. He'd pieced together enough these two weeks. It was now time for faith. It was time to make his own life. Before Lyman was a face with a strong jaw, broad brow, and skin toughened by weeks outdoors, no longer the face of a boy. Lyman stuck his hand out. "I'm sorry, Wes."

Wes clamped his free hand onto Lyman's shoulder. "You done good by us, Lyman."

Before Lyman could say anything else, Wes pointed toward the pitcher's box. "Get back there."

The high afternoon sun showered the field with a playful light that snuck under bent blades of grass and danced in the green of the trees. Lyman watched his men out in the field pawing the ground impatiently for the first pitch, the Rebels sitting in knots, urging on E. Simon Weed. A fertile smell rode the breeze, a promise that there would be many more days like these before autumn and the cold, that these hours of warmth and light were just the first spoonful of so much more to come in this season and this life. Lyman drew in a breath and smiled at the wonder of it.

Lyman could walk away and start again somewhere out West in Chicago or on a homestead. He could go back and listen to the parlor clock tick and his wife's sighs, or he could live his old life in a new way, as a man who chooses to take a stand no matter the cost to himself.

He saw Victoria, saw her as she deserved to be seen, laughing as she once did so often, with her eyes hidden beneath joy, fingertips pressed together in savor of whatever was so deliciously funny. She was all movement and curves, and Lyman pictured her in a line with a hundred women but all he saw was her, and he realized that what made her laugh so was *him*, his small jokes, the slow, affectionate touch that dissolved her into that young girl he had been watching since he was six years old.

Lyman reached out his hand and pulled her from the line, as he decided he would do every day, to select her as his wife, to know that it was within his power to make her happy.

A line of boys then appeared. At the end was one with a dozen pounds of baby fat and a sheepish look, as though he'd been caught out at something. His boy. Mysteries sat in that boy's head. Lyman could not create him whole, but that was *his* son, who even now looked out from this line of all boys in the world with an expression of hopefulness and wonder at the question of what a man was and how he could become one. Who would teach him? Sorry boy, standing eager and repentant, wet and soft in all ways and still able to kiss his father. This boy whose vision of the world was formed around the small thoughts and interests Lyman had conveyed as a pearl is built around a grain of sand.

Placing a finger in the dent of Ernie's chin, a depression identical to his, Lyman pulled him forth into his arms and felt the thin bones of the boy's back under his hands. This was *his* son and Lyman would choose him, too, every day, and lead him forward.

In the seconds it took for Wes to get back to the plate and E. Simon Weed to find the bat, Lyman embraced his life. He reached out to the wonder of Victoria's smooth lips and Ernie's dirty nails. The shop, his father, his friends, all passed through his mind, and to each he held his hand and pulled them closer, made them his home in a churning, smoky world whose song was not whistled by birds anymore but by steaming locomotives and the rushing looms of factories. They were life in this land of metal, his garden for the coming darker age, and he had to actively tend them for the colors to bloom.

Lyman closed his eyes and squeezed Ernie's ball in his hand. He whipped a practice throw at Wes. "Let's get into our work, goddamnit!" Burridge held up nine fingers, one for each Rebel hand left.

Weed came up next. Leaving the bat on the ground, he clasped his arms together and said, " 'A *new* covenant, he hath made the first *old*! Now that which decayeth and waxeth ole is ready ta vanish away!' "

The game stopped briefly, as even the most dissolute Rebels like Deal nodded and added their own assent. Kingsley said, "Hebrews 8, vuss 13." Seeing all the Rebs suddenly banded together on this, the Yankees looked to Willie and Stives. Willie pointed toward Stives. "Don't look at me. *That's* your man." Stives scratched his wild mane, eyes rolling. Both sides waited to see if the Union could muster a repulse to Weed's scriptural assault.

Wes whispered, "Hurry up, Stives. We don't got the whole day. Think of something."

The baker mumbled to himself, then froze. He slowly lowered his head and when he raised it again, he was smiling. " 'So the king of the north shall come, and cast up a mount, and take the most fenced cities; and the arms of the south shall not withstand!' Daniel 11!"

Weed looked at all the Union men, and in a soft tone with his hands at his sides he asked, " 'What hast thou to do with me, that thou art come against me to fight in my land?' "

The field became still. Rather than a plea to heaven, Weed's tone made this a simple question posed to the Yankees, something gone long unasked between friends.

No one spoke. Karl's watch ticked loudly. Everyone had his own answer, words that were impossible to say out loud and to the Rebs' faces. Men coughed and some shuffled their feet until Stives finally stepped forward, closer to the pitcher's box, and gave a calm reply. " 'Thus saith the Lord, for three transgressions of Israel, and for four, I will not turn away the punishment thereof; because they sold the righteous for silver, and the poor for a pair of shoes.' " He folded his arms. "Amos, chapter 2, verse 6."

The field remained quiet. Weed had pressed his eyes closed as if struck and now he slowly nodded. He had no response. The Rebs did not threaten this inning. It was still 4–3.

	1	2	3	4	5	6	7	8	9	R	H	E
CONFEDERATES	2	0	0	1	1	0	0			4	13	0
UNION	0	0	0	1	2	0				3	9	1

The Yanks had the top of the order coming up in the seventh. Newt ground out to Emmitt Welch and there was one out. Eight more and the Rebs had the series and their choice of a future. Burridge had stopped checking the timepiece—the troops were due any moment. They were now on borrowed time.

Arlette bore down, squeezing the ball in his hands. "Bring on the Dutchman!"

He soon regretted the request—Karl tripled and the Yankee challenge finally surged forward. The Rebs rose up behind Arlette, trying to firm the wall. If the Yanks caught up, it would be all over. Teddy took the bat.

The first two pitches came in low.

Newt and Lyman applauded Teddy's patience; Arlette had to throw a strike on the next pitch and he did. The ball cut straight over the sack and Teddy pounced on it, knocking it on a line to deep right field. Karl jogged home and Teddy beat the throw to second. The score was tied at 4.

Shots cracked off to the north, not too far away. A few voices could be heard.

As they had in the second match, men of both sides scrambled and dove for their weapons; guns pointed in every direction. Together they waited for the end. Silence drifted back over the field.

Then there was a quick movement toward the Union line. Micah's voice growled, "Stop there!" Mink halted and raised his hands as soon as he noticed the rifles pointed at him. "Come on back here and finish what you started. We don't got no other first baseman."

The lieutenant seemed to weigh all this, then dropped his hands and came back to the match. Brockington and his high cavalier's boots were put in charge of guarding him. Lyman and Breese looked at each other. The

Union man shrugged his shoulders. Micah nodded and picked up the ball. "We gotta know." The rest of the match would be a race.

Arlette went right to work on Tiger, who tapped a weak roller that stopped halfway toward first base. Tiger reached safely and Teddy took third.

Wesley had a chance to break the game open, but he could only pop out to Weed, leaving it up to Burridge.

The lieutenant saw the ball leave Arlette's fingers and slowly float toward him, getting larger and larger. He hesitated at first—was it going inside?—but then he decided to swing. Striding forward, Burridge put the bat right on the growing target, the only sound in his ears the crack of bat on ball. The ball bounced once, then twice on the left side, and then past Emmitt Welch. He sprinted toward first as Teddy crossed with the lead run.

Cowles was just touching the ball as he rounded the base, so Burridge decided to go for two. Coming out of the turn and heading toward second, he suddenly went sprawling onto the dirt. A Reb near him called for the ball. As he rolled over, he felt the tag. Mink's contorted face loomed over him. "You are out." Mink had tripped him. Burridge laughed at the traitor's desperate face.

	1	2	3	4	5	6	7	8	9	R	H	E
CONFEDERATES	2	0	0	1	1	0	0			4	13	0
UNION	0	0	0	1	2	0	2			5	13	1

Now the Yanks began counting outs, as Lyman's combination of speed, snap, and hesitation took control. Tidrow's slow grounder to Newt was one; Welch's tricky fly to Del Rio, frightening as it was, made for two; and Denton's spinning pop to Lyman was three.

The Union side came back up and the Rebs had barely had a breather. Arlette had to stop them this inning. Del Rio opened with a single and Stives struck out. Lyman came up with a man on first and one out. Before facing Arlette, he extended a hand to Breese. "May the best team win."

Breese shook it, but scowled. "How often does that happen?"

"Not often. That's why I'm asking." Try as he may, Lyman could see nothing but that towering home run, the clout that people talk about for years afterward, the kind that young boys re-create on early evening streets as the fireflies begin to glow. He set himself and though he meant to wait, the first pitch looked so inviting that he had to swing. The ball took two crisp hops toward Kingsley and though it should have been an out at second, Del Rio beat him to the bag. First and second—one out.

Arlette's face was red and his shirt as wet with sweat as it had been with water two days before. He took off his cap and wiped his brow, then came in tight on Newt. The Yankee pulled a grounder to Welch, who tagged third for the second out.

Eager to finish the inning, Arlette had hardly let Karl get into the box when he shot in another inside speed ball. This one, though, was much too inside. It bounced off Karl's hands and now the bases were loaded and Teddy was coming up.

Arlette held his head in his hands, and he started when Harlan Deal put his hand on his shoulder. "We behind ye, brother." Deal trotted back out to center.

The first pitch was low. Teddy fouled off the next.

Deal shouted in, "He can't hit you!"

Teddy snorted, tensing his muscles to wallop the third pitch, but it was a ball high. Everyone took a breath.

Arlette wound up and delivered a speed ball down the heart of the plate. Finn reared back and swung.

Strike three.

	1	2	3	4	5	6	7	8	9	R	H	E
CONFEDERATES	2	0	0	1	1	0	0	0		4	13	0
UNION	0	0	0	1	2	0	2	0		5	15	1

Union 5, Rebels 4. Top of the ninth. Three more outs for a Union victory. Arlette to lead off. The friendly interchange between teams had stopped.

Arlette swung and missed the first pitch, took a ball, then aired one ⁀ep to left that Teddy hauled in on the run. Newt held up a finger and ⁀ked around his turf, saying, "That's one!"

Sidney Mink was next. Wes called for a snap to start him off, but it broke outside. Wes called for another one. Lyman thought he was crazy, but he gave it to him all the same and Mink went with it, poking the ball into right for a single.

Burridge focused on the next batter, but he could not hide from Mink. The Rebel edged off first as Deal came up, hissing into Burridge's ear. "My efforts are to save *your* life, as well, weak little man that you are." Lyman tossed one inside for a ball. "Your treachery will be discussed. You'll be lucky to have a job when you get back. The end of a promising career." Deal lifted the next pitch deep to right, where Del Rio was waiting. Two outs, but Mink didn't stop. The coming end to the match only increased his viciousness and his attacks began to find their mark. "You will be penniless. No job. No wife. Begging for coal." Weed took a strike. "You are nothing and you will remain nothing until you die. And do you know what the worst part of your hell will be? You're smart enough to know what a horror it truly is."

The pock of Weed's bat echoed in Burridge's head, a gavel slammed by a higher judge. The ball dropped into right center. Mink made it to third and Weed took second on Del Rio's throw to the plate.

Second and third, two outs, Micah Breese at the plate and Burridge saw none of it. Mink's brutal words bore into him. What happened now would forever define him as a man.

Micah did not force Burridge to wait. He ground Lyman's first pitch right at him, an easy roller that made Burridge smile. He could do this, he thought with relief. This was simple, just like the play he'd made to end the last match. He bent over, his hands eight inches off the dirt.

But the ball stayed lower. It rolled under his fingers, through his legs, and Mink howled with laughter as he crossed the plate. Weed scored the lead run and knelt in the dirt on the side, offering loud hosannas. Burridge knelt in the dirt as well, his face cradled in his hands.

Del Rio held Micah to a single, but the damage had been done. Rebels 6, Union 5. Kingsley popped to Newt and now it was the Yankees who were down to their last three outs.

	1	2	3	4	5	6	7	8	9	R	H	E
CONFEDERATES	2	0	0	1	1	0	0	0	2	6	16	0
UNION	0	0	0	1	2	0	2	0		5	15	2

Tiger gripped his gut as he bent over to pick up the bat, his arms tensing. Arlette whipped a strike in. The cramp throbbed once. The next pitch was outside, but he went after it anyway and dumped a single into right.

The Rebs told Albert to get into his work. Wesley watched two balls bounce on the sack, then he took a smooth swing at the third. The ball shot past Weed into left and now it was first and second, no one out, and Burridge up.

Mink, at first base, laughed and repeated over and again to Burridge—"Nothing." Numb with shame, knowing he'd let his men down once again, Burridge had no thoughts of heroism anymore. He stood up at the plate and took a whack at the first pitch.

The ball arched into right, the sloppy swing having put a spin on the ball, and though Tiger and Wes had held up, the ball dropped in front of Tidrow and now the bases were loaded. Burridge and Mink did not speak at first.

The air tingled. Rebs circled around Arlette as Del Rio came up.

The first pitch was high. Both sides clapped.

The runners stepped off. A fly ball would tie it. Arlette wound up. The ball arched outside.

Newt yelled, "Wait him out!"

The third pitch looked good to Del Rio. He flicked his hands forward and the ball popped harmlessly in Arlette's hands. One out.

Stives held up his arms and opened his mouth to deliver the quote to end all quotes, but Weed shouted, "Shut the fuck up and play ball!" Stunned, Stives watched three perfect strikes cut the plate.

Two outs. Bases loaded. Union down by one. Bottom of the ninth. Lyman at the plate.

Boys—and men—dream of such moments, but few have them and when they do, they are revealed. A man batting in the bottom of the ninth with the bases loaded and down by a run knows that there will be no excuses if he fails, just as he will not claim an excuse if he succeeds. A man cannot hide in the bottom of the ninth; he will learn how strong his body is, and his mind and his heart.

Heart pumping, Lyman dug in. Tiger, Wes, and Burridge on base. The Rebs nervously tromping in the grass and dirt. Sun high and in his face.

Lyman heard every voice. Before he was fully set, Arlette wound up and strike one ripped over the plate.

Lyman took a breath and stepped back while the Rebels cheered. He closed his eyes and pictured the ball cresting far over Deal's head, then planted his foot again. Arlette scowled, pulled back his arm, and the toss came in at his eyes.

This was going by so quickly, Lyman thought. Micah threw back the ball. He had to swing. Lyman grabbed a breath when Arlette's hand let go and swung wildly at the approaching ball as it seemed to avoid his bat. The ball ticked his bat and went foul.

Two strikes now. He closed his eyes and again saw the dream home run. One swing left to get it. Mindless, anxious chatter piled up on the field, rang in his ears. He heard Danny's voice in there and his head swam as Arlette bent over, ready for the next pitch. Then he heard Wesley's voice, a clear and true sound from second base; a request. "Bring me home, Lyman. Just bring us home."

Arlette wound up and released. The ball came in fast, but it was a good pitch and as he stepped in, Lyman's intention to keep an eye on it and analyze where it would go and how quickly it would get there disappeared like a mist. It was just him and the ball. He didn't think about pulling it or putting it in one place or hitting a fly; he just swung and connected.

It shot past Arlette's left on the fly, then bounced hard on the dirt between Mink and Kingsley.

Neither man could reach it.

Tiger scored, screaming all the way. Wes rounded third as Tidrow scooped up the ball.

The throw was wide.

Union 7, Rebels 6.

	1	2	3	4	5	6	7	8	9	R	H	E
CONFEDERATES	2	0	0	1	1	0	0	0	2	6	16	0
UNION	0	0	0	1	2	0	2	0	2	7	19	2

Wesley crossed the plate and a massive flock of crows burst out of the trees and wheeled overhead. Heads turned and there was Lieutenant Linden

Stewart, grinning. The short muzzle of a revolver poked out from his right hand and once the initial shock of his appearance, expected though it was, passed, he strode toward the frozen field of men, raising the gun higher.

Mink rushed toward him with his hands up. "I'm a Union man! Don't shoot! Don't shoot me!"

Stewart pointed his gun at the nearest Rebel, which happened to be Micah Breese. Mink had no interest in Micah's ultimate fate, but the show of force did stop him. Stewart said, with obvious pleasure, "There's a line of skirmishers coming this way. Union skirmishers. I would say they'll be here in two or three minutes and at that point I will give them an order to shoot into this field and kill whomever they see. Irrespective of uniform. You are *all* traitors." Micah shifted his feet. Stewart thrust the revolver forward. "Stay where you are."

Lyman had been trotting back to the side when Stewart had stepped from the trees and froze him at his place. He glanced at his Rebel friend, who was returning the stare of the muzzle pointed at his head. As the only parts of him allowed to move, Lyman cast his eyes about for a solution and the only possibility he saw was Burridge's rifle at his feet.

He looked at Burridge, who was standing next to him. The lieutenant met the gaze, then flicked his eyes sharply at the rifle. Lyman gave an almost imperceptible nod. Burridge nodded back, very slowly.

Lyman wondered if it was it loaded. Burridge's stare could not answer that question. There was a cap next to it, but he would never have time to put it on the nipple; Stewart would shoot him before he'd be able to load up and pull the trigger.

But he *could* fake it. After all, he thought, it didn't matter if it was real or not, did it? In one swift motion, Lyman bent over, picked up the rifle, pulled back the hammer, and trained it on Linden Stewart. "Take the gun off him."

Stewart turned, an eyebrow raised and his doughy face kneaded into a sneer. The lieutenant moved his arm to the right and now the muzzle of the revolver pointed directly at Lyman's chest. "As you wish, Mister...?"

"Alder. Lyman Alder."

"You realize, Mister Alder, that as a soldier threatening to discharge a weapon at a superior officer, you are not only certain of court-martial and life imprisonment, but it would be completely within my rights to shoot you. You see that, don't you?"

Lyman's life did not scroll before his eyes. He did not see his family and he did not ponder large questions. Lyman tensed his finger on the trigger of this harmless gun and swallowed. His throat was dry. "Yes. I do."

"Well, then you understand that for the good of this regiment, this army, and, truly, this nation, I must do this."

Stewart hooked a thumb over the hammer of his revolver and drew it back. As the lieutenant squinted his eye to aim and began to squeeze, Burridge dove in front of Lyman.

The shot echoed through the trees, a sharp crack not unlike the crack of bat on ball. Burridge fell back against Lyman, then slid to the ground clutching his chest.

The smoke cleared around Stewart's face and as he saw what his first bullet had done, the corners of his lips rose a trace. "A heroic deed, but I still have five bullets. He was not a man to well consider a problem."

As Stewart pulled the hammer back again, another gun fired and Stewart's head burst open as Danny's had, the body tumbling down and the hands grasping wildly, no longer under human control.

Every man in the field stood stunned.

Then Mink sprung forward toward the Union lines off to the south. Brockington hurriedly tried to pour another round into his rifle, but Mink had a good jump and was well on his way to surrender and the oath before the bullet ripped harmlessly by him. The spy had escaped.

The churn of approaching men sifted through the trees. Mink's gray blur had snapped everyone into a frantic state and they were now too consumed by the need to escape from the coming skirmishers to worry about his desertion. The Worms ran off to try to intercept the threatening forces.

Lyman looked hopefully at Micah. "A deal's a deal, brother."

Micah picked up his pack. "I hope everything in life ain't a game."

Lyman shook his head, releasing the Reb, then he looked at him. "Last chance, Micah."

Micah flipped the base ball to him. "This belongs to you."

They would never see each other again, but they were never meant to see each other across the flames of the Wilderness. Lyman nodded once, then paused a beat; a luxury they spent taking a final image of each other. "I want us to be on the same team."

Breese looked nervously around and jogged his pack up and down in his hand. "Well, if'n we ain't now, we will be." He shrugged his shoulders. "Someday."

An unfamiliar voice could be heard coming closer, followed by dozens of feet dragging through the dirt on the other side of the trees.

Lyman leaned his head toward the sound. "You better get going."

"Yup." Micah slipped his pack over his shoulder and caught up to the rest of his men now sprinting toward their lines, as yet unseen by the skirmishers, Deal with Newt's bat in his hand. Bits of paper flew out of Arlette's pocket as he ran. Huey winced, watching the scraps flutter and skip across the grass like butterflies.

Stives folded his arms. " 'The righteous shall inherit the land, and dwell therein for ever.' "

Disgusted, Willie looked up from Burridge's body. "Psalms, chapter 37, verse 29. But Oliver? Who *are* the righteous?"

Stives scratched his beard. He did not answer, but he slipped his pack underneath Burridge's head and dabbed at the blood seeping forth from the fatal wound.

John Burridge could hear men talking around him, but their words were indistinct and their voices little more than the distant, busy hum of stevedores to an impatient traveler already staring over a rail toward the other, unknown shore. At the bullet's impact, his thoughts had gone careening, but as his heart strained to pump a final rhythm, he had settled into the realization that it was too late for regrets and too late for second-guessing. His father's face appeared, eyes half closed, nodding in certainty that his son had done the right thing; a wise appreciation of serious action that Burridge had never thought possible from a father he had deemed facile, but the lieutenant admitted at this time of all truth that he had never earned such a look before. Not until now.

A sharp pain sliced through Burridge from stomach to spine, and when he tried to move in a way that would relieve it, he found his body unwilling to comply. Clearly his end was very close. The short review of one's life that Burridge had expected sped by and left few definite images amid a sense of comforting light; though every wrong now pricked his heart like a thorn, his sacrifice had made some forgiveness possible, had made a salve for the hundreds of wounds he'd caused his own soul. The best kind of death, he reflected, was not the kind Caesar described that night before the Ides, though swiftness had its merits. No, the best kind of death had been described by another man of that time who in the end became a God of stronger powers.

He felt a head close to his, a hand upon his cheek, but he was too weak to take a last look. The final thought in his mind was of his body wrapped in white linen, laid upon the top of that broad mahogany desk. As the breaths came in longer and deeper waves, Burridge sensed that he was floating, and as he looked once more for the kind face of his father, the desk slipped its moors and began its long journey over the sea.

Micah looked back one more time, just as the skirmishers hit the field and found it full of Union pickets doing nothing more than their duty. The Rebels had reached the relative safety of their lines, sneaking in through a high thatch of dogwood before the trees to the west, and Micah stood there for a moment, staring back toward a kind of life he could not choose, toward a nation whose forgiveness he could not bring himself to ask. Lyman saw that hulking figure, wreathed in flowers as it had been in flames, one hand held up in parting. He waved back, then wiped his eyes. When he looked up, Micah was gone.

EPILOGUE

On the twenty-first of May 1864, a file of three hundred men marched east along the Mattaponax Church Road, en route to Ginney's Station on the F. and A.C. railroad alongside the wagon train. Their caps were scarlet and beneath layers of blood, sweaty grime, and dust, their trousers were loose, made blousy by the gray tattered leggings some men still had around their battered shoes. The jackets, blue and brimmed with red, fastened at top and bottom to show a stained vest the same deep scarlet as the trousers. The hems of most were singed by fire or shredded into soft fringe. Instead of their bayonets, the moon caught the gold buttons, shining like small fires. Every man had a beard and mustache; many had scars, open wounds, or a limp.

A stout man, cap tipped so the brim stretched far over his eyes, rolled on his thick legs out just ahead of his company as though trying to get home that much quicker. He leaned over to the thin blond-haired man next to him and said, "I think he'll make a fine butcher. He's got the size."

"What will Alder Senior say?"

"We have to expand. That's all there is to it."

Newt nodded. "I think we'll be hiring, too, once the war is over."

Lyman felt a tap on his shoulder; it was Huey. He reached for Lyman's hand and dropped the base ball into it. "I thought you wanted to give this to Barnum."

Huey hung his head a bit. "Well, I, I just don't think base balls belong in a museum. It's just a game, you know."

Lyman held the ball up close so he could look at it in the dim moonlight. Grass stains and deep brown mud mottled it; stitches had popped loose in places and there were many indentations where the bat had slammed into the leather. He fingered one spot—was this where he hit the last single, he wondered. Or was this Covay's home run in the first match?

There was no way of knowing.

Lyman stuffed the ball deep into his knapsack and looked north toward home.